SESSIONS

Heather Leese

For everyone who has felt alone...

CHAPTER ONE

'So, tell me, how's life been since I last saw you?

Francesca hated visiting Jenny. It was nothing personal, except that she had been her supervisor for the whole eight years she'd been a psychologist and she knew her too well.

'Come on, you know I don't bite! I'm here to help. We'll cover your private life first then move on to your professional role.'

Francesca tried to talk her way out of speaking about herself. 'You know I hate talking about myself. I'd rather discuss my clients. That's what I'm here for isn't it, so that you can supervise me professionally?'

'Nice try, but you've known me long enough to know my work involves looking at the balance of your professional and private life. 'Jenny took a sip of her chamomile tea, and waited for Francesca to start talking, but she didn't say anything. 'Let's simply catch up first with the kids and David. How've they been?'

'Mia's knee deep in exams and Mark is in his second year at university, living the student life by the looks of him. He comes down to see us when he can – when he's not hung over from his escapades...' Francesca paused.

Jenny waited, expecting Francesca to get onto the subject of her husband, David.

'So shall we move on to my work?' Francesca didn't let Jenny answer but carried on talking, in an attempt to control the direction of their session. 'You know Roger, the client I've been seeing for a while now, well he...'

'Whoa, whoa, hang on a second. You haven't told me about David...I haven't seen you for a few months! Surely he's been up to something during that time. Has he finished his project at work?'

Francesca, uncomfortable at the mention of David, shifted in her chair. Jenny could see she was uneasy. 'David and I, we've... we've split...separated.'

'OK...' Jenny knew there had been issues in the relationship which she'd put down to a complete lack of communication between the two of them. When they'd discussed it last session Francesca was going to try and make things work, practise responding to him instead of reacting to him. She was surprised to hear the turn of events. 'What's happened? I mean this is a big change...'

Francesca interjected. 'It's the best change I've ever made!'

Jenny contemplated the notion that Francesca was going to be resistant to her support. She moved in her chair to prepare herself and to feel more comfortable. She straightened her back and crossed her legs. 'Start from the beginning. What's gone on? What's changed?'

Francesca had just finished seeing a client. He was a regular who had been coming to see her for a couple of years to address the OCD issues he'd been struggling with.

She strolled along her office corridor behind him, towards the reception area and saw him out. Julie, the receptionist, who had worked with Francesca since she'd qualified, gave her a warm smile and handed her some notes across the desk.

'Sorry.' She felt bad giving Francesca more work, she knew how hard she worked and how much she had to get through already, but the phone and emails hadn't stopped whilst she'd been in session.

Francesca flicked through the notes surprised and dispirited with the amount of calls that had come through in the past hour. Holding on to them she turned to walk back to her office.

'Oh and Mia phoned...'

She stopped half way down the corridor and turned back to look at Julie. 'Is she OK?'

'She needs you to go home and pick up her science notes. She's left them on her bed, she thinks!'

'It's Friday and I told her I was working all day. She should know I can't be running around after her. She's so disorganised, it's unbelievable!' Mia, her daughter, was so unlike her sometimes it worried her. All her life Francesca had been organised, on time and in control. Sometimes her friend Laura would take the

4

mickey out of her and call her anal. She'd say such things as 'Cesca your life is so organised, I reckon you must even shit on schedule!'

Julie looked at her appointment calendar on the computer. 'Actually you could pick her notes up if you go now.'

'No, I've got Mrs Gurney, my two o'clock...'

Julie pointed to the notes in Francesca's hand. 'Look at the messages.'

Francesca looked down to see written on the top note in Julie's neat handwriting, 'Mrs Gurney. 2pm cancelled'.

'She apologised and will phone next week for another appointment. So you've got a free hour for the first time in ages!'

Twenty minutes later, after Francesca had caught up with her paperwork, she picked up her car keys, mobile phone and jacket, in case it was chilly outside, and walked down the stairs and into the street. The weather was warm and bright but still with a bit of a spring chill, so she put her jacket on. Her mobile phone started to ring. She took it out of her pocket and glanced down at the screen. It was he daughter, Mia.

'Hello...'

'Mum, where are you? I need those papers. My exam starts in forty minutes and I need to read over my notes before...' She could barely get her words out quickly enough, she was so anxious.

'Mia, relax! I'm on my way over to the house to pick them up now.'

'Thank you and hurry!'

The phone went dead. Mia was too nervous and panicky to even remember to say goodbye. It was something Francesca had come to accept recently. At first she took it personally, but when she became aware of how stressed Mia was with her studying, she let it go, hoping it would pass once she'd finished her exams.

Francesca pulled her Range Rover up onto the family drive. They lived, as a family, in a spacious, four bedroom house, near town, in a quiet area, but it wasn't the family house the children had grown up in. David, or more David's mother, had insisted they sell the old house and buy one that was more 'substantial'. What she really meant was a house that reflected their increased wealth and income. Her mother in law, Celia, was one of the most conceited people Francesca knew. She was the kind of person who did her weekly shopping in Aldi, but packed her food in Marks and Spencer bags for appearance sake. When Francesca had to spend time with her she'd always bitten her tongue at her off the cuff remarks and funny ways, partly because she was the grandmother of her children but also because she didn't want to rock the boat. To start something with Celia you knew you would be in it for the long haul and she just didn't have the time or effort to go in to battle with her.

She reached the front door to her house and rummaged in her handbag for her front door keys. It took her a few seconds to find them, as always, at the bottom of her bag. She opened the front door and walked in to the hallway noticing David's work shoes on the floor, the same make and style he had worn for the last twenty years. She threw the keys on the side cabinet and began to walk upstairs. It wasn't until she was about half way up that she heard a noise, footsteps, as if someone was walking in the room above her.

'Hello?' There was no answer. She didn't even consider being in danger - that maybe an intruder had broken into the house. She just carried on to the top of the stairs, onto the landing, and headed straight for her and David's bedroom, where the noise seemed to be coming from. As she got closer to the bedroom door, she heard a different sound, a muffled giggling and thudding. It didn't take Francesca long to click the thudding was actually the sound of the headboard hitting the wall. She put her hand on the door handle and swung the door open to find David and Melanie, his twenty four year old secretary, having sex in their marital bed.

Both of them were so engrossed with one another that they didn't notice Francesca watching them. Melanie was sitting on top of David, straddling him, both of them panting and breathing heavily from exertion. She stood, shocked and horrified, in the doorway as Melanie made a squealing noise of pleasure.

Francesca had seen and heard enough. 'Excuse me! Have I interrupted a business meeting?' Her voice was cold but calm, David nearly jumped out of his sin when he heard her.

'Fuck! Francesca! What are you doing here?' He pushed Melanie off so quickly and roughly, it looked as if she'd tried to attack him, as if her sitting on top of him was against his will. 'This isn't what it looks like Cesc...' He didn't know how he was going to talk himself out of it, but he knew it was worth a go.

'Really, David? How stupid do you think I am? Because it looks like you've been shagging your secretary!'

Francesca stared across at Melanie, who was still in shock, sitting on the other side of the bed. Melanie had never felt so awkward in her whole life. She'd come round a bit after dismounting from David and could see Francesca wasn't going to leave the bedroom for her to get dressed. She scrambled out of the bed and walked, totally naked, across the room, picked up her clothes from the floor and hugged them to her body, ironically, to try and cover her modesty from Francesca. 'I'd better leave you two to it.' She didn't dare to look at Francesca as she squeezed past her out of the bedroom.

Francesca calmly walked over to the side of the bed opposite where David was sitting and sat down on the new, soft mattress they had only just bought a few weeks ago.

David felt vulnerable. He was caught off guard and naked. The fact that Francesca was so quiet after walking in on them un-nerved him even more. He covered his naked body with the bed sheets as if for the last twenty two years she'd never seen him naked. Francesca settled herself. She bit the bottom of her lip and stared at him, wondering what to say.

'How long has it been going on?' She wanted to know the details - how long he'd been unfaithful?

'I can explain!'

'How long David?' She didn't want to hear his excuses, not on his terms. She just wanted him to answer her question truthfully.

'About two weeks, that's all.' He said it as if two weeks wasn't long, nothing to write home about, but Francesca knew as soon as he'd said it, as soon as the words had come out of his mouth that he was lying. She almost always knew when he was lying. His giveaway was that his voice went up a couple of octaves. It was something that frustrated him. He was aware of it and would try to control it, but it always made his voice sound stiffer, and the lie even more obvious and Francesca could tell when he was being dishonest. She'd had enough of the lying and the years of just carrying on, suppressing her own feelings. She knew their marriage wasn't great and hadn't been for a long while, but she would never have dreamed of cheating on him. She had bitten her tongue over the years for the amount of stupid things David had done, but what she had walked in on was one thing too many.

'I can't believe you! In our house... In our family home? What if it had been Mia who had come home to find you? It's our house David, our bed! What were you thinking?'

'Please Cesca I can make this up to you.' He tried to grab her arm as she got up from the bed.

Francesca couldn't stand to be near him and turned to face him. 'What, like you did after the first time you cheated on me?'

'That was twenty years ago...' He was angry with her for bringing up the past again. Getting out of bed, he began to get dressed. He put one foot into his trousers and then the other and tugged them up to his waist. He put his shirt on not bothering to button it up. 'We weren't even married then.'

'Oh yes, sorry, I forgot that made it OK!'

'Well you knew about it and you still married me.'

Francesca could feel the rage bubble up inside. She thought, as usual, he was trying to turn it around – her problem, her fault, her issue. 'That's because two weeks later I found out I was pregnant!' She took a few deep breaths to try and calm down. As she took her last deep breath she remembered Mia's notes and her short time limit to get them to her. She didn't want to waste any more time hearing what he had to say so she walked out of the bedroom, leaving David standing there looking at her. She headed across the landing towards Mia's bedroom.

'Where are you going?' He followed her, frustrated with her just leaving, and saying nothing, half way through their argument.

Francesca paced across Mia's bedroom to her desk. She found her notes on the top of a pile of magazines and picked them up. As she went to walk back out David was still standing in the doorway waiting for her to say something. 'I came here because Mia forgot her science notes. I'm glad she asked me now and didn't come home herself to see her father's balls deep in some other woman!' She barged past him and went downstairs to leave.

Jenny looked at Francesca after she'd finished speaking. 'You never told me David had cheated on you before.' She wondered why Francesca would hold back on such an important piece of information about their relationship.

Francesca knew she hadn't mentioned it. She'd done it purposefully because she wanted to put it behind her. A lot of water had passed under the bridge since then. She was a completely different person, more mature, who actually had a voice now. 'I thought I had.' She didn't want to have to explain herself. 'It was just a one night stand with some random girl from university...' She underplayed how much it had hurt her at the time. David had cheated on her when they were dating and she only found out about it because her friend had seen him leaving a party with another student. She confronted him the following day and he confessed. He spent the next four weeks begging her to stay with him, telling her that he was nothing without her. He was her first serious relationship and in the beginning she had loved him but, after the cheating, she felt betrayed, as if his actions had fragmented them in a way that could never be put back together again. If she hadn't found out she was pregnant a week later who knows what would have happened. Maybe she would have felt it was easier to leave him. 'I knew it didn't mean anything. He was drunk and under a lot of stress and pressure from his parents.' She wasn't sure why she was trying to justify his behaviour to Jenny.

'Still it's not a pleasant thing to discover about your partner.'

'It is what it is. I'm glad I found out this time. I'm not as naïve or stupid as I was back then. I know I'm not going to stay with him this time, not again.'

'So you stayed with him when he cheated on you the first time but you won't after the second. Have I got that right?'

Francesca didn't answer the question.

Jenny tilted her head to the side to try and get Francesca's attention. 'Is that what you would advise or expect a friend, or let's say a client to do in that situation?'

Francesca looked up at her. 'It depends on the circumstances.' She felt self-conscious, like Jenny was judging her decision. 'I was pregnant the first time.'

'Lots of women bring up babies by themselves. Did you have the time to consider any other possibilities?' Jenny was questioning her to try and grasp what the situation was and what was going through Francesca's head at the time.

'David was with me when I found out and he'd told his mother before I had even come to terms with the news myself. At the time, yes, I had more options, but I was too young and unsupported by my own family to know what to do, other than keep the baby and stay with him.'

Jenny could hear how defensive Francesca was by her tone of voice. 'I'm not judging you Francesca. I was just trying to get clear in my mind what was going on.' She could see how tense Francesca was talking about it, so she decided to ease up a bit and change the direction of the conversation back to the split with David. 'How have the children taken the news?'

'Mark was happy. As you know he and his father have never seen eye to eye, but Mia... well she's finding it hard.'

'And you? Are you finding it hard?' It was apparent to Jenny that Francesca still hadn't discussed her own feelings. 'Have you stopped working to let your new personal circumstances settle?'

Francesca knew she would ask her that question so she'd made sure, last night, that she had her answer lined up. 'No, I'm still working. I'm still very competent at my job!' It came out more abrupt and defensive than she would have liked.

'I'm not questioning your competence. I'm questioning your emotional stability and how it can be challenging, at the best of times, to have boundaries with clients let alone when you're going through your own personal problems at home.'

Francesca paused, not quite sure what Jenny was implying. She frowned 'What? Are you saying that I shouldn't be working?'

'I'm just saying think about taking some time off, even if it's just a week. Have some time to address your own feelings which is what, as your supervisor, I would suggest. If you do continue to work be careful with your clients and pay extra attention to any projections or transference that may occur.'

After an hour or so Jenny glanced at her watch and saw it was time to wrap the session up. 'Just so you know, I'm going on my travels for the next four months...' She pulled out a card from the back of her diary and wrote a name and number on the back of it. She handed it over to Francesca. 'This is a colleague of mine. If you need to speak with someone, in my absence, he's an excellent listener.'

Relieved the session was nearly done Francesca took the card from her and quickly glanced down at it. 'I see you every three months anyway so four doesn't make much difference...' She put the card in her trouser pocket planning not to need or use it. 'I'll be fine.'

Jenny wasn't completely convinced but she knew only time would tell. There was a possibility that Francesca would just be one of those people who fly through the whole process of splitting up. She had known clients that had and some that had completely lost their identity and standing in the world. If being a therapist had taught Jenny anything it was that you couldn't make someone feel feelings they weren't ready to acknowledge or address.

'Are you going anywhere nice for all that time?' Francesca liked, and wanted to get to, the small talk which always started just before she could leave.

'My partner and I are going over to Australia. My daughter, who we haven't seen for a long time has just had a baby boy and we want to go over to help them settle. I think it's taken her by surprise, just how much work having a baby is.'

Francesca smiled and got up from her seat with the intention of leaving. 'That's lovely.' She straightened out her shirt which had creased up a little from sitting down. 'Well I hope you have a safe journey over and a fantastic time. I'll see you when you get back!'

Jenny put her notes on Francesca down on the floor and got up giving a warm smile. 'That's if I haven't decided to retire by then. I can see myself enjoying the outdoor lifestyle over there!'

They said their goodbyes and Jenny watched Francesca leave knowing that, at some point, some time, she was going to have to face her feelings and let go of trying to control them.

CHAPTER TWO

I t was a busy Friday night at Yani's bar, a relaxing and popular restaurant in the middle of town. It was popular because it was one of the only places that served great tasting food with a modern, relaxed atmosphere. In the evening the tables in the restaurant were lit by candles and fairy lights, which were strung in their hundreds across the ceiling. Shay, who had just turned twenty four, had worked at Yani's, her Uncle George's place, for the past four years. She'd moved over to the United Kingdom from France, her birth place, after her parents had gone their separate ways. George, her father's younger brother, with whom she had always got on, had offered her a job and a bed to sleep in, to help give her some stability so she could get her life together.

'Shay, table five need their drinks.' Frank, one of the waiters at the restaurant had caught Shay's attention as they'd walked past each other by the bar. She didn't look up at him. She knew what he was going to say before he'd said it.

'*Oui*, I've got it!' She walked over to one of the side tables, in a booth, which were always cosy and a favourite with customers. The booths created an intimate, private space and most nights they were usually the first to be taken up.

Four men in their early thirties, wearing business suits, were sitting at table five, having spent the day in the office where they worked together. Their shirts were creased and crumpled, and their ties were hanging loose below the neck. A mixture of old deodorant and body odour was coming from each of them, mixing together and making an unpleasant smell. They were all laughing as Shay approached them with a tray full of the drinks they had ordered. As she approached they all went quiet and watched her as she picked up the first drink from the tray.

'Beer?' One of the younger men motioned to her so she put the drink down in front of him and picked up the second bottle of beer. The man in the corner put his hand up to claim it. Shay had to reach over one of them slightly to put it on the mat in front of him. 'Pardon.' Her soft French accent came out stronger when she spoke softly.

'No worries love, you can bend over me any day!' All the others, except one, laughed at his remark.

Shay tried to ignore it and carry on. 'Diet Coke?' She stood there with the cold glass in her hand but nobody said anything. 'Nobody order a Diet Coke, *non*?'

Barry, the man who had made the crude comment, and the only one without a drink, spoke. 'No darling, I ordered a Coke, not a Diet Coke,' he said in a patronising tone, as if she didn't speak fluent English.

Shay forced a polite smile. '*Pardon.* I'll get that sorted for you now.' She put the drink back on the tray and hadn't even walked out of earshot when the men started talking about her.

'Man, what a sexy accent. I'm totally hitting that tonight!' Barry said as he licked his lips.

'Whatever Baz, but you've got no chance!' His workmate Chris, grinning, wasn't convinced.

'No chance? You know I have a cool tongue and I can talk the ladies into my bed… or up against a wall!' He laughed, believing he was God's gift to women. 'I'm better with women than any of you lot!'

Shay walked back over to the table with the Coke in her hand and placed the drink in front of him. She tried to remember the service course that her uncle had sent her on, before he decided to give her the job…always be polite and civil with the customer no matter what the situation. She looked at Barry, tensed her jaw, and forced a smile. She'd had a bad day as it was. She was tired and sore and just wanted to curl up in bed.

'So when are you going to bring it to me?' Barry was staring at her with a smirk across his face. Shay assumed he was talking about his food but, when she looked at him, she could tell by his face that wasn't what he was insinuating. 'Your telephone number?' He looked her up and down as if she was a piece of meat and continued. 'It's pretty obvious you're into me, so we might as well exchange numbers now, don't you think?'

Shay attempted to be diplomatic and just laugh off his joke. She turned around and left them to it, relieved to be walking away from their table. The others started laughing and one of them, Pete, stared at Barry and shook his head. 'Dude she just totally burned you!' He took a gulp of his beer. 'No chance...'

'Shut up man...' Barry punched Peter playfully on the arm.

'She's playing hard to get, that's all. I bet she's dying for it!'

None of the men had noticed that Shay was serving another table, nearby, and heard every word Barry had said. She'd had enough, not just tonight but in general, with men like him coming in and treating her or Faith, another waitress she worked with, disrespectfully. She finished serving the other table and charged into the kitchen and headed straight for one of the cupboards in the corner. Sam, the chef, who'd been working at the restaurant since it had opened six years ago and had become a good friend of Shay's, watched her.

Shay turned around with a pot of hot chilli powder in her hand and looked at the food prepared, on the counter, ready to be served. 'Is this the order for table five?' She walked over to it with the chilli in her hand.

Sam looked at her concerned. 'Why? What are you planning?' He knew how wild Shay could be. She wasn't always logical but would go with her heart and emotions and act on impulse.

Before Shay could answer him, Faith walked into the kitchen from the restaurant, visibly upset. 'What a bunch of morons! Why do Friday nights always bring out the pricks?'

Shay knew straight away who she was talking about. 'Table five?

'Yes...' Faith put the dirty plates on the side board. 'Complete idiots!'

'So you won't protest about me doing this, then...' Shay lifted her hand and vigorously sprinkled the hot chilli powder on to the chicken dish.

'Shay!' Sam's voice echoing through the kitchen and stopped her from sprinkling any more on. 'You can't do that! George isn't going to like it.'

Shay grabbed the plates of food and smiled, 'You're right, he won't, but he'll get over it!' She walked back into the restaurant, her hands full.

Sam, still a little shocked, looked across to Faith. 'You know she wouldn't get away with that if she wasn't George's niece.' He knew it was hopeless to try and stop her. When Shay wanted to do something she would do it.

Faith shrugged her shoulders 'Perks of working with family I guess?'

Shay served the first plate of beef burger and chips, consciously leaving the chilli coated chicken until last. Faith caught up with her, at the table, holding the rest of the food. She waited for Shay to serve the chicken, but Shay gave her a nod to go first.

Shay waited with the chilli chicken in her hand, holding it up slightly. 'Spicy Chicken?' She looked at Barry, knowing full well it was his order.

'Yes, darling, that's me.'

Shay put it down in front of him. 'Enjoy sir! I put a little extra on there for you.' She winked at him and walked off with Faith following behind her.

Barry puffed his chest out and turned to Peter. 'I told you she was into me! Did you see the way she winked at me? I knew it! Sometimes you've just got to let these girls warm up a bit!' Thinking that he was in for a great night, Barry picked up a chicken wing and took a huge bite. It took him a moment before his mouth registered just how 'hot' the chicken was. His eyes began watering and his face began to flush as the chilli hit his taste buds. 'Jesus…. Jesus this is …' He started to cough, almost choking from the heat in his mouth.

Peter started tapping him on the back, thinking, maybe, he was choking on a bit of chicken. 'Dude, are you alright?'

Shay heard his coughing from behind the bar and waltzed back over to the table with an accommodating smile on her face. 'Is everything OK with your meals gentlemen?'

Trying to breathe and let the fire from his mouth out, Barry saw the smug look on her face. He looked down at the chicken on his plate. 'What the hell did you put on this?'

'I thought you could take the extra heat… you know, as you have such a cool tongue, *oui?*'

'You bitch!' He took a couple of gulps of Coke to try and cool his mouth but the fizzy just made it seem hotter on his tongue. 'I'll have you fired for that!'

Shay smirked at him and walked off, leaving his mates to try and help him cool his mouth down. She didn't care. As far as she was concerned he deserved it!

The next morning Shay arrived at the restaurant with a heavy, blurry head. She'd had a terrible night's sleep, tossing and turning, agitated about the chilli incident.

'Shay! Get over here!' George, her Uncle, was sitting in his usual corner table going through the previous night's takings and till receipts. She had hoped he wouldn't call her over because, if he did, she knew that meant he'd got word of what she'd done last night, and the last thing she wanted or needed right now was a lecture from him. 'Take a seat...' He wasn't impressed.

Shay sat opposite him and gave him her doe-eyed look of 'please don't shout at me'.

George knew her too well to fall for it. 'I take it, by that look, you know what you've done?' George was forty five years old and was not only a friend but also a father figure to her. Usually he was chilled and easy going and Shay could have a laugh with him, but she could tell by his body language and face that now wasn't one of those times. She'd pushed the boundaries too far this time.

'I don't know what you're talking about Uncle George! This is my normal face.'

He ignored her sarcasm and continued. 'I wasn't born yesterday Shay. I've known you since you were a baby so I know the faces you pull!' He shook his head in disappointment. 'What the hell were you thinking?'

Shay tried to play dumb. 'I honestly don't...'

'The French bitch spiked my food?' He read from the piece of paper he had in his right hand 'This is a serious, official complaint made by the customer you served last night.'

Shay joked, trying to lighten the atmosphere and situation. 'How do you know he was talking about me...? I'm not the only bitch that works here!'

'Maybe so, but last time I checked you were the only 'French' one!' George was determined not to be distracted by her light heartedness. 'This is serious Shay! You can't do things like this. What if he had pressed charges?'

She didn't see what the big deal was. It wasn't as though she'd physically assaulted him. 'For what? Putting a little extra chilli on his chicken?'

'For tampering with food.' George picked up all the receipts he'd spread across the table and tucked them into a folder. 'You need to sort yourself out. I know you're hurting, but you can't take your frustration and anger out on other people.'

'He was an idiot!'

'I don't care what he was. You need to get some help for...'

'Don't even go there Uncle George...' Shay stood up, angry at where the conversation was going. 'It was over twelve years ago and I'm over it.' She stomped off and headed for the cloakroom at the back of the restaurant. As she entered Faith was already in there talking to her boyfriend, Dean, on the phone.

'Yes, I'm going out tonight, Dean. You went out last week, so why shouldn't I?' They'd been going out for the past eight months and Dean was struggling with his jealousy. He knew Faith was a catch and he didn't want to lose her but he hated it when she went out without him. Shay couldn't hear what he was saying, over the phone, but she could tell Faith was unhappy because she had her irritated face on. 'Look, some people can go out, drink and have a good time without sleeping with someone at the end of the night...' She looked across at Shay and rolled her eyes, totally fed up with his complaining. 'No Dean, I'm going out! Bye.' She hung up the phone, making sure he couldn't have the last word. 'God! I see why you love them and leave them! Being in a relationship is hard work!'

Shay smiled and wandered over to her, she leant in close to Faith. 'Is that you saying you would like to visit my place for a bit of 'easy' work?'

Faith pushed her back playfully. 'We've already been there Shay and you know how that worked out!'

'Yeah it was great sex that we could have continued for longer if I hadn't gone travelling...'

'No... I mean yes, it was great sex, but I told you...' looking at Shay's face, Faith cottoned on that she was only teasing her and enjoying making her squirm. She stuck her tongue out at her. 'You're such a wind up, Shay!' She put her phone away and hung her bag on one of the hooks on the wall. 'So tell me, was George angry with you about last night? What did he say?'

'I don't want to talk about it... not now, later.' She didn't want to risk George walking in on them. She felt guiltier about what she'd done now, she hadn't thought it through or considered how the incident would reflect on his name or business.

'How about meeting later for a few drinks at Juice nightclub? Tonight, ten o'clock?'

'I'm in.' Shay hung her jacket up on her usual hook and walked back into the main restaurant to start laying out the tables for lunch.

CHAPTER THREE

Julie quietly tapped on Francesca's office door. She opened it and peered around the door frame. 'Sorry Francesca, Dr Sims is on the phone and he would like a word.'

Francesca looked down at her watch. It was late in the afternoon, nearly evening. Officially she shouldn't still be working. 'Can you tell him to ring me back tomorrow morning?'

'I tried but he says it's urgent!'

Francesca scratched her scalp, hesitating whether to take the call or not. 'OK, I'll take it in here.' She waited as Julie walked off back to her reception desk. She could hear Julie speaking for a while when the phone on her desk flashed with an incoming call. She picked it up and leaned back in her black, leather chair. She tried to sound more upbeat than she actually felt. 'Hello Dr Sims, how can I help you?'

'I'm sorry to bother you Dr Draw...' Dr Sims was a G.P in his late sixties. He should really have retired a few years ago, but he was dedicated to his job and always put his patients first, so he'd carried on working at his local surgery. In the past few years he'd referred a few patients to Francesca. He trusted her as a therapist and the way she worked was proven successful by the patients. A high percentage had come back to see him, looking and behaving like a completely different person after seeing Francesca. 'I appreciate it's late and probably out of hours for you, but I'm off on my holiday break for three weeks tomorrow and I don't want to leave my patient in the lurch.' He paused to see if she was keeping up with him and listening.

'Don't worry Dr Sims. I can hear its urgent, go on.'

'Well, her name is Jasmine. She's a fifteen year old young lady who is going through a bit of a hard time at the moment. I really don't have the time to get to know her. Fifteen minutes a patient just isn't enough, as you well know! It's been a challenge to try and find her a suitable person to talk to. Her mother is worried and found her a couple of counsellors but she just doesn't seem to get on with them.'

'Is she seeing a counsellor now?'

'Well that's why I was phoning you! You're one of the best I know, especially when it comes to adolescents. I don't suppose you have any available spaces?' He didn't sound very hopeful but he knew it was worth a try.

Francesca picked up her diary and scanned the pages. She found an available slot. 'I could see her on Wednesday if that's any help? We could meet to see if she would be interested in talking to me.'

'Oh that's great!' He breathed a sigh of relief. 'That's a weight off my shoulders knowing she's going to be in good hands. Thank you. I'll send you over her details.'

After their phone call Francesca made a note in her diary of the new appointment. She wrote Jasmine's name with the words 'new client' underneath. She put her diary away, moved over to her laptop and caught up with her work making some extra notes on the clients she'd seen during the day.

Francesca was on the last client's notes when Julie popped her head around her office door again. Francesca put her finger up in the air so Julie didn't start speaking, she wanted to finish typing her sentence before she lost her train of thought. She finished writing and looked up at Julie.

'Don't you think you should be leaving?' Francesca looked confused, trying to think where she was supposed to be by now. Julie raised her eyebrows as she spoke, 'Mia's play? It's starting in twenty minutes.'

'Oh shit…!' Francesca jumped up from her chair and rushed to get her jacket, which was hanging up in the corner of the room on an antique stand. 'Am I going to get there in time?'

'You might if you don't bump into any traffic.' Julie watched her fluster getting her things together. She held Francesca's car keys up in the air. 'I think you'll need these!'

Francesca grabbed them and headed for the door. 'Thank you! What would I do without you?' She rushed out of the office.

The weather was rough outside. It was raining heavily making for poor visibility. Francesca drove the route she usually took towards Mia's school but by the time she hit the second roundabout she found herself behind a huge line of vehicles that had built up from the bad weather and the road works the local council had created by widening one of the roads. 'You are joking! Come on...!' She beeped her horn under the illusion that it would somehow make the traffic go faster. For the fifth time in the last four minutes she looked down at her watch to check the time. She was already ten minutes late and knew she would probably miss the first fifteen or twenty minutes of the play.

After another ten minutes had passed the traffic had still barely moved. 'Come on! She's going to kill me!' Knowing how much the play meant to Mia, and how much acting meant to her, she was anxious about arriving late seeing as their relationship was strained at the moment. Francesca had secretly hoped it wasn't just because of the split with David but also about Mia being a teenager and having hormones flying around her body.

CHAPTER FOUR

Mark was sitting in the audience next to his father, David. The play was about thirty minutes in and it was tense between the two of them, more so from Mark's side than David's. He hadn't seen his father for a few weeks, which suited him. He couldn't stand him at the best of times. To have to sit next to him for so long wasn't something he would have chosen but Mia had reserved the seats together for them.

The school hall was packed full of people, a mixture of parents, locals and teachers. Mark knew he was biased but he thought Mia outshone all the other pupils in the play. For him, they all seemed like classic school amateur actors, wooden and nervous, but Mia was something else. She showed real promise and he knew how hard she'd worked on her dialogue and understanding of her character. For the past couple of months she'd been on the phone to him most days, running it by him, asking him what he thought. Really he didn't know the first thing about the acting process. He just knew it was nice to see and hear Mia so passionate and animated about something. He was aware she was finding everything else going on at the moment tough.

He looked down at his phone screen to check the time. Francesca was more than late. He gazed over to the hall entrance, wishing his mum was there now to see and watch how well Mia was doing on stage. He whispered under his breath to himself, 'Come on mum.' Mark started fidgeting his right leg, bouncing it up and down. David, irritated by it, pinned Mark's leg to the floor with his hand.

'Will you stop fidgeting?' He whispered in his son's ear.

Mark, annoyed at his father telling him what to do, turned slowly and looked at him. 'Take your hands off me!'

David could hear the annoyance and aggression in his voice. He moved his hand off his leg.

'Don't start Mark...'

'Me don't start? That's rich coming from you! I didn't realise you wanted us to play happy families still, put on a show for everyone, pretend you didn't shag your secretary!'

David was paranoid about people knowing and was aware Mark was speaking too loudly. 'That's enough!'

A woman sitting in the audience in front of them coughed lightly and awkwardly, she shuffled in her seat pretending it was just out of discomfort. David leant closer to Mark's ear and whispered even lower. 'Keep it down! Not here Mark. Now's not the time. Tonight is about Mia.' Mark wanted to tell his father he should be the one to keep it down...it being his penis, but Mia came back onto the stage and briefly broke the rising tension between them.

Mark saw Mia glance across to where they were sitting in the audience. He saw the disappointment on her face as she noticed the empty chair that had been reserved for Francesca. He knew no one else would have understood her look because it was only slight, but he saw it. He knew his little sister too well not to see it.

Francesca parked the car outside the school. It was still pouring with rain so she ran across the school yard, holding her jacket over her head, into the old school building. Damp from the rain she crept as quietly as she could into the hall. The play was in the middle of a scene so she crouched down and tried not to block anyone's view or draw attention to herself. She scanned the audience and looked for an empty chair, when out of the corner of her eye she spotted Mark trying to get her attention as subtly as he could. He'd heard the door creak open a few times during the play, each time hoping it was Francesca. She smiled at him and half raised her hand to let him know she'd seen him. She did her best to get to the seat next to him without disturbing anyone.

She reached the empty chair and sat down quietly, putting her wet jacket, along with her handbag, on the floor by her feet.

Mark spoke softly into her ear, 'Where have you been mum?'

'I know. I know. I'm sorry. I got held up.'

'You know she's going to...'

'Never forgive me? Yes I know.' Francesca looked across Mark's body at David, whose attention had been distracted by a text message on his phone. He was so transfixed he hadn't even noticed or realised Francesca had arrived. 'What's he doing here?' She whispered a little bitterly into Mark's ear.

'Mia invited him.'

Francesca pulled a surprised face. 'Really?' David had never been interested in Mia's acting before.

'Yes, really, mum! That's what's going to keep happening if you keep lying to her. She should know what dad did. He sure as hell isn't going to tell her!'

Francesca went to say something, but somebody next to them hushed them with a look of disapproval and annoyance.

Francesca and Mia were alone in the car as she drove them back home after the play. Mark had told them he was stopping off at a friend's house before he came home, otherwise Mia would have gone home in his car, to save herself from having to be in her mother's company. It was painfully tense between them as the heaters on the dashboard blared out some well needed hot heat. Mia was in a mood and had barely acknowledged Francesca for the whole evening, even after the play when everyone was talking and mingling.

Francesca tried to ease the tension by breaking the silence. 'That was a nice surprise, Mark driving back from university to watch your play...' There was no response, so she tried a different angle. 'You were brilliant tonight Mia.'

Mia took her phone out of her pocket and started playing with it. She looked through old photos and messages. Anything to ignore what Francesca was saying.

'Look Mia, I'm sorry I was late. I got held up at work and...'

'You're always held up at work, mum. I'm lucky if I even get dinner these days!'

'You're nearly seventeen Mia and more than capable of making your own dinner!'

'Whatever!' She knew her mum was right but, for her, that wasn't the point.

Francesca felt guilty after saying it. She knew her break up with David had been tough and out of the blue for Mia and she hadn't really had a proper conversation about it with her yet because every time she'd tried Mia had always shut her down, not wanting to acknowledge the separation. She would tell Francesca that it was her fault and she should just find more time for David.

'I know it's not ideal what's happen with me and your dad, especially so close to your exams, but things will come right eventually... it's hard for me too, your dad leaving. Everything feeling like it's been tipped upside down...'

Mia jumped in, 'So why don't you get back together? Tip it back the right way again?'

Francesca could hear the desperation in Mia's voice. She was desperate for her parents to just get back together again, so it could be how it used to be. Francesca felt another pang of guilt and put her hand on Mia's leg to try and calm her. 'It's not as easy as that sweetheart.'

'Why not? Why can't you make it that easy? Just tell him he can move back in again...'

Francesca didn't know what to say. She squeezed Mia's leg which only riled Mia even more because she knew it was an 'it's never going to happen' squeeze of pity.

'Do you know what...?' She pushed Francesca's hand off her leg, 'Forget it!'

There was five more minutes of awkward silence between them in the car before Francesca pulled up on their drive. She cut the engine and decided to make one last effort to make amends with Mia.

'Why don't we order a pizza and watch a movie, just the two of us, like we used to?'

'No thanks, I'm tired. I've got studying to do.' Mia got out of the car and slammed the car door behind her. She had only been studying for an hour or so when Stacey, one of her friends at school, texted her to come over. Mia got her things together and ran down the stairs. As she opened the front door Francesca caught her in the hallway.

'Where are you going Mia? It's late!'

'I'm studying over at Stacey's.' She didn't give Francesca a chance to disapprove. She just walked out and slammed the front door behind her.

CHAPTER FIVE

Shay was relaxing in her flat, reading a magazine on her sofa. She'd finished her evening shift an hour ago when a text from Faith came through on her mobile.

U COMING OUT 2NITE? XX

She turned and looked at the huge pile of washing up in her kitchen sink and weighed up her options. She hadn't washed up for the past five days or so and it was building up into a mound by the sink. She texted Faith back knowing how she would prefer to spend her time.

PICK ME UP AT 9PM XX

The line outside Club Juice was the longest Shay had seen in a while. She was glad to see it was Nathan on the door as he was one of the bouncers that had worked there for years. He knew Shay well from when she had worked at the club herself as the D.j. Faith followed her as she strolled to the front of the line, confident Nathan would let them straight in.

When they got there Nathan was busy with two young ladies who were causing a bit of a commotion. 'Look girls you're not coming in! I wasn't born yesterday and there's no way you're twenty one.' He handed back the fake ID's to one of the young ladies. 'You should have tried eighteen first.'

'This is a joke!' The two young women were Stacey and Mia. Stacey had invited Mia over with the lure of studying but when she'd got to her house she had informed her they were going out clubbing with the new fake ID's she'd ordered from her brother's friend, Freddie, who had promised he was the best at procuring fake ID's. Mia hadn't cared where they went as long as it wasn't back to her house. If she was honest she'd had enough of trying to cram in more studying and wanted a break.

'Come on, let us in! Look, look the ID's. We're twenty one.' Stacey refused to give up convincing the bouncer they were old enough to enter. She fluttered her eyes to try and charm him and held the ID's out again to show him, but he was having none of it.

Shay watched them, feeling a little bit sorry for them. When she was younger she had experienced being turned away in front of a crowd of people many times, with a fake ID. She had glanced at the ID's as they had been held out and thought they look pretty genuine, but Nathan, after years of experience, was a professional at spotting them.

Shay caught Mia's eye as she turned around to see all the people being held up by them. She gave Shay a bashful smile feeling embarrassed by how full on Stacey was being with the bouncer. If it was up to Mia she was happy just to leave.

Faith, who was watching behind Shay's shoulder whispered into her ear. 'I used to try that one when I was under age!' She would always try and play the cute card when she was younger, hoping her sweet and innocent, but sexy, face would get her into clubs.

Nathan had had a few underage people trying to blag their way in and he'd always given them a blatant no, but for some reason he decided to play with Stacey and Mia a little. He wanted to see how well they had planned the whole thing. 'What year were you born?' he asked.

Stacey tried to look at the dates on the ID's so they matched, but Nathan snatched them from her before she could. He stared down at her, 'No, without looking! What year were you born?'

She hesitated too long which did nothing but confirm his suspicion. 'Nineteen... ninety...uh... SIX!' Stacey was still trying to do the maths in her head.

Nathan, humouring her, glanced down at the dates on the cards. 'I thought you said you were twenty one?'

'We are!'

Mia knew Stacey's mistake. Maths was never her strong point. 'That would make us twenty not twenty one.' It was the first verbal involvement Mia had had in the conversation and Stacey wasn't impressed by it.

'Shut up Mia!' She looked at Nathan again. 'Yeah, well, whatever! It still makes us old enough!'

'Mia? Is that your name? How come neither of these ID's has the name Mia on them?' He handed the cards back over to Stacey. 'Nice try ladies! Now stop wasting my, and everyone else's, time and get out of the line!' He looked up at the line of club goers to check the next people in the line when he spotted Shay and Faith standing off to the side of the crowd. He smiled at Shay and gave her a nod and gesture for her to go on through.

Shay and Faith headed for the entrance. When she approached Nathan they shook hands and gave each other a quick hug.

Nathan ignored Stacey and Mia and checked the next group of people waiting to get in. Giving up, they pulled away from the line and began to walk away from the club.

'That was embarrassing! Matt better give me a refund for these stupid ID's. He charged me thirty quid each for them!' Stacey was more than annoyed. Her whole night was ruined as far as she was concerned.

'Why don't we try and get someone to buy us some alcohol next time and have our own party? It seems a lot easier than going through all that again.' Mia's suggestion helped Stacey get over her mood. Thinking it was a good idea she stopped and looked at Mia.

'Yeah, maybe your brother would?'

It wasn't exactly what Mia meant but she was happy for Stacey to believe it, as long as it meant she wasn't going to be in a grump with her all night.

Club Juice was busy and bustling with people. The noise from the music thumped through the hot stuffy air. Shay and Faith had been dancing together in the themed strobe lighting for an hour or so when Faith moved away and started dancing with a man who was part of a stag party. Shay decided now would be a good time for a drink. She walked through a crowd of hot, sweaty bodies over to the bar. She saw a gap and got served straight away. The bar man nodded at her for her order. She shouted over the music so he could hear.

'Shot please mate.' He served her a shot and Shay downed it in one. As she slammed the empty glass down on the bar she ordered another one. Not knowing he was helping her drink into her feelings of numbness the barman topped her up again. Shay picked up the second shot glass and turned to take in the crowd. She lent her back on the bar and spotted a woman standing across the room staring at her. She downed her second shot and noticed the woman was now smiling at her, as if she knew her. Shay turned to put her empty glass on the bar again and waited for the barman to come back over.

'Hey..!' It was the woman who had been staring at her. She purposely stood close to Shay's body as she spoke. 'I'm Jade.'

'Shay.' For some reason Shay didn't feel that interested, which was very unusual for her. The woman was a hot, sexy, twenty something who wasn't shy in showing, by her body language, that she had taken a liking to Shay. Any other night Shay wouldn't have hesitated to go to bed with someone like her, but what George had said to her, about sorting herself out after the chilli incident, was still distracting and bothered her.

Jade put her hand out. 'It's nice to meet you. How are you?'

Shay shook her hand to be polite. When she tried to let go Jade playfully held on to it for a bit longer and stared into her eyes. 'I've seen you around here before. Don't you DJ here sometimes?'

Shay made sure to hold her own physical space. She could feel Jade's fiery energy pushing against hers, trying to pull her body in. 'Yeah, I used to, but I don't anymore.'

She combed her hair back with her fingers. Jade took it as an invitation to move in closer against her body.

'That's a shame! You always played the best beats... and you always looked good!'

Shay had thought she was closed down physically but she could feel herself begin to respond. Jade's body was pressed right up against hers, she'd taken over her personal space now. She was impressed by Jade's confidence. 'Really?'

'Really...' Jade held her gaze with a strong intensity. 'So do you want to go somewhere?'

Shay paused as she looked Jade up and down, imagining how she could work her body. 'That's very tempting because you're beautiful and seem nice, but I would warn you not to get involved with me. I'm trouble and a mess rolled into one!' She felt she had given her fair warning...a chance to walk away, but Jade wasn't bothered. She put her lips to Shay's ear and whispered loudly.

'I've wanted to talk to you for ages...' She kissed and nibbled on shay's earlobe, 'and for the record, I like trouble!'

Shay grabbed Jade's hand and walked her over to one of the private side rooms. As soon as they entered Shay closed the door and started to kiss her. She pushed Jade up against the wall and reached under her dress. Squeezing her buttocks with her hands she pushed and thrust Jade's pelvis towards and against her own. Excited and aroused Jade moaned.

Back in the middle of the dance floor Jade's friends were oblivious to where their friend was and what she was doing. Lucy, one of Jade's best friends, was swaying along to the music completely entranced by it, when she was grabbed by the arm from behind and interrupted.

'Where's Jade?' It was Jade's boyfriend Charlie, a self-centred and jealous man that, if they were honest, none of Jade's friends liked.

'I don't know...' She pulled his strong, large hand off her arm and tried not to look too disgusted. 'She went to get a drink at the bar and she hasn't come back yet.' Lucy was surprised to see Charlie there as she was sure Jade had told her he wasn't coming tonight.

'I thought you couldn't come tonight?'

He gave her a sickeningly sly grin. 'I lied. I wanted to surprise her.' He walked away from her and went over to the bar where he spotted the barman, who he knew, and greeted him with a wink. 'Busy tonight huh?' He didn't wait for the barman to reply. 'Have you seen Jade?'

The barman wondered whether or not to say anything. He was friends with Shay and didn't want to put her in a compromising position, but everyone knew Charlie was an idiot who thought he was some kind of demi God. The barman had despised him ever since he found out he had slept with his ex-girlfriend, when he was still dating her. They had broken up in the end because of it a - six year relationship ruined from just that one night that he suspected Charlie probably didn't even remember, but he decided Shay was a strong enough woman to stand up for herself and nodded towards the side where the booths were. 'Last time I saw her she was heading for the VIP booth.'

'Cheers mate.' Charlie went to shake his hand but the barman pretended he needed to pour a pint so he didn't have to make any kind of contact with him.

Shay had moved to kissing up and down Jade's neck. Jade grabbed Shay's hand with an urgency and put it under her skirt, between her legs. She groaned and tilted her head back as Shay hit a sensitive spot with her finger.

Shay had her back to the door and didn't see Charlie open it and enter the room. Jade bent forward, unable to take the amount of pleasure building in her body. She opened her eyes and gasped, Charlie was staring at her.

'Oh shit!' Shay didn't stop. She assumed Jade had said it because of how she was touching her.

Charlie stormed over to them, his face red with anger, and pulled Shay away from Jade. He glared at his girlfriend. 'What the fuck Jade? I come here to surprise you on your birthday, and you're letting some chick feel you up?' He glared over at Shay who was standing holding her hands up in the air, not wanting any trouble.

'Hey, she never said she had a boyfriend.'

Charlie, furious, grabbed Jade tightly by the wrist and tried to pull her out of the room, back into the club. Jade tried desperately to pull back. 'Get off me Charlie, you're hurting me!'

'Pardon...' Shay kept her cool. 'Let her go! She obviously doesn't want to be touched... not by you anyway...' Shay couldn't help herself with having the last comment.

Charlie let Jade go and walked over to Shay. He squared up to her and tried to intimidate her using his body and size.

Not willing to even entertain his aggression Shay turned away and headed for the door. 'I don't have time for this shit!' she mumbled to herself.

Charlie shouted at her. 'Hey! Where are you going? I didn't say you could leave!' Shay ignored him, opened the door and walked back into the club. The loudness of the music hit her eardrums straight away.

Charlie, not satisfied with her just walking away, followed her out. He caught up with her and grabbed her from behind by the upper arm.

Shay pulled her arm forward to make him let go but it just made him hold on tighter. 'Get off me!' He didn't let go and carried on gripping her arm. Furious and triggered by his physical restriction on her she exploded. 'I said get the fuck off me!' She punched him hard, straight on the nose, and felt it crack against her fist. Blood started to pour out and dripped onto his shirt making a large red patch. In pain, he let go of her and put his hands to his nose.

'You just assaulted me, you bitch!' He screamed and made a scene knowing the other clubbers must have seen it all and were witnesses. He turned to look around, 'Did you see that?' No one said anything. They just watched. The music was turned down by security who were aware something was going on in the club, though they hadn't located where yet. Faith, who had still been dancing with her stag party man, pushed through the crowd to see what the commotion was. She saw Shay standing, holding on to her swollen and bruised hand. She looked at Charlie, who was attempting, with no luck, to try and stop the bleeding from his nose.

'Shay, you OK? What's going on?'

'Nothing! This arsehole just didn't listen to me!' She felt calm again, now he wasn't in her personal space or holding her back.

'The bitch just broke my nose...' Charlie shouted, having heard Faith's question and Shay's answer. 'That's what just happened!' Somebody standing by him in the crowd could see Charlie was still bleeding badly and passed him a cold beer bottle to put on his nose to help the blood clot more quickly. Charlie snatched the bottle from him as he glared at Shay. 'You're going to pay for that! I'll have you for assault!'

'Do what you want, I don't care.' She walked off, out of the club, leaving the crowd behind her stunned with what had just happened.

CHAPTER SIX

'Good morning. How was the play?' Julie was her usual chirpy self when she greeted Francesca, who wasn't in a good mood. Mia had blanked her all through breakfast refusing to talk to her. She was grateful Mark was there to make it seem a bit less awkward and tense between the two of them.

Julie didn't need an answer. The look on Francesca's face was enough for her to know. 'Oh... Well your first client is here.'

In her office, Roger, a 49 year old man who Francesca had been seeing for the past nine months, was sitting down on the sofa in front of her. She sat in her usual chair opposite him. Roger never needed any prompting to start talking and today was no exception. 'I just don't understand what women don't see in me? I mean look at me... I'm handsome...' He wasn't handsome at all, even if you could see through the challenging personality he was still one of those men who'd been mollycoddled for far too long by their mother. The clothes he wore didn't help his case rather, he had no sense of style or colour co-ordination. 'I'm smart, rich... what more could a girl ask for?'

Francesca tried to stay present and actually listen to what he was saying but it was the same story with Roger every week. The only two things he ever talked about were himself and women.

'I think you mean, what more can a woman ask for. Last time I checked Roger you were a forty nine year old man.'

'Yeah but really I feel like twenty five!'

Francesca had heard that so many times. More or less every man that had come into her office having a midlife crisis would proclaim the same thing. She decided to challenge him about it.

'You feel like you're twenty five, or you want to be twenty five? Because there's a big difference...' He laughed at her question thinking she was teasing him. She wasn't.

'Touché, Dr. Francesca! You see, this is why I come to you, because you understand me... besides what else would you do on a Monday!'

'I don't know Roger, probably twiddling my thumbs wishing and waiting for you to come back!'

He completely missed her sarcasm. 'Really?'

'No Roger. I would be seeing other clients.'

Roger sighed. 'So tell me doc... what do I do? How do I find a woman good enough for me?'

In that moment, for some reason, Francesca was willing to humour him. She looked down at the hand written notes from their last session and scanned the page.

She saw the words, another woman, another date, written down next to all her doodles.

'You had a date with a woman last week, didn't you? How did that go?'

He brushed his purple suede trousers, which he had owned for over thirty years. 'Who, Susanne? No that's over.'

'Why, what happened?'

He re-adjusted his bright red tie. 'It was going well, or so I thought, until she flipped out on me out of nowhere!'

Francesca put her notes down on her lap and looked at him like a mother would a naughty child. 'What did you do?'

'What makes you think it was me that did something?' Roger wasn't usually easily offended but he was a little offended by her assumption.

'Because your track record with women is that you usually do or say something that isn't always appropriate.'

He puffed his chest out with pride, 'I think I'm very appropriate...'

FIVE DAYS AGO.

Roger was on a first date with a lady called Suzanne. He'd chosen a restaurant he knew and liked and felt comfortable in. As he sat opposite her, on the table for two, he checked out every woman in the restaurant as they walked by. Suzanne was quite tolerant and let the first couple of glances go but by the third, fourth and fifth time she had really had enough. They had only been seated for five minutes and he had made it clear, even though they were supposed to be on a date, that he was still keeping his options very much open. He picked up the glass of red wine he'd ordered and swilled it around the glass. He took a sip and put the glass back down.

'So how old are you?' It was always one of his first questions on a date.

'Actually it's my birthday next week...' Suzanne was quite upbeat about answering, she thought maybe this was the part during their date when she actually had his attention. 'I turn thirty one. I'm hoping to go out to New York with some of my friends and live it up a bit.'

'Oh sounds nice.' His voice went flatter as if he had no interest in furthering the conversation. He went quiet as he took a few more sips of wine.

Suzanne looked at him, waiting for him to ask something else. 'Is something wrong Roger?'

'No. It's just that I don't usually date women over twenty nine...' He was completely oblivious to his rudeness and didn't even register Suzanne's look of disgust. He proceeded to ask her another question. 'So do you like jazz?'

'I'm more into pop or electro music myself...' she tried to give him the benefit of the doubt, that maybe it was a one off comment.

'I can't stand electro music. I don't see the point of it. It just sounds like noise to me.' He spoke over her before she could even finish her sentence.

Suzanne gritted her teeth feeling that Roger was starting to sound like noise to her. She was relieved when the waiter came over to take their orders.

Roger ordered the rib eye steak and Suzanne ordered the vegetarian meal. He stared at her. 'Do you not eat meat?' The waiter, knowing what was likely to happen, saw his chance and walked off. He knew Roger and his tactlessness with women, having served him the last three times. He'd been in with a different date each time and none of them had ended well.

'No. I've been veggie since I was a teenager.'

'Oh dear, we're not having a good start!'

Suzanne grimaced at him and uttered under her breath, 'I've had better as well.'

Roger didn't hear her and continued to vocalize his thoughts. 'I mean we don't seem to be doing well compatibility wise.' He paused to take another sip of his wine. 'Maybe it's best for us to have sex tonight, you know, make sure we are at least sexually compatible!'

Suzanne, who was offended and had reached her limit with him, stood up and threw her glass of water over him. The whole restaurant looked round to see what was going on when she began screaming at him about how disgusting he was and how every single woman on the planet deserved better than him.

Francesca winced hearing his story. She felt sorry for Suzanne and for every woman that had endured a date with him. 'You honestly can't see why she did that and ended the date?'

'Well yes, obviously it must have been that she wasn't too happy with the fact that I eat meat... which is a shame as I was willing to see past the vegetarian thing. She was gorgeous... for her age.'

Francesca exhaled, astonished by Roger's level of narcissism. She looked down at her watch to check the time and was relieved to see that the hour had gone. She moved forward in her chair. 'Well that's it for today's session I'm afraid.'

'That's a shame. It went really quickly...' Roger got up to leave as Francesca mumbled to herself, 'For you it did.' He put on his ugly leather jacket which he wore to every session.

'I'll see you next week then, unless I find my 'wife to be' before!'

He left and Francesca was glad to see the back of him, for at least another week or so. She lay down on the sofa in her office and attempted to relax a bit when her mobile went off. She got up and walked over to her handbag, took her phone out and saw David's name on the screen. At first she hesitated, but then decided to answer.

'Hello.'

'Oh, so you are talking to me then!' He made it sound more of an accusation than a question.

'Yes I'm talking to you David. I answered the phone didn't I?'

'Well, at Mia's play you didn't really speak to me. I thought we were going to make an effort, for the kids, to keep things civil?'

'I wasn't not talking to you it's just that it was late. Trying to have a conversation while a play is on isn't exactly the best time for a chitty chat!'

He huffed, feeling she was purposely patronising him. 'You know what I mean.'

Francesca felt impatient and annoyed. She knew David was phoning for a reason but he was taking his time to get to the point. 'What do you want David? I'm busy. I've got work to do.'

'I was just checking with you, if it's OK for Mia to stay around my place next weekend?'

Francesca's initial answer would have been a no but she didn't want to antagonise their relationship, much as she disliked him. 'If she wants to, it's OK with me.' It felt hard for her to get the words out 'Do you want me to ask her..?'

'No, it's OK. I know she wants to since she was the one who suggested it.'

Francesca felt a little hurt and a bit embarrassed that they had already discussed and organised it all. 'Oh right, OK...' She went quiet. She could hear David's breath down the telephone line.

'I'm sure she would have asked you.' He wasn't trying to reassure her he was just trying to fill the silence. 'I'll text her and say it's on. I will see you Friday next week? You haven't forgotten have you?'

Francesca had gone blank and couldn't remember what they had arranged for Friday. 'What's happening next week?'

David huffed again knowing she would forget. 'My mother's having a dinner to celebrate her birthday.'

Francesca flicked through her diary to see if she had written it in, she had. She didn't know why because she didn't really want to go. 'Don't you think it's time you told your mother we've split up?'

'No Cesca! She's an old woman with a weak heart. She doesn't need to know yet!'

'She needs to know at some point David. I'm not going over there and pretending.'

He became short with her. 'I realise that but there's a time and a place.'

She didn't really want to argue with him over the phone. It was one more evening with her soon to be ex mother-in-law. 'I assume that Mark and Mia are invited?'

'Of course. Mia wants me to pick her up.'

Francesca gasped. 'Am I that awful she doesn't even want to be in a car with me?'

David stayed silent and said nothing.

Francesca circled the date again in her diary so it was more obvious to the eye. 'I guess I'll see you next week then. What time?'

'Seven. I'll see you then.' He put the phone down and finished the call.

CHAPTER SEVEN

Julie was sitting behind reception, at her desk, typing some appointment letters when Shay walked through the door. 'Shay Bentley?' Julie gave her a smile. She was expecting her as Francesca's next client.

'That would be me.'

Julie stopped typing and gave Shay her full attention. It's nice to meet you. I'm Julie, Dr Francesca's receptionist.'

Shay was a little confused by the doctor's name mentioned. 'I thought I was seeing a...' she looked at her appointment letter she'd been sent through the post, 'a Dr Draw?'

'Dr Draw is Dr Francesca. We're pretty relaxed here and use first names.'

'OK.' Shay nodded.

'If you would like to take a seat Dr Francesca will be with you in a minute.'

She smiled at Julie. 'Just the one!'

'Just the one what?' Julie frowned not understanding the joke.

'Just the one minute!' Shay winked at her with a cheeky grin.

Julie realised the joke and in that moment she decided she liked Shay and her cheekiness. She smiled at her, 'Well, maybe two!'

Francesca left her office and walked into reception. She didn't see Shay tucked in the corner of the waiting room. 'God what a day...' She squeezed the back of her neck with her hand to try and loosen the tightness in neck muscles.

Believing they were alone Julie could tell Francesca was about to let off steam. 'Your next client is here Dr Francesca, Shay Bentley.'

'Oh right, OK.' A little surprised her next client was here already Francesca turned around.

Shay popped her head around the corner and smiled at her. Francesca hesitated a little when she saw her. They were both silent as they took one another in for the first time. Francesca felt an immediate discomfort and unease in her body. Shay felt an immediate intrigue and attraction.

Francesca realised they were staring at each other for a little too long, she cleared her throat. 'Shay, I'm Dr Francesca. Would you like to come through?'

Shay checked Francesca out from behind as she followed her down the corridor to her office. Francesca reached the end of the corridor and stopped in the door way. She turned to face Shay and motioned for her to go in a head of her. She couldn't be sure if it was her who hadn't left enough room, or whether Shay had purposely moved in closer towards her, to intimidate her, but as Shay walked past she was closer than Francesca felt comfortable with. She cleared her throat again and turned away from Shay. 'Please take a seat.'

Shay sat down on the sofa as Francesca closed her office door. Shay observed and watched her every move from the sofa. 'You're not how I had imagined!'

'How did you imagine me?' Francesca sat down on her seat and made sure her skirt was pulled down.

'I don't know...a lot older...a man maybe?' She raised her eyebrows and smirked 'Not so hot!'

Uncomfortable with the compliment, Francesca squirmed in her chair. 'Thank you...' This time she pretended to clear her throat. 'So what can I do for you?'

Shay remembered why she was there and, unintentionally, went a little cold and defensive. 'Nothing. You can't do anything for me.'

Francesca paused and waited to see if Shay said anything else but she didn't. She just stared at her holding her eye contact. Finding her gaze too intense Francesca got up and walked over to her desk to try and create a bit more physical space between them. Before, she'd never felt her chair and the sofa the clients sat on were too close together, but right now she was contemplating moving her chair back a little for next time. She reached for Shay's notes and the letter sent from the court and walked back to her seat and sat down holding the letter in her hand. 'That's not what this letter says.' Her tone was a little sharper than usual.

'What does the letter say?'

Francesca looked at the piece of paper. 'That a court order, after an incident in a club, has requested you see me for some sessions. After we've completed the sessions together you can be signed off, if we reach satisfactory results, otherwise you will go back to court and face a time in prison for assault...' She looked up at Shay, 'Prison doesn't look good on anybody's record...'

Shay tried to dodge the seriousness of the court order and the situation she found herself in. She had managed to stay clear of shrinks for most of her life and there was no way was she going to start talking about herself now. 'So I need to satisfy you, *oui*?' She moistened her lips with her tongue and raised her eyebrows at Francesca.

Francesca knew what she was insinuating and tried to ignore it. 'I guess you could say that...' Shay could tell by Francesca's body language that she made her nervous. She liked it.

Francesca attempted to take charge of the conversation. 'Shall we start? Why don't you tell me how you managed to get this court decision in the first place?'

Shay didn't really want to talk about it but she knew the sooner they started the sooner they would finish and she could leave. 'I broke a man's nose. It's as simple as that really...' she acted as if it was no big deal 'Right, done. Now can I go?'

Francesca ignored her request. 'Right, tell me more but in a bit more detail.'

'I ended up in a club a little drunk. Some man grabbed me and he wouldn't let go, so I punched him.' She paused and scratched her nose. 'He pressed charges and the judge thinks I have anger issues, so here I am *voila!*'

The room went quiet as Francesca waited for her to say more. Shay just sat there picking at the frayed knee on her jeans.

'Is that it? That's your version of events?'

'That's it.' Shay shrugged her shoulders, 'Why, do you want more?' She raised her eyebrows again.

Francesca did her best not to react and looked at the judge's letter again instead. 'Well it says here that the judge is under the impression you've had a couple of angry outbursts recently...' She searched the page for an example. 'There was a restaurant incident with a member of the public?'

Shay, annoyed, became defensive again. 'Why are you asking me questions that are obviously already answered on that letter?'

'Because I want to hear your perspective on things. I'm here to help you Shay, if you'll let me?'

Provoked by the word 'help.' Shay scoffed. 'Why? Do you want to hear me pour my heart out about what's really going on?' She leant forward so the space between them was even closer. 'Does that make you feel better, hearing people's sadness and fixing it?' She was trying to provoke her but Francesca stayed quiet and held her space. Getting no response, Shay leant back against the sofa. 'It sounds like whatever you want to know about me, you just need to ask the Judge in charge of my case because he seems to think he knows me...'

'Is that you trying to tell me you're feeling cornered...sad maybe?' It was a reach but Francesca thought it was worth a try to nudge her into talking about her feelings.

'Fuck you!' Shay felt that Francesca was toying with her.

The room went quiet again and Francesca knew she'd pushed too soon. She played with her ear, something she always did when she was nervous or uncomfortable and took a couple of deep breaths to try and decrease the intensity in the room. She looked at Shay, who stayed completely silent.

Francesca knew from Shay's body language that she had had enough. 'Look it's obvious you don't want to be here. Can't we just try and work through this?'

Shay's only response was to uncross her arms which Francesca interpreted as a bit less defensive, maybe even acceptance. She continued. 'Tell me about the man you punched. Is that your usual response to someone that grabs you?'

'*Non.* He was a big guy who was angry and threatening and I was protecting myself.' As she answered the question Francesca jotted down the words Shay used to describe him.

'Why was he so threatening?'

'Probably because he caught me with his girlfriend!'

Francesca lingered before responding to be sure that she'd heard correctly. 'He caught you with his girlfriend?' Shay nodded. 'Did you know she had a boyfriend?'

'*Non.* I assumed she didn't. She was the one who came onto me.'

Francesca didn't know why she felt so uncomfortable, as she pretended to jot down more notes. 'So you were kissing this woman?'

'We were doing a bit more than kissing!' She smirked, knowing Francesca was trying to hide her discomfort at discussing her sexual antics.

'So you're gay?'

'*Non.*'

Francesca tried again. 'Bisexual?'

'*Non.*'

'What do you identify as?'

'I don't identify with anything but the moment I'm in, and the person I'm experiencing that moment with.'

Francesca thought she had it. 'So you're pansexual then?'

Shay laughed. 'You shrinks are funny! You have to tick your boxes. You can't just let things be in a space of possibility...' She got up from the sofa and walked around the room, to take in the new space. She walked over to Francesca's desk and spotted a picture frame on the edge. Shay picked it up and looked at it. It was a photo of Francesca and her family taken a few years ago. 'Is this your family?'

Francesca felt uneasy with Shay standing behind her. She turned so she could see her. 'Yes.' A bit of her wanted to be annoyed at her for picking up the photo, but she knew that if she didn't want people to see it she should have taken it out of her office. No one else had ever mentioned it to her before.

Shay pointed to David in the photograph and turned the frame towards Francesca. 'Your husband?'

'Yes.'

She turned the frame back around and studied Francesca in the photo 'You don't look happy.'

The observation made Francesca feel uncomfortable. She felt as if she was being analysed. It was true what Shay had noticed, she wasn't happy in the photo and hadn't been for a good few years before it had been taken.

She got up and walked over to Shay and took it from her grasp and put it back on the desk before she could notice anything else in the photograph. 'We're not here to talk about me. We're here to talk about you.' She felt off track with this client and flustered. She took another couple of deep breaths and walked back over to her chair.

Shay knew and liked the fact that she'd got under her skin so soon. She went back over to the sofa and sat back down. Staying silent she stared at Francesca.

Francesca could feel her eyes burning into her 'What?'

'Nothing.' She smiled, teasing her some more.

'No, go on, you've obviously got something to say!' Francesca crossed her legs and then her arms, waiting for Shay to talk.

'I just totally pissed you off then, didn't I?'

'No you didn't piss me off...' She tried to stay calm and professional. 'It's fine. Lots of people have commented on that photo.'

'Bullshit! You frowned and your nose crinkled slightly. My ex-boyfriend used to do exactly that when he was pissed off. It was quick but I saw you do it... it was kind of cute.'

Francesca felt Shay was goading her. 'You're very observant of the people around you, aren't you?'

'I have to be. That's how I survive.' Shay brushed her hair back, away from her face, with her fingers.

'Survive what?' Francesca asked.

'Life and the unfair bullshit it can throw at you.' Francesca stayed quiet so Shay would continue. 'Don't tell me you don't have bullshit going on in your life right now that makes you think, why me? Not again.'

'Yes I do, I think we all do.' Feeling that she had an opening, Francesca put her pen and note book down. 'Tell me a bit about yours.'

Shay thought Francesca was challenging her, as if she wouldn't dare tell her story to her. 'You want to know my story?'

'Yes I want to know your story Shay.'

'My father didn't love me. He cared more about work than me, and my mother was an alcoholic. Enjoy the story?' She tried to sound as if it didn't bother her, but Francesca saw straight through it. She could hear and see the underlying hurt and the closed off walls that Shay had created around herself as protection. She recognised it because she did it herself.

'I'm sorry.' Francesca genuinely meant it.

'For what?' Shay tried to bluff that she didn't know what Francesca meant.

'That you didn't feel like you had the love you deserved... I'm sure your father loved you in his own way.'

Shay scoffed. 'If he did, I never felt it...' She could feel emotions she'd blocked out for years, rising up in her. She didn't like it and wanted to change the subject. 'Can we talk about something else?'

Francesca was happy to ease off a bit. It was only their first session and they had plenty of time together and right now she felt a little bit more in control of the session. 'What do you want to talk about?'

Shay glanced at one of the paintings hanging on the office wall. 'That's a nice painting.'

'You like art? Do you paint?'

'I love art. My mother got me into it. She would take me to a gallery every week so we could spend some time together. She taught me how to paint and even encouraged me to sell my work.'

Francesca couldn't help but notice how different Shay was when talking about her mother compared to her father. 'I would love to see some of your art. It can be very revealing seeing someone's work'

Shay laughed whilst still studying the painting. 'That's why I don't show my work...' She tilted her head to the side to take in the art from another angle. 'You see that painting? The person that painted that, I would say, by their strokes and how heavy they are must have been frustrated at the time,' She studied the different strokes used in the painting, 'and you see the circular movements?' Francesca found herself looking again. 'They are symbolic of the artist feeling that they're going around in circles...' Shay got up and walked over to the painting to take a closer look. She combed her hair back with both hands and leaned forward towards the art piece. 'See how the artist hasn't quite mixed the colours but has stuck to keeping them apart? That's telling about their need for control.' She tried to make the signature out in the bottom corner of the piece but she couldn't. 'Who's it by?' She turned and looked at Francesca.

'It's one of mine.'

Shay headed over to her uncle George and Aunt Kate's house after her session. George was out shopping with the three boys so Shay helped Kate peel and chop the vegetables ready for dinner.

'They should be back any minute...' Before Kate had finished speaking the kitchen door swung open and in came Toby, eight, George and Kate's eldest, followed by the two four year old twins, Jordan and Noah. They bounded in having seen Shay's car, a blue mini, parked outside the house. They ran straight over to her, excited to see her. Shay smiled and picked the twins up. She gave each one of them a kiss and then put them back down.

'Calm down kids, what have I told you about being calm in the kitchen...' Kate tried to be the voice of reason knowing it was always chaos when they first saw each other, 'there might be sharp knives about.'

Shay did nothing to help calm the boys down since she was just as excited and thrilled to see them. She hugged Toby and kissed him on the cheek. Toby wrapped his arms around her neck and squeezed her hard. 'Why don't you go into the living room and set the television up Tobes? I've brought a DVD over for us to watch together.'

His face showed disappointment. 'I hope it's not colour spaces?' Colour spaces was the twins favourite program to watch but Toby was bored with it and felt he was old enough now to watch something a bit more grown up.

Shay laughed at the face he was pulling. '*Non*. I promise you it's not colour spaces!'

'Cool!' He ran into the living room to set up the DVD player with the twins following him, excited at the prospect of watching something new as well.

Kate called after them. 'Hang on, what have you done with your dad?'

George entered carrying a load of shopping bags in each hand. 'I'm here! These bags are heavier than they look! They make them so bloody cheap these days. All the handles snap!'

Shay teased him. 'Are you sure it's not because you're in your forties now and time's catching up with you?' She gave him a cheeky smile knowing how paranoid and obsessed he was with trying to stay young. George gave his reply with a soft 'watch it, you' look.

Shay walked over to help him with the bags which were weighing him down. Kate saw how many bags he was carrying in each hand as he passed them over.

'Oh my god George, what have you bought? I only sent you out to buy milk!'

George didn't answer, knowing she knew what he was like when he saw a bargain that he couldn't resist. He lifted the bags he was left carrying and began unpacking them. He reached into the first bag and pulled out the milk, he plonked it in front of Kate on the kitchen table.

'Here you are! Two pints of milk as requested!' He was more than pleased with himself for accomplishing the job she had asked him to do.

Kate glanced at the milk and knew straight away it was the wrong colour. 'It's semi-skimmed!'

George scrunched his face up. 'That's what you asked for isn't it?'

Shay smiled as she watched them. Even she knew Kate and the boys drank whole milk.

'No darling I asked for whole.'

'I could have sworn I heard you say the word 'semi'.' He frowned in confusion.

'Yes, probably, when I said 'don't' get semi skimmed!'

'Whoops!' He gave her a kiss as an apology and to soften her up a bit. He turned to look at Shay who had started emptying some of the other shopping bags. Shay had lived with them a couple of years ago, when she'd first moved over to the United Kingdom, so she knew where everything went.

'So kid, how did it go?' He asked.

'How did what go?' She put a box of cereal in the top cupboard.

'This morning, with the shrink? George handed her a box of cornflakes to put away in the same cupboard.

Kate finished peeling the potatoes and started on the carrots. She'd completely forgotten Shay's first appointment was today. 'Sorry Shay, I should have asked, I completely forgot...'

'No don't worry... It saves me having to talk about it twice!' She moved onto emptying another shopping bag. 'It was how I imagined it to be, pretty pointless. It was boring so I teased the doctor a bit to entertain myself and make time go faster.'

'Shay! You didn't?' Kate stopped chopping a carrot to look around at her. 'Talking about things might really help you. It helped me going to see someone.'

Shay was surprised to hear Kate had seen a therapist. 'Really? You never said. I mean I never knew you...' She stopped putting the shopping away and sat opposite Kate at the kitchen table.

Kate started chopping the vegetables again. 'Yep, after I had Toby I was referred by my doctor who thought I had a bit of depression after the pregnancy.'

George was listening to their conversation as he walked back and forth putting the rest of the shopping away. Kate had never really openly spoken to him about the help she'd had after her pregnancy.

'How long did you go for?' Shay reached across the table and took a bit of raw chopped carrot from the chopping board. She bit into it looking at Kate.

'About a year. It would have been less if I hadn't mucked around, pretended that I was OK and coping for so long...' Kate was like a mother to Shay. She had been there for her, like her uncle George, through the good times and the bad. She couldn't believe she didn't know, that Kate hadn't told her before now. 'I was embarrassed to admit that I needed help, though I shouldn't have been.' She finished prepping the vegetables and put the knife down to look at Shay. 'Not everybody gets the opportunity you're being given, Shay, to get help. Maybe it was a blessing you punching that guy!' She gave her a soft smile.

George walked up behind Kate and squeezed her shoulders gently as a sign of support. 'What's this shrink like anyway?' He looked at Shay, interested to know. 'Is he an old man with glasses who wears a waist coat like a right proper educated chap?'

'Actually her name is Dr Francesca Draw.' Shay went quiet as she thought about Francesca and what Kate had said about being given the opportunity of help. 'She's alright really. I should probably give her a chance...' On reflection she felt a bit guilty about her behaviour with her in the session and how she'd acted towards her. She knew she'd been challenging by being overly suggestive but she couldn't help it, it was something she did as part of her defence mechanism. 'I just find it hard being in that kind of room, in that environment. Feeling like there's nowhere to run or hide, I can't help but close up... the thought of having to talk about mum and Tommy...' Her voice broke slightly saying her brother's name, 'I've tried so hard to put all that behind me.'

Kate took her hand from across the table and squeezed it. 'It's understandable you want to try to protect yourself. You're hurting still, but you can't keep taking what happened out on yourself or others.'

George had filled Kate in about the restaurant incident. She hadn't been surprised, she'd been worried about Shay for the past few weeks and could see her struggling.

'Easy.' Shay smiled, 'You nearly started to sound like the shrink then!' They laughed, lightening the mood in the room a bit.

George let go of Kate's shoulders and walked over to Shay. He playfully put her in a headlock. He'd done the move, ever since she was a child, as a term of endearment. He held the headlock loosely so she didn't get hurt, and messed her hair up using his free hand.

'You're a good kid Shay. Why don't you give this woman a chance?'

Shay squirmed and extricated herself from the headlock quickly. She'd had many years of experience, George was never able to hold on to her for long.

She flipped her hair back to try and make it look less messy. 'I'll think about it.' She walked towards the living room, remembering the boys were waiting for her to watch a DVD together. On her way out Shay hadn't realised her top had ridden up during the headlock. George could see the tattoos that covered her back and hips.

'Pull your top down...' He shouted playfully at her. 'I don't want the kids seeing those and getting ideas!'

Shay knew exactly what he was referring to. 'Too late! Toby's already shown me the design he wants!' She grinned at him and strolled out.

George walked back over to Kate and hugged her. He pecked her on the lips. 'Honestly, when did she get so cheeky?'

Kate put her hands on either side of his face and looked into his eyes. 'When she started spending more time with you!'

CHAPTER EIGHT

Francesca hadn't seen her friend Laura since splitting up with David. They'd been in contact via text but not face to face so she'd only been able to give Laura minimal details about the affair and separation. Laura was an experienced sex psychologist and they'd been friends since the beginning of Francesca's career, when Francesca had done a month's work experience with her. Francesca liked her because she never held back. She was always honest and spoke her mind. Whether Laura agreed with her or not, Francesca knew she would get an honest opinion. They hadn't seen each other for so long because Laura had been on holiday with her husband Mike and had only returned a few days ago. Out for dinner together, at the restaurant Laura had booked, they were catching up with one another, something they tried to do as frequently as possible.

They sat at a table for two by the window and Laura had ordered a bottle of red wine to share while they waited to look through the menu and order.

'So come on, tell me, how are you?'

Francesca looked through the restaurant's menu. She didn't want to look up at Laura because she knew she would pick up on something, as she always did. 'I'm OK, busy at work...'

Straight away Laura knew Francesca was evading her. She waited silently until Francesca gave up on the menu and looked up at her before she asked her next question.

'You're not angry?'

'About what?'

Laura was bemused by her answer and her lack of anger over what David had done.

'Jesus Christ, Cesc, you must be busy at work...' she paused, 'or in denial... have you actually taken some time to begin processing what's happened? If you haven't you should.'

Francesca said nothing so Laura carried on. 'Have you seen Jenny? Surely she advised the same?'

'I saw her. She said it was fine to carry on working, if that's what you mean.' Francesca told herself she wasn't lying to her friend. She started playing with her napkin so she didn't have to look her in the eye. 'People separate and survive!'

'That surprises me.' It went quiet between the two of them as Laura tried to figure out what Jenny's angle could have been. She let it go and carried on questioning Francesca. 'So have you seen David since? If Mike ever did that to me I would make his life a living hell!'

'We're trying to keep it amicable, for the kids. There's big changes going on as it is with Mark at University and Mia studying. I don't want to rock her world even more. Having exams and your parents splitting has to be stressful enough!'

'Does Mia still not know why you've really split?'

'She still thinks it's my fault and that I'm being unreasonable.'

The waiter interrupted them with their bottle of wine. He poured them each a glass and left saying he would be back for their food order.

Laura continued with their conversation. 'Why don't you tell her?' She wasn't sure if it was a good idea to keep it from Mia.

'Because she loves her dad and I think it would break her heart if she knew the truth.'

Laura took a sip of her wine. 'So you're just lying to her then? You don't think that will break her heart when she finds out?'

Francesca knew she had a point and was probably right, but with what was going on at home and the day she'd had at work, she just wanted to try and relax and unwind. 'Can we talk about something else?'

'OK, but I'm just saying, I think Mia should know. Maybe she wouldn't be so difficult with you then.'

Francesca started to fidget in her seat. 'Let's stop talking about me and talk about you! I haven't seen you for ages. How was your epic cruise?'

Laura rolled her eyes to the ceiling. 'Oh god, don't remind me!'

'Why? I thought it was supposed to be your and Mike's holiday of a lifetime?'

The same waiter came over to take their food order before Laura could answer Francesca's question. He took a tablet out and put their orders through electronically to the kitchen.

Laura answered the question after the waiter had walked off. 'It was, until I got on the ship! Mike was sea sick for the first week until he summoned the courage to see the on board doctor. You know what he's like with medical stuff and the threat of needles! Then for the last three weeks we both had the shits and shivers because of some virus on board!'

Francesca tried not to laugh. 'That sounds romantic!'

'Don't laugh! Do you know how traumatic it is being trapped in a cabin the size of a shoe box? War can break out when you're both competing for the same toilet!'

After they'd finished laughing about the trip from hell, Laura went straight for the gossip. 'So are you seeing anyone?'

'Laura! I've only just split up with David!'

'That was months ago! You know what I tell my clients in the sex clinic? It's good to get back on the horse...' She grinned... 'And ride it!'

CHAPTER NINE

Maggie was twenty eight years old and pregnant for the first time by her boyfriend Jamie. She had arranged to meet up with her friend, Olivia, at the corner bistro. Olivia didn't know her news yet and Maggie had been dying to tell someone about it.

'Oh my God!' Olivia could barely contain herself when Maggie told her. 'So how far are you? Does Jamie know yet?'

Maggie smiled, pleased that her friend was so happy for her. She hadn't been seeing Jamie for long and was worried that her pregnancy, which hadn't been planned, had come too soon. It had certainly come as a surprise to both her and Jamie. They'd only found out because Maggie had been fainting at work and gone to the doctors.

'They think I'm about fourteen weeks. Jamie knows, I told him last week.'

'How did her react? Is he pleased? I bet he is!'

Maggie went a bit quiet and hesitant. 'He was...'

The way she answered made Olivia calm down. She could tell something wasn't right.

'Was?'

'When I told him he was over the moon but then, the next morning, he was really moody and quiet and he's been like that ever since.' She began to get emotional. 'I'm starting to think maybe he doesn't want the baby... or me anymore.'

Olivia took her friends hand. She hated to see Maggie so upset. 'Maybe it was just a bit of a shock for him. How long have you been dating him? It's only about four months isn't it? He could just be getting his head around it because it happened so fast and wasn't planned.'

'Maybe...' She wanted to believe her but she wasn't convinced 'I just wish he would talk to me... open up to me... so I know what he's thinking, how he feels.'

Jamie was working on an extension to Francis' house. She was having it built on the back of her kitchen so she had more space to cook. Jamie had been on the job with his boss, John, working alongside him. All morning John had noticed how vacant Jamie had been.

Jamie was like a son to him. He had been working for his small building business since he was fourteen and he, more or less, felt like he'd seen him grow up into a man. When Jamie had worked for him as a youngster, at the weekends, he would give him simple jobs to do. When he reached sixteen, and finished school, he went to work for John, full time, on all his building projects, he knew he could trust Jamie to do a good, honest job.

John had waited for their lunch break to start before he asked Jamie how he was.

'You've been miles away, what's wrong lad?'

'Sorry.' Jamie took a bite of his shop bought cheese and pickle sandwich.

John looked at him and waited expecting him to say more, but Jamie wasn't giving anything away. 'What's up with you? Lady Trouble?' The last time John had known him to be this quiet was when he was arguing with his ex-girlfriend. He put two and two together 'How many times have I told you to always nod your head so it looks like you're listening!'

Any other day Jamie would have laughed but, today, he was too involved and sucked in by his thoughts about Maggie and the pregnancy.

John nudged him in the side playfully. 'Jamie that was a joke! You're supposed to laugh!'

Before Jamie could say anything Francis interrupted them with two cups of hot tea, one in each hand. She passed them over making sure John got the cup with two sugars in it.

'Can I just let you know, if you're bringing any rubbish, supplies, or whatever through the house, could I ask you to take care not to hit the piano in the hallway? It was my late husband's and is very precious to me.'

'No problem.' Jamie nodded and gave her a reassuring smile.

John and Jamie drank their tea and ate their sandwiches outside in silence. After about five minutes Jamie couldn't take the pressure that was building up inside him from not saying anything. 'Maggie's pregnant.' He blurted out.

'Well that's great news lad! You must be excited!' Really pleased for him, John embraced Jamie in a tight hug. When he pulled away he could see Jamie looked neither excited nor pleased... just anxious. 'Or maybe not?'

'I am...' Jamie exhaled. 'It's just I'm scared...' He hesitated. 'I'm probably just not used to the idea of it yet. I mean it's something I've wanted... a family. I love Maggie and, let's face it, I'm thirty six and not getting any younger.'

'When Frieda fell the first time it took me a while too. I promise you though, Jamie, as soon as you see that little face, those tiny fingers and toes, you forget everything that ever came before having that little person in your life. It's a special thing to be a father.'

John stayed another couple of hours with Jamie on site and then left him to finish off another job he had in town. Jamie didn't get home from work until later that evening. As he walked through the front door of his house he saw Maggie's trainers in the hallway. He'd given her a spare key a couple of weeks ago so she could let herself in when he wasn't there. Tired and drained from work and not being able to stop thinking about the baby, he walked into the kitchen and over to the fridge to get a beer. As he pulled out a cold can of beer he could hear the shower running in the back ground. He opened his beer and took out his phone from his back pocket. He scrolled through his phone contacts and rang a number he'd found online when he'd typed in 'local therapist' in the search engine.

'Hello, Dr Francesca Draw's office. How may I help you?'

Jamie was surprised to hear how professional Julie sounded answering the phone. He didn't want to go anywhere too serious. He just wanted some help. He checked he could still hear the water running in the shower, so Maggie wouldn't hear him. 'Eh hello... I was wondering if I could book an appointment.'

'Of course. Have you been before?'

'Eh no.' He thought about putting the phone down. He was so nervous, it felt more real all of a sudden, actually speaking to someone.

'OK...' Julie scrolled through Francesca's available dates on the computer. 'Can you do Wednesday?'

'No, sorry I have work then.'

'No problem. How about Friday at 12.30pm?'

'I can't, I work a full day Friday as well...' If Jamie was honest he would probably be so busy with work, with the dry weather, he didn't really know when his next day off would be. He started to panic, thinking he should have thought, before calling, about his available times and dates.

Julie looked on the screen again. 'I'm afraid that's all she's got at the moment. The only other option is to give you a ring if we get a cancelation. How about that?'

Jamie stayed quiet as he thought about it. 'You know what, book me in for the Friday at 12.30pm.' He changed his mind knowing that if he didn't go now it would be too easy never to go.

With the panic and quick change of his mind he didn't see or hear Maggie walk into the living room from behind him. She wondered who he was talking to. She could hear a woman's voice on the other end of the phone.

'Are you sure? You're definitely able to come on that day?'

'Yes, honestly that's fine. I'll find the time to come. I need to talk to...' He turned to pick up his beer when he saw Maggie staring at him accusingly. He put the phone down and picked his beer up wondering how much Maggie had heard.

'Who was that?' She had her towel wrapped around her wet body.

'No- one. Nobody.'

'Well you were speaking to someone!' She didn't know if it was her hormones but she felt really insecure and emotional. 'Who was it Jamie? Who are you meeting?'

'Leave it Maggie. It was just a man I'm going to meet about some potential work.' He picked up his wallet and keys knowing that he wasn't in the mood to be grilled by her. 'I'm going to get some bread for breakfast tomorrow. I'll be back in a bit. Do you want to stay for dinner tonight? I could cook us something?'

'I'm going over to my sister's tonight...' she said with a downcast voice. Maggie knew she would never get anywhere with him when he was like this.

Jamie kissed her on the cheek and left the house before she could question him more about the phone call.

CHAPTER TEN

Maggie dried herself off and dressed after her shower. She drove over to her elder sister Jessica's house angry and upset at not being able to control her thoughts and imagination about who Jamie was meeting up with. She rang the doorbell on the front door twice before Jessica answered the door.

'He's seeing someone else!' She burst into tears on the doorstep.

Jessica, surprised, pulled her in for a hug. 'I caught him on the phone talking to some woman! When I asked him about it, he said it was no- one, just some guy.' She wiped the tears falling down her face and looked at her sister. 'I could hear it was a woman...'

'Mags, calm down. Being this wound up isn't good for you or the baby.' She tucked a strand of Maggie's hair behind her ear. 'Are you sure? I haven't known Jamie for long, but he doesn't seem the type of guy to cheat. He absolutely dotes on you!'

Maggie had brought Jamie over to Jessica's house a few times for dinner, she knew after her sister's history of dating jerks she had found a good guy, who her sister was head over heels in love with.

'Then why did he lie, Jess?'

'I don't know...' She couldn't be sure but she didn't want Maggie to be upset and get herself in a state about something that may not be true. 'But try not to jump to conclusions. There's been no other signs of him cheating, right?'

'Right. But what if he's just good at covering his tracks?'

Jessica got her to sit down on her sofa. 'Just try to hold back a bit. Your body's going to be raging with hormones right now. That phone call could be something really innocent.'

Maggie tried to calm down and rationalize the situation but she felt so upset by Jamie's strange behaviour that she didn't know what else it could be.

CHAPTER ELEVEN

Francesca had finished with her last client just before lunch. She walked down to reception to check in with Julie. 'Any messages?'

'Three.' Julie handed the messages over to Francesca. 'Oh and Laura phoned just to remind you that you're meeting her for lunch today. She said she'd pick you up from here.'

Laura arrived five minutes later and took her to one of the new cafés that had recently opened in town. They sat on a side table and studied the menu. It didn't take Laura long to decide what she was having. She looked over at Francesca who was still browsing through.

'I need the toilet.' She got up from her chair. 'I'll leave you here to decide what you're having.' Laura walked off to the rest room at the back of the café.

Francesca had her back to the restrooms, she didn't see Shay come out of the ladies as Laura went in. Shay strolled over to a table at the back where she was sitting with a 'friend' Greg, who was drinking a beer and waiting for her to come back. She sat down at the table and Greg immediately became very physical and touchy feely with her. He couldn't help himself, the fact that Shay had been away for a few minutes had only made his desire to touch her worse.

A couple of minutes later Laura came back to find Francesca still hadn't decided what she was having.

'Bloody hell, Cesca, I'm starving! Make your mind up already will you!'

Francesca smiled at her. 'I love how even though my whole life is upside down and out of control I can still count on you to be the most constant thing!'

'Oh finally, we've come out of the 'I'm OK' story now?' Laura paused and sat down at her seat. 'Also, is that you implying I'm boring and predictable?' She tried to pretend to be upset but Francesca saw right through it and laughed at her.

'It means your impatience when it comes to food is always the same and I love that about you!'

'Yeah, well, do you know what I love about you?' She leant towards Laura and whispered. 'That I always pay for lunch!'

Laura pretended to be offended again but she couldn't stop herself from grinning. 'Maybe that... but I love you more when you know what you're going to order!'

Francesca put her hands up in defence. 'Right, OK, I've decided.'

Starving, Laura got the waiters attention straight away. He walked over with his pad and pen in hand.

Laura made sure she gave her order first. 'Can I get the steak, medium rare? Does that come with onion rings?'

'No, it comes with chips madam.'

'OK. I'll have the steak with chips... and onion rings on the side please!'

The waiter scribbled the order down and looked in Francesca's direction. 'And for you?'

'I'll have the chicken salad, please, with hummus.'

He wrote down Francesca's order and smiled at them before he walked off to the kitchen.

Laura pulled a face, hearing Francesca's healthy choice. 'Francesca! Live a little would you? Your order puts me to shame. Salad? Really?'

Their food order arrived ten minutes later. Half way through their meal Laura glanced up towards the back of the café where Shay and Greg caught her eye. She watched Greg kiss up Shay's neck. He moved up on to Shay's lips.

'See! You should find yourself a guy like she has, to do that to you!' Laura raised her eyebrows.

Francesca didn't bother looking around, she wasn't interested in seeing what she assumed would be two love birds making out.

'Don't tell me there's a loved up couple in the honeymoon phase, sitting behind us?'

Laura glanced over at them again. 'Actually I would say they're the 'just sex' phase kind of couple!'

Francesca carried on eating her salad. 'How can you even know something like that?'

'Cesca, I've been a sexual psychologist for twelve years now. I know body language!' As she finished her sentence Greg got up from the table to leave.

Leaving a small tip on the table, Shay followed behind him.

Laura lowered her voice. 'Here they come, they're leaving!'

As Greg walked past their table, heading for the exit, he accidently knocked Francesca's napkin from the table. He didn't notice and carried on towards the door, out of cafe.

The napkin fell on the floor directly in Shay's path. She saw it and bent down to pick it up, her short t-shirt top revealing the tattooed and tanned skin on her back.

Francesca, not knowing it was Shay, found herself staring at the tattoos as she grabbed the napkin and turned to put it back on the table. Shay looked up and caught Francesca's eye. Both of them paused as they gazed at one another.

Francesca felt herself blush slightly from shock and embarrassment. She was caught off guard seeing Shay again, especially outside her office.

Shay put the napkin in front of Francesca on the table and walked off before Francesca could say anything. All she could do was stare as she watched Shay follow Greg out of the door.

'Cesca?' Having seen their interaction, Laura tried to break Francesca's daze and get her attention. 'Francesca?'

Francesca couldn't answer, her brain was trying to process what had just happened. She wondered if Shay had felt her staring.

'Do you know her?'

Francesca came out of her daze and cleared her throat to answer Laura's question.

'No.' she wondered why Laura was so interested, what she had seen. 'Why?'

'Well because the two of you totally had a moment and now… you're blushing!'

'I'm not blushing!'

Laura just looked at her.

'I'm not!' She carried on eating her salad in an attempt to brush the whole subject aside.

Laura got out her mobile phone and changed the subject. 'Anyway, I'm going to help you out. There's this friend of Mike's that wants to go on a date with you. I said I would pass his number on to you.'

'Laura! I don't want a date. I'm too old to start all that again.'

Laura scoffed. 'Francesca, please! You're forty two and in your prime. Look at you, you're gorgeous. Men would give their right arm to date you and predominately most men are right handed so that would mean their wanking hand…'

'OK thank you! I hear what you're saying!'

Laura skimmed through the numbers on her phone. 'You've met him, at Mike's birthday. Garth? He was the tall, dark, handsome one! Look…' She took Francesca's phone off the table. 'I'll put his number in your phone.' She continued to type the numbers in Francesca's contacts, despite her obvious doubts. 'In case you change your mind.'

CHAPTER TWELVE

Greg took Shay back to his apartment, after leaving the café. As soon as they walked through the front door he started kissing her again.

Shay tried to enjoy it, but it was difficult for her when all she could see in her head was Francesca's face in the café. She couldn't stop wondering Why Francesca hadn't said anything to her.

Greg realised her attention was elsewhere. He couldn't really feel her kissing him back, so he stopped what he was doing and looked at her. 'Where are you? Do you want me to stop?'

'No. no, I'm right here.' She kissed him to reassure him she was still interested.

Greg didn't need any more encouragement than that, he pulled her t-shirt up over her head to take it off. Shay teased his mouth with her tongue and moved back a little so she could unbuttoned his shirt. She pushed him down on the bed and straddled him whilst undoing the button and zip on his jeans. She felt numb as she roughly tugged his trousers down and touched him.

After they'd finished they lay in the warm bed next to one another. Shay felt uneasy in her body, she'd hoped having sex would get rid of the feeling but it hadn't, she still wasn't satisfied. All she wanted to do was get out of there and be alone. She sat up sharply and got out of bed to get dressed.

'I don't think we should do this anymore...' She put her knickers back on and then her jeans. 'This was the last time.'

Greg sat up confused. 'What? Why? Wasn't I good?' As far as he was concerned he and Shay had had mind blowing sex for the past five weeks they'd been seeing one another.

'You were fine... and it's not that. It's just... I don't do relationships. I don't want you to get hurt, so I'm ending it now.'

'I'm a big boy, I can handle just sex. I don't do relationships either.'

Shay could tell he was lying. She knew for the past week or so he was falling for her. He had that doe-eyed look in his eyes when he saw her, the one she always ran from when she saw it coming.

'People say that, Greg, but then feelings get involved and before you know it, you're in a relationship, moving in together. It's just not me, and its clearer this way, no ties, no drama, no distractions. Sorry.' She picked up her bag from the floor and left him lying in his bed.

CHAPTER THIRTEEN

Mia sat in her maths classroom studying for her exam she was taking the next day. Everyone else had gone on their lunch break but she had stayed to try and cram in some more revision.

Josh, one of the boys in her class that she'd become friendly with in the last few months, walked in. He saw her at the back of the classroom, walked over to her and sat next to her at the desk. 'I thought I'd find you here.'

Mia didn't even look up. She just concentrated on her books and work, writing notes down.

'Mia come on, don't you think you're over doing it a bit?' He was worried about her. He could see she was over working and had noticed she was starting to lose weight from skipping lunch to study more.

Tired and hungry Mia snapped at him. 'We can't all be as brilliant and brainy as you Josh! Some of us actually need to study and work to get good grades!'

'That was harsh!' He was a little hurt by the way she'd said it. 'I was trying to help you.' He got up to leave when Mia realised how sharp she must have sounded. She liked Josh and she didn't want to fall out with him.

'Josh, wait. I'm sorry...' Josh stopped where he was. 'I didn't mean to snap at you. Look, I'm stopping!' She threw her pen down on the desk as proof.

He smiled at her, pleased he'd got her full attention. 'Have you had lunch yet?'

'No. Not yet.'

He closed Mia's study books. 'Come on, I'll treat you to a burger or something.'

They walked to the school canteen and ate lunch together. After the bell went for fifth period they separated and Mia walked by herself to her next lesson, English. She sat down at her desk and began to get out her books.

Stacey walked into the classroom and spotted her, she sat down beside her. 'So I see you and Josh are getting closer!' She'd seen them sitting and talking to one another at lunch.

Mia knew by her tone what Stacey was trying to insinuate. 'We're just friends and that's all.'

'Good, because you know he's a loser. You could do so much better with someone older and better looking!'

Mia didn't like the way Stacey was talking about Josh. He was a nice guy, as most of the pupils and teachers in the school would tell you, but Stacey, for some reason, had an issue with him.

Stacey saw Mia's face and changed the subject. 'So are you going to Louise's house party this Saturday?'

'No I'm busy this weekend.'

Stacey hated it when people didn't go along with her and her ideas or plans.

'Whatever Mia... sometimes you're a real bore!' She turned away and began chatting to a couple of other girls on the table next to her.

Mia got to science, her worst subject and her last class. After one of the slowest hours of her life the bell rang for home time. She left the classroom and headed for the school gates. As she reached them Stacey nudged her in her side. She'd seen Mia and had run to catch up with her.

'Hey, little Miss boring!' Mia stopped walking and turned around to face her. 'If you can't do this Saturday then how about this afternoon? I've managed to nick some vodka from my brother so we could go to the park and drink it.' She acted completely normal as if Mia had never annoyed her in English class.

Mia knew it probably wasn't the best of ideas but she found herself agreeing. Stacey was surprised at her answer, she thought she would decline and say 'no' again.

'Cool! Wait for me here while I get my jacket.' Stacey spun round and ran back towards the school to collect her things.

Francesca couldn't stop thinking about Shay. She sat at the kitchen table looking through the details of her file to see whether it could help her understand her, if there was anything that might help her bring down Shay's walls. She wasn't having much luck. By the looks of the notes about Shay, she had never given much away.

Francesca put the file down when she heard the front door open. 'Mia?' There was a silent pause as she waited for an answer.

Mia heard her mum call. She walked towards the kitchen and stopped in the door way. Not saying anything she stared at Francesca and waited for her to say whatever it was she needed to say.

'Where have you been? School doesn't finish at 8pm!'

Mia slumped against the door frame. 'I was studying.' She'd made sure she hadn't got too drunk with Stacey, just a little bit tipsy. She knew if her mum found out she'd been drinking in the park she would be grounded for a year, at the least.

It wasn't a good enough answer for Francesca. 'Where?'

'With Stacey, at the library.' Mia's moodiness helped her seem more sober than she actually was.

'Well can you ring me and tell me next time? I was starting to get worried.'

'Whatever.' Mia was too tired to be bothered with a lecture. She walked away and went upstairs to her bedroom.

The next day, after school, Mia arrived home to find Mark back from university. He was only staying for the night, it was one of his old school friend's twenty first birthday and he'd been invited out with them to celebrate. They were all going on a pub crawl but Mark wasn't going to go mad and drink too much, though he knew his friends would. He knew he would have to drive back to university the following morning and he didn't want to do it with a heavy hangover.

Mia was elated to see him. She gave him a big hug and they chatted in the living room for hours, catching up on everything, as though he had never been away.

By the time she'd looked down at her watch it was 6pm already. Mia hadn't eaten lunch and was hungry for dinner. She went into the kitchen and checked the cupboards and fridge for food but both seemed empty to her, there was nothing that inspired her to eat something. Mark offered to walk with her to the supermarket to buy something a little more exciting than cupboard food. He didn't have to be at the first pub until 9.30pm so had plenty of time.

In the supermarket they spent about half an hour debating what to get, pasta, pizza or burgers? They decided on a stuffed crust, meat feast pizza because it was frozen and simple to cook. Mark carried the cold pizza box as they walked home.

'When are you going back? I miss you. We hardly spend time together anymore, since you started university.'

'I know. I miss you too.' He took hold of her hand. 'I know it's hard with mum and dad with what's going on right now...'

'Why can't they work it out?' It was all so simple in Mia's eyes. 'If mum stopped working so much then they could actually spend a bit more time together. Dad wouldn't feel so lonely then.'

Mark frowned, he stopped walking. He looked at Mia. 'How do you know that's how he felt?'

'It's what he told me. He said he tried to work it out but she was too busy with work to listen.'

Mark knew he couldn't say anything. She didn't know he knew exactly what had happened, that David had cheated. He started walking again, annoyed by his father's lies. 'You shouldn't believe everything that man tells you.'

They walked a couple more streets before they reached their house. Mark put the key in the front door and went to open it, when Mia asked him a question.

'Why do you hate him so much?'

He turned the key and opened the door so that he didn't have to answer her question. As soon as they'd stepped over the door step Francesca called to them.

'Kids! Can you come here for a second please?'

Following the direction of her voice they both wandered through in to the living room. Francesca was watching television with her feet up on a stool. When she saw them enter she turned the television off. Pleased to see Mark, she embraced him. She went to hug Mia as well but Mia backed off not wanting her mum to touch her. 'Just a reminder, your grandma's got her dinner this Friday at seven. Mia your dad will pick you up after school.'

'Why?'

'Because he said you wanted to go over and stay at his during the weekend. You could stay Friday night as well then.'

'OK...' Mia was a bit miffed. She knew she'd been a bit harsh towards her mum. She wasn't sure why she would let her stay over at her dads.

Francesca noticed Mia's quiet response. She'd expected her to have acted a bit more excited. 'What? Is something wrong?'

'No, I just didn't think you would agree to the sleeping over at his idea.'

Francesca hated being alone in the house, it always seemed so quiet and empty when neither Mia nor Mark were there. 'Why would I say no? I'm not going to stop you from seeing your father.'

'I wish you would stop him from seeing me!' Mark grinned.

'Mark!' Francesca knew he was half serious and half trying to cheer her up. She knew when it came to Mark, whose back he had, it was hers and not David's.

CHAPTER FOURTEEN

Another day in the office and Francesca had a new client in session.

Francis sat nervously on the sofa, twiddling her hands, hoping Francesca wouldn't notice how broken and how much emotional pain she was carrying.

Francesca took one look at her and saw it written all over her face. 'Would you like to tell me why you've come here today?' She had the feeling to tread carefully with her.

Francis could feel her tears coming as soon as Francesca had finished the question. She'd only just kept it together for the past few months or so.

'Why hasn't it gone away?' She could barely get her words out.

Francesca crossed her legs. From the movement her pencil skirt rode up her thigh a bit so she pulled it back down. She looked up to concentrate on Francis.

'What do you want to go away?'

Not able to hold it in any longer Francis began to cry. 'The pain... my husband, he passed away...'

Francesca could see Francis was struggling to keep it together. She passed her the box of tissues she kept on her side table.

Francis gratefully took a couple of them.

Francesca gave her a few moments to try and compose herself. 'How long were you married for?'

'Thirty six years....' Francis took a deep breath. 'I nursed him before he died, for eighteen months at home, all on my own. The doctors said he would only live six months because of how the cancer had spread, but he managed more.'

Francesca made some notes on timings from the information Francis was giving her. 'How long has it been since his passing?'

'It's been eight months now... but it still feels like only yesterday.' She sobbed even harder and took another few tissues to wipe her face and blow her nose. As soon as she stopped blowing her nose she started crying again.

'What is it Francis? Can you tell me what it is, exactly, that's upsetting you so much?' By the amount of grief and tears Francesca could see there was something else going on.

'He just deserved so much better, so much more than...' Francis couldn't finish.

'A lot of people deserve better when it comes to the way they leave this life but all we can do is try to make them comfortable...'

Francis interjected. 'No, you don't understand! He deserved better than... cancer of course but he also deserved better than me.'

Concerned that Francis would hyperventilate if she didn't calm down and breathe, Francesca put her note pad down and moved to the edge of her seat, so she was closer to Francis. 'I'm sure you did the best you could. By the sounds of it you were there for him.'

Francis dropped her head with guilt. 'No I wasn't.'

'Wasn't what?' Francesca was unsure what she meant.

'I wasn't there for him... I left him... maybe not physically but emotionally.'

TEN MONTHS EARLIER.

Francis was on the cancer ward in hospital with her husband Jack. He was 59 years old, two years older than her and having his chemotherapy session. Francis sat by his bed and watched, feeling hopeless. Never had she imagined this happening to them, Jack being ill. He'd always been such a healthy, outgoing man.

They'd been given a private room which was small and stuffy, like any typical hospital room. Jack was groggy and tired. The medication going through his system made him sick. Francis held the bedpan as he vomited for the third time. Feeling completely exhausted and having nothing left in his stomach Jack leaned back on his bed and rested his head on the pillow.

Francis tried to tidy him up a bit by wiping his chin with a damp cloth. He grimaced and grunted at her, he found it unbearable to be touched when his whole body felt like it was on fire. Francis hesitated and contemplated putting up with his bad mood but the nurse on duty, who'd been looking after him, walked in and took over from her.

'Here, Mrs Jones, let me do that.' She took the bed pan and cloth out of her hand. 'I can sit with him while you have a break.' She looked down at Jack, 'you'll be all right with me won't you Jack?'

'Yes. You'll do a better job than her.' He didn't even turn to look at his wife.

Francis' face dropped, she'd never felt so unwanted and in the way.

'There you are then, it's sorted.' The nurse ignored the growing tension between the two of them to keep the energy in the room positive and chirpy.

Francis wasn't comfortable with leaving Jack, It felt like her job to look after him. She looked at the young nurse. 'Are you sure? I know how busy you are.'

'Honestly its fine...' She tried to reassure Francis whilst still fussing over Jack, making sure he was comfortable in bed. 'There's a meeting downstairs. Chris won't mind if you join late.'

'What kind of meeting?'

'Oh didn't you know? There's a family and friends support group that they run in the hospital twice a week. It's run by a gentleman called Chris, who is very nice.' She fiddled around with Jack's drip to up his fluids as the doctor had suggested. 'It's a good place for people to talk and share their cancer experiences and get some support. They're up on the fifth floor. You should go and check it out.'

Francis wasn't sure, seeing other people was the last thing she wanted to do. A couple of minutes went by when Francis decided to leave the hospital room to get some air. The nurse finished what she needed to do and followed her out.

'You know that's not him talking to you like that. I mean all the drugs and medication going around his body will have an effect on his mood.'

Francis tried to hold her tears in. She didn't want to show how much she was struggling. 'I know, but knowing that still doesn't make it any easier.' She left the ward and went outside to sit on one of the hospital benches near the entrance. Francis watched as people walked in and out, she wondered what they were going in for and what they might be going through.

After about ten minutes Francis felt too cold. She re-entered the hospital and walked over to the lifts to go back to the cancer ward. The lift beeped as the doors opened. She walked in and looked at the numbers, she was unsure which level she'd just come from, Francis's head was so foggy she couldn't remember if it was floor eight or floor six. She pressed six and the doors beeped again as they closed shut.

The lift made a noise as it travelled up. It stopped and the doors opened. Francis smiled at a lady who was standing in the corridor waiting for the lift. The lady entered as Francis left, trapped in her thoughts of dread about seeing Jack again. As she walked away from the lifts it took her a few minutes to realise she was on the wrong floor and completely lost. Francis walked down the corridor hoping to find someone to help her. Ahead of her she saw a young woman walk into a room. The sign on the door into the room had a notice with 'Cancer Group for Loved Ones' stuck to it. It was the group that the nurse, who was looking after Jack, had mentioned. She looked closer and could see a group of people chatting, eating biscuits and drinking tea. Francis thought nobody would see her hovering behind the door but one of the men in the group gave her a warm smile and walked over to her.

'Don't be shy! Come on in!' He had the nicest, kindest smile Francis had seen in a long time. He was quite young looking, with short salt and pepper hair and a dark stubby beard. 'We haven't started yet so you can grab a biscuit and cup of tea. What's your name?'

'Francis.' She tried to sound more confident than she felt. The stranger put his hand out, as they shook hands she felt a shock of electricity go through her body. Francis looked at him and wondered if he'd felt it as well. His face gave nothing away.

'I'm Chris, it's nice to meet you Francis.' He kept her eye contact as he spoke. 'To have a new face in the group is always nice.' All of a sudden he became aware that he was still holding her hand. He let go and turned to face the group. 'As you can see, we're not a huge group.

So hopefully you won't find it too overwhelming. Let me introduce you.'

'He took me around the whole group, introducing me to everyone. He never left my side and I felt so looked after, so safe. Chris was just one of those people... you know when...' Francis changed direction, 'when he took my hand, I felt relief for a while. The kindness, his reassuring words, it felt like... for a change, someone was looking after me. I felt he was concerned about me. I know it sounds silly... my life had started to seem like everyone who came over to the house, or who I met out and about, would ask about Jack. How he was or how he was doing, was he coping all right with his diagnosis... not once did anyone ask me how I was feeling or how I was coping.'

'That's not silly at all.' Francesca wanted to reassure her, lessen her guilt. 'How were you coping?'

Francis paused and took a deep breath as she tried to compose herself before she answered.

'I wasn't coping. I was crumbling.'

NINE MONTHS, THREE WEEKS EARLIER.

Francis went to the group again. It was more or less the same group of people as the last time but there was a couple of new faces. Everyone was happy to see Francis there again.

Chris saw Francis enter and walked over to her, to hug her hello. The hug was a bit awkward and stiff, which they both felt. Chris pulled away and they both attempted to ignore it and carry on, but after the embrace neither of them knew what to say to one another, they ended up just looking at each other in silence.

Chris tried to make it less awkward between them by coming up with an excuse to leave. 'I better go and sort the drinks out.'

Francis felt a little embarrassed as she watched him walk across the room to the drinks table.

'Hi! Francis is it?' Francis turned around to see a young woman in her thirties smiling at her. 'I'm Hannah. I wasn't here last week. I'm usually a regular visitor here...' Hannah stopped, she was worried she was talking to fast. 'Anyway I just thought I would introduce myself. Chris told me all about you. He's lovely Chris...' Francis followed Hannah's gaze over to him. 'He's helped me get through some tough times with my daughter's chemotherapy. I don't think I could have managed, especially with understanding all the medical jargon.'

'I'm so sorry! That must be so hard when it's your child. I can't imagine...'

'I think it's hard for everyone where cancer is concerned.' Hannah wanted to lighten the conversation, lately, she felt like she talked about how awful cancer was with nearly everyone she'd met and she'd had enough. 'Do you want to go get a cup of tea?'

Francis smiled at her as if she'd read her mind. 'Sure.'

She walked with her over to the drinks table, passing Chris on her way. He smiled at her and Francis timidly smiled back. She couldn't understand why she felt so shy around him and so nervous.

'He liked you? You liked him?' Francesca didn't need Francis to answer. 'How old was he?'

'Younger than me...forty six. We started talking more and more each week. He told me he lost his wife to breast cancer five years ago. That's why he started the group. He felt he had nobody to talk to and when he did, he found it easier to talk to people who were going through or had been through a similar situation.'

Did you feel you could talk to him about your situation?'

'Who, Chris?' Francis laughed a little. 'Of course! I looked forward to speaking with him, all of them. They became like a second family to me. Hannah only came every other week because she had other commitments but we had fun and a laugh when we saw each other. I told her how odd it felt to laugh...'

'What did she say to that?'

'She hugged me and said I had to laugh as much as I could because laughing is what gets you through the tough times.'

The room went quiet for a while as they both contemplated.

'Did you laugh a lot with your husband, Jack?'

'Yes, we had our moments. We laughed, we cried and shouted! It wasn't a perfect marriage but we made the best of it.'

'How did you meet?' Francesca was intrigued to hear their story.

'We met at a dinner and dance evening. I was nineteen. He was with his mates mucking around when they dared him to ask me to dance.' She grinned. 'He reckoned it was love at first dance. We married the following summer and Hilary, our daughter, arrived a few years later.'

'Do you have just one daughter?'

'Yes. Jack didn't really want children, but I did, so we compromised with having just the one.'

Francesca made a note of it. 'How was that for you?'

'I was upset at first because I'd always imagined having a huge family but after Hilary arrived I realized that having just one child was probably better. I soon learnt the idea of having a child and the reality of it are worlds apart... I think being a mother is both one of the most challenging and rewarding things I've ever done!'

Francesca couldn't agree with her more. 'It is a bit of a challenge isn't it?'

CHAPTER FIFTEEN

Friday came around quickly for Jamie. He had felt nervous about going to see Francesca for therapy. Having to speak about things he hadn't told anyone else before, disclose things he'd spent years trying to cover up.

'Did you find the place OK?' Francesca gave him a warm smile to reassure him. She could tell he was nervous. 'Some people tend to walk straight past us.'

'Yes, thank you.' He hesitated a bit. She was a complete stranger to him and he didn't know what he was supposed to say or do.

Francesca picked up her pen and note pad. She wrote Jamie's name and the date across the top. 'Was there anything in particular you wanted to talk about today? What made you come and see me?'

'I um...' He still wasn't sure where to start. 'I wanted to...' His nerves had got to him so much that he couldn't find his words. The words he manage to find he fumbled. 'Sorry.'

'That's OK. You're doing fine. I understand it's daunting having therapy for the first time. It can take some time to find your feet in a situation like this.' She paused, trying to think of a way to put him more at ease. 'Do you want me to start with some easy questions?'

Jamie nodded his head as his mouth was too dry to speak.

'OK. So how old are you Jamie?'

He leant forward for the glass of water on the table in front of him, took a swig and gripped on to the glass as if it was a safety blanket. 'I'm thirty six.'

Francesca wrote all his answers down as he answered. 'Are you married?'

'No, I don't want to get married. I saw how my mum and dad were... I never want to be like that.'

She could hear how strong he was with the statement and wanted him to elaborate a bit more 'Why? How did you find your parents' marriage?'

'Dysfunctional, to say the least! As a child I always remember them arguing most nights. If it wasn't about money or my dad's drinking it was something that my sister Lucy or I had done.' He took another swig of water. 'My dad would just blow, as if everything we did wrong was on purpose and to piss him off. We were just kids and we didn't know any better at the time.' He paused as he remembered a memory from when he was ten years old. 'I would go into Lucy's room. She was four years younger than me. I would sit with her, on her bed, and put my hands over her ears so she couldn't hear what our parents were screaming at each other. Every time they argued you could hear them through the walls... I wanted to protect her.'

'That must have been hard only being a child yourself and feeling that you had that kind of responsibility?'

Jamie hadn't really seen it like that before. 'I didn't mind. It felt natural to me. I was her big brother... she would get so scared when dad came back drunk...'

Francesca noticed how much he was talking about his sister's feelings and not his own. 'What about you? How did you feel? Were you scared?'

He went quiet as he thought about it. 'I told myself back then, as a child, that I wasn't scared. I couldn't let myself be scared or feel fear. I made myself strong for Lucy.' He looked down at the floor. 'But now I keep feeling as if I'm being haunted by the memories and feelings I tried to block as a kid.' Anxious, just talking about it, he started jigging his leg up and down. 'There's this intense anxiety whirling around inside me... it's got worse since... since finding out my girlfriend's pregnant.'

OK.' She could see how wound up he was becoming. His breathing had changed and become more rapid. 'Just take a breath for me... you're doing really well.' She waited for him to look back up at her. 'If I asked you what your biggest fear is right now, what would you say?'

'That I'm going to be like him.'

'Your father?'

'Yes, my father.' He let out a long breath. He'd kept the worry of becoming like his father for so long that he felt relief getting it off his chest and telling someone.

'Have you spoken to your partner about your fears?'

'No, not really. She doesn't know anything about my parents or childhood. We haven't really been seeing each other for that long, so every time she's asked I've managed to dodge the questions. But now that she's pregnant, she's starting to ask again, wanting to know things.'

Francesca played with the pen in her hand. 'How far gone is she?'

'Over twelve weeks.' Jamie hung his head in his hands thinking about the baby. 'How am I supposed to cope if I'm like this for just the beginning bit? I can't sleep and I'm drinking to try and cope with my nerves.' He took his head out of his hands and looked directly at Francesca. She could see the desperation on his face. 'I don't want to spiral down into that world like my father did. I don't want to be anything like the parent he was to me.'

Francesca tried to acknowledge and soothe his anxiety. 'It's natural that your imminent fatherhood is bringing up your childhood and how you were parented... but just because your parents brought you up in and around a certain environment, doesn't mean you'll do the same with your child and your family.'

The room went silent as Jamie thought about what she'd said.

Francesca wanted to explore the drink problem thinking it was obviously a family pattern, a way they had learned to cope.

'Was your father drinking throughout the whole of your childhood?'

'The times he was there, yes, more or less. Although the times he didn't drink he actually was quite a sweet man. Those were the times when I could see what my mum saw in him, why she fell in love with him, but sober days were rare. The people who knew him and the people on our street called him a functioning alcoholic.'

'Did he ever get help for his problems?'

'Not apart from reaching for the bottle, no.'

Francesca nodded. 'OK then, there you go! Already you're different from him.' She thought it was important to draw attention to that fact. 'You're the one here today, making steps to try and change. You're willing to address your issues, fears and anxieties. Something your father never did!'

Jamie wanted to believe her but something in him was resistant too.

Francesca could see he wasn't totally convinced. 'Are you comfortable with telling me a bit more about your childhood?'

'Yes.'

27 YEARS EARLIER.

Jamie was 9 years old and his little sister Lucy was five when they both had been banished to their garden to play. Their mother, Joan, was in one of her emotional, fragile states and couldn't cope with the noise they were making in the house. She'd ushered them outside so they would get the hint she needed space and time alone.

Half way through cooking the spaghetti bolognaise for dinner, Joan began to set the table. She counted the knives and forks and laid them out on the kitchen table and went back to the cupboard to count the plates. As she walked across the kitchen with them, to place them on the table, the just seemed to slip out of hands. It was as if her brain had told her hands to give up. All but one of the plates shattered as they hit the hard tiled floor. Straight away she collapsed to the floor with the pieces of sharp, smashed plates and started crying. She couldn't go on. For the past week or so she knew she was on the verge of having a nervous breakdown. Smashing the plates had tipped her over the edge.

Having heard the noise of the plates smashing Jamie ran in from the garden. He saw his mother crumpled and curled up, breaking down on the kitchen floor and it felt like a punch to the stomach to see her that way.

'After that day most of my childhood was filled with trips to the hospital with her. She would have breakdowns, paranoia, all kinds of things. As children we never had a safe foundation around us. It was always uncertainty and some type of abuse.' He lowered his voice when he used the word abuse.

'What kind of abuse?'

'Physical, mental and emotional. My dad would come home late, after having had more than a few pints after work. Mum would leave his dinner on the table and we would wait, anxiously, for him to come home. Some nights he never came, but I remember one night, he came home really late and still expected his food to be hot on the table. It had gone cold and he blamed it on mum. He accused her of not respecting him enough by giving him cold food. He could never see reason when he was that drunk. So he punished her.'

Francesca took a slow breath out before she asked the question. 'How did he punish her?'

Jamie's father, Richard, stumbled home from the pub late, after a session of drinking with a couple of his friends. Joan heard him open the front door and quickly told Jamie and Lucy to go upstairs to bed. She didn't want to risk them getting under Richard's feet as she knew what he was like when he was drunk. Everything was heightened and if anything kicked off there was no way of making Richard see sense. Lucy listened to her and went upstairs to her bedroom but Jamie only went up the stairs and stayed at the top on the landing. He crouched down quietly, to keep an eye out for his mum.

Richard stumbled in and didn't even acknowledge his wife. He went straight to the dining room table where he expected to see his food, but there was nothing there.

'Where's my food?' He was agitated and annoyed, not just by the alcohol in his blood but after the day he'd had at work as well.

Joan felt more on edge with the way he was acting and tried to sound as nice as possible when she spoke to him.

'You had your food love, before you left...'

Richard grabbed Joan behind her neck. Jamie hesitated, unsure whether to go downstairs or not. He knew sometimes his father would back off and would just blow hot air, threatening her.

'Don't tell me what I have and haven't done 'love''
he said sarcastically. 'If I say I'm hungry then I'm
hungry!' Spit flew from his mouth as he barked the words
at her.

Joan looked up at him and tried not to wince at the
smell of alcohol coming from his breath. She was scared
and uncertain what to say. She didn't want to provoke
him.

Richard slapped her hard around the face, insulted
by her silence. She shrieked and whimpered as her face
quickly heated up and turned red where he'd hit her.
Before Jamie could get down the stairs Richard backed her
into a corner. He raised his hand to strike her again when
Jamie leapt on to his father's back. He started hitting him,
trying to get him to put his arm down.

'Leave her alone you bully!' Jamie screamed,
letting out all his anger. He'd seen his mum being
battered and bruised too many times.

'I'm a bully am I? I thought I was the man that
puts food on this table and pays the bills.' Richard reached
behind him and pulled Jamie off his back like he was just
some ragdoll. He turned to square up to his son.

'You obviously think you're man enough to protect
her so show me… go on, let's see what you've got?'

Jamie just stood there frozen on the spot, not sure
whether it was a trick or not.

Joan was scared and uncertain about what Richard
was going to do to their son.

'Richard please, he's just a boy.' She tried to
protect him but Richard hit Jamie square across the face.
Jamie crashed to the floor with the force of his father's
hand. Crying, he looked up at his dad

. A flash of remorse and guilt went through Richard as he looked at his young son on the floor, holding onto his bruised face. He knew he had gone too far but he couldn't bear to see the weakness and vulnerability on his sons face.

'Come on! A man would stand up and hit back. Be a man Jamie!'

Jamie stayed down on the floor knowing he would have no chance against his father.

Francesca stayed silent for a while. She found it challenging to hear Jamie's childhood experience. 'Did you tell anyone, back then, that your father was physically abusive?'

'No. Mum didn't want anyone to know. She said she didn't want pity or anyone to feel sorry for her...for us.' He paused as he thought about his mother. 'When I was nineteen she passed away from cancer, I just wanted to move on so I never brought it up or told anyone. I buried it deep...' He became a little emotional and overwhelmed but still tried to continue. 'Burying my head in the sand doesn't seem to be working anymore. That's why I came here, because I can't tell my girlfriend. I don't want to stress her with the baby on the way.'

'Have you told her you're here, having therapy?'

'No.'

Francesca was a little confused. 'Where does she think you are now then?'

'At work. That's where I would usually be at this time. I will tell her... when I'm ready.'

CHAPTER SIXTEEN

Francesca, David, Mark and Mia sat around the dining table at David's mother's house. Celia's birthday family dinner had come around quicker than Francesca had expected or wanted. She'd left straight from work to get there on time as she knew how Celia felt about late comers.

The atmosphere was so tense that Francesca struggled to eat the meal Celia had prepared. She had cooked chicken, potatoes and vegetables for them all. Well, that was what Celia had told them but Francesca knew she had probably brought them from a shop ready prepared.

'So Mark, tell me how university is going?' Celia asked the question being the only one happy to be there. Mark was so tired from driving the two and half hour journey from university that Mia had to nudge him, to make him realise she was talking to him. 'Are you enjoying your course? What is it you're doing again?'

'I'm doing chemistry, grandma, and it's going well thank you.'

'Good, I'm pleased to hear that. You're a good boy, like your father was.' Celia sliced a new potato on her plate and put it in her mouth to chew.

Francesca tried not to throw up her food. She'd suffered years of listening to Celia's blind admiration for her only son. Out of the corner of her eye she noticed Mark looking at his father with disgust and contempt. She knew being compared with his father was his number one hate.

Celia finished her mouthful of potato and swallowed loudly. 'What about you Mia?' Her tone was different when asking, as if she didn't really want to ask, but felt compelled to.

'I'm studying for my A levels at the moment and then I'm hoping to study performing arts, focusing on acting.'

Celia wasn't impressed by her grand-daughters answer. She saw acting as a waste of time and money, It wasn't something she would be bragging about to her friends when they asked her on their Friday lunch get together what her grandchildren were up to.

'Well I guess we can't all be scientists can we!' She made no attempt to hide her judgement of what Mia was hoping to do. 'Could you please pass me the wine Francesca?'

Francesca wanted to throw the wine over her, not pass it to her. She gripped the neck of the bottle hard so she wasn't tempted. She passed it to David and gave him a look for him to say something to his mother and stand up for his daughter. Mia was visibly upset by her grandmother's brashness but David didn't say anything, he just took the bottle off Francesca and poured Celia another glass, as if she was the queen of Sheba.

Francesca couldn't bear to see Mia's upset face, she felt she had to say something if David wasn't going to.

'Mia was brilliant in her school play. The school says she's got a real talent for acting.' Francesca made it clear how proud she was of Mia and her accomplishment so far, but Celia ignored her and carried on eating her food.

Mark gently nudged Mia in the side to try and cheer her up and encourage her.

'She was amazing...' Mia couldn't help but smile a little bit at Mark but it didn't last long. Her eyes begin to water up.

'Excuse me, I need the toilet.' She got up to leave the table.

Celia corrected her statement. 'It's lavatory Mia. We're not French! And don't forget to wash your hands afterwards.' Mia hung her head in shame as she walked away. Oblivious, Celia started telling David about her new neighbour who had moved in next door a few weeks back.

Mark looked at Francesca across the table and they both glanced in Mia's direction.

'I'll go mum.' He whispered to her.

Francesca stayed seated at the table waiting for David or Celia to realize what was going on and how upset Mia was but neither of them do, they were both too stuck in their own bubble talking to one another.

'So David, how's accounting going these days? I suppose you'll be noticing a difference on the books with the way the economy's going at the moment?'

Francesca reached breaking point. Years of anger, that had been suppressed, flooded her body, she could no longer stay silent.

'Wow! Celia you are truly a piece of work! You know that? You have no tact...'

'Excuse me?' She was shocked and surprised at Francesca's outburst.

'Cesca, don't.' David tried to stop her.

'No David, I have waited years to tell your mother how I feel about her so right now I'm not going to bite my tongue.' She looked at Celia with a face full of anger. 'I won't watch my daughter be crushed by your snobby nosed opinions which, frankly, nobody wants to hear.' Celia turned to David appalled by the way Francesca was talking to her. 'She's a young woman...' Francesca continued, 'trying to find her way in a world where people, like you, will try to crush her dreams. I let you do it to me to keep 'your David' happy but I won't let you do it to my daughter!' She threw her napkin onto her plate of food, not willing to eat any more of it.

'You needed direction Francesca. Marriage was the best thing for you and, besides, you were pregnant. I saved you from a certain reputation.'

'Reputation?' She felt her face burn with anger. 'Don't act like you've ever cared about me or my reputation. The only reputation you've ever cared about was, and is, your own!'

'David, you're not going to let your wife speak to me like that are you?'

David didn't know what to do. He felt stuck between the two of them.

Francesca got up from the table and headed for her jacket and handbag. 'Actually I will soon not be his wife, so he can't stop me doing anything anymore!'

Celia became hysterical. 'David what is she saying? What does she mean she's not going to be your wife anymore?' She clutched her chest as if she couldn't breathe properly.

David was worried she was about to have another heart attack and tried to calm her down. 'Don't worry mum, calm down, breathe, I was going to tell you...'

Mark and Mia came back into the room. Mark had managed to reassure Mia and she had felt ready to join them again.

Francesca looked at them. 'Come on kids! We're leaving!'

'What? Why? How come?' Mark was confused. He could see his father breathing with his grandma as if she was giving birth.

'Because I've just realized how much of a bitch your grandma really is!' Francesca had wanted to say that, call her that, for years.

Celia did a high pitched, over dramatic squeal as if her heart could take no more.

'Only just now?' Mark said under his breath as he put his jumper on.

On the drive home Mia rode in Francesca's car. Mark had packed his car full of furniture to take back with him to university, so there was no room for Mia to ride with him. Twenty minutes into the hour's journey back Mia spoke for the first time.

'I was supposed to go back with dad.' She wasn't complaining. She'd just remembered she was supposed to be staying over at his apartment afterwards.

'I know. Sorry. I didn't plan to blow up at your grandma like that and walk out.'

They both started laughing, thinking about Celia's face and the way she'd acted.

'Don't worry. I didn't want to stay there any longer. Anyway, Dad's probably going to stay over there with her now, knowing him.' Mia's stomach rumbled. 'God I'm starving!' She had hardly eaten any of the food on her plate and her body was just realising it.

Francesca checked her middle mirror to see if Mark was still following behind her.

'Why don't you ring your brother and see if he wants to stop for some food. I could do with a hot, greasy burger... and the lavatory!' They both laughed, remembering Celia's choice of words.

The next morning David rang Francesca on the house phone. He made sure not to call her on her mobile because he knew she would see his name and probably not pick up.

'Hello...'

'Why did you have to do that?' He went straight for her. 'You know she has a weak heart. She could have popped her clogs there and then!'

'Do we actually know she has a heart condition?' Francesca kept her tone calm and didn't rise to him. 'I mean I wouldn't put it past her to make something like that up.' It wouldn't have been the first time Celia had stretched the truth. She had a history of doing it.

'You're unbelievable!' David was more than irritated with her.

'Well, have you seen any documentation from her doctor or the hospital?'

'No. I trust her. Anyway, why would she make something like that up?' He was too naive, when it came to his mother, to think badly of her.

'She lives an hour away. How many times did you go over and see her before, compared to after she said she was ill?'

He started to work it out in his head and realised Francesca actually had a point.

'Still, you had no right to speak to her the way you did.'

'What? But she had the right to speak to Mia the way she did? You should have stuck up for your daughter!'

'Don't start Cesca! You can't talk! My relationship with Mia is in a better place than yours...'

Francesca felt it was totally off topic and below the belt. She put the phone down on him, cutting him off, she wasn't prepared to have an argument with him over the phone.

CHAPTER SEVENTEEN

Jasmine rushed out of the classroom as the bell rang. She felt sick and queasy, as if she could faint any second, she didn't want to collapse in the classroom or the corridor and have the whole school talking about her the next day. She was only fifteen and had too many more years to get through at school to be known as the girl who face planted the floor and passed out during class. She liked flying under the radar and had been like that all her life. The last thing she ever wanted to be was the centre of attention in any situation.

She got to the main school corridor where the girls toilets were and began to sway slightly. As she walked her eyes began to blur and she bumped into the blue lockers that covered the whole right hand side of the wall. The school shirt she was wearing was damp with sweat and she could feel the material sticking to her back. She tried her best to walk normally towards the toilets so as not to draw attention to herself, but with each step her vision was worsening and it made her feel completely off balance. She could just about, by squinting her eyes, make out two girls walking towards her. She wasn't sure if she recognised them or not.

She knew who they were as soon as she heard them snigger at her. It was Denise Kelp and Bonnie Freeman, two girls in her year, the ones that had ridiculed her at school for the past few months. In school Jasmine had always done her best to avoid them but, now, she had to walk past them to get to the toilets.

'Careful Dee, here comes the druggie!'

'Eh gross...' Bonnie moved out of the way as if Jasmine was contagious. 'What's the matter? You need another hit Jazzy?'

Jasmine put her head down and tried to blank them so that she could concentrate on putting one foot in front of the other. All she could hear was her heartbeat racing and pounding in her ears. She couldn't believe how sweaty her palms had become and how wobbly her legs were. She was so close to the toilets.

'Nearly there...' She whispered to herself.

Other pupils started filing out of the classrooms into the corridor. They soon filled it, causing mayhem and chaos. Jasmine looked up at the hustle and bustle of the other kids. It wasn't what she wanted. She had hoped to be in the girls toilets before the crowds came so she wouldn't have to use more energy and effort pushing through them all. The only good thing was that the influx of pupils got Denise and Bonnie off her back. They had seen one of the boys they liked from the year above enter the corridor and they made a b-line for him.

Jasmine was only metres away from the toilets when she tripped slightly on a rucksack that had been left outside a classroom. She would have hit the floor if a hand hadn't reached out and stopped her. The person helped Jasmine to steady herself.

When she was as steady as she could be, Jasmine looked up.

'Are you OK?' It was Mia.

'Yes, sorry. I just lost my footing...' Jasmine looked at Mia. She knew her as one of the older, popular girls in school, but she had never actually spoken to her.

Mia was concerned about the way Jasmine seemed and how rough she looked. She looked at her as if to say she didn't quite believe her.

'I'm fine... really.' Jasmine could barely get the words out, her mouth was so dry. She quickly thanked Mia and rushed in to the girl's toilets.

Mia stared after her. She wondered if she should follow her into the toilets and check on her when Josh approached.

'Are you OK? What were you talking to Jasmine for?' He didn't let her answer. 'You know the whole school talks about her. They say she's a proper hard core drug taker...'

'Really? The *whole* school?' She teased him on his choice of words.

'OK, so Hailey from year eleven, she said she saw her shooting up in the toilets once during P.E. Hailey said she had forgotten her jumper so she'd run back to the changing room. On the way back she went for a pee. Jasmine was behind one of the doors in the stalls taking a hit, so she says!'

Mia didn't really believe the gossip. There was always new gossip going around the school most days. She felt sorry for Jasmine who she'd noticed a few times recently at school because she looked like she was carrying the weight of the world on her shoulders.

'Don't believe everything you hear Josh. You're seventeen and should know by now people talk a lot of shit!'

'Yeah, yeah, I know.... but you've got to admit she does look pretty rough!'

When Jasmin got into the girls toilets she couldn't hold her vomit down any longer. It had been building up in her stomach, burning her insides. She flung herself at the toilet and dropped to her knees as fluid shot out of her mouth and hit the toilet pan. Feeling a sense of relief, almost as if her anxiety and emotions had come up and out with the vomit, she stared at the discoloured liquid floating on top of the water in the toilet.

She sat up and wiped her mouth with her sleeve to get rid of the residue on her face and brushed the cold sweat off the palms of her hands onto her trousers. She rummaged through her school bag, pulled out a bottle of water and took a few big gulps. She could tell her body was dehydrated by the way it responded to the fluid. It was as if she could have carried on drinking forever. She finished the bottle and rummaged through her bag again, she found what she was looking for and pulled it out of her bag, it was a syringe needle filled with a clear liquid. In the morning she had made sure she'd filled the syringe before coming to school. A few weeks ago she had nearly been caught in the toilets injecting and wanted to make sure, this time, she was more discrete and quick.

As Jasmine put the needle into her skin she took a deep breath. She pressed the plunger on top of the syringe and her body swallowed up the liquid. It rushed through her bloodstream, she could feel herself respond and relax as it entered her circulation.

Jasmine got home later than her mother liked. She hadn't done it on purpose, she'd just missed the bus trying to stay out of the way of Bonnie and Denise at school, she'd hung back and made sure they had left so they couldn't approach her again. She put her key in the door and walked into her two up, two down, council house where she had lived for most of her life. Her mum, Debra, had moved there when she was just six months old.

'Jasmine, where have you been? I've been worried sick!' Debra rushed to the front door having heard it being opened.

'Sorry mum. I had after school detention so I had to stay behind.' Jasmine couldn't tell her mum the truth, that she was hiding from two girls who, on the best of days, made her school days a living nightmare. Jasmin worried about her mum because she had too much to deal with as it was, paying the bills and finding a way to get food on the table being just a couple. Jasmine's father, Debra's ex-husband who she hadn't seen for twelve years, contributed towards his children but he wasn't reliable and the money would be less than was needed and very sporadic.

'Detention?' Debra wasn't impressed, 'What did you do?'

'Nothing. I was just cheeky to some teacher.' She walked past her mum over to her little brother Paul, who was sitting at the kitchen table doing his homework. 'Hey kid.' She scuffed the top of his head with her hand and kissed him. She had done it since he was a baby and it had become a habit every time she saw him. It was one of her favourite things to do and Paul loved it just as much.

'Hi Jazz!' He was always excited to see her. Jasmine's self-esteem was so low that she never understood why and how he could love her so much. Sometimes it was hard for her to look at him, because she could see how much she meant to him and it was too much for her to take. She felt guilty that his love and admiration for her wasn't enough for her to feel content, or enough for her to want to live and watch him grow up.

'I got a merit at school today!' He carried on writing as Jasmine sat down next to him. He was the only thing or person in her life that actually made her feel something. Sometimes it was only a little spark but it resembled a feeling inside of still being alive.

'Jasmine! Please don't ignore me. Detention is serious!' Debra had followed her in to the kitchen. 'I hope you apologised for saying whatever you did to the teacher.'

'Yes of course I did mum!' She knew her mum could never tell when she lied. It was a gift she'd mastered, the art of being one of the best liars in the world.

'Good...' Debra felt a little less upset knowing her daughter had at least apologised. The school had already been in touch with her about Jasmine's attendance, she didn't want them on her back about her behaviour as well.

'Are you thirsty do you want a drink?' Reassured, she was back to normal mode straight away.

'I am, but don't worry I'll get it.' Jasmin got up and went to the cupboard for a glass. She strolled over to the sink and ran the cold tap. The water had to be really cold otherwise she felt like she was drinking warm water so she left it running and went out of the room.

Debra stayed in the kitchen. She opened and began rummaging through one of the cupboards. It was what they referred to their 'junk cupboard' which had things like batteries, their first aid kit, medicine and tablets, along with all other kinds of random debris that got stuffed into it.

'I'm sure I only bought a new packed the other day!' Debra said, talking to herself. She couldn't find what she was looking for.

Jasmin heard her mum talking and came back into the room. She turned to look at Debra.

'What are you talking about mum? What did you buy?'

'Paracetamol.' She scratched her head in confusion. 'I thought I'd bought a packet when we went into the chemist to get you're...' She paused and started to doubt her memory. 'Never mind.' Debra thought maybe she was just over tired because of the amount of night shifts she'd done at the care home she worked for. 'I must have just thought I bought one, silly me!'

'I can pop down to the shops now if you like. It won't take me five minutes.'

'No we don't have time. You've got your appointment in ten minutes.'

'What appointment?' Jasmine filled her glass up from the tap and took a sip. It was just about cold enough for her.

'You've got a meeting with a doctor.' Debra closed the cupboard and went over to the fridge to get something to snack on.

'I don't want to see another doctor. I like Dr Sims...'Jasmine assumed Debra was talking about going to see another G.P, a different one to usual.

'No, not that kind of doctor. She's a psychologist who Dr Sims recommended, I told you last week about it. 'Jasmine couldn't remember any conversation they'd had about it but she was aware that, recently, she'd picked up the bad habit of pretending to listen. She noticed herself doing it most of the time lately, when someone would say something to her and she would just give an answer hoping it was a yes or no kind of question.

She took another few sips of water. She wasn't so sure about seeing someone new as she didn't like meeting new people or having new people come into her life.

'What about Paul? Who's going to look after him?'

'Don't worry about your brother, Jasmine. I've got that sorted.' Debra had organised for Paul to go over to the neighbours. He was friends with one of the girls who lived there and they always played well together and enjoyed each other's company.

Debra drove in to town within about ten minutes. It should have taken longer but she had a heavy, impatient foot when it came to driving.

When they were outside the door to Francesca's building, Debra turned to her daughter.

'Do you want me to come in with you for your first time? I won't come in to the actual session, but I mean wait with you until you're with her?'

'Would you? Do you have time?' She didn't want her mum to hang around if she had work to go to, but she was so nervous she felt it would help her knowing her mum would be so close.

'Of course I have time Jazz!' She stroked a loose bit of hair back behind Jasmine's ear.

They made their way up the two flights of stairs. Jasmine opened the glass door and walked into the reception area with Debra behind her. Julie greeted her with a big smile which helped her feel a little less anxious. Before she'd left home she'd imagined the place as scary, with scary people, but now she was there the reality of it was different. It was nicer.

'You must be Jasmine...?' Julie was behind her desk and had just finished making herself a cup of coffee. 'How are you? Can I get you or your...?' Not wanting to presume she paused to let Debra finish her sentence.

'Mum.'

Julie smiled, 'You or your mum a drink?'

Debra and Jasmine both agreed on having a glass of water and Julie directed them to the waiting room on the left hand side of the reception area. It was quite a small waiting area, but open and airy with a lot of light coming in through the window. Depending where you sat you could see through to the reception area and down a bit of the corridor that led to Francesca's office.

Debra and Jasmine had only been sitting for a few minutes when Francesca appeared. She introduced herself to both of them and then invited Jasmine into her office. As Jasmine walked down the corridor, behind Francesca, she realised how sweaty she'd become due her nervousness. Her whole body tensed up as she took a seat on the sofa in Francesca's office.

Francesca gathered herself together and picked some paperwork off her desk as Jasmine took in the room, waiting to start. The desk was at the back of the large, carpeted room in front of a small window. The window looked out over the town and let a lot of natural light in, making it seem cosy.

Jasmine took a quick glance at the walls which had large canvas paintings hung on each of them. The paintings brought a soft colourful brightness to the room.

'So...' Francesca had sat in her chair, opposite Jasmine, ready to begin. She put her file and note pad down on the small table beside her. She looked at Jasmine and smiled. 'I just want to tell you everything said in this room is confidential, just between us, unless you tell me something that I believe puts you or someone else in danger. Is that OK?'

Jasmin could only manage a nod in agreement. She could tell already that Francesca was nice but she was still unsure about why and where she was.

'So...' Francesca said again as she leant back in her chair and crossed her legs, 'do you want to tell me why you think you're here?'

The room went quiet. Jasmine played with the cuffs of her sleeves and stared down at the floor, too shy to look up and half hoping Francesca would say something else.

That was what usually happened when she didn't answer someone. They just carried on with whatever they wanted to say.

Francesca held the silence in the room, until Jasmine couldn't take the quiet any longer, she answered the question.

'I guess... my mum's worried about me?'

Francesca could see instantly how much of a struggle it was for Jasmine to speak, she decided to try a different angle and start off a little more casually with her questions.

'I see you've got your school uniform on. Did you come straight from school?'

'Yeah... well kind of...'

The easier question seemed to work, Jasmine felt a lot less pressure answering. 'We got some food before we came here.'

Francesca smiled at her warmly. 'Anything nice?'

'Just some chicken and salad. My mum always worries about what I eat.'

'Sounds like your mum worries about you a lot. Do you know why she worries so much?' She wasn't sure whether Jasmine would answer the question but it seemed like a good opening.

Jasmine wavered slightly but then answered the question. 'Because the doctors say I have depression.'

'Do you think you have depression?' It was a genuine question with no right or wrong answer.

'I guess so... I stay in my room a lot, most of the time, when I'm at home. That's probably why she brought me here because she thinks I'm up there taking drugs or something?' She laughed nervously.

'Are you on drugs?' Francesca didn't really like asking her but she took it as an opportunity to ask. She was a little surprised when she first saw Jasmine, she had looked pale, tired with bloodshot eyes. She knew there could have been many reasons for her appearance but she wanted to rule out drug taking as one of them.

'No. She shouldn't be worried about things like that. 'Jasmine shifted on the sofa as if she was uncomfortable.

Francesca noticed but didn't push her on her visible discomfort. She just made a mental note of it. 'Is there anything in particular you think your mum 'should' be worried about with you?'

'I don't know... I talk about death and dying a lot so I think she worries about that.'

'That's quite a heavy subject to talk about...'

Jasmine jumped in before Francesca could finish. 'Not really. Not for me... I think about it a lot...' She hesitated wondering if she could trust Francesca or not... she took the risk.

'When my Grandpa died I couldn't stop thinking about where he'd gone or what the point of living was if, ultimately, we just disappear? Why do we build and create these connections and love for people when they just end up leaving you?' As she thought about her grandpa, she could feel her eyes begin to burn with sadness. 'All the special moments you share with them, they just end up becoming nothing but vague memories...' A tear dropped down her cheek as she let a deep breath out. 'When I was little my grandpa... we were really close and we did everything together. He was my best friend. When I got upset he was the one who told me everything was going to be OK. I knew he couldn't possibly know that, but I didn't care because I felt safe when he held me… I could turn to him for anything.' She wiped away the tears that had fallen down both cheeks with her sleeve.

Francesca passed her the box of tissues. Jasmine pulled the top one out and scrunched it up to dry her cheeks.

'We would always go to a pub on a Sunday for lunch. He would pay and always say to me and my little brother Paul, 'have whatever you want. It's all on me!' By the end we would feel sick with the amount of food we had eaten!' She couldn't help but smile at the images the memory brought back. 'He would always order a pint of beer and it would come, frothing, straight from the tap and he'd let me sip the froth off it every time. Mum never liked it, but he still let me do it, because he knew how much I loved it. It wasn't even the beer I loved it was just that it was our thing we did together, you know?'

Francesca nodded. 'Sounds like you have some wonderful memories of him.'

The smile quickly dropped from Jasmine's face and her body slumped, already reacting to her next thought, 'When I think about him now… I feel guilty, because all I feel is anger… anger over him leaving me. I can't help it. It just seems to overtake me and I find it harder and harder to remember the good times.'

Francesca could see she was obviously struggling with her feelings and emotions with the loss of her grandpa, she felt sorry for her. The room went quiet again whilst Francesca gave Jasmine some space and time to be with hers feelings, knowing how raw they still were.

'Can you remember one good time?' Francesca asked her softly.

She thought about it and one memory came to her mind. 'Yes.'

'Well I would say that's what is important. Hold on to that one memory, the happy one and promise yourself you won't let it go or let it be tarnished by anything or anyone. We can do it now if you want to? Can you tell me the happiest memory you have of him?'

Jasmine grinned thinking about it. 'His favourite place was the beach. Every Friday he would pick me and Paul up. Paul was only small so he would pick us up in his car and park a short distance from the beach. If we hadn't been with him he probably would have walked all the way to the beach from his house. When he was 70 he had a triple bypass and the doctor had told him 'once we do the operation you're going to have to do a lot of walking, at least a mile a day to start off with.' I remember him being really stroppy with the doctor about it but, three months in, it turned out he loved going out in the morning and fitting in a five mile walk!'

Francesca smiled warmly hearing her story and seeing the delight on Jasmine's face re-telling it, she wanted to see it more. 'What would you do at the beach?'

'We would walk down the beach together holding hands with me on his left side and Paul on his right.' She looked down at her hands, 'He had such warm, big hands. I can never forget because his hands were about four times the size of mine.' She looked back up at Francesca. 'We would go to the rock pools and watch the tiny fish caught in the water, the ones that had to wait for the tide to come back in to get back to the sea. We'd splash about together until we were so wet and cold we had to go home because my lips would always begin to go blue...' She paused and swallowed hard, trying to control her emotions. 'On my eleventh birthday he said he'd come and pick us up. I waited for him, looking out the living room window, but he never...' She gasped, too overcome by grief to carry on. She began to weep.

Francesca sat forward in her chair, hoping it would somehow comfort Jasmine in some way. She was unsure whether to go over and sit by her, make contact with her to reassure her. She knew some therapist's insisted on no contact with their clients but she wasn't one of them, especially in instances like this when the client was so upset. Before she had time to come to a decision Jasmine began to speak again.

'He was walking to his car to come and pick us up, but had a heart attack about ten yards from his front door... the neighbours heard him drop to the floor and tried to help, but it was no good, he was gone.' She paused. 'I've never felt so alone. When mum told me, it was like a huge hole was created inside me and each day it grew bigger and bigger... at first it felt empty, like I didn't really exist anymore. My whole reality had changed and I didn't even want to imagine what my life would be like without him, and now... well... that emptiness is just filled up with anger, sadness and loneliness...'

Francesca stayed silent as a wave of her own loneliness hit her completely out of the blue. She felt unnerved by it. She knew she had experienced loneliness on and off for years since her mother had died, but she had managed to ignore it and carry on like most people did. She was surprised that her body was choosing to bring it up and feel it now. She shrugged her own feelings away to concentrate on Jasmine's.

'Had you ever experienced any of these emotions so strongly before the passing of your grandpa?'

'I guess so. Since I can remember, I've always had this feeling of not feeling at home here, in this world, in this body, around people. I don't understand them and they don't understand me.'

'You know, if people were honest with themselves I think they would say that at some point in their lives they've felt like they don't fit in.'

Jasmine looked at Francesca. No-one had ever said something so reassuring and honest to her.

'Is that why people act like they do? Like everything is OK and normal? All I see is dysfunction and insanity and people rushing around trying to run away from their real feelings. Trying to fill that emptiness inside them with whatever they can find... alcohol, drugs, sex... work...'

Francesca knew she wasn't directing the 'work' comment at her because they had only just met, but it made something inside her flinch. She shuffled, uncomfortable in her chair, as Jasmine continued.

'People just lash out because they can't deal with, or don't want to deal with, their own pain. I don't want to be like that.'

'What do you want to be like?' She was intrigued to know what a young lady, who in her opinion seemed to have a high level of emotional intelligence and sensitivity, wanted to be like.

'I want to be free!' Jasmine's body language completely changed, she sat up straight. 'I don't want to be like them.' But as quickly as she'd changed for the better she changed back again and became heavy in her body and voice. 'Some days I spend the whole day in the supermarket just watching people walk in and out. I wonder what it is they're rushing to and from. They don't seem to see what's happening there and then, because they're already thinking ahead.'

Francesca looked at her and tilted her head to the side. She wanted to understand Jasmine's experience of life a bit more. 'What do you mean?'

'Well, one couple had a small child who must have been about three or four. She was upset and crying because she didn't feel very well. Her parents just ignored her and told her to 'hurry up' because they had somewhere else to be. She had warned them but they still got angry with her when I saw her throw up in the car, all because they didn't want to be late. The amount of people I've seen cradling a pack of beers or bottles of wine. One man seemed so desperate for a drink that he hadn't even got outside before he had opened a can and started swigging it. I could see the desperation in his eyes and his body and his hands wouldn't stop shaking.'

'Do you watch people a lot?'

'Only when I bunk off school. I learn way more watching people than sitting in a classroom all day. Schools boring, why would I like somewhere that tries every day to take away any individuality I have left? A place that wants you to fit into their system and conditioning that only ticks their boxes? All they want you to do is turn into a capable working machine that will be qualified enough to have a high paid job with ridiculous hours because, to them, that's what the 'real' world is. It's shit!'

Francesca couldn't really disagree with her. 'I know it is, and I agree with you there, but the positives of school are things like socialising and making friends. Do you have any friends that would make school a little less boring?'

Jasmine thought about the kids at her school. If she was honest she hadn't ever really made an effort with any of them. 'No not really. I keep myself to myself.'

'You don't go out and meet boys and girls your own age?'

'No.' she said it in a very matter of fact way as if friends had no bearing on her life.

'What do you do in your spare time then?'

'I read...' Francesca noticed her light up again. 'I'm into things like philosophy and that kind of stuff.'

'Just some light reading then!'

She laughed at Francesca's irony. Francesca noticed how Jasmine's face completely changed when she smiled, it was lovely to see.

Their session together ended after an hour. Francesca walked Jasmine back into the reception area where Debra had sat and waited the whole time. She had passed the time reading a few of the out of date magazines left on the corner table.

'So I'll see you next time, Jasmine...' Francesca gently touched her on the shoulder to give her some extra physical reassurance. 'Call me any time before if you need me, OK?'

'OK, thank you.'

Debra put her magazine down when she heard her daughter's voice and walked over to them.

'How did it go?'

'OK actually. Mum do you mind if I go to the car? I'm tired.' Debra looked at Francesca to see if their appointment was completely over.

'Yes, that's fine with me, Jasmine. You've done your time, so to speak! I need a quick word with your mother anyway about what dates and times you can do.'

Jasmine gave her a half smile with the side of her mouth and took the car keys from Debra.

'I'll see you in a bit love.'

They watched her walk out and begin to descend the stairs. Francesca encouraged Debra to follow her down the corridor to her office. She breathed a sigh of relief as she entered the room, she'd been so anxious about Jasmine seeing someone new.

'How did it go? Was she OK?'

Francesca was searching her diary for next week's appointments, 'I'm sorry but it's up to Jasmine if she wants to say how it went or give any details about today. Our work is confidential so I can't discuss anything.'

'No, no, that's fine, sorry.' Debra felt a little embarrassed, 'I wasn't trying to pry or anything. I'm just worried about her. She can be so quiet and reclusive.'

Francesca empathised with her, knowing she would be just as worried if it was Mia. She tried to reassure her.

'I will tell you this about your daughter though, she's a very intelligent and observant young lady and very wise for her young age.'

'That's what I worry about! I know I can't protect her. She's so sensitive and so aware. Sometimes it scares me.'

CHAPTER EIGHTEEN

Francesca was out on her lunch break. She'd eaten a light lunch at one of the deli cafes and was on her way back to the office. She stopped off and bought Julie a muffin from one of her and Laura's favourite bakery's.

When she got back she placed the muffin on Julie's desk.

Julie grabbed it. 'Oh, lovely! Aren't I a lucky girl! Blueberry I hope?'

'Of course! Would I dare bring anything else?' Once Francesca had turned up with a lemon curd muffin and Julie had given her such a face of disgust that she'd never made the same mistake again.

'Speaking of lucky, it's your lucky day as well!'

Francesca leaned on Julie's desk to take the weight off her feet slightly.

'What? Can you give me back the twenty years of my life I wasted with David?' She didn't even have the energy to sound sarcastic anymore when it came to him.

'Oh OK, maybe it's not your lucky day then!' Julie went off track, 'How are things? Have you heard from him?'

Francesca scoffed at the question. 'I think I've heard more from him recently than I ever did when we were married! It's probably because he wants to talk about the divorce agreement. He reckons he has the right to have the Range Rover!'

Julie frowned, confused. 'Didn't he buy that for you? For your birthday?'

'Exactly! Anyway tell me, why is it my lucky day?'

'Roger's not coming in today because he's got...' She picked up the piece of paper with the whole message on, 'another last minute appointment that's come up for tonight, no pun intended, he said! Although...' She pondered over the message, 'I don't understand why something that's come up for tonight effects his three o'clock appointment with you?'

'I'll explain to you in Roger's world what that means. He's telling me he's got a date with a poor unfortunate soul who doesn't know what they're getting themselves into, and he won't be able to make it later this afternoon because a date night for Roger means preparing himself the whole day before!'

'What does he need to do that takes him so long?' Julie was completely baffled but also slightly interested at the same time.

Francesca stood up straight again. 'You don't want to know! Plus, client confidentiality, I shouldn't have really told you anything.'

'I like him. Yes, he's quirky, but he's always charming with me.'

Francesca couldn't believe what she was hearing. 'Quirky, yes. Charming?' She left Julie's desk area, and began walking towards her office. 'I think you've been working here too long Julie!' She smiled to herself at the thought of Julie liking Roger. 'Who have I got coming in next?'

Julie shouted the answer down the corridor in Francesca's direction, 'Shay Bentley!'

Francesca turned the corner into her office. 'Great' she mumbled to herself. The smile went from her face, she had totally forgotten today was Shay's appointment. She shut her office door and sat at her desk dreading the next five minutes she had to wait until Shay's arrival.

The five minutes wait turned into nearly half an hour. Francesca was about to give up, thinking Shay wasn't going to turn up, when her office phone rang. She looked at it. It was Julie's line ringing through. She picked it up and put it to her ear and heard Julie's voice at the other end. 'She's arrived.'

Francesca opened her door slowly to give her a bit more time to prepare herself and walked down the corridor through into reception where Shay was sitting in her usual seat, but with a guilty look on her face. Completely unimpressed with her lateness and lack of communication Francesca kept her face neutral and her voice low when she spoke to Shay. 'Come on through.'

Francesca sat down and crossed her legs in her chair. Her skirt rose up her leg a bit too far so she pulled it down a bit.

Shay watched her, aware that Francesca hadn't really looked at her yet. She felt like she'd been called into the principal's office again after annoying one of her teachers.

Francesca looked down at her notes as she spoke to Shay properly for the first time. 'You're late. Where have you been?'

Shay answered her slightly allusively. 'Sorry, I got caught up and lost track of time.'

'Caught up? It must have been important to make you nearly...' Francesca looked at her watch knowing full well how late Shay was, but she wanted to make it clear to Shay that their meetings weren't a joke, 'half an hour late for our appointment!'

Shay didn't react to her mood. 'No it wasn't important. It was just one of those things that happens!' She winked at Francesca and gave her a cheeky smile. 'Sorry miss, it won't happen again!'

'Shay I'm not your teacher! This isn't school. I just want you to hold accountability for your lateness...' Francesca was trying to be serious but she could see Shay was having none of it.

Shay looked at her and completely changed the direction of the conversation.

'Did you have a nice meal?'

'Excuse me?'

'The other day you were eating out. It looked like you were having lunch with a friend?' Francesca tried not to let on that she knew what Shay was talking about, 'You

143

know, the day you blushed when you saw me!' She bit her bottom lip and smiled suggestively.

Francesca scoffed. 'I didn't blush.'

'No?' Shay smiled again, she enjoyed winding her up too much.

'No!' Francesca said more sternly than she needed to but she wanted to stop Shay from continuing with her games.

'I know when someone is blushing and you, for sure, blushed!'

'Shall we just agree to disagree and move on?' She was embarrassed that Shay had seen her blush at the café and just wanted to move on as quickly as possible. 'We don't have much time left or many sessions, so let's just make the most of it while we can, yes?'

Shay stared at her. 'You like changing the subject when it's about you, don't you?'

A phone started ringing before Francesca could answer her question. It was Francesca's mobile, she'd left it on in her bag without realising. She got up from her chair, slowly, paranoid her skirt would lift again in front of Shay, and went over to her desk. She found her phone in her bag just as it stopped ringing and went to pick it up. She looked at the screen, it was a missed call from David. Francesca could tell he'd left an answer phone message, no doubt about meeting up to talk. She was about to switch it to silent when It started ringing again. David's name came up on the screen. Francesca could feel the fire in her belly heat up with annoyance, she decided against putting it on silent and switched it off instead.

'Sorry I thought I had switched it off... where were we?' She walked back over to Shay and sat back down in her chair.

'We were on you and how you like to change the subject!'

Francesca had lost any tolerance she had left after seeing David's name on her screen, she went straight to the point with Shay.

'Do you know what? I think you like being sexually forward, flirtatious and suggestive to test and push people's boundaries, especially mine!'

'Damn Doc! Break it to me gently why don't you!' Shay could see she wasn't impressed with her teasing but she couldn't help but carry on. She noticed Francesca wasn't wearing her wedding ring. 'Marriage problems? You're not wearing your ring today.'

'That's none of your business!' Francesca could hear the shortness in her own voice, 'can you just stop mucking around so I can actually help you?'

'I'll tell you my story, *oui*? If you tell me yours! Otherwise, how am I supposed to know if I can trust or relate to you?' It was an offer Shay assumed Francesca wouldn't take, but tired of getting nowhere and pushing against the way Shay wanted to do things, Francesca tried another angle by being honest with her.

'My husband and I have split. That's why I'm not wearing my ring. Happy..?'

Shay stayed quiet, she looked at Francesca with wide eyes.

'What?'

'*Non*, nothing...' She was the flustered one out of the two of them now. 'I'm just surprised. I didn't expect you to tell me!'

Francesca un-crossed her legs and leant forward in her chair. 'Look Shay, I'm willing to be open and honest with you, if you can do the same for me. I'm here to help you. I want to help you...' she leant back, conscious she was too close to Shay. She straightened her back against her chair, 'so come on, I held my side of the bargain now it's your turn! Tell me, when was the first time you remember feeling angry?' Francesca asked the question knowing she was still a bit taken aback by her personal disclosure. It made her feel a bit more in control of the session.

Shay started to answer. 'I'm not an angry person...' Hearing her tone Francesca thought she was still not going to cooperate, but Shay surprised her as she continued. 'It's just sometimes this energy of frustration builds up inside me, like it's squeezing me from the inside, so I have to release it any way possible.'

'How long have you felt this way?' Do you know when it started?'

'*Oui*... It started after...' She wasn't sure if she was going to be able to say his name, 'after Tommy died.'

'Tommy?' Francesca wrote the name down on her notes.

'My little brother.'

'Would you tell me about him...? What happened?' She asked softly.

Shay combed her hair back with her fingers and took a deep breath. She felt emotional just speaking Tommy's name. 'He would follow me around like a shadow. He liked what I liked, wanted to go where I went. He always wanted to do what I did.' She tried to clear the lump in her throat, 'he was six years younger than me... and, if you can believe it, twice as cheeky and definitely twice as sweet!' Francesca smiled to encourage her to carry on, she could see Shay was struggling with her unacknowledged emotions. 'He didn't deserve to...' she held her breath to try and stop her voice from breaking with grief. She became aware Francesca's full attention was on her and it was too much. Shay stood up and started to pace the room, hoping it would move the strong emotions bubbling up inside her. She was completely out of her comfort zone.

Francesca encouraged her again. 'It's OK. Take your time.'

As Shay paced the room, she spotted one of the pictures on the wall by the door. It was hanging in a slightly wonky fashion so she walked over to it and straightened it up. She stayed by the door because it made her feel a bit safer, as if she could make a quick exit if things got too much.

'My mum and dad met in school when they were still only young, they married when they were both twenty years old. Dad got a job where he had to travel a lot. Mum got fed up with moving, what seemed like every six months, and wanted to settle so she gave him an ultimatum. It was either her or the job. The company didn't want to lose him so they offered him an office job which required no travelling, no moving, just simple nine to five. The only thing was, it was in France... they moved three months later and another three months later mum became pregnant with me. We lived over there until I was fourteen and Tommy eight. *Voila!* Hence the accent! All through their marriage I remember them having rocky patches but somehow, after every argument dad would always know how to make mum stay. He would convince her that their relationship would get better if she could just give him the time to show her.' She paused. 'I think she was lonely, had enough of living abroad. None of her family ever came out to see her. They used the excuse of not having enough money, but she knew, really, it was because they couldn't stand my father.'

Shay's legs began to feel a bit tired standing. She'd worked a shift beforehand and had been on her feet for a long time so she leant against the wall. 'Dads work company folded so we moved back here to the U.K.'

'How did you feel about moving?'

'I didn't care where we were, as long as I was with mum and Tommy...' She felt her eyes burn and her stomach tense as she hung her head. It made her hair fall forward so she combed it back again. 'God! I don't know what's wrong with me?'

Francesca could see Shay's emotions peaking out over the surface. She tried to sound as understanding as possible. 'Tell me what happened, Shay.'

TEN YEARS EARLIER.

Shay, Tommy and their mother, Sara, were in the car on the way to the local supermarket. It was raining,

pouring down, and hitting the top of the car roof. Visibility was poor, the thick grey clouds in the sky dulled and blocked the natural daylight making it seem like the evening and not the afternoon.

Shay was sitting up front listening to her CD player and Tommy was behind her in the back, staring at the rain smashing against the window. Sara slowly took a left turn and pulled up outside the supermarket. Barely anyone was shopping because of the state of the weather, so the car park was practically empty.

Sara parked the car and cut the engine.

'Mummy, mummy can I get the dinosaur cake this year?' Tommy was barely able to keep his excitement in. It was his eighth birthday and Sara had promised him the best day ever. She didn't answer his question straight away because she was too stressed about having to rush into the supermarket to get the cake and then to drive on to the soft play venue, which she had booked for an hour and they were already five minutes late.

'You had a dinosaur cake for your last birthday so why would you want another one?' Shay teased him a bit, she knew why he wanted one, he was mad about dinosaurs.

Tommy gave her one of his looks. He knew she was being silly on purpose.

They all got out of the car and ran, through the rain, into the supermarket. By the time they had been in and picked up the cake the weather had eased off a bit. Sara walked back to the car and sat in the driver's seat while the kids put the trolley back. Even though they had only needed one item Tommy had insisted on going around in a trolley.

Shay pushed him across to the trolley tunnel.

'Shay, will you come on the big slide with me? Kasper says it's really high! You know I don't like heights.' Kasper was one of Tommy's friends from school. He always tried to scare Tommy so he would seem like the strong and brave one in their group of friends.

'Why would you want to go on it then?'

'I don't mind heights when I'm with you...' He grinned up at her as though she was his hero. 'I know you will protect me!'

Shay smiled and grabbed him under the arms to help him out of the trolley. She let Tommy connect the chain of the trolley to the one in front and pull the euro back out of the slot.

As they walked back across the car park it started lightly raining again. Shay and Tommy, both in sync, started running. They both began giggling as they turned it into a race. Shay having the longest legs won and got back to the car first. She was slightly damp from the rain as she opened the front passenger door. She hesitated and looked back at Tommy who had only just made it back. She didn't take her usual seat.

'Tommy you can sit up front.'

Tommy looked at her, unsure of the offer. He wondered if it was some kind of a trick. 'But you never let me sit up front!'

'I do...' Shay insisted.

'No you don't! Only when mummy tells you to!'

It was true. Shay did always sit up front unless she was told otherwise.

'Look do you want to sit upfront or what? I'm getting soaked here!'

Tommy was getting just as wet standing by the car and he didn't care if it was a trick or not. He jumped into the front seat.

'Here you go.' Shay passed Sara Tommy's booster seat for him to sit on. As Sara strapped him in and belted up, the heavens opened fully again. It was heavier than when they had first started out. The sound of the rain hitting the windscreen hard echoed through the whole car. Sara started the car engine and put the window wipers on the fastest speed for better vision of the road. She pulled out slowly from the supermarket car park and headed for the main road.

'It's like the car wash mummy!' Tommy was mesmerised by the speed of the car wipers.

'It is, isn't it sweetheart!' Sara didn't do her usual glance over to look at him so she could concentrate on the road in front of her.

As they drove through a small village, a few miles from their destination, a black cat ran out of nowhere across the road. Sara saw it late and slammed the brakes. Thinking she was still going to hit it she automatically swerved to try and avoid it. The wheels locked from the amount of water on the road and the car skidded across to the other side of the road. Frightened, all three of them screamed. The car eventually came to a stop on a grass verge by the side of the road. Flustered and with all the colour gone from her face, Sara checked Tommy, who had screamed the loudest, to make sure he was OK and not too traumatised with the near collision.

'Tommy darling, are you OK?' She looked over at him. He was unhurt, but visibly shaken.

'Uh huh, mummy.'

'Shay?' She turned and looked at Shay in the back.

Shay could taste blood in her mouth. She put her hand to her lip. She had bitten it and cut it when her mum had slammed on the brakes.

'Oh my God, Shay!' She was shocked to see the bright red blood coming from Shay's lip.

Shay patted her lip with her sleeve. She felt that it was nothing, the blood from the small cut was already clotting. 'I'll be fine mum.'

'You're bleeding Shay!' Shay may have been the one bleeding but out of the three of them Sara seemed the most traumatised by the whole thing. 'Right, sorry Tommy, but I think we're going to have to call your friends and tell them we won't be able to make it. We can go another time. For two hours next time.' She felt guilty and was trying to make it up to him. 'It's too dangerous for me to carry on driving when the rain is this hard.'

'What are you going to do?' Shay was worried about her. She had never seen her mum look so pale.

'I'll just slowly pull up over there by the side of the road and wait for the rain to stop.'

Shay looked to see where Sara was talking about. There was a lay by fifty yards ahead of them where they would be safe to park.

It took about half an hour for the rain to stop so they played games and sang songs together to make the time go faster.

It was nearly five o'clock and it hadn't rained heavily for the past five minutes so Sara decided she felt confident enough to start to drive again. She got the kids to put their seatbelts on and started the engine. Before she pulled off she switched her headlights on because the light had begun to fade even more with the evening coming on.

Sara didn't attempt to do a three point turn, she knew there was a roundabout about half a mile further on and it wasn't worth the risk. There weren't many vehicles on the road but the ones that were passing them were appearing out of a fog of rain water and mist. She approached one of the junctions before the roundabout. A white van, travelling at speed, didn't see them on the road and smashed straight into the front passenger side of the car. The force of the impact pushed their car over into the next lane with a crippling sound. The last thing Shay heard was the sound of the car horn going off, ringing in her ears, before she passed out.

'Hello? Hello can you hear me?'

Shay couldn't tell if she was hearing things or if she was asleep and in some horrible wet and cold nightmare. She tried to open her eyes to see who was talking to her but she couldn't see anything. Every time she opened her eyes lights flooded her pupils and blinded her. She turned her head from side to side and mumbled, 'Turn the lights off…' She was aware of other people talking but she couldn't make out what they were saying. All she knew was her head was throbbing and it hurt.

'I'm one of the paramedics. Can you move your legs?' The paramedic opened the car door which was pretty smashed and deformed from the impact. He wanted to assess what state Shay was in but, before he could do anything, she got out of the half crushed car as if nothing had happened. Her brain and the adrenaline rushing around her body was telling her that everything was fine and normal. Shay attempted to walk, but she swayed heavily.

'Whoa, hey steady, there's no rush.' The paramedic grabbed her arm and guided her to the back of his ambulance.

'Take a seat there and I'll take a look over you, OK?'

Shay's blood rushed back to her head as she sat down on the edge of the ambulance. Her eyes started to focus a bit and clear. It was dark and only the lights from the emergency vehicles lit up the road.

As the paramedic checked her arms and legs for any obvious injuries Shay looked across the road, over to her left, where another stationary ambulance was parked. She saw her mum on a trolley, being prepared to be lifted into the back of it. It took Shay a few seconds with her sore head to actually register what had happened and what was going on. The last images she had before the crash played out in her head, she saw the van hit the car from the side, all the images in her head ran silent.

The paramedic touched Shay on one of her bruised ribs, which brought her back into the present moment.

'Mum!' She shouted across to Sara, 'Mum!' Sara couldn't hear her because her calls were muffled out by a helicopter landing nearby. Everything was in slow motion for Shay, her brain couldn't catch up as she witnessed her mum being lifted into the ambulance and the door closing behind her.

A police officer and one of the other paramedics on the scene walked over to the side of the ambulance Shay was in, trying to get some cover from the drizzling rain.

They shouted to one another over the noise and chaos. They had no idea Shay was sitting at the back of the ambulance and could hear every word.

'The mother's gone off in the first ambulance. She's pretty beaten up but will recover. The young lady who was in the back has taken a few cuts and bruises and has quite a deep laceration to the torso that may need stitches, potential concussion, but nothing too serious. I would say by the looks of it she was saved by sitting in the back.'

'What about the young boy?' The police officer knew it wasn't good by the look on the paramedic's face.

'He took the brunt of the collision. It doesn't look good. The team are working on him and he's going by air ambulance to hospital.'

Shay looked over to where their car was. The front passenger side was almost completely crushed into the driver's side. Dread overtook her body and she screamed. 'NO... NO!' She pushed the paramedic treating her away and started running towards the helicopter. All she could see were the blur of lights from it shining through the rain.

The paramedic treating her shouted for her to come back, but Shay just kept on running as fast as she could. It wasn't very fast because her adrenaline was wearing off and heaviness in her body was beginning to settle in.

'Shit! She heard everything!' The police officer heard the shout and realised what was going on. Feeling responsible, he chased after her and grabbed her from behind by her arm, the same way the man at the night club had.

'*TOMMY!*' She screamed from the top of her lungs as she watched the helicopter take off.

'*It's better this way. He'll get to the hospital sooner.*' He could feel the resistance in Shay's body as she was trying to wriggle out of his hold, it just made him hold tighter. '*Come on, take it easy, look you're bleeding!*'

Shay knew he was talking about the cut on her side, she hadn't realised how deep it was. '*Let go of me! Let go of me!*' Her voice broke with emotion. '*You don't understand...*' Her body gave way from exhaustion.

The police officer did his best to hold her up off of the wet floor. Shay could do nothing but cry with despair. She knew it was hopeless to reach Tommy now.

'*He doesn't like heights... I have to be there with him...*'

'I wish... I wish still to this day, I had had the strength to swing around and hit the policeman holding onto me...' Shay turned and faced the wall. She clenched her right hand in a fist and pushed it against the wall, shoulder level. She wanted to punch it. 'If I had done what I did to that guy in the club, hit him, maybe then he would have let go of me and I could have been with Tommy.' She let tears silently fall down her face. She didn't want Francesca to know she was crying. 'I should've been with him in the helicopter. I should've been with him to make sure he wasn't alone or scared when he... when he died.' She took her fist from the wall and pulled it back. With some force she punched the wall.

Francesca sprang from her seat and instinctively rushed over to Shay. She caught Shay's arm before she could punch the wall again.

'Shay, I won't let you hurt yourself.' She slid her hand down her arm and held onto her wrist gently. She brought Shay's hand up so she could check it for any bruising or broken skin. Her knuckles were a bit swollen from the hit but they weren't cut.

Shay let Francesca hold her wrist as she leant her forehead against the wall. It was quiet between the two of them. Shay considered hitting her head against the wall to stop the pain she was feeling inside but out of the corner of her eye she could see Francesca's concerned face looking at her. Shay turned her face away from her.

Francesca knew it was a move to try and block her, push her away. She purposefully, gently, held on to her swollen hand, letting her know she was still there.

Shay started speaking again. 'I was so angry... he wouldn't let me go, he wouldn't listen to me, I never got to tell Tommy he would be OK...' Her voice broke again and she broke down, tormented by the thought of how scared Tommy must have been.

Francesca could feel the emotions radiating from her and she found herself becoming tearful. She impulsively pulled Shay into her body and held on to her tightly. Shay's body was stiff at first as she clung onto Francesca's shirt but she finally let her body give in to the embrace and security of Francesca's arms.

Francesca felt her own tears silently fall down her face as she stood there holding Shay.

About ten minutes after Shay left, Francesca sat at her desk trying to stop thinking about her and their session together. She picked up her mobile and flicked through looking for Laura's number. She stopped at Garth's name and stared at it. She'd forgotten Laura had given it to her that day at the cafe. Her finger hovered, hesitantly, over the call button, deciding whether to press it. She pressed it and his phone rang about five times before he picked it up.

'Hello, Garth Chambers, how can I help you?'

As soon as Francesca heard his voice she regretted calling him. She was a little embarrassed thinking how desperate he was probably going to think she was, phoning him up.

'Hi Garth, I got your number from Laura, Mike's wife?' Garth didn't say anything. 'It's Francesca....' She winced at her own awkwardness and wondered if it was too late to hang up, but then it clicked with him who it was.

'Francesca?' He hadn't expected her to call. He had hoped, but he hadn't held his breath. 'I can't believe you've called me but I'm glad you did! Ever since Mike's birthday party I've been meaning to ask you out...'

'Well I guess I got there first! I'm free tonight, if you want to do something?' She knew it was soon but she wanted to strike while the iron was hot, otherwise she knew she would never do it.

'Tonight? Yeah great! I could take you out for dinner. Do you like Indian?'

'Sure, I love Indian. I'll meet you in town for seven thirty?'

'I look forward to it.'

Garth opened the door to the restaurant for Francesca. She thanked him and they walked over to their table. He pulled the chair out for her, making the point of being a gentleman. Francesca wasn't sure how she felt about it. She didn't know whether it was too much and over the top, or if it was just that she wasn't used to it, having been married to David for so long. They ordered their drinks and Garth ordered some samosas to share, for starters. He started their first proper conversation off once they had both settled.

'So tell me, when did you last go on a date?'

'I haven't been on a date since I met my husband, or ex-husband I should say! So that would be a total of about twenty one years!' She smiled at him and took a sip of her wine. 'How about you, do you date much?'

'If I'm honest, yes. I've seen a few people but nothing's ever come of it, you know? No butterflies in the tummy feelings but maybe that's about to change!' The comment was a bit forced and awkward, Francesca laughed it off, wondering if he said it because he was just as nervous as she was.

'So tell me a bit about yourself.' Garth leant towards her across the table. 'I never really got to speak to you much at the party. I just admired you from a distance! Mike said you're a psychologist. I guess that must be a bit intense and rough at times?'

'It has its challenges, ups and downs.'

'A guy I used to work with had a partner who was a counsellor. He used to get jealous of how involved she would become with her clients.' Francesca wondered where his story was going. 'Eventually she had to stop because she couldn't keep her home life and work life separate.' He picked up a samosa and took a bite of it.

Francesca could tell by his face it was still a bit too hot so she decided not to take a bite of her one until it had cooled down more. She took another sip of her wine instead.

'You need good boundaries and balance between the two, otherwise it can take over.'

'Do you have that?'

She hesitated before she answered. His question had caught her a bit off guard. She was used to only talking to Laura about work.

'Most of the time I would say so, yes. But I can't say the odd client doesn't affect me in some shape or form. It's an intense, intimate environment where strong emotions and feelings come up. It's a challenge to not be affected by some of the stories I hear.'

'Do you touch your clients?' Garth heard how his question might have sounded. 'That doesn't sound quite right! What I mean is, if they're upset or something, would you touch them to comfort them? Or do you try and stay detached?'

Francesca thought about it. 'I mean... it depends. I think touch can be an important part of connecting, reassuring someone and even help in part with the healing process, but it can also blur the lines with some people if you don't stay objective. Some people really don't want to be touched when they're processing strong emotions or reactions.'

Garth smirked at her. 'I would want you to touch me if you were my therapist. I like a cuddle too much!'

Francesca didn't know what to say and felt awkward again. She bit into her samosa not caring if it was still too hot.

They sat talking and eating in the restaurant for an hour and a half. Francesca didn't know what it was about him and wondered if it was more herself, but she just didn't find him as attractive as she thought she would. When she'd been at Mike's party all the women were going on about how handsome he was, he was very good looking, she couldn't deny that, but something was missing.

Garth paid for the meal and drove her back home. Francesca was too drunk to worry about him knowing where she lived and the kids seeing anything. She hadn't got drunk on purpose. She just wanted to try and relax a bit, but now, at the end of the night, she was probably a little too relaxed.

Garth pulled up by her house and they sat in the car, in the dark. Francesca waited for him to say something and looked across at him. He took it as an invitation to kiss her. She didn't move away from him but let him kiss her. It was graceless and new, neither of them knew each other's technique or movement.

After a while Garth went for a little more and tried to touch her breast.

'Garth, sorry...' She stopped him. 'I'm tired and my kids are asleep upstairs. I don't think it would be appropriate...'

'Oh right, OK.' He backed off completely and leaned back in the driver's seat. 'Well I really enjoyed tonight. I'd love to take you out again if you'd let me?'

Francesca wasn't sure. The only thing she knew she was sure on right now was that she wanted him to leave so she could climb into her bed and sleep. 'Yeah, why not...' She decided to take the quicker, easier option.

'Great! I'll text you to organise something.'

Francesca smiled and got out of his car. She entered her home and went upstairs straight to bed. Lying down on her bed, on top of the covers, she got her phone out to text Laura.

JUST BEEN ON A DATE WITH GARTH xx

Laura was still up and replied back in seconds.

AND... TELL ME ALL!? Xx

Francesca didn't know if it was sharing the news with Laura like an excited school girl would after a date, or because she'd had the time to look back on the date and realise it wasn't that bad as first dates went. She sent another message feeling a bit more optimistic about him.

HE KISSED ME. I'M SEEING HIM AGAIN x

Laura took longer to text back, Francesca assumed she must be brushing her teeth. Her phone beeped.

LOOK AT YOU 'MISS I DON'T WANT TO DATE!' xxxx

CHAPTER NINETEEN

I t was the afternoon and Julie was sitting at her desk when Roger walked in through the reception door. She was confused to see him as she knew he didn't have an appointment today.

'Hello Mr Rowland. Can I help you?'

Roger was flustered and un-grounded as if he had an emergency. 'Hi, yes, Julie is it? Please call me Roger. I need to see Dr Francesca urgently!'

'I'm sorry Roger but she's in with a client at the moment.' She could see how worried he looked and didn't want to leave him so perplexed. 'Is there anything I can do to help?'

Roger considered it. 'Maybe you could help.' He got out a handful of tourist attraction leaflets. 'If one wanted to take a lady out for a nice getting to know you date, where would you choose?' He handed the leaflets over to Julie who was relieved to know it wasn't as serious as she was presuming by his behaviour. She was a little taken aback by the question but took the pile from him and shuffled through them. She pulled out the local zoo leaflet. It was her favourite place to go on her day off.

'Here... It has a lovely little café. It's only forty minutes drive away and perfect for having a conversation about all the animals! I mean, who doesn't love animals? I l certainly do!'

Roger smiled at her. 'I love animals as well!'

She handed the leaflets back to him and he smiled at her again. He'd never really met someone who had something in common with him. He never managed to get to know them well enough to get to that point.

'The Zoo it is then!'

Julie looked at him. She could see the twinkle in his eye. They were interrupted by Francis arriving for her appointment with Francesca so Roger left, leaving them to it and wanting to prepare for his date.

Francis entered Francesca's office. She sat down on the sofa and noticed a dust mark on her right trouser leg, above her knee. She licked her finger, ashamed, and tried to rub it off.

'I'm so sorry, I didn't realise I had dirty trousers on! I'm having building work done...' she rubbed the fading mark again, 'the dust and muck seems to get everywhere!'

'Don't worry we've all been guilty of wearing dirty clothes out! My son's trick is usually leaving the house with tooth paste down his top!'

Francis laughed knowing she'd done that a couple of times herself. 'You have a son?' She didn't know that about her.

Francesca nodded as conformation. 'And a daughter.'

'How old are they?' Francis didn't want to seem as if she was prying, but she was genuinely interested.

'Twenty and sixteen. My daughter's nearly seventeen. Not my baby anymore, so I can't tell her what to do. That's what she likes to remind me all the time anyway!'

Francis empathised with her. 'That's how my daughter Hilary was at that age! She was convinced she knew best and could argue black is white...' She paused and thought about her daughter who she loved to bits. 'Actually she's still a bit like that now!'

'Do you see your daughter often?'

Francis's body stiffened. 'Not as often as I would like. We fell out after her father died. I don't think our relationship will ever be what it was.' She felt sad saying it. Never in her wildest dreams did she imagine their relationship to be as estranged as it was.

'What happened between the two of you?'

Francis lowered her voice. 'I wasn't there in time...'

NINE MONTHS EARLIER.

Francis took Jack up to the chemotherapy ward. He wasn't pleased and kicked up a fuss when the nurse told him the doctor had requested a new chemotherapy port in his chest. It took about an hour for Francis and the nurse to convince him it was necessary, that the doctor wouldn't have asked for it otherwise. Francis didn't want to leave him so unsettled so she stayed with him for longer than she'd planned or expected.

She checked her watch as she stepped into the hospital lift knowing she would be lucky to catch the last five minutes of the group meeting. The lift reached her floor and she walked the usual corridor towards the meeting room. When she reached the door it was quiet. She peered through the window and saw the room was empty. Disappointed, she went to leave.

'Francis?'

She turned to see Chris walking towards her from the other end of the corridor. He was pleased to see her.

'I thought that was you! How are you?' He approached and stood in front of her.

She could smell his aftershave mixed in with his natural scent and, for some reason, it felt comforting to her. 'I missed you...'

Chris smiled at her answer. Francis blushed realizing how what she said might have sounded to him. She tried to correct it. 'I mean I missed the group!'

Chris found her flustering endearing, he could see her bashfulness and wanted to make her feel a little more at ease. 'Don't worry I knew what you meant!' It went quiet between them so Chris carried on. 'We eh, finished a little early this week. Did you hear?'

Francis frowned at him. She didn't know what it was she was supposed to have heard.

'Unfortunately Hannah's daughter died this morning. She got the call to go back up to the ward.'

Francis couldn't believe what he'd just said. 'Oh my god! But she was only twelve!' She didn't know what to say as she tried to come to terms with the news. 'How's Hannah? Is she OK?'

'I don't know yet, I hope so.'

Francis hadn't seen Hannah for a couple of weeks and she had no idea her daughter had gone downhill so quickly.

Chris, seeing how upset she was, stepped forward, closer to her, and offered a hug. She automatically leaned into his body for the embrace. He put both his arms around her and she could feel the strength of his chest as her head pressed up against it.

After what seemed like only a few seconds he loosened his arms and pulled away from her. It felt abrupt to Francis when he let her go and she wondered if she had done something wrong. She looked up at him for reassurance but Chris said nothing. It became awkward and silent between them when they both realized they were alone in the corridor.

'How's Jack doing? Is he in for chemo today?' He wanted to break the tension that was building up between them. Their hug had felt more than just an embrace between friends. He asked about Jack so it was clear to Francis he wasn't trying anything with her and that he knew she was married.

Francis became more emotional at the mention of Jack's name. In the last few days she'd noticed how quickly he was going downhill. She'd known it would happen, but she hadn't expected it to happen so fast and so drastically. He wasn't able to eat properly and had lost three stone in weight, becoming weaker with every day.

Francis tried to answer. 'He's ah...' she clenched her fist to try and help her hold herself together, the last thing she wanted was to cry in front of him. 'He's...' Her eyes started to sting. 'He was given six months. It's been fifteen into his treatment, so I guess you could say he's doing well...' She felt relief to have got through saying it but as soon as she'd finished a lump of emotion began to build at the back of her throat. 'Sorry I have to go...' She turned, but only got a few yards away from him before she burst into tears.

Chris rushed over to her and put his arms around her. He had never seen her so upset before. 'Francis! Let me help you.'

They walked down to the hospital canteen together. Francis sat at one of the tables feeling a bit calmer but still emotional. Chris went over to the drinks machine and bought her a hot, sugary cup of tea.

'Here.' Their fingers slightly brushed as he handed the plastic cup full of weak tea over to her. He sat in the seat opposite her. 'It's probably not the best tasting tea you'll ever have but it's got sugar in it for the shock.'

'Thank you.' She put her hand to her temple feeling a bit bashful at how upset she had been. 'This is so embarrassing, I'm so sorry. You don't have to stay. Please go if you need to.'

'Are you trying to get rid of me?'

'No it's just...' She didn't know what to say.

Chris reached out and touched her hand from across the table. 'That was a joke Francis!'

She felt a small sense of relief but she was aware at how nervous she felt. They both looked down at Chris's hand resting on Francis's. He pulled it away. Francis nervously sipped her tea trying to ignore how close they were sitting opposite one another.

'Do you want to talk about it?' He wanted to help her but didn't want her to feel he was being pushy.

'I just... I just feel exhausted. I've turned into a full time carer. My days are filled with sickness, changing beds, emptying bedpans, among a million other things.' It all came out at once. She'd kept it in for so long that it was a release to share it with someone. 'I don't get a minute to myself without some doctor or district nurse are after me, wanting to know about Jack's medication, bowel movements, water intake...' She felt guilty but she needed to let it out. 'I've lost my husband and I'm looking after a man I barely even know anymore. Now... now I feel like I'm losing myself.' Francis looked down and stirred her tea, as Chris continued to listen. 'The most awful thing is I'm beginning to resent him. I think I could have done six months. I could have managed. But he keeps on going...' She began to cry. 'I know I should be grateful... I get more time with him, but he's so sick and he's so grumpy and aggressive on the medication. He just doesn't seem to want to let go...' She wiped her tears with her sleeve and gave a huge sigh.

Chris looked at her and, without thinking, grabbed her hand again, he squeezed it tightly. 'I understand Francis, I do. I would keep on going if I had a woman like you looking after me...' A bit surprised by his comment, Francis looked up at him. 'Sorry, I shouldn't have said that. That was totally wrong of me.' He let go of her hand again.

'No, don't worry about it.' She could see he was upset with himself but she honestly hadn't minded him holding her hand. If anything she minded more that he had let go of it. She'd felt comforted by his strong, warm grip.

They were silent again, Chris put his hands under the table and clenched his fists so he wouldn't be tempted to hold her hand again. He tried to think about how he could help and support her as he watched her drink a few more sips of her tea.

'Maybe you just need a little extra help so you can take some time off for yourself. Why don't we arrange to meet up? I could take you around some of the local hospices? Some centres can only take patients for half a day, or a few hours, but it would be something.'

Francesca had listened intently to Francis talk.

'How did you feel about that?'

Francis thought about Chris holding her hand. She could still feel his heat. 'I thought it was a good idea. I liked it.' She paused. 'When he held my hand it felt like the world had stopped. For that one moment I felt as though it was possible for my pain to go away. His touch was kind and reassuring. I felt listened to, as if someone was looking after me, making sure I was OK. It felt nice.'

Francesca realised how Francis was when she talked about Chris. It was as though her whole demeanour softened.

'What happen after that?' She asked.

'We sorted out a hospice to take Jack twice a week for a few hours each time. Chris and I, we gradually met more often in and outside the group. Each time our attraction grew stronger. It was hard to ignore, alongside my anxiety!'

Francesca reflected on what Francis had said for a moment.

'Do you think his friendship brought up your need for companionship?'

Francis held back her answer for a while. 'My need... and my want.'

Francesca stayed silent for a bit. She wanted Francis to sit with and feel what she had just stated.

'What was the tipping point between the two of you? Did you admit your attraction to him or...'

Francis exhaled before she answered. 'We met up for a coffee...'

TEN MONTHS EARLIER.

Chris and Francis were in Yani's restaurant at one of the booth tables. It was about the eighth time they had met up outside the cancer support group and each time they'd met she had naively hoped the attraction between them would die down, that it was only there because they didn't properly know one another yet, but it only became more intense and Francis found herself looking forward to their meet ups, so she could get to know more about him and his life.

In the restaurant, for some reason, the atmosphere seemed a bit cold and brittle between them.

'So how have you been?' Chris was more nervous than usual. He could hear it in his own voice. 'How's Jack doing at the hospice?'

'He's OK. I think he's enjoying it. He doesn't seem to complain anyway!' She noticed how tense he seemed and how unusual it was for him to be that way. 'Thank you... for helping me to find a place. It means a lot to me.' She glanced up at him sensing he had something he wanted to say.

Chris caught her glance and couldn't hold back any longer. 'Francis listen, I need to talk to you about something. We've been getting to know each other and I...'

'Chris, don't...' She knew by his face and his tone what he was about to say. She didn't want to let him say it because then she would have to acknowledge her own feelings and thoughts about him.

'I have to.' He got up and sat next to her on her side of the booth. He shuffled closer, right up next to her. 'I've never felt this way about someone, not since my wife... I know you're married still but I can't stop thinking about you.' He looked into her eyes and slowly leaned in towards her.   Francis didn't make any motion to move away from him, he took it as her approval and kissed her gently on the lips. He could feel her lips respond to his, it confirmed for him that he had made the right decision.

Francis enjoyed the warmth of his mouth on hers until he slowly pulled away. He looked at her again, not caring if anyone else in the restaurant could see or hear them.

'Will you come home with me?'

Every bit of Francis wanted to. She wanted to be wrapped up in his arms, in his bed, but she was supposed to be back at the hospital within the next hour or so.

'I can't...' She lifted her hand and caressed his face. 'I have to get back...'

Chris kissed her again, out of desperation. He didn't want to hear her say she was going to have to leave.

As they kissed passionately once more Francis couldn't bring herself to pull away from him. She gave in and let him take her back to his house.

Chris held on to her hand and guided her up the stairs. They entered his large, airy bedroom and stood facing each other at the end of his bed. He tenderly kissed her and this time it didn't feel so new or raw to either of them, it seemed natural, like, from the couple of kisses they'd shared at the restaurant they already knew each other's mouths.

Chris began to take off her cotton top. Francis became nervous and self-conscious at the thought of him seeing and touching her body, naked. She stiffened under his touch and he felt her body go from relaxed to frigid.

He stopped, worried he was doing something wrong. 'What's the matter?'

She thought about lying to him, saying nothing, leaving him to feel that he was doing something wrong, but she wanted to tell him the truth and be honest with him.

'I don't want you to see my body.' She felt ashamed admitting it to him.

'Why not?' He took in Francis's body with his eyes. He couldn't understand why she would feel that way. 'From where I'm standing you have a beautiful body.'

Francis dropped her head and took a step away from him. 'That's what you think with clothes on... I have wrinkles and stretch marks and...'

He interrupted her, 'Do you think I don't? That I'm not terrified right now to show you my body? Reveal my insecurities?'

'Really?' She found it hard to believe him. The way he looked and the way he conducted himself, it had never even have occurred to her that he would have his own insecurities.

'Yes! Really!' He took her hand and held it. 'Full disclosure, before I take my top off, one of my hang ups is... I have a third nipple.'

Francis laughed thinking he was joking to try and lighten up her mood.

'Honestly really, I do.' He took his top off.

Francis stopped laughing when she saw a small extra nipple on his chest. She couldn't believe she'd laughed at him. 'Sorry I thought you were...'

He smiled and stepped towards her so their bodies were closer again. 'Don't worry I was half joking! Your turn!'

Francis started to lift up her top but then she stopped and looked at Chris.

'I want you to do it!'

Chris grinned as he slowly peeled her top off and threw it on the floor. He took his time to properly look at her body.

'You're beautiful Francis. I wish you could see that.'

By the look on his face Francis knew he meant it. She knew he wasn't just saying it to please her. A tear fell down her cheek. She'd never felt so vulnerable.

'I haven't... I haven't had sex in a while.'

Chris gently pulled her in to rest against his body. She could smell the scent of his skin. 'You tell me what you want and don't want me to do. I don't want to rush you.'

Francis felt a flicker of excitement in her stomach. She kissed him and led him around the side of the bed.

Francis left Chris asleep, naked in his bed, after they had made love twice. She'd never felt so special, so safe, and secure with someone.

It took her twenty minutes to drive to the hospital, she rushed up towards the ward, half an hour late. The nurse looking after Jack was just finishing her break and spotted Francis pacing down the corridor. She ran after her and pulled her to the side just before Francis was about to enter the ward.

'Mrs Jones, where have you been? We sent a search party out for you around the hospital.'

Francis could see the concern on the nurse's face, even though she was trying to hide it. She didn't beat about the bush with her.

'I'm afraid your husband has taken a drastic turn for the worse.'

Francis felt the euphoria going around her body from being with Chris suddenly turn to darkness. She knew today was too good to be true.

'Where is he?'

'We've moved him to a side room.' The nurse lowered her voice, 'Mrs Jones, I must warn you he's unresponsive now. The doctors have been in to see him and they think this is it. He hasn't got long now.'

Francis walked on to the ward and was shown into a side room. She expected to see Jack hooked up to all kinds of machines, but he only had a heart monitor and a morphine drive attached to him.

Hilary was next to him holding his hand. She looked over at her mother, full of a mixture of emotions, anger being the strongest one. The nurse left so they could have some private time together as a family. Francis could see how enraged Hilary was.

'Where the hell have you been? You were supposed to be here!' Hilary had felt scared and alone sitting there without her mother.

'I'm sorry. I lost track of time...' She didn't know what to say. She couldn't explain why. She just hoped Hilary would forgive her. 'How is he?' She sat down on the other side of Jack's bed and took his cold clammy hand.

'He's dying. The doctors say they can't do any more other than help him with the pain. It's just a matter of waiting.'

Francis stroked his hand, riddled with guilt.

'Oh Jack! I'm so sorry. I'm so, so sorry. I'm here now.' She began to cry.

Jack opened his eyes, as if he'd heard her voice, he took one last look at her, smiled and closed his eyes again. The heart monitor beeped as his heart rate dropped then flat lined as he passed away peacefully.

Francis couldn't control her crying. Francesca pulled a couple of tissues out of her tissue box and bent over to pass them to her. She touched Francis's knee with her hand to try and reassure her and comfort her a little.

'I'm sorry Francis.'

'Don't be sorry for me.' Francis blew her nose. 'Be sorry for Jack. He thought he had a loyal, loving wife.' She dropped her shoulders. 'How could I, in his last moments be with...' She couldn't finish, her grief was too much.

Francesca broke contact with her knee and leant back in her chair to try and bring some objectivity to the situation.

'By what you've told me, the Jack you married had disappeared a while ago. Maybe the woman he married had as well?' Francesca paused. 'You were doing what you needed to do, to stay sane. There's no shame or guilt in that.'

'I had no right. I made a promise to him. I was selfish, too self-involved in my own pain, when there was Jack struggling, doing his best to stay alive.' She was telling herself off.

Francesca thought about it. She wouldn't normally re-confirm affairs or sleeping with someone other than a partner, but, for her, the situation and the circumstances were different with Francis.

'You were just trying to cope, to feel supported, wanted even. That's a natural need and desire... for all of us.'

Francis couldn't take her words of support or validation. She felt she had to finish her story.

'A few months after Jacks funeral Chris got in contact again. He wouldn't stop calling and insisted on seeing me face to face. Then he would stop, he said...'

7 MONTHS EARLIER.

Francis saw Chris sitting outside the café where they had agreed to meet. It felt strange for her seeing him again. He looked good, better, with the tan he had got from the recent sunny weather. She strolled over to him aware she needed to be strong, to resist him and whatever it was he wanted to say to her.

Chris stood up as soon as he saw her approach.

'Please, sit down...' It was awkward, he felt flustered as he waited for Francis to take her seat. He sat back down. 'How are you?' His voice shook with nerves. He had waited for what seemed like forever to see her again and to get the chance to speak with her.

Francis got straight to the point. 'I'm not staying for long. I've just come to ask you to stop calling me, to leave me alone. Whatever we had Chris, it's over! It's done!'

'Francis, please. I know you're hurting but you don't have to push me away and be alone right now...'

She jumped in. 'How do you know how I feel?'

He lowered his voice to reply. 'I lost my wife too, remember?'

Francis knew their meeting up wasn't going to work and decided the best thing to do was to get up and leave.

'Yes, but you weren't having an affair with someone else when she was dying though, were you?'

Chris was desperate. He knew he wasn't going to get through her wall of protection with words. He stood up and kissed her, hoping she would remember what they had between them.

Francis didn't immediately pull away from his kiss, she tried to saviour the feeling of it for one last time.

'I can't.' She pulled herself away and left.

Chris didn't stop her. He stood by himself outside the café as she walked away down the street.

Francesca put her note pad down and shuffled forward in her chair. She'd tensed up so much listening to Francis that her back hurt and she needed to relax a bit. She waited for Francis to make eye contact with her.

'I can see the guilt and hurt you're feeling and holding on to.' She paused as Francis began to sob harder. 'But do you think Jack would want you to carry on feeling this way?'

'No. He would forgive me in a heartbeat. That was the kind of man he was. Before the... Sometimes I think it's me who can't forgive myself.' She took a couple of breathes. 'Why did I do it? I know if Hilary ever found out... She was angry at me for not being there at the hospital. Imagine how she'd feel if she knew where I actually was. Who I was with and what I was doing.'

CHAPTER TWENTY

I t was a slow, steady night at Yani's restaurant. Faith was helping Shay sort out drinks for her table of six. A group of girls were out celebrating their friend passing her driving test after four years and her tenth attempt. Shay was still exhausted after her session with Francesca and was hoping nobody else would come in to eat so she could get home early and have a bath and an early night.

'So how did your last session go? You haven't mentioned anything about it. Did you intimidate the doctor with your sexual prowess?' Faith hadn't really had a chance to speak to Shay since their shift had started, but she had noticed through the evening that Shay didn't seem herself, she seemed down.

Shay only just about managed to answer as she poured herself a glass of water behind the bar.

'Something like that.'

'Come on then, spill the beans! I'm intrigued!' She tried to keep it upbeat but Shay wasn't responding.

'I can't. I need to take table five's order.' She took a sip of her water and strolled off leaving Faith to finish her table's drinks order.

She served her table of two and walked into the kitchen. She took off her apron that was wrapped around her waist and threw it on top of the side counter.

'I'm off on break. Frank's covering my tables.'

She didn't wait for an answer from anyone but left the hot kitchen straight away, by the back door. She was relieved a little and felt she could breathe properly when the fresh air hit her face.

It was Laura's and Francesca's dinner date night and they always dressed up and made a night of it when it came around. They were both smartly suited and booted as they strolled in the town centre towards the restaurant Laura had booked.

'So come on out with it! How did the date go with Garth?'

It was the last thing on Francesca's mind after the past few days that she'd had at work, and if she was honest, it was the last thing she wanted to talk about, even if it was with Laura.

'Like I said in the text I sent you, it was fine and we'll be meeting up again sometime.'

'That's all you're going to say?' Laura was disappointed with the lack of details from her.

'It was only the first date Laura. I promise you more details after the next one. How about that?'

Their conversation finished as they reached the entrance to Yani's. Laura opened the door and let Francesca walk through first.

They both waited to be seated at their table. 'I've never been here before. It looks nice.' Francesca took her jacket off and folded it over her arm as Frank approached them.

'Hello ladies! Table for two is it? Please come this way.' He took them to one of the booth tables in the corner so it was more private. The table was lit nicely with a warm purple candle and fairy lanterns weaved above their heads from the roof. Frank waited by the table while Laura and Francesca looked at the drinks menu as he had no other tables to serve and was in no rush.

'What can I get you ladies to drink?'

'Your biggest bottle of red wine with two glasses please!' Laura needed no time to decide for both of them.

Frank didn't need to write the simple order down so he just left them to it and headed straight towards the bar.

'God, I've been gasping for a drink all day.' Hearing herself Laura paused. 'Do you think that makes me an alcoholic?' Francesca smiled at her remark which pleased Laura. 'Ah that's a start, that's the first joke you've smiled at tonight!'

'Sorry, I don't mean to be miserable, it's just that I had a pretty intense session with a client the other day...' She tried to shake work off. 'It's fine though, I'm fine.'

'Are you sure? Do you want to talk about it?'

'No, it's fine...'

Before Laura could prod a bit more Frank came back over with the wine. He put the bottle down on the table along with two large glasses.

'This will help with my day!' Francesca poured herself a glass and took a couple of swigs.

After a couple more swigs and Laura staring at her, Francesca started talking about what was bothering her.

'We had this pretty big break through. That's what made it so intense, I think.' She could feel anxiety in her belly when she started thinking about Shay's session. She tried to ignore it and put the feeling down to hunger.

'Well that's great! When that happens that's when you can really get to work together.'

She knew what Laura was saying was right, but she felt something just didn't sit right.

'Yes. It's just... It doesn't matter.' She tried to shake away the image of Shay in her head and move on but Laura wasn't going to let her get off that easily.

'No, we're not doing that one! Come on, out with it!'

'I don't know what it is...' She stared into her wine and played with the stem of the glass, twisting it between her fingers. 'Have you ever had a client that seemed to be able to really push your buttons, you know emotionally, mentally...'

Laura could see her discomfort and wondered why.

'Physically?' It was a wild guess.

'Laura, I'm talking about a client!' Francesca was surprised Laura would even suggest it.

'Cesca, you're telling me, after all these years, you've never fantasized or been attracted to a client? Transference is perfectly normal and sometimes it's even expected in a therapy space.'

Francesca couldn't hide her defensiveness, 'No I haven't...' She went quiet and took another sip of her wine. She looked at Laura. 'Why have you?'

Laura's voice went high and excitable. 'Hell yes! I have! I'm stuck in an office talking about sex all day! It starts to get a lady going!' She calmed herself down a bit and continued. 'Even though, of course, I'm happy with my Mike and our time between the sheets, it livens things up a bit fantasizing about other people.'

'Really?'

'Yes, and if I was like you, not in a committed relationship, I would take every opportunity to go wild with my imagination. Why not? It's never going to happen in real life so that's the whole point and fun about a fantasy!'

'It's different with sex therapy.'

Laura didn't agree. 'Psshh! No it's not. It's just as intimate when you're talking with someone about their life and emotions. In fact it's probably more intimate.' She wondered who it was that was affecting Francesca so much. 'Your client isn't a douche bag is he? No offense but I know your type!'

'No, she's not a loser.' The words just came out automatically.

'SHE! Now we're talking!' Laura's interest in the conversation sky-rocketed.

'Hush, keep your voice down Laura!' She was paranoid about the other customers hearing their conversation.

'What? It's nothing to be ashamed of. I've always told you, you should dip your toe in the lady pond! Tell me more!'

Francesca nervously started to play with her napkin.

'Laura can we be serious for a second?' She attempted to convince herself that it was strictly platonic between her and Shay. 'I'm not attracted to her and I'm not fantasizing about her! I find her cheeky and...' She realised it sounded like she was trying to justify their professional relationship. 'It's not a sexual thing. I'm just trying to understand how she knows how to push my buttons so easily, so well.' Francesca became more serious as she tried to figure it out. 'She watches and studies me. I can feel it and it puts me on edge. She sees me somehow... her intensity sometimes it...' She didn't finish her sentence but sat with her thoughts.

Laura waited for Francesca to come out of her head and look at her. 'Are you sure you're not attracted to her?' She asked.

'I'm sure.' Francesca felt more sure when she answered. She reached over the table for the bottle of wine to top up her glass but, instead, knocked it over. The bottle chinked as it hit the table and the red wine ran out over the cream table cloth.

'Oh shit!' Francesca flipped the bottle back up as fast as she could but about a third of it had already spilt.

Frank heard the noise from across the restaurant and rushed over to their table. He saw the red fluid on the cloth and grabbed a cloth to try and soak it up.

'I'm so sorry!' Francesca was genuinely embarrassed by her clumsiness.

'No, don't worry. It happens all the time. I'll send someone over to re-set the table for you.' Frank left the cloth on the table to soak up the excess liquid and left.

Francesca noticed Laura's dress from across the table. 'Shit Laura! It's gone on your dress!'

Laura looked down to see a small patch of pink on the cream dress she had bought only last week, but she stayed calm as though she wasn't too bothered about it.

'Don't worry, I'll ask for some white wine at the bar and try to wash it out in the bathroom.'

'Does that actually work?'

'We will soon find out!' She left Francesca alone at the table, which looked a complete mess and headed over to the bar.

Francesca, hopelessly, tried to soak up some more of the wine with her napkin, to limit the damage, but there was too much liquid on the thin table cloth. She stopped trying when another member of staff came up from behind her and started soaking it up with a new bigger cloth.

'It's OK madam, I can do that!'

'I'm so sorry. I'm so clumsy sometimes! I didn't mean to...' Francesca stopped talking and looked up to apologise.

'Shay!' She was too surprised to hide the shock in her voice, she couldn't believe she hadn't recognised Shay's voice.

'I didn't... you work... I didn't know you worked here!' She was slightly lost for words.

Shay calmly carried on cleaning the table and soaking up the wine with extra cloth and a smile broke from the corner of her mouth.

'That's because you only know the things I tell you!' She glanced at Francesca to wink at her but they both caught each other's eye and stared at one another.

Shay cleared her throat to break the silence. 'Where's your date?'

Francesca attempted to compose herself a bit more before she answered. She picked up her handbag and pretended to search for something in it so she didn't have to look at Shay or risk catching her gaze again.

'I'm not on a date. I'm just here with a friend...' She put her bag back down feeling, all of a sudden, it was a stupid idea. 'She's gone to try and wash the red wine out of her top.'

'She might be there for a while then! Wine isn't the easiest to wash out, especially red! I'll take that...'

Francesca saw Shay looking at the sodden cloths on the table. They both went to pick them up and their hands touched. Francesca pulled her hand away and broke contact.

Shay continued to take everything off the table and clear it. She scrunched up the wet table cloth and peered at Francesca.

'I'll go get you a clean one.'

When she returned the atmosphere between them was more tense and awkward as she re-laid the new, clean, table cloth.

'I have to tell you something... I feel a little embarrassed that I didn't hold it together the other day, you know during our appointment? I should have held it together a bit more.'

Francesca was surprised to hear Shay's admission. She always seemed so laid back to her but looking at her now she could see it had really bothered Shay how she'd responded in their session. Her honesty broke the tension between them a bit.

'You have nothing to be embarrassed about Shay. Besides 'holding it together' isn't really what we want to achieve when in therapy.'

'What, so you usually hold your clients while they cry like a baby?'

Francesca smiled, she felt a lot more comfortable talking about work related things. It was her comfort zone and she knew what to say. She didn't have to come up with awkward every day chit chat.

'I try to support all my clients the best way I can.'

Shay tutted playfully. 'Here I was thinking I was special!' She sat down opposite Francesca and tilted forward over the table to speak with more privacy. She looked directly at Francesca.

'Really though, joking aside, I want to thank you.'

Francesca had to focus on what Shay was saying because most of her awareness was on the fact that their legs were touching underneath the table.

Shay continued. 'You made me feel safe. I've never felt safe with any...' She changed direction, realising she was maybe becoming too deep. 'I know I fought it at first, but what I'm trying to say is it was a relief to get all of that off my chest, so, thank you.'

'I was just doing my job.' Francesca said in matter of fact way, as if they hadn't shared anything personal.

It hurt Shay a bit but she tried not to show it. She didn't open up to people like that every day. She shook it off when she saw Laura walking across the restaurant, still wiping at the damp patch on her dress.

'This must be your friend coming back.' She got up to leave. 'I'm glad you're not on a date. I would be a little bit jealous if you were!' She smiled and winked at Francesca, who tried not to smile and encourage her.

'Shouldn't you be working?'

Shay smirked and walked of, smiling at Laura as they crossed paths on her way back to the table.

Laura took her seat and glanced back at Shay. 'Wasn't that the woman we saw making out with her boyfriend when we were out for lunch?'

Francesca tried to play it cool, as though she didn't really know who Laura was talking about.

'Was it? I don't know. I didn't really notice her.'

'Sure! How come you were grinning like the cat that's got the cream when I walked over here?'

'I was pleased to see you!' She knew Laura saw straight through her.

'Then why was she smiling just as much? You both looked like horny teenagers discussing the best time to meet!'

'Laura you're sex obsessed!' Francesca was trying to bluff and make it seem it was all in Laura's dirty mind.

'Yes thank you! I know. That's exactly why I got into the psychology of it!'

It went quiet between them as Laura stared at Francesca again, waiting for an explanation. In the end, she could take it no longer.

'She's one of my clients if you must know...'

Laura looked over at Shay again. She turned back to face Francesca and thought about it for a second. 'Is that the one that, you know... pushes your buttons?'

Before Francesca could deny or reply, Shay walked back over with another full bottle of red wine. She placed it down on their newly set table.

'Here you are and don't worry. It's on the house so we won't charge you double!' She smirked at Francesca and teased her. 'Just don't spill it this time!'

Laura watched and studied their interaction with one another.

'Thank you, that's really kind.' Francesca wasn't expecting the free bottle of wine.

'No problem. Is there anything else I can get you?'

An orgasm? Laura thought to herself. She grinned at the blatant chemistry Francesca was trying to deny. She answered her question.

'No I think we're OK thank you.'

Shay nodded at them both and walked off to clear another table.

'Ding, ding!' Francesca knew Laura would have something to say. 'That, my dear, is the sound of ALL your buttons being pressed!'

'Laura!'

'You can't deny it now, not to me...' Laura raised her eyebrows. 'I've just seen it with my own eyes!'

CHAPTER TWENTY
ONE

Jamie had come home from work for lunch. Maggie had made a fresh salad with lasagne which they were eating it together, Maggie at one end of the table and Jamie at the other.

'Your father phoned today.' She wasn't sure how he would respond so she'd waited until he had nearly finished his dinner, with the hope that he would be calmer on a full stomach.

'What? What did he want? How did he have your number?' Jamie was confused. It was the last thing he had expected Maggie to say.

'I gave it to him. He approached me at the supermarket and knew who I was. He asked how you were...' She was surprised Jamie hadn't kicked off about her talking with his father but she took it as a good sign. 'I told him about the baby...'

'You didn't, did you?' She saw his jaw tense. 'Tell me you're joking?'

'Yes Jamie I did and he seemed really pleased. I don't know why you have such a problem with him because he seemed like a nice man to me.'

Jamie stopped eating, leaving the last few mouthfuls. He dropped his knife and fork down on his plate and the noise of it made Maggie jump a little.

'You don't know him like I do.'

'If this is about what happed when you were a child, he seemed really sorry about it. He said...'

He didn't let her finish. 'What did he say?'

'He said he was sorry for being a drunk and not being there for you or your sister. He wants to be there now, with the baby coming. He is this baby's grandfather...' She looked down and softly rubbed her belly. 'He does have some rights...'

'He lost his rights years ago...' Jamie, feeling more than mad, got up and took his plate over to the sink, he threw it down into it. 'Don't see him behind my back again OK?' He wasn't asking her, he was telling her. He walked out of the kitchen and through to his living room, he picked up his jacket to go out for some space and fresh air.

Maggie followed him, upset and livid with the way he'd just spoken to her. 'You can bloody talk! Seeing people behind backs!'

'What are you talking about?'

She confronted him outright about her suspicion that he had been cheating. 'Who is she?'

'What?' He was totally puzzled and thrown off by the question.

'The woman you've been seeing! When I asked you who was on the phone you said it was a work thing, but I know it was a woman, I could hear her!'

He realised she must have been talking about the phone call with Julie when he was organising his appointment to see Dr Francesca.

'You've no idea what you're talking about. You're just like my father!'

'So then tell me! You've gone all secretive Jamie. Talk to me?'

He didn't want to say anything so he slipped his shoes on and walked out the front door leaving Maggie alone in his house.

Jamie drove over to his Aunt's house. He didn't have any plans to go back to home while Maggie was still there, he thought he may as well do some of the work he had promised his Aunt a while back. He started to plaster a wall in one of her spare bedrooms. It took him longer than usual because he was still so pumped up from his fight with Maggie and the thought of her meeting his dad, that he couldn't keep his hand steady or the plaster as smooth as usual. When he was about done with the first wall his Aunt checked in on him with a fresh, hot cup of milky tea in her hand.

'You're a good boy Jamie. I don't know how to repay you.' She handed him his tea with a gentle smile.

'Don't be silly Aunt Jane. You don't need to do anything to re pay me. It's me who owes you for all those times, as a kid, when I would come over starving and you would give us food. Food you could barely spare yourself.'

She had flash backs in her head of Jamie and Lucy arriving at her front door hungry and cold. 'Your father was a bit of a bastard for drinking away the money and letting you go hungry.' She took a sip of her tea, glad those days were over.

'He was a bastard in general. Still is!'

She saw the look of bitterness and resentment on Jamie's face as he said it.

'You've seen him?' She was slightly surprised since she, herself, hadn't seen her brother in almost ten years and the last person she imagined would go looking for him was Jamie.

'No. Maggie ran into him at the supermarket and, by the sounds of it, he tried to play the ''I'm a saint card. I'm a changed man now.'''

Jane thought about the little brother she used to know. 'You know, your dad *was* a saint, as a boy I mean!'

Jamie was fed up with people saying what a good person his father was. 'I find that hard to believe. You must have known a different man.'

'I don't blame him for turning to the drink. I can't really. That's why I always tried to help you out when I could. Going through what he did...'

Jamie interrupted her. He didn't want to hear his father's sob story. 'I'm sure it was no worse than what I went through, having him as a father.'

She could tell by his lack of empathy that he must have no idea what his father went through a child, growing up. 'He never told you? I thought you knew.'

'Knew what?'

She back tracked a little. 'It's not my story to tell... you need to ask your father if you want to know the truth behind why he drank so much.'

CHAPTER TWENTY TWO

Francesca looked at her mobile phone as it rang with Garth's name up on the screen. She put the paperwork down on her desk and answered the call with an apology.

'Hi! Sorry I never got back to your message but I've been really busy.'

Garth nervously laughed. 'Don't worry about it. I probably messaged you too soon after our first date so I wouldn't blame you for thinking I'm too keen.'

'No. Not at all.' She lied because she had thought exactly that.

'Good. Well, I'm phoning to see if you fancy going to the cinema this Friday night?'

Her first instinct was to say no, but she looked down at her paperwork and saw Shay's name written on the top of a sheet of paper. It had somehow got into the wrong pile. Francesca stared at it and decided to give Garth a chance.

'OK, sure, I can't remember the last time I went to the cinema. What time?'

'It starts at eight but, if I pick you up at seven, we could have a couple of drinks before?'

'Sounds good. I'll see you then.' She put the phone down and stuffed Shay's sheet of paper to the back of the pile. She leaned back in her chair and wondered if she was just leading Garth on, giving him false hope, because there wasn't really any attraction on her side. He liked her more than she liked him but she knew what Laura would say, 'Give it a chance. A fire doesn't roar straight away!'

After finishing her paperwork for the evening Francesca headed for her bed. On her way up, in the hallway, she noticed the house phone flashing with a message. Being so tired after work and desperate to finish, she'd completely missed it on her way in. She pressed the play button.

'Hi Francesca, its David. I've spoken to my lawyer and he thinks, under the circumstances, it's best we get the divorce proceedings under way as soon as possible. If you could let me know when you're available to meet, that would be great! Don't tell the kids yet. I think we should tell them together, when it's finalised...' The machine caught the sound of knocking at the door in the background. 'That will be Mia now! Speak to you soon.' The message finished with a loud beep.

Francesca stood still, angry at his message. Yes, divorce was on the cards, and an eventuality, but it felt strange that David was the one instigating it, when she was the one who had been cheated on.

CHAPTER TWENTY THREE

Mia had expected to be able to spend time with her dad but when she got to his apartment, within half an hour, David was doing his work.

She watched television, entertaining herself whilst waiting for him to finish, but it didn't look as though he was going to finish anytime soon. He had a load of work piled up on the table.

'When are you going to finish dad? I'm bored! I thought we were supposed to be hanging out tonight? That doesn't mean me watching you work!'

He finished a page and signed it at the bottom. 'I did tell you next week would have been easier for me, because I have so much work to catch up on, but you insisted...'

Mia aimlessly flicked through the television channels. 'That's because I don't want to spend all my spare time stuck in the house with mum!'

David stopped writing and looked over at Mia. 'Don't be so hard on your mum...'

'Why not? She tells you to leave, and breaks up the whole family. I'm not going to let her off that easily for doing that!'

He wasn't going to tell Mia the truth, but he didn't want her to take it out on her mother either, since he knew how she could be when she was focused on something.

'Just promise me you won't be too hard on her?'

Mia pulled a 'yeah, whatever face'. She didn't really want to get into it with him, it was supposed to be their time together and she didn't want to spend it talking about her mother. Mia found a programme she liked and stayed on the one channel, but shortly after she received a text from Stacey.

BORED, ALONE AND FRUSTRATED! WANT TO COME AND RESCUE ME?'XX

David heard the message alert. 'Who's that?'

'My friend, Stacey. She wants to know if I can go out with her tonight.'

Only half listening and interested in Mia, David opened another set of accounts and began to look through them.

'God, look at the state of these!' he mumbled to himself. 'Sorry sweetheart, but I think it's going to be a long one tonight! We can do something tomorrow.'

'This better not be what the whole weekend's going to be like! Otherwise what's the point of me coming over to stay?'

Another text came through from Stacey.

U COMIN OR WHAT? XX

Mia glanced up at her dad. 'If we're not hanging out this evening can I go and meet my friend?'

'Does your mum usually let you go out on a Friday night?'

'Of course!' She lied. 'I'm not a baby dad!' She knew he was likely to say no but she felt she had some leeway with a guilt trip due to the little time he was actually spending with her.

'Does she have any rules if you go out?' He made a mistake in his working out, trying to concentrate and speak with her at the same time. He stopped what he was doing so he could register the rules Francesca had set for Mia.

'No sex, no drugs etc. and be back no later than midnight.'

David thought it would be a good idea to get her out the apartment for a few hours so he could finish his work without distraction. 'I don't see why not then.'

Mia couldn't believe her luck. 'Yes!' She texted Stacey back with the good news and turned the television off with the remote. She got up from the sofa and picked up her jacket.

'Mia, wait...' David called.

She thought he'd thought about it some more and changed his mind.

'Make sure you eat something,' he continued as he got his wallet out and passed her a ten pound note. 'And if your mum asks, I cooked for you!'

Mia met Stacey in the town centre, by the bus station. They walked down the street which was lit up by the street and shop lights.

Stacey was like an excited puppy out in the big wide world for the first time. 'I can't believe your dad let you go out! Your mum will kill him if she finds out!'

'She won't find out.' Mia was sure of it.

Stacey pulled her to a stop outside one of the late night newsagents and raised her eyebrows.

'Want to get pissed?'

'No. I'm not getting those dumb, fake Id's out again. It was humiliating enough the first time.'

'No, I was thinking that we can get someone to buy it for us. Lots of people walk past here! Surely we can convince someone?'

Mia felt resistant to the idea but ended up going along with it after Stacey had begged her for the past ten minutes.

Stacey approached and asked more or less every person that walked past them, if they would buy them some alcohol. Three people ignored her and acted as if she wasn't there and a couple came out with a simple abrupt 'no'.

After over an hour of trying Mia was cold and fed up with standing still and not moving.

'This is useless! Can we just go back to your place and watch a movie or something?'

Stacey wasn't ready to give up. She grabbed her by the hand and pulled her forward into the middle of the street. 'No way, come on, I know a better place.'

They walked for ten minutes down the street to one of the small supermarket chains that was open 24/7, and casually strolled in, with Mia lagging behind and dragging her cold feet.

'Stacey...' She was about to protest again but Stacey grabbed her by the arm and pulled her in close so she could whisper in her ear.

'I've got a plan b...'

The checkout man, working in the supermarket noticed the two of them walking in straight away. He watched them on the CCTV monitor until a customer approached his till. It was Jamie out on a late night shop. He put a few items down on the counter, milk, bread, butter and a few bottle of beers.

'Hello sir, how is your evening?' He was practising his customer service since his boss had sent him on a course a couple of weeks ago, after just starting the job.

Jamie managed to mumble an answer. 'Good thanks...' He wasn't in the mood to be friendly. He just wanted to get the few things he needed and get back home. 'Can I get a packet of smokes as well please?'

'Sure. Which ones sir?'

'I'll have a packet of Marlboro.'

The checkout man turned and took a packet down from the shelf and put it through the register.

'Stacey what are we doing here? Come on lets go.' Whilst Jamie was paying, Stacey had taken Mia to the alcohol aisle. She took a quick glance left and right down the aisle, making sure nobody else was around and grabbed a bottle of vodka from the shelf, quickly stuffing it into Mia's bag.

'What are you doing?' Mia was frozen with shock at what Stacey had just done.

'Getting us some alcohol...' As far as Stacey was concerned the job was done and she pushed Mia forward. 'Now walk!'

Mia began to walk towards the supermarket exit, self-conscious with the weight of the bottle in her bag.

Stacey followed behind her and tried to usher Mia out of the supermarket but, as they reached the end of the aisle and turned the corner to leave, the checkout man stepped out in front of them.

'Can I help you ladies?'

Mia's tummy flipped with anxiety. She felt as though her bag was see through and he could see what she had in there. She started to panic and broke out into a cold sweat.

Stacey stayed as cool as a cucumber. She'd shoplifted a thousand times before. 'Eh, no thanks... you don't have what we're looking for.'

'I'm sorry to hear that. Maybe you can help me find what I'm looking for...' He looked directly at Mia and then at the bag hanging from her shoulder. 'The bottle of alcohol you have in your bag. The one you haven't paid for!'

CHAPTER TWENTY FOUR

Francesca was asleep in bed when the phone rang. The sound of it echoed through the empty house. Blurry eyed and still half asleep, she stumbled down the stairs. '

Hello?' Her throat was dry as she spoke.

'Hello. Am I speaking to Dr Francesca Draw?' The voice on the other end of the phone sounded very serious and official to her. She rubbed her eyes with her spare hand and yawned. 'Yes. Who is this please?'

'I'm sorry to phone you so late but this is Constable Owens from the police. Could you please tell me the whereabouts of your daughter Mia?'

'She should be over at her father's...' Francesca's tired brain caught up, dread took over her body. 'What's going on? Is she OK?'

'I think you should come down the station as soon as possible.'

Every possible scenario rushed through Francesca's head, Mia getting hit by a car, being assaulted, being taken...

'Your daughters OK...' It was as if Constable Owens had heard her thoughts. 'But she's been involved in an incident.'

Francesca arrived at the police station twenty minutes later. It was late and most of the roads where clear for her to drive through.

She reached the entrance and walked into the station. It was busy with the usual drunks and wayward people but she was able to walk straight up to an officer on the reception desk.

'Hi, I've been told my daughter Mia Draw is here?'

'Give me a moment please, I'll find the sergeant that brought her in.' He left the desk and came back a couple of minutes later with Sergeant Travers walking behind him.

'Hello, Dr Draw...' She shook Francesca's hand. 'I'm Sergeant Travers, I brought your daughter in tonight.'

Francesca was surprised at how young she was. She thought she must have only been in her late twenties.

'What's happened? Has she been arrested?'

Sergeant Travers gestured for Francesca to come through and follow her towards the holding cells. 'No, she hasn't been arrested, just a warning and a caution. She and a friend were caught trying to shop lift a bottle of vodka...' She saw Francesca roll her eyes in annoyance. 'I wouldn't be too hard on her. By the looks of the CCTV her friend instigated the whole thing. I spoke to her and she seems like a good kid, compared to the ones that usually come in here!' She held the last door through to the cells open for Francesca to walk through as she continued. 'She probably could just do with better judgement when it comes to friends.' They entered the holding cells corridor and Sergeant Travers opened the door to the third cell.

Francesca peeped in and saw Mia sitting on the bench bed. She peered sheepishly up at her mum with a mixture of guilt and relief on her face.

Francesca didn't say one word to Mia on the drive back home. When they got back to the house she threw her car keys on the side unit in the hallway.

'Get to bed. I'll speak with you in the morning!' Her voice was flat and un-impressed.

Sullenly, Mia began to walk up the stairs, she paused half way up feeling she needed to explain herself. 'It wasn't my fault. I didn't...'

'I don't want to hear it Mia! I don't know who I'm more upset with, you or your father?'

'It wasn't his fault. I told him I would be back by midnight...' She didn't want to give her mum even more reason not speak to her dad.

'That's no excuse! He shouldn't have let you go out!' She glanced at the clock on her phone. It was already 1am. 'It's one in the morning! If you said midnight why hasn't he phoned you to check where you are, see if you're OK?'

Mia was about to reply when Francesca's phone started ringing. Francesca looked down at the screen.

'This is your dad now! Up to bed.'

Mia carried on up the stairs to her bedroom. Francesca waited to hear the door shut before she answered the phone.

'What were you thinking?' She was too angry to do 'hello's' with him.

'Is she with you?'

'What do you think you were playing at? You were supposed to be looking after her!'

'She's sixteen Cesca. She doesn't need a baby sitter.' He wasn't going to take responsibility or let her blame him for whatever had happened.

'Well, evidently she does after tonight!'

'What's happened?'

'She got cautioned by police for trying to steal a bottle of alcohol.'

'Shit!' He hadn't thought it would be that serious, 'That doesn't sound like something Mia would do! Why do you think she did it?'

Francesca was tired, emotional and ready to break after the night she'd had. She let rip at him. 'Why? I don't know! Pick any reason! She's a teenager, she's under stress with exams and, oh, her family is falling apart! Is that enough for you, David?' After the split Francesca had wanted, and planned, to be more civil with him but there was just too much between them and only so much she could take.

'OK, ease up Cesca! It's not my fault!'

She raised her voice over the phone. 'It never bloody is, is it?' she said, indignantly as she cut the call.

CHAPTER TWENTY FIVE

Francesca and Jasmine had been in their session, talking, for the past twenty minutes. Francesca had noticed Jasmine wasn't looking too good when she first walked in and thought she was looking gradually worse and worse as the session had gone on.

'Are you OK Jasmine? You don't look so bright today?'

'Yeah, I'm fine. I wish people would stop asking me that!' She didn't mean to be short with her but she'd come in feeling worse than she had for a very long time. Her whole body felt like lead, heavy, aching lead.

Francesca backed off a little, not wanting to upset her. 'Sorry. I only asked because I'm concerned about you...'

'Don't be. I can look after myself.'

Silence broke out between them. In the quiet Jasmine's head started to feel like she was swaying on a boat, she felt a wave of heat flush through her body.

'Do you want to carry on then?' Francesca thought it best to just continue.

'Can I have some water first please?' She could feel her tongue trying to stick to the roof of her mouth.

Francesca stood up and walked over to her desk to pour her a glass. Jasmine sweated profusely as she watched Francesca walk back towards her. Her eyesight started to blur and Francesca started to sway in her vision.

Francesca was about to pass her the glass when she noticed Jasmine's head flop to the side.

'Jasmine...Jasmine, are you OK?'

Jasmine tried to stand up from the sofa but her legs buckled beneath her as she collapsed onto the floor. Francesca panicked and rushed over to her.

Jasmine did her best to try and communicate but her voice was faint. 'I...I think I'm going to be sick...' Her eyes rolled back and she passed out.

Francesca dropped the glass of water and ran to shout for Julie. She rushed back to Jasmine and kneeled down next to her, trying to gently stir her by tapping her on her cheek. 'Jasmine, Jasmine have you taken something? What have you taken?'

Half conscious, all Jasmine could do was mumble, her eyes kept rolling to the back of head.

Julie appeared at the door unaware of the severity of the situation. She saw Jasmine and Francesca on the floor.

'Call an ambulance!' Francesca screamed.

Julie didn't ask any questions. She ran back to her desk and picked up the phone, leaving Francesca still attempting to stir Jasmine. 'Stay with me... stay with me Jasmine!'

Jasmine tried to open her eyes and look towards the bag she had left by the sofa. 'Ba... bag... my bag...in my ba...'

Francesca glanced over at where she was staring. She saw the bag and dragged it over. She began to rummage through it. Jasmine's phone, wallet and a bottle of water were on top, she threw them out and reached for the last item. It was a plain metal tin that she assumed was a pencil case. When she lifted it out Jasmine made a noise of acknowledgement, Francesca opened it up to find a needle and syringe inside.

CHAPTER TWENTY SIX

The hospital waiting room was stuffy and packed full of people. Francesca had been sitting, for a couple of hours, waiting to hear news about Jasmine. She spotted Debra walk pass the waiting room towards the toilets and hurried over to her, anxious for news.

'Is she going to be OK? How is she?'

Debra was surprised Francesca had waited for so long. She had assumed she'd gone back to work. 'She's going to be OK. She'll have to stay in overnight on a drip. The doctor said she is pretty dehydrated.'

'I'm sorry. I didn't know she was taking drugs. I should have known. A little bit of me suspected but...'

Debra had never seen Francesca so flustered. 'Whoa, hang on a second Doc! What are you talking about? You've lost me!'

'When I went through her bag she had a syringe and needle...'

'She's not on drugs... she has type one diabetes.'

Francesca couldn't hide her shock. 'What? Why didn't she tell me? Is that why she fainted because of the diabetes?'

'Yes. Her levels went way too high. They think maybe she had a virus going around her body pushing her sugar levels up. That and the dehydration can cause havoc in the body, apparently.' Debra looked down at her watch and worked out how long Francesca had been waiting for. 'I'm sorry you've been waiting here for so long. It was kind of you to stay.'

Francesca hadn't even thought about leaving until she knew how Jasmine was. 'Is she awake? Can I see her?'

'She's asleep at the moment but I'll tell her you were asking for her. The doctor said she should be right as rain in a few days.'

Francesca reluctantly left the hospital. She got into her car and gripped on to the steering wheel to let out a sigh of relief that Jasmine was going to be OK. She put the key in the ignition and started the engine. Before she drove off she noticed the car clock showing six o'clock. She couldn't believe it was that late already, she pulled the sleeve up of her shirt and checked her own watch to make sure. It was the right time. She only had an hour until Garth would be picking her up for their date.

CHAPTER TWENTY SEVEN

Shay had picked a bunch of roses and a toy car, she thought Tommy would have liked, from one of her local shops and headed towards the cemetery. She hadn't been for over five years and was nervous to go there again after such a long time. She used to visit Sara and Tommy's grave regularly but stopped suddenly believing it was stupid visiting a grave, talking to a head stone with nothing but their names on. Talking to Francesca during therapy and speaking about it had changed things for her. Discussing Tommy had made her realise how much she'd missed just sitting by the headstone and being with something physical that reminded her of them, whether they could hear her or not.

She entered the cemetery gates and walked to the spot where she knew they were buried. The grass was slightly damp when she sat down by the side of the grave. She thought the grave site would have been overgrown and a bit of a mess, but the council had got in a groundskeeper to make sure each grave looked well-kept and tidy. She laid the roses on the ground in front of the head stone and placed the toy car on top. 'I'm sorry I haven't visited.' She could hear the emotion shaking in her voice. 'I miss you guys, more than you can imagine. The boys said to say hello, they want to come and visit you someday too!' She paused and looked at her mother's name engraved in bold italics, 'You'd be proud of me mum. I'm getting help. Seeing someone, so hopefully I can move forward and not feel so much anger.' She stayed in the cemetery watching people come and go, visiting their loved ones, and outstayed them all, until the light completely faded.

CHAPTER TWENTY EIGHT

Mia, Mark and his friend from university, Brad, were in the lounge watching television. Mark was back for a few days so Mia let him watch what he wanted because she was just glad to have him there.

Francesca was upstairs in her bedroom not sure what to wear for a drinks and cinema date with Garth. She ended up putting on one of the dresses that she'd worn when she and Laura had gone out for a cocktail evening a couple of months ago. She only just about had time to put her make up on and rushed to grab her heels. She ran down stairs into the living room looking for her handbag.

'Wow mum! I thought you were just going to the cinema!' Mark was impressed with how dressed up she was.

'Drinks first, then the cinema...' She found her hand bag by the side of one of the settees. 'Are you sure you guys will be OK?' She felt guilty leaving them. 'I totally forgot you were coming home tonight. I should have cancelled...'

'Mum chill! It's not like I'm never going to be home again. Go out and enjoy yourself. Brad, Mia and I can go out for dinner or something.'

Mia jumped in. 'I can't go out, I'm still grounded!'

Francesca didn't want to spoil their brother and sister bonding time, she knew how much Mia had missed him. 'I'll let you off...' Mia's whole body perked up. Her mum hardly ever let her off when she was grounded. 'But only for tonight, as you've stuck to the rules. Well pretty close anyway.' It was a bit of a peace offering. She was fed up with the minimal and awkward interaction she and Mia were having.

Brad hadn't been able to take his eyes off Francesca since she'd walked into the room. 'Hey, Mrs D, I mean Dr D, you *should* go out! You're too fit not to! If I was like ten years older...'

'Dude!' Mark wasn't impressed with him slobbering over his mum.

'What? Your mum's fit. You must know that!'

'She's my mum!' He was about to rip into Brad more but a car horn from outside interrupted him.

'That's him.' Francesca checked she had her front door key. 'Make sure you take a pair of keys with you if you do go out. I don't know what time I'll be back. I think the film finishes around ten but I'm not sure.' She was starting to feel a bit more anxious about the date as she walked out into the hallway to put on her jacket.

'Mum...' Mia had quietly followed her out.

'Yes?

She felt self-conscious and guilty all of a sudden for giving her mum the silent treatment for so long. 'Nothing... you just look nice, that's all.'

Francesca could tell it was Mia's way of making amends, she walked over to her and gave her a kiss on the cheek. 'I'll see you later darling.'

After Francesca had left Mia walked back into the living room, relieved they were on better terms. She found Mark and Brad play fighting in the middle of the room over Brad's comment.

'Brad, seriously! I'm not going to invite you again if you keep perving on my mum.' He had Mark in a playful head lock.

'Boys! Come on, stop fighting. What are you like, twelve? I'm starving! Let's go somewhere to eat.'

CHAPTER TWENTY NINE

The three of them entered Yani's restaurant and found a table. None of them had been there before but they had decided to give it a try.

Shay was working a shift and saw them take a table. She waited a couple of minutes as they looked through the drinks menu and then strolled over.

'Hey! Can I get you some drinks?' She glanced quickly at Mia and thought she recognised her, but she couldn't place where she'd seen her before.

'Can I get a beer? Brad what do you want?' Mark didn't get an answer from him though because he was too busy drooling over Shay. 'Brad?'

'He'll have a napkin by the looks of it!' Mia quipped as she quickly scanned the drinks menu again. 'Can I get a lemonade please?'

'*Oui.*' Shay scribbled down the second order on her pad.

Brad managed to lift his jaw off the floor to speak and give his order. 'Yeah I'll have one of those as well please.'

'A lemonade? *Oui*.' She repeated it out loud as she scribbled it down.

'Eh no, no, a beer I mean... *merci*.' Brad smiled at her. He knew his school French would come in handy at some point.

Shay humoured him and smiled back at him, '*Bien*.'

As she sorted out their drinks, she kept glancing over at Mia. It was still niggling her that she couldn't place where she'd met her before. Faith walked over to join her wondering who it was she was staring at. She looked over at Mia's table.

'It's not fair! You always get the hot young blood to serve!'

'If you're talking about table three, the two guys and the young lady, they look barely eighteen!'

Faith wasn't bothered by their age. 'Yeah and? Eighteen's legal Shay! Any way, you can talk! You've been staring at the girl since she came in.'

'I know her but I just can't remember how...'

'Did you sleep with her?'

'Faith!'

'What? You like sleeping around, there's nothing wrong with that, Miss love them and leave them. I'm sure you gave her the night of her life!'

Shay still couldn't place Mia but she knew she hadn't slept with her. 'She's probably just some kid I've walked past in town. And for future reference I'm not doing that anymore. I'm not sleeping around. I'm over it.'

Faith paused before she replied. 'Don't tell me this shrink you're seeing is actually working? Are you saying you actually want to have real life relationships with people?' She was half sarcastic and half serious.

'Maybe!'

Having prepared the drinks Shay left Faith behind the bar and took them over to their table. As she placed Mia's lemonade in front of her she realised where she knew her from.

'I've seen you before...' Mia looked up at her. 'You tried to get into the club with your friend using the fake Id's!'

'I was hoping you wouldn't recognise me! That was really embarrassing.' Mia's cheeks flushed a little, thinking back to that night.

Shay remembered how sorry she'd felt for her. 'How about if I say your lemonade is on the house, to make it a little less embarrassing? You were one of the lucky ones not to get in. The music was shocking that night! She smiled at her and served the boys their drinks and walked off to another table.

Mark glared at his little sister. 'Mia you used fake Id's to get into a club? Mum would kill you if she knew!'

'Relax! I didn't get into the club and I won't be using them again, that's for sure!'

Brad wasn't interested in their conversation and he couldn't take his eyes of Shay serving the other table. 'How cool is she? I totally have a thing for French chicks.'

His comment stopped Mark from lecturing Mia. 'You have a 'thing' for all chicks. Get real! You're like a puppy on heat!'

Brad didn't even register his remark. He was now too involved, in his head, with the daydream of how he and Shay would live happily ever after together.

'We totally came to the best place tonight. I think she might like me. Do you think she likes me?' He wanted their validation on the situation before he figured out his next move.

'Brad, dude seriously! You need a muzzle or something. Get a grip!' Mark nudged him playfully in the ribs.

CHAPTER THIRTY

The movie, Red, turned out to be the worst film ever. It was a low budget, soft porn movie. As they left the cinema Garth couldn't help but feel he needed to apologise to Francesca for putting her through the film

'I am so sorry. The boys at work must be having a right laugh at me now! I can't believe I fell for it!'

Francesca actually found it quite funny. 'Well at least you can say you've given me my first porn film date! We probably should have guessed by the title!' She could tell he was completely mortified by the whole experience and tried to reassure him. 'It wasn't that bad.'

'Really?' He was hoping that meant the film hadn't put her off him.

'OK, it was pretty bad!'

They were both laughing at how awful the movie was as they reached his car, Garth suddenly became nervous knowing what he was about to ask her. 'Do you er... do you want to come back to mine?'

Francesca answered quickly, 'I'd better not.' She'd thought of a legitimate excuse beforehand just in case he suggested anything. 'I've left the kids at home without food so they're probably starving by now!'

'I thought you said they were going out for something to eat?'

'Did I?' Francesca kicked herself for not making a more concrete excuse.

By the time Garth pulled up outside Francesca's house it was pretty late. The house looked dark, as if the kids had already gone to bed. Garth killed the car engine and paused before he said anything.

'Francesca, have I done something wrong?' She'd been quiet with him for the whole of the journey home.

'No.'

'You seem a bit off me. If it's something I've done I'd rather know now so we can sort it. Are you not interested in me?' He hoped that wasn't the issue and made a joke so she couldn't confirm his fear. 'Is it my driving or my choice in films?'

'I'm sorry. I'm just tired. I had a rough week at work. It's not you, I promise.' She turned to look at him and looked into his eyes. He wasn't a bad guy really. A lot of women would see him as a good catch, she thought. 'Maybe...' Before she could finish her sentence Garth pressed his lips onto hers. She let him kiss her and even attempted to kiss him back, but she couldn't feel any attraction or spark, she pulled away from him. 'I'll see you soon.' She opened the car door and rushed to her front door. Garth watched her from the car, making sure she got in safely.

CHAPTER THIRTY TWO

The next morning Francesca headed over to Laura's house for a catch up. Surprised, but pleased to see her, Laura invited her in.

'Mike's out, so we've got the house to ourselves!'

'Where is he? I thought he's usually home at the weekend.' She followed Laura through into the kitchen.

'He's got a mate who's just bought a new BMW so he's gone over to play with it and then probably after seeing it, he'll play with himself! I don't get it! What is it with boys and their toys?'

'Girls like cars too!'

'You're right! Always the diplomat! So spill...how did it go with Garth? Is he the sex god I imagine him to be?'

'You've imagined him as a sex god?'

Laura reached for two mugs out of the cupboard. She filled the kettle and switched it on. 'I know! Since I've gone part time I've got too much time on my hands! So, don't leave me in suspense what...'

'I haven't slept with him.' Francesca couldn't get the statement out quick enough.

Laura was disappointed to hear it. 'What? Why not?'

'Because I hardly know him.'

'Yeah and...'

'And? Like I said, I barely know the guy.' It was a good enough reason for her, but Laura still wasn't convinced.

'Yeah, like I said, and? Cesca the game's totally changed since you last dated.' Francesca pulled a face at her. 'I'm just saying that nowadays people have sex before marriage!'

'I'm not that bad Laura! I had sex before marriage. How do you think Mark appeared?' She tried to justify herself. 'I just like to know someone before I jump into bed with them.'

The kettle stopped boiling and Laura filled the cups up, she watched as the water turned a light brown as it hit the tea bags.

Francesca sat quietly at the kitchen table and watched as Laura took the tea bag out and added milk. She brought the hot mugs over and passed one to Francesca. She sat down opposite her, wondering, the whole time, how to get through to her.

'Have you never just wanted someone? You know to scratch an itch you might have, or just because you're attracted to them and your body wants them? It's called desire, passion!' Laura became animated just thinking about it but Francesca just sat hugging her mug of tea, waiting for it to cool down a bit. 'When did you and David have sex last, I mean before you split?'

'Er...' She was a bit embarrassed by the personal question. 'I don't know. We would try and have sex about once a month...'

'Oh my God! It gets worse! Try? Are you serious? Please tell me doing it only once a month you at least were having orgasms?'

'Sometimes... not really, I mean not all the time...'

Laura covered her face with her hands in disbelief.

Francesca tried to explain herself. 'It was just sex... No big deal. I can go without sex.'

Laura took her hands away from her face and gawked at Francesca. 'Go without sex! Are you kidding me? Stop Francesca, otherwise next you're going to tell me you don't even get yourself off!'

The silence that fell confirmed Laura's fears. 'Oh Jesus! I never realised your sex life was so dire! I've been a bad friend. I'm a bloody sexpert for goodness sake and my friend is literally drying up! No wonder you're not that interested in Garth. How do you expect to find him sexy if you're not keeping your engine running?' She realised she was talking like her husband Mike, who would always talk about their sex life compared to how a car worked. 'Find some time in the shower or bath or something. You need some passion in your life woman! Try putting your focus on yourself for once and not on other people. Get out of you head and into your body! Francesca laughed at Laura's rant. She couldn't believe she thought her sex life and orgasms were so important. Laura saw Francesca's doubt and hesitation by the look on her face. 'Trust me. It will help with your stress!'

Francesca took a sip of her tea and looked at Laura. 'How is it we've been friends for so long?'

'Because I give you the best advice!'

Francesca didn't say anything she just smiled at her reply.

CHAPTER THIRTY THREE

'So I gather you had a date when you cancelled our appointment...' Francesca had more patience with Roger today for some reason. She surprised herself and thought maybe it was because she hadn't seen him for a couple of weeks. 'How did it go?'

Roger rolled his sleeves up on one of the worst shirts Francesca had ever seen him wearing.

'Well...' He made a point to clear his throat. 'Actually Doc, it was a great success. We're moving in together!'

Francesca thought he was joking at first, but the look on his face let her know he was one hundred per cent serious, 'Don't you think that's a bit fast, maybe?'

'Maybe for most people, but not for Penelope and I.' He puffed his chest out with pride. He felt he had the whole relationship thing sorted out.

'Penelope, is that her name?'

'Yep, she's twenty eight...' Francesca tried to keep a straight face, she wondered where he was going with this. 'I took your advice on finding someone older. We just fell in love. Aren't you happy for me?'

'I'm happy for you Roger.' She genuinely was. She believed everybody deserved to be happy with someone, even Roger. 'I'm just a little shocked at the speed because moving in together is a big commitment for anyone.'

'I'm glad you're happy for me Doc. It makes this easier.'

'What easier?'

'Me leaving you! I wondered for a long time why, when it came to finding a partner, a lot of the advice you gave me never worked.'

She was confused where he was going with the conversation and went to speak. 'Roger...' but Roger started speaking over her.

'And then suddenly I realised it. You were trying to sabotage me and my dates, because you want me for yourself...'

Francesca gasped. 'Roger I can assure you that isn't...'

Wanting to finish his big speech he hushed her. 'It's OK Dr Francesca. I'm going to walk out this door and never come back. It's going to break your heart, otherwise, to carry on seeing me when you know I'm no longer available. I want you to know I'm committed to Penelope and I can't, I won't, let you come in between that.' He stood up to leave, Francesca was so bemused she couldn't even reply.   He walked out, leaving her completely shocked.

Julie had seen Roger leave prematurely and poked her head around the office door. 'Is everything OK? I saw Roger leaving early.'

'Apparently I'm in love with him! He's sparing my feelings by leaving me so I don't have to be around him when I can't have him!'

Julie frowned confused. 'OK... have I missed something?'

'Obviously you have... and I have to!'

Half an hour after the Roger revelation Francesca had an appointment with Francis.

'So, I haven't seen you for a while. How have you been?'

Francis was tired and she looked it. 'I'm OK thank you.' She went quiet. 'Sorry, I don't really know what to say. I can't remember what we talked about last time.' She didn't want to repeat something she'd already told Francesca last week.

'You were speaking about how Chris wouldn't stop calling. You had arranged to meet him to call everything off.'

'Oh yes.' It all came flooding back to her, 'He's stopped calling and trying to see me, so I haven't seen him. After all that though, Hilary's stopped talking to me.'

'Why? What happened?'

Francis paced over to Hilary's house. It was a warm humid day and they were meant to have met up for their weekly lunch. Francis had waited for over an hour for Hilary, but she never showed at their usual meeting place. She'd tried calling her but there was no answer when she'd rung. As she turned into Hilary's street she could see her car was parked in the drive, which usually meant she was in. She walked up the four steps to the front door and rang the bell. It took Hilary about ten seconds to answer the door, almost as though she was expecting her, Francis thought.

'Thank God you're OK! I've been worried sick! Are the kids OK?'

Hilary was very short and blank with her. 'The kids are fine.'

'Well, why didn't you answer my calls, my messages? We were supposed to be having lunch...'

Hilary couldn't hold back her anger. She was too mad at her mother. 'I saw you mum!'

Francis hesitated, she didn't know what she was referring to, but she figured it out when she saw the way Hilary was glaring at her. Somehow she'd found out about Chris.

'Hilary, listen. It's not what you think!' Francis had dreaded this moment.

'Really? Because it looked like you were very comfortable with each other. Comfortable enough to kiss him! When were you going to tell me you were seeing someone?' She was fuming, 'I can't believe you!'

232

'How... when did you... I can explain...'

Hilary had heard enough. 'Don't bother mum. I've decided I don't want to know.' She shut the door in Francis's face and left her on the doorstep.

Francesca looked at Francis. 'Do you know who told her or how she found out?'

Francis sighed deeply. 'She found out, probably, one of the worst ways possible.'

NINE DAYS EARLIER.

Hilary and her two children Zach, seven, and Noah, four, were walking down the high street after Hilary had done some shopping. The boys had got her to stop at every toy store on the way back so they could look through the windows and see all the new toys.

'Look mummy that's the new Lego I want!'

She could hear the excitement in Zach's voice, but wasn't really concentrating on what he was pointing at, she was too concerned about getting back to the car before the parking ticket ran out. She encouraged the boys to speed up. 'Maybe you can have it for your birthday sweetheart.'

'Oh mum, but my birthday isn't for ages!'

'Zach honey, I don't have time to argue with you. Your birthday will be here in no...' She was about to say 'time' but something caught her attention across the

street. She spotted her mum sitting at a table outside one of the cafés. Hilary smiled to herself and contemplated going over to surprise her, but then she noticed she wasn't alone. She watched from across the street as Francis stood up, she watched as Chris kissed her. A rush of heated anger ran through her body, so powerful that the boys could feel it.

'What's wrong mummy?'

Hilary didn't want to risk either of them seeing anything so she pushed them on. 'Nothing, sweetheart. I just want to get back to the car.'

Francesca winced as she heard Francis explain how Hilary had seen them. She knew what it was like when you caught someone in a potentially compromising position. 'Was that the last time you spoke to her?' she asked.

'No, I went back a couple of days later because I didn't want to leave it too long. It was Zach's eighth birthday party and I wasn't going to miss it, no matter how uncomfortable it might be, since I'd promised him I would go. She only let me through the door because Zach saw me. He ran up to me and dragged me in, but it didn't take him long to run off back to his friends. I just sat in the kitchen and watched the chaos. Have you ever organised a children's party for twelve eight years olds?'

'Absolutely not!' Francesca had taken Mia to one once, many years ago, and saw the state the child's mother was in by the end so she'd decided against ever having to organise something like that.

'I don't think Hilary realised how much stress and work it would be, but it worked in my favour. She came into the kitchen looking for me. I could tell she was nervous.'

'What did she say?'

'I thought she was going to ask me to leave but she asked me to help her with the cake.'

TWO DAYS EARLIER.

Francis was in the kitchen when Hilary walked in. She barely looked at her mother as she walked over to the fridge and opened the door to take out a large bowl of butter icing she'd made earlier in the morning. Francis thought she was going to ignore her all day, but Hilary proved her wrong and walked over to her. She put the butter icing bowl in front of her and went to get the chocolate cake she'd made. She put it on the table and looked at Francis. She silently handed her a knife. As Francis helped ice the cake she wondered if Hilary letting her do it was her way of a peace offering, but she couldn't be sure. She decided not to say anything and just let Hilary take the lead.

As they finished icing the top of the cake together Hilary broke the awkward, tense silence that had built up between them.

'Do you remember on my tenth birthday when dad went overboard and got me that huge four tier cake?' They both laughed softly. 'It was a discounted wedding

235

cake and it took us about two months to get through that monster!' Her memory was as if it was only yesterday.

Their laugher soon went quiet again as silence fell between them. Hilary dipped her knife in the remaining butter cream to start to ice the sides of the cake, but she stopped and began to sob quietly. 'I miss him mum.'

Francis put her knife down and instinctively hugged her. She held on to her tightly, relieved to be able to touch her daughter again. 'I know darling. I miss him too.' She whispered into her ear.

Hilary pulled away a bit so she could see Francis's face. 'I miss you too. I'm sorry for how I lashed out and ignored you. You did all you could for dad. You stopped living your life to look after him. I realise that now.' Francis became teary. 'You know I'm bull headed... dad's gone and you deserve to see other people. I was just surprised at how soon...'

'You were right to be upset. What you saw with me and Chris was...' She wanted to explain herself but Hilary interrupted.

'You don't have to tell me. It's none of my business if you're seeing someone.'

'I promise you I'm not seeing him anymore, so you don't have to worry.' She pulled Hilary in for another embrace, happy she wasn't still mad at her.

'What? Why?' Hilary was confused.

'I don't want to lose any more of my family and I felt that, if I kept on seeing him, that's what would happen.'

'You won't lose me mum. I want you to be happy and I want us to be able to be honest with each other.'

'So you were on good terms?' Francesca was pleased to hear they had eventually become reconciled.

''Were' being the operative word! When she said about being honest I knew I had to come clean otherwise it would hang over me. I told her the day her father was dying I was with Chris... in his bed.'

'How did she take it?'

'What you would expect really. She told me to get out. That she never wanted to see me again. That I was selfish and disgusting for not even being able to wait until my husband was dead before jumping into another man's bed.' She paused as she remembered the look on Hilary's face as she screamed at her. 'It was nothing I haven't already told myself.'

Francesca empathised with Hilary's impossible position. 'What you told her would be a really challenging thing for anyone to hear, but it was also a brave thing for you to do.'

Francis exhaled deeply as she thought about it. 'I don't feel brave.' She scratched the top of her head. 'I thought I would give her some space before I even attempt to try and speak with her.'

'It might be a good idea to let her make contact first. Space, in a pretty intense situation like this one can be what's best and what's needed.'

CHAPTER THIRTY FOUR

After a busy day at work Francesca met up with David. She was fed up with trying to dodge him and prolong the inevitable talk about their divorce. They'd arranged to meet at one of the sleek bistros in the centre of town.

As Francesca entered she spotted David already at one of the tables, drinking coffee. She approached him and sat down opposite him. The atmosphere between them was still icy after Mia's police station visit. They didn't even greet each other.

'Why did it take you so long to agree to meet me?'

Francesca noticed, as he spoke, that he had dark stubble growing through on his face. For all the years she'd known him he'd always been clean shaven. She wondered if it was a sign of stress.

'Don't start. I'm here aren't I? Let's just get this over and done with shall we?'

David pulled the divorce papers out of his bag and passed them over to her. She'd seen and read a copy of them beforehand but wanted to keep David waiting, so she slowly pretended to read through them.

When she got to the last paper she could see David had already signed at the bottom. All that was left to do was sign the space where her signature needed to go. 'Do you have a pen?'

He passed her a black biro pen from his shirt pocket. Francesca signed her name next to his for the last time. She gathered and shuffled all the papers together and passed them back to him across the table. 'So I take it you're going to drop these off at the solicitors?'

'Yep. You will hear back from them when it's all gone through and finalized.' He put the papers back in his bag and the pen back in his shirt. 'When are we going to tell the kids?'

'I thought we were going to wait until it was done and dusted and then tell them together?'

Francesca hadn't expected him to ask that question. She'd assumed they would figure the details out after the divorce had officially gone through.

He recalled saying it to her. 'Right, OK, yes that was what I said...'

'What *we* said!' The comment reminded her how it was always about him when they were together.

David shrugged off Francesca's correction. 'Just give me a call and let me know when you know what you're going to tell them and how.' On anything else Francesca would have declined doing all the work but, on this occasion, she wanted to be the one to figure it out so David couldn't mess it up. She got her bag and jacket together, ready to leave. She'd signed the papers and didn't want to stay any longer than necessary.

'I hear you're seeing someone? Mia mentioned it.'

Francesca heard it as if it was an accusation...that she'd moved on quickly. She was so riled and offended that he'd thought he even had a right to ask about her personal life that she sounded as if she was spitting the question at him. 'Are you still seeing her?'

'Yes.' He stated the answer to her question with no remorse.

Francesca stood up and glared at him, telling him straight. 'It's none of your business who I see, or what I do.'

'OK Francesca, you don't have to be so shitty with me!'

'I think I have every right to be shitty with you, don't you?' She left feeling a mixture of emotions. Relieved that it was done but a bit sad that all those years they'd spent together, all those years people spend together, can end up with just a signature on a piece of paper.

CHAPTER THIRTY FIVE

David entered the apartment he'd bought when he and Francesca had split up and she'd asked him to move out. It was in the middle of town, in a posh, swanky area, where all the people that wanted to have some kind of status lived. He'd just got back from the meeting with Francesca and walked straight to the fridge for a glass of white wine. Melanie, his girlfriend, was in the living room reading a magazine when she heard him come in and open the fridge door.

'How'd it go babe?' She strolled into the kitchen assuming he'd just come back from a business meeting.

'She can be such a shit to me sometimes!' He poured the wine to the very top of the glass and swigged some.

'Who?' She walked over to him and gave him a quick kiss on the lips.

'Fucking Francesca!'

'I don't understand why you're phoning her and meeting up with her. What's the point?' She didn't like the thought of them together, she'd heard him speaking on the phone to her a few times and got jealous. 'If I was paranoid I could start thinking you still want to be with her.'

David didn't reassure her by saying he would never even consider getting back with her.

'She wouldn't take me back. She hates me.'

'Great! So what you're saying is you would get back with her if she wanted to!'

He leaned over and kissed her softly. The gesture made Melanie feel a bit better, as if he did care about her. 'I want to be with you...' He stared down at her stomach and caressed her small, swollen, pregnant belly. 'Both of you.'

CHAPTER THIRTY SIX

Francesca was feeling pent up in her office, waiting for her next appointment. She decided to walk down to reception to try and move some of the energy building up in her body.

'Julie, have I got any messages?'

'Yes. Jasmine's mother, Debra, phoned. Jasmine's out of hospital. They kept her in longer just as a precaution. She left her mobile number. I wrote it down somewhere...' She searched her desk, looking for the piece of paper and found it under the phone book. She passed it to Francesca just as Shay walked through the door for her appointment.

Francesca put Debra's number on her desk, in a safe place, while Shay made herself comfortable on the sofa. She sat down on her usual side, the one closet to Francesca's chair, and watched as Francesca walked towards her to take her own seat. After Francesca sat down she leaned back and squeezed the back of her neck, preparing herself for the next hour.

'So, I want to acknowledge last week because we went pretty deep talking about your family and Tommy. I wonder if it's possible to continue from where we ended. Could you tell me a bit about how your family were after Tommy's death?'

'Where's the foreplay? You're not even going to warm me up this week?'

By Francesca's body language and expression Shay could tell she wasn't in the mood to play games. She took a deep breath in and let it out slowly to calm herself, before she spoke. 'There's nothing much to tell really. We each broke down completely, in our own ways. My father became even more distant... my mother started drinking...'

Francesca interjected. 'That's hardly nothing, Shay.' Silence filled the room. Francesca realized Shay hadn't shared how she'd broken down. 'What did you do? How did you cope?'

'I found my own way...' She paused and went quiet.

Francesca tried to encourage her to explain a bit more. 'Which was?

'I don't know... sex... tattoos.'

'Tell me about your tattoos?'

Shay looked down at the tattoos on her arm and ran her fingers over them. 'These? I got these when I felt numb. When it felt like no one was at home inside me... the pain and the sting would bring me back into my body. When the needle touched my skin, I enjoyed it.' She purposely made eye contact with Francesca to show just how much she'd enjoyed the pleasure of pain. Francesca shifted her gaze to her skirt and pretended to try and brush something off it. Shay smirked to herself, enjoying how nervous and on edge she could make Francesca feel with certain comments. She carried on talking. 'The soreness afterwards, the physical pain, helped me cope with the emotional pain I was feeling.' She looked down at the tattoos on her arm again. 'It wasn't just about the pain though, each one means something to me though.'

Francesca looked at the tattoos on her lower arm. 'How many do you have?'

'Probably around eighteen now, I think. I've lost count! The biggest one I have is on my back.' She stood up and lifted her top to show Francesca her back. 'It's a piece of my mum's art work...'

Francesca studied the black tattoo with a few splashes of colour. It covered at least a third of Shay's back and was like a mixture of scripture, patterns and delicate flowers rolled into one. She was amazed at the detail. She didn't usually like tattoos on people but this one suited Shay as if it was made for her. Shay turned slightly more to the side to try and look at it herself and the movement took Francesca's attention to the inch thick, foot long, white scar running down the side of her torso. She hesitated whether to ask about it or not.

'Is that scar from the...'

'The accident? Yes.' Feeling vulnerable that she'd noticed her scar, Shay dropped her top and sat back down.

Francesca noticed the big change in her demeanour. Now it was Shay who couldn't look her in the eye. 'You know we all have scars, Shay. Some of them we can't hide and some of them we can. Well, we try to!'

Shay wanted to change the subject. She didn't want to talk about her scars. 'Are you going to ask me about the sex?'

'We were talking about scars. Why have you switched to sex? Do you not want to talk about your wounds?'

Shay flipped the question around. 'Do you want to talk about your wounds?'

Francesca didn't answer. It was a fair point.

Shay continued. 'You asked me about the tattoos but not about the sex...'

'That might not be appropriate to talk about today but...'

She didn't let Francesca finish.

'That moment when you orgasm, when you come, everything disappears into this feeling, this moment of freedom, aliveness, pleasure!'

Francesca shuffled in her chair, uncomfortable, and not prepared to talk about the subject. Shay continued. 'You lose yourself completely... lose control and you just don't care! That was the feeling I started to chase. That connection you can create with someone, or something, which is higher than yourself.' She brushed her hands through her hair and pulled it back away from her face and looked directly at Francesca, who was still slightly lost for words. 'Have you ever had that feeling when you're in someone else's hands? You give them your body because you know, if you do, if you can trust and let go, they can make you feel alive ...' Shay leaned forward, intensifying their gaze and the distance between them. 'And I mean really alive... even for just a moment?'

Francesca tried to hold Shay's gaze, she didn't want to give her any satisfaction by reacting. She swallowed the lump in her throat and attempted to play cool, not let Shay have the upper hand.

'So, you're chasing the feeling of being alive?' She managed to keep her voice steady when she asked the question but Shay didn't want to let Francesca carry on without her answering her question first.

'You didn't answer my question!'

Francesca rubbed the back of her neck and started playing with her ear so she didn't have to look at Shay directly. 'Shall we move on?'

Shay stayed quiet. She didn't say anything or move but waited for Francesca to look at her.

'Do I make you uncomfortable, Francesca?'

Francesca looked up at her.

'Can I call you Francesca or do I have to call you doctor first?'

'No, you can call me whatever you want...' She realised how her statement sounded. 'I mean Francesca is fine.'

'I make you a little uncomfortable!'

Francesca quietly cleared her throat. 'What makes you say that?'

'Because I've noticed you touch and play with your ear a lot, when you're nervous or uncomfortable, the same as you squeeze the back of your neck when you're tired or stressed.'

Francesca realised she was still playing with her ear and stopped. She'd had enough of feeling that Shay was goading her.

'You were being purposely provocative. How am I supposed to act?'

'Maybe... but you deflected my sex and feeling alive question!'

'I didn't deflect it...'

Shay could hear the anger in Francesca's voice.

'I chose not to answer it. There's a difference.' She stated.

For the rest of the session they got nowhere. They both went back and forth deflecting each other's questions, when Shay did answer, it was with a sarcasm and allusiveness. Francesca was relieved when it was over.

CHAPTER THIRTY SEVEN

Francesca sat in her office at her desk working on her laptop when she heard a funny noise. After about the third time she realised it was her mobile vibrating. She'd forgotten to re-adjust it after putting it on silent during her appointments. It was Mia calling.

'Finally! I've been trying to reach you. Your mobile keeps going to answer phone. I was wondering if you fancied curry this Thursday night.'

Straight away Francesca was suspicious of the offer, and how particularly chirpy she was when asking. 'I thought we were having curry for your birthday?' Mia's birthday wasn't on Thursday night.

'So this is what I wanted to talk to you about...' Francesca knew it. Here it comes she thought. 'I want to go over to dads for my birthday.'

Francesca went silent.

'Mum?'

'But it's your birthday and I thought we could do something together after I've finished work?'

'Yeah, but you won't finish work until what, 7 or 8 o'clock? That's more or less the whole day gone! I could go straight to dads from school and hang out and he said he would take me out for a birthday dinner.'

Francesca was disappointed with the change of plans, but she didn't want to cause any more tension between the two of them. 'OK, I guess it's only fair you get to spend your birthday how you want to.'

'Thanks mum! We can do something together another time, I promise.'

CHAPTER THIRTY EIGHT

'So, how are you?' It was the first time Francesca had seen Jasmine since her collapse in her office.

'OK.' It was a tired answer.

Francesca could tell she was low in her mood.

'You had me worried last time. How come you didn't tell me you were diabetic?'

'I'm not diabetic. I have diabetes. There's a difference!'

'Sorry...' Francesca hadn't meant to offend her. She asked the same question again but corrected herself. 'How come you didn't tell me you have diabetes?'

'I didn't think it was that important.'

'Diabetes must be a huge part of your life! It's 24/7. Anything that takes that amount of attention is important.'

Jasmine said nothing. She just sat there staring at the floor.

Francesca attempted to reach her. 'Your mum said the doctors think you're passing out was due to a virus and your levels going off the scale.'

Jasmine scoffed. 'That's what she wants to believe!'

Francesca picked up on her tone and the way she said it. 'Is there something you're not telling me Jasmine?'

Jasmine slumped back against the sofa and pushed her back against the cushion. 'I don't take my insulin all the time...' she tried to play it down. 'It's no big deal.'

'What do you mean? You forget, or you don't take it on purpose?' Francesca wanted to be clear on what she was actually telling her.

'On purpose. That's why I became so sick.'

Francesca paused, a little shocked at the revelation. 'How long have you been missing your insulin for?'

'A few weeks, on and off.'

'Can you tell me why?' She was concerned. She hadn't been able to get the image of Jasmine, collapsing on her office floor out of her head and how ill she'd looked being put in the ambulance.

'I just had enough. Enough of never being able to have a break from it and enough of my mother asking me what my sugar levels are all the time, when I'm tired, or if I'm grumpy... and if that isn't frustrating enough then the doctors start on me about it. I'm tired of trying to control something that has no reasoning to it.'

'What do you mean by 'reasoning'?'

Jasmine tried to explain her reality. 'One day I can do something and my levels are fine. The next day I do the exact same thing and, nope, my sugar levels are all over the place. Do you know how frustrating that is?'

'No. I can't pretend to know either.' Francesca attempted to tread carefully, 'Do you think maybe that's what could be adding to your low mood? There's a strong link between diabetes and depression...'

'I had depression before I had diabetes!' Jasmine was irritated by the question, it ended up with silence between them.

Francesca contemplated what to say next. She didn't want to upset Jasmine even more, and take two steps back with her, but she was concerned for her health and safety.

'Jasmine, not taking your insulin is really dangerous. You could die!'

'Don't you get it? I don't care! I already feel dead inside. I don't feel anything. And besides, when I don't take my insulin it makes me feel more alive...'

Francesca shook her head. 'I don't understand?'

'My body aches and it hurts like hell, like I'm working on empty. Every movement is an effort, a focus, a purpose... It makes me feel something and that's better than nothing. The only time I feel something is when... is when I'm struggling.' She finished and went quiet again.

Francesca looked at her, wishing she could help her more, that she could make her see herself and her potential. She leant forward and lightly touched Jasmine's knee. It made Jasmine look up at her.

'When someone is living with depression, to feel any emotion, other than numbness, feels better. I understand that. Trust me.' She squeezed Jasmine's knee. 'But I promise you, Jasmine, you *can* feel something and you *can* feel alive without struggling and without jeopardizing your health, your life...'

'Don't you get it? Life 'is' struggling to me... It's never been any other way.' She moved her leg not wanting Francesca's hand on her knee anymore.

Francesca leaned back in her chair and took a deep breath. 'I guess what I'm trying to say is, it doesn't have to be.'

'Can you make me feel different? Erase my past? Make my body work properly again? Can you make me see the world differently?' It was intended as a rhetorical question but Francesca still tried to answer.

'No but...'

'You can't make me feel better then! I have a disease I'm stuck with for the rest of my life...'Jasmine became teary. 'I was only twelve when the doctors told me I was responsible for keeping myself alive. They seed fear with threats of losing limbs, heart disease, losing your eyesight...' A couple of tears fell down her face. 'No kid should be told that or given that much responsibility. And the depression? Well I've had that long enough to know I can't run away from it. None of it's fair... but that's life...'

'You're right, it's not fair. I haven't known you long but I can see you're a strong, intelligent, young lady. You can work through this Jasmine and come out the other end. I know it doesn't seem like it at the moment but you can and will feel better...'

'What if I don't want to feel better? What if I've felt this way for so long, I'm tired of fighting to try and be any other way?'

Francesca could hear the exhaustion in her voice, not just physically but emotionally as well. She gave it one more shot to try and get through to her.

'What would your grandfather say if he were here, now, talking to you?'

Jasmine stayed silent, staring at the wall behind Francesca, too tired to respond anymore. As she stared, a sparkle of light appeared by the wall right in front of her eyes. It was like a flash from a camera but a lot slower. Jasmine squinted at it, thinking she was so tired she was seeing things but out of nowhere, from the middle of the light her grandpa appeared. He was younger than she remembered him and he looked a lot healthier, he had a warm light glow all around his aura. He gave her a warm smile before he spoke.

'You're my granddaughter...my flesh and blood. We don't give up and we don't give in!'

'I can't do it anymore grandpa...'Jasmine's voice was desperate and exhausted. 'I'm tired of pretending I'm OK. I'm tired of seeing other people pretend they're OK. I just want to be with you.' Even though he was standing across the room, away from her, she felt the heat of his hand caress her cheek.

'I know kid. We will be together again... one day. All of this, what you're feeling right now, will be the making of you, I promise you. It will make you stronger.' He paused. 'Remember when you broke your arm that day at the beach?'

She remembered, it was too painful for her to forget. He continued. 'It hurt and you said it felt as though the bone was screaming with pain, and do you remember what I told you? I said if you're patient and give the bone a chance, it will realize it can heal itself, not only that but it will heal stronger and the pain will pass. People will tell you that being broken makes you weaker, but it's not true. Until you're broken you don't know what you're made of. It gives you the ability to build yourself all over again, stronger than before. Everything evolves and *changes if you can hold on and let it. Give it a chance and this will pass, kid.'* He smiled and blurred, dissolving back into the light he had come from.

Even though he had disappeared Jasmine could still feel a warmth in her heart and she knew he'd put it there, like a parting gift. It made her feel stronger in herself and a bit more resilient.

'Jasmine, are you OK?' The sound of Francesca's voice brought her attention back into the room. She felt a bit dazed wondering if what she'd just seen had been real or not. 'You're staring into space!' Francesca continued.

Jasmine smiled. She didn't care if it was real or not. She felt a new sense of strength and hope that made her want to keep trying. She answered Francesca's very first question about her grandpa.

'He would tell me... not to give up!'

Francesca was surprised at how she said it, as though she'd had some quick turnaround that she hadn't been part of or aware of. She didn't know what had happened or what Jasmine had thought when she was staring into space but she could see, within the space of a minute, that Jasmine had completely changed. As if she had her fighting spirit back in her again. She felt a sense of relief and calm herself.

'Do you think you can do that, for your grandpa?'

'I guess so. I'll try.' Jasmine exhaled.

CHAPTER THIRTY NINE

Mia had caught the number six bus to her dad's apartment. One of her teachers had called in sick at the last minute, so the whole class were free to leave and have a study afternoon. She'd had enough of studying and had decided to surprise her dad by showing up early at his apartment.

She reached his building's front door and went to buzz his number when a group of people walked out. One of the men in the group recognised her from the few times she'd been before. He gave her a friendly smile and held the door open for her. Mia smiled at him, as a thank you, and walked on through towards the lift. She pressed the button for the fourth floor.

It didn't take long for the lift to arrive at David's floor. She strolled down the wide corridor to number twenty four and knocked, excited to see his surprise at seeing her. She waited a while but nobody answered so she put her ear to the door. She could just about make out her father's voice and someone else's. Assuming he was watching television she knocked again but this time harder and louder.

David opened the door and was shocked to see her. 'Mia!'

He shouted louder than she thought necessary and didn't invite her in but stood behind the door almost hugging it to his body.

'Hey, dad.'

He made sure the door was only open slightly so that Mia couldn't see in. 'I, eh, wasn't expecting you.'

'I thought I'd surprise you as Thursday's your day off. I have a last minute study day so I thought we could hang out?'

'Thursday?' He was trying to buy time. 'Yes it usually is, but not today, I'm eh, working from home. Could you maybe come back another day? I don't mean to be rude but I'm busy.'

Mia was suspicious of the way he was acting. Something didn't seem right for her. David didn't say anything else but just stood there waiting and hoping she would leave.

'David.... David?' He dropped his head knowing Mia would have heard Melanie call him.

'Who's that dad? I heard...'

'Mia...' He tried to passively push Mia back by taking a step forward, out of his apartment.

'David?' This time Melanie's call was louder. By the look on Mia's face David knew it was pointless to try and continue so he stepped back and allowed Mia to walk in.

'Who is it babe? Tell them to go away!' Melanie didn't know Mia was in the apartment as she walked in from the living room. She froze as soon as she saw Mia by the entrance.

Mia looked down at her growing swollen belly. 'What the hell dad?' She turned around to face him.

'Mia, listen honey, this isn't what it looks like. I can explain!'

Upset and embarrassed, she didn't want to listen to what he had to say. She was so angry it set a ringing off in her ears. 'I see what Mark means now! He always said you were an arsehole but I just didn't see it! Well I see it now!' She stomped past him to leave, he tried to stop her but she shrugged him off and slammed the door behind her.

David glared over at Melanie who was still standing in the same spot. She pulled a face at him. 'Whoops! I guess she had to find out sooner or later right?'

'Francesca is going to kill me!'

CHAPTER FORTY

Francesca and Jamie were forty five minutes into their session, their conversation flowed, he didn't see her as a stranger so much now and felt more comfortable talking to her.

'I stayed over at my friend's house a few times when I was a kid. It was the first time I realised other people's fathers weren't always walking around obliterated by alcohol. I always got fed and slept well at their houses, I knew I was safe.'

'Did you go hungry a lot?'

'Yes and no. I think my body just adapted.'

Francesca felt sorry for him. She couldn't imagine letting her children go hungry. 'Where was your mother when you were hungry and looking for food?'

'Most days she barely came out of her bedroom. Her nerves were shot and the tablets the doctor had her on, more or less, left her comatosed. I would take Lucy over to our aunt, my dad's sister, who was ten years older than him and had a family of her own. We only went over there when we got really hungry because I didn't want to bother them. They were struggling, in their own way, as well.' It was the first time Jamie had spoken about his Aunt to Francesca.

'How come there was such a big age gap between the two of them?'

'My grandma was pregnant a few times after my aunt, but she couldn't carry the babies to full term. Apparently my dad was a miracle!' He didn't hide the irony in his voice saying it. 'She didn't expect to carry him to full term either. I used to wonder if maybe it would have been better if she hadn't.'

It went quiet. Francesca waited to see if he was going to say something else but he didn't.

'Are you close to your aunt?'

'I help her out now and then with jobs around the house. I was over there the other day and she mentioned something about dad. She thinks I should give him a chance to explain why he was the way he was.'

'Do you want to give him a chance to explain?'

'I don't know...' He looked down at his feet and shuffled them with angst. 'I don't know if I can.'

'We could consider inviting your father to one of your sessions. It would be a safe space to explore with him what was going on and it might help you move on'

Jamie wasn't sure his father would want to show up at a therapy session, let alone if it would be helpful.

CHAPTER FORTY ONE

The reception door swung open with some force which startled Julie, who nearly spilt the cup of milky coffee in her hand. Mia walked in with a face like thunder, it didn't take a genius to tell she wasn't happy about something.

'Mia darling, what's the matter? What's happened?'

'I need to see mum!'

'She's in with a client but after...'

Mia ignored her, not prepared to wait, and rushed down the corridor towards Francesca's office. Before Julie could even get out from behind her desk Mia was at Francesca's door and barged in to her office.

'I need to talk to you!'

Francesca was shocked to see her daughter in her office doorway.

'In a minute Mia, as you can see I'm busy...' She tried to remain professional, for Jamie's sake and her own.

She got up and walked past Jamie and gave Mia a warning glare as she approached her. Mia stepped back, out of the door, knowing her mum was less than impressed.

Francesca closed the door and went back to her seat, apologising to Jamie for the interruption.

'I'm so sorry, Jamie. That shouldn't have happened...' She sat back down and picked her notes up. 'My daughter is very stressed at the moment with exams.'

'No problem...' He glanced down at his watch, completely unfazed by the interruption 'We were finishing anyway.' He stood up to leave.

'Will you think about what I said with regards to inviting your father here?'

'I'll think about it.' He took his jacket from the back of the sofa and left.

As soon as he exited Mia rushed straight back in, too angry and upset to care about the consequences.

'What do you think you were doing?' Francesca was fuming. 'I was in a private session, that's supposed to be confidential, with a client. Don't you ever do that again, you hear me?'

Mia didn't care that her mum was angry. 'Why didn't you tell me?'

'Tell you what?'

'That dad's got a girlfriend!' she shouted.

Francesca calmed down now that she realised why Mia was in such a state.

'Listen sweetheart, your dad and I were going to tell you but we were just waiting for the right time.'

'The right time?' Mia was the one raging now. Francesca had never seen her so angry. 'And when might that be? When the baby's here?'

'What? What are you talking about? What baby?'

Mia could tell, by her mum's confusion, that she had absolutely no idea about Melanie's pregnancy.

'You don't know? You haven't seen her? She's pregnant, mum!' She burst into tears.

Francesca hurried over to her and hugged her tightly.

'I'm sorry, I should have told you about his girlfriend. I was just trying to...'

Feeling betrayed Mia, abruptly, pulled away from her hold.

'I can't trust you, either of you!' She turned to leave.

'Mia, please...'

Mia didn't wait. She stormed straight out just as quickly as she'd stormed in.

As soon as Francesca finished work she drove over to David's apartment. She was just as angry with him now as she was two hours ago when Mia had told her about the baby.

She buzzed his apartment and waited for him to answer. David didn't pick up to speak with her, he saw her standing there in the camera and buzzed her up. He'd expected her to show up, sometime soon, after Mia had left. He took the time, before Francesca reached his door, to figure out exactly what he was going to say to her.

Francesca paced straight in and said nothing at first. She took a long glance around his apartment.

'Is she here, your girlfriend?' Her voice was lower and calmer than he had imagined it would be.

'No.'

'Good...' She raised her voice. 'What did you do?'

He suspected, by her level of annoyance, that she knew about the baby.

'I'm sorry. It's not how I wanted things to go...'

'She's pregnant?'

'Yes.'

'I can't believe you! I hope you realise that what you've done has destroyed our family.'

'That's rich coming from you Cesca. You were the one who started it!' Incensed, he raised his voice to match her level. 'You never really loved me. You never let me in. I always loved you more. You were the one who became distant. After the kids you totally ignored me... I needed to get the love and attention from somewhere, someone.'

Francesca couldn't believe what she was hearing. It was as if he was trying to make out he was the poor, hard done by husband that got no affection or attention.

'I was looking after our children David! You go off and have an affair because I didn't *let you in?* So it's my fault!'

'I was lonely Cesca. I needed to feel loved.

Her voice started to break with emotion. 'I can't, fucking, believe you! This whole marriage has always been about you. I more or less brought the children up by myself because you were still away working, living the 'bachelor' life with all you friends. Not once did you offer to put the kids to bed, take them to school, cook them dinner...'

He was upset by the accusation. 'I made them dinner...'

'When? Tell me when?'

He didn't reply. He couldn't think of a time. 'That's not the point Francesca!'

'No, that's not the point! I think the point is that you having an affair has saved me from putting up with you and your bullshit for any longer.' She went to leave.

'Whatever! Look at yourself, Francesca! One day you're going to break! *Miss perfect* can't last forever. Even you will make a mistake one day.'

She didn't bother to look back at him. 'I already made a mistake. It was marrying you!'

Mia went home after leaving Francesca's office. She spent ten minutes trying to calm down but felt she needed to talk to Mark. She ran straight up to her bedroom and called him on her mobile.

'I've just seen dad. He's got some woman pregnant!'

Mark was shocked. 'I can't believe he's got her pregnant. I feel sorry for the kid already!' He'd forgotten Mia didn't know he knew about Melanie and he kicked himself for the slip.

Mia was silent at the end of the phone. 'You knew about her?' She couldn't believe it.

'I knew about the affair but I didn't know about the baby.' He knew it wasn't going to make any difference, Mia was going to be angry with him for keeping it from her.

'Why didn't you tell me?'

'I'm sorry Mia. I just didn't want to upset you with you taking your exams and...'

'I wish people would stop talking about my exams!' She was tired of it being used as an excuse by other people. 'I can't believe you Mark! I thought, at least, you would tell me the truth! You're just as bad as them. Treating me like a kid as well!' She put the phone down on him and began to pace her room, when she heard the front door open and the sound of footsteps running up the stairs. Francesca knocked and opened her bedroom door.

'Mia, listen. I'm so sorry! I know you're probably feeling really angry right now and that's understandable...'

'Don't bloody shrink me right now mum! I'm not one of your patients, clients, whatever you call them!' She grabbed her bag and headed for the door, to leave.

'Where are you going?'

'I'm going to be around people who I trust, who tell me the truth!'

Mia took the number nine bus to Stacey's house. Stacey was surprised to see her. She didn't want to stay at her house, it was full of her mother's friends, so they agreed to go into town.

Mia didn't say or talk about anything regarding her family. She didn't really feel that Stacey was the kind of friend to talk about things like that because her own family was so dysfunctional. Instead, she suggested they go to the cinema to watch a movie and just hang out.

They both stood outside the cinema while Stacey took the last few puffs of the cigarette she'd stolen from the packet her mum had left in the kitchen. As she stubbed it out she noticed Josh walking towards them from across the street, grinning at Mia.

Stacey put two and two together. 'What did you invite him for?'

'Relax, he's cool when you get to know him.' Mia had texted him to see if he wanted to come.

Josh saw Stacey as he approached Mia, he was a bit disappointed she was there as well since he didn't like her much, but he didn't want it to spoil his time with Mia.

'Hi, Mia. I brought you this...' He handed her a present wrapped in birthday paper, 'for tomorrow, so you can open it on your birthday!'

'Thank you. You didn't have to!' She was too embarrassed to open it in front of them so she put it straight in her bag, to open later.

'Hi Josh!' Stacey pretended to be overly friendly toward him.

'Stacey.' He didn't play along, he kept his tone low.

Stacey lost interest with him and looked over at Mia. 'If it's your birthday tomorrow, that's perfect! Do you know why? It means we can celebrate and I've got just the thing...' She opened the top of her bag and revealed a large bottle of vodka. 'We can drink it while we watch the movie!'

'You're not seriously going to drink that?' Josh thought it was one of the most stupid ideas Stacey had ever had.

'You don't have to join us, Joshy! Come on Mia.' She dragged Mia into the cinema by the arm. Josh followed behind them wishing, even more, that it was just him and Mia watching the movie and not Stacey as well.

By the time the film had finished the girls were pretty drunk, having drunk at least half of the bottle. They left the cinema with Josh tagging behind them. He was concerned about Mia and wasn't happy with the state she was in. As she raised the bottle to her mouth again, to take another swig, he tried to grab it from her, but she pushed him away and, purposely, took a bigger gulp just to spite him.

Josh looked at her. 'Don't you think you've had enough?'

'You're not my father, Josh, so leave me alone!' She stared at him and took another swig.

'Yeah Josh!' Stacey took the bottle from Mia and took a swig for herself.

Josh had had enough. He wasn't prepared to stay and watch them get drunk and rowdy. 'Whatever, I'm not going to hang out with you if you're just going to get even more rat-faced.'

'You may as well leave now then because I have no plans to stop drinking!'

Three older men, in their thirties, who'd been walking behind them when they left the cinema, had watched the interaction between them and noticed how tipsy Stacey and Mia were. One of the men in the group saw an opportunity and decided to approach them.

'Hi there! You look like you're having fun! My friends and I would love to take you lovely ladies out for a drink. What do you say?'

Stacey, drunkenly, leaned on the stranger's shoulder. 'See Josh, some people want to have fun!' She put her arm around the man and looked at Mia. 'You coming, Mia?'

Josh panicked when he saw Mia consider it. 'Mia you can't seriously go off with these guys when you don't even know them. Let me take you back home.'

'No, Josh. I'm going with them.' She walked away from him and went with Stacey and the stranger to join his friends, leaving Josh feeling helpless as he watched them stroll away.

CHAPTER FORTY TWO

Stacey and Mia walked down the street with the men. One of them finished his cigarette and daggled his arm around Stacey's shoulders.

'Come on. Let's get some food. I'm starving!' He leaned over and kissed Stacey on the cheek.

They ended up in Yani's, it was one of the only restaurants still open. They strolled and took the empty corner table nearest the window. Shay had been working the whole day and was close to finishing her shift when she walked over to take their order. Straight away she recognised Mia and noticed how much older than her the men were. She wondered how Mia knew them but she didn't say anything. She just kept an eye on Mia as she took their order and served them their drinks.

Nathan, who was sitting next to Mia, put his arm around her and encouraged her to drink the beer he'd ordered for her. Mia could smell his aftershave and body odour as he leaned in closer.

'Come on, darling, drink up. We've got a good night ahead of us!' He winked at his mate sitting across the table.

Mia went to take a sip of the beer but was distracted by the vibration of her phone in her pocket. She took it out and had to focus her eyes to read the screen. It was a text message from Francesca.

Please call me. I'm worried about you. Please don't do anything stupid. I love you. Mum xx.

Remembering how annoyed she was with her whole family, she tucked her phone back in her pocket and swigged the beer. The men cheered and toasted her as she aimlessly glugged half the bottle in one. When she put it back down on the table, for the first time, she started to feel woozy, as though her head was spinning at a 100mph. The mix of spirits and beer were taking their effect on her body.

'I don't feel so good...' She mumbled.

'Come on Mia! I've had way more than you. You can't stop now!' Stacey didn't want to finish the night there, and she, certainly, didn't want Mia to chicken out either.

Nathan spotted Shay walking back towards them.

'Ah here comes the waitress! Let's have another bottle of wine and three beers.'

Shay had finished her shift and wanted nothing to do with them but she was worried about leaving Mia with them. 'I'm off duty now so you'll have to ask another member of staff.' She looked at Mia and Stacey. 'I just came to check on the girls before I go.' She touched Mia's arm gently who could only just about lift her head to look at her. 'Are you OK?'

Nathan answered for her. 'Of course she's OK. They both are, aren't you girls? They're grownups. They can handle a few drinks!'

Shay ignored him and kneeled down at Mia's level so she didn't have to lift her head again. 'What's your name?' she asked softly.

'Mia.'

'Hi Mia. I'm Shay.' Shay smiled to try and reassure her. 'How old are you?'

Mia didn't answer so Stacey spoke for her. 'She's twenty one. We both are.'

Shay didn't believe her, she squeezed Mia's arm a little to try and get her to focus. 'Mia look at me. How old are you?'

Mia slowly turned her head towards Shay. 'Sixteen.' She mumbled it but it was clear enough for Nathan to hear, he quickly pulled away from her.

'What the fuck! You never said you were that young!'

Mia slurred her words. 'You never asked...'

Stacey saw the look on Nathan's face as the man with her took his arm from around her shoulders. She was annoyed with how quickly things had changed. Before Mia had opened her big mouth they'd all been having fun, as far as she was concerned.

'She doesn't know what she's saying! Look at her, she's drunk!' She sounded as if she was pleading with them.

Nathan stood up and pulled his wallet out of his back pocket. He threw a few notes into the middle of the table and glanced at Shay, who was still holding onto Mia's arm. 'For the bill, keep the change.' He looked around at the others. 'Come on guys...' His friends got up to leave with him. 'We don't have time to babysit school kids.'

'I'm not a kid. She's sixteen but I'm older!' Stacey didn't want to be left behind.

The man she had thought was interested in her turned around. 'Whatever! Call me when you're at least eighteen!' They left the restaurant, leaving Stacey speechless.

Shay could feel Mia shivering so she took the jacket that she had put on to leave, and put it around Mia's shoulders to help try and keep her warm. Stacey came around from her shock and looked at Mia.

'Nice one! You're a loser Mia!'

Shay glared up at her. 'Hey, watch your mouth! Can't you see she's not well?'

'Whatever, I'm out of here.' Stacey left, leaving Shay by herself to help Mia up from her seat. She was wobbly and unsteady so Shay put Mia's arm around her neck, to help support her. They left Yani's and got about two streets away from Shay's car when Mia jolted forward and vomited on the pavement before she passed out. After a long shift Shay was too tired to hold her up, she had to let her slowly collapse onto the ground so she didn't seriously hurt herself.

'Shit, Mia... Mia?' Shay could see the mist come from her mouth as her breath hit the cold, dark, night air, she gently tapped Mia on the cheek to see if she would stir, but she didn't make any movement. 'How much have you had to drink?' She knew she was talking to herself, Mia was out cold.

Francesca hadn't heard from Mia and she couldn't sleep. In bed, she couldn't settle herself or switch her brain off because she was thinking about her. Completely awake, she got out of bed and started to clean the kitchen, something she would always do when she couldn't sleep. She'd sorted a couple of the cupboards out and was about to clean the fridge when her mobile rang. Out of habit she'd brought it down with her. She quickly pulled her rubber gloves off and picked it up. She could see it was Mia calling. 'Mia? Thank god! Please come home so we can talk...'

'Hello? Francesca is that you?'

Shay recognised Francesca's voice straight away. She'd found Mia's mobile and had looked through her contacts to find the number. Francesca was surprised and confused to hear Shay's voice on the other end of the phone.

'Shay?' There was a pause between them, 'why do you have my daughter's phone?'

'I'm at the hospital with her. She had a bit too much to drink and collapsed...'

Francesca felt her heart drop into her stomach with fear. 'Is she OK? I'll be there as quick as I can!'

She got to the hospital and asked one of the nurses on duty where her daughter was. The nurse led her to a side room where Mia was in a bed, connected to a drip feeding her fluids, and a mask giving her oxygen. Shay was next to her in one of the arm chairs brought in for visitors to use.

Francesca rushed over to Mia's side, took hold of her hand and looked at her. Mia looked as pale as a ghost, her sweaty hair stuck to her forehead. Francesca couldn't really take it all in. She was just too relieved to see her.

Mia opened her eyes to see who had grabbed and was holding her hand. She saw it was her mum and lifted her oxygen mask.

'Mum. I'm sorry...I'm sorry...' Her voice was rough and dry.

'It's OK... I'm sorry... I'm sorry, sweetheart.' She stroked her hair back from her forehead. She could feel the sweat under her fringe as she tucked it behind Mia's ear, but as she gazed into her daughter's eyes they begin to roll back. 'Mia? Mia? Nurse...' Francesca shouted with complete panic. 'Nurse!' Nobody came in. For the first time she looked across at Shay, who jumped up, as if she knew what she was asking, and ran out of the room. She found a doctor and nurse talking, half way down the corridor, and called to them.

'We need some help!'

They both rushed directly into Mia's room and found her fitting in the bed. The nurse ran straight to the alarm behind the bed and pressed it, while the doctor began to check Mia and her vital signs. Shay and Francesca could do nothing but watch helplessly.

'Looks like it could be alcohol poisoning...' the doctor said to the nurse, he turned to Francesca and Shay. 'I'm going to have to ask you to leave.'

'No! She's my daughter. I'm not going to leave her!'

The doctor hadn't got time to argue with her. Shay gently took Francesca's hand from behind and encouraged her to the side of the room. Francesca gripped Shay's hand, full of fear, as Shay spoke gently and confidently in her ear.

'Let them do their job. She'll be OK. Just let them work.'

They left the room as another doctor and two more nurses entered.

A porter showed them into a private family room. Shay shut the door behind them. The room went completely quiet as Francesca paced up and down unable to stand the silence or stillness of the room.

'That's my baby! She's my baby... I wasn't there for her!' She began rubbing and squeezing the back of her neck to try and release some stress. 'I wasn't... I wasn't. I've just been working, ignoring... carrying on...' Her body gave in to the shock and adrenaline and she began to slowly sink to the floor.

Shay saw what was happening and rushed to catch her before she hit the ground. She pulled Francesca back up onto her feet and held her. As Francesca gripped and clung to Shay, she began to cry.

Shay whispered into her ear. 'I've got you... I've got you...'

Francesca cried harder and released the weight of her body onto her. Shay held her, supporting her, not letting her go.

It took Francesca about forty minutes to calm down and stop crying. Shay went to fetch her a cup of tea while they were waiting for news of Mia. She cautiously passed it to Francesca.

'Careful! It's hot! I mean of course it's hot... It's a hot cup of tea, right?'' She felt nervous, all of a sudden, as she'd had time to assimilate what had just happened between them.

Francesca took the hot cup from her. 'Thank you.'

Shay sat down next to her. The seats were so close that the side of their legs touched. The room fell quiet again and they both became aware of the silence and the closeness of their bodies next to one another.

Shay felt Francesca's body stiffen.

'I must look a complete mess. Crying for so long...' She wiped her red, swollen eyes.

'You look great, I mean nice... It makes a change that you're the one crying and not me...' Shay couldn't seem to control her mouth. 'I realise how that just sounded. Obviously I don't want you to cry...' She was fumbling for her words and it made Francesca smile a bit. She could appreciate the situation they were in.

'No?'

'No, *oui*.' Shay wished she could stop herself. 'I'll stop talking in a minute!'

They both laughed from the awkward tension of not knowing what to say. It dawned on Francesca how vulnerable she'd just been with her.

Shay tried to think of something sensible and useful to say.

'She'll be OK, you know. She's in the best hands.'

Francesca took her first sip of her tea. 'How can you be so sure?'

Shay contemplated whether or not to tell Francesca how she knew. 'My mum... she fitted a couple of times after she'd drunk too much. I brought her into A&E. They would pump her stomach and send her home a couple of days later. It wasn't pleasant to see and she was pretty groggy afterwards, but she was OK.'

Francesca looked up at her. She had no idea she had witnessed that kind of thing with her mother. Shay stared at her, waiting for her to say something. 'Shay, I...'

They were interrupted by the door opening as the doctor walked in. 'Sorry, I didn't mean to disturb you...'

Francesca was confused. Why he would think he was disturbing them? It took her a few seconds to realise how close she was to Shay, almost as if she was leaning in towards her.

The doctor continued. 'I thought you might like to know she's OK.'

Francesca leaped up from her seat. 'What happened? Is she awake?'

'Your daughter's drunk a lot of alcohol and it's poisoned her system. That's why she started fitting. We had to pump her stomach and we're pushing fluids through her. She's very drowsy but awake. You can go back in and see her when you're ready.'

Francesca felt that she could breathe out for the first time in a long while. 'Thank you, doctor.' He smiled at her and left the room.

Shay picked up Francesca's jacket, from the back of the seat, and passed it to her. Their hands touched momentarily, making them both aware they were alone again.

'I'd better be going. I'll leave you to it.' Shay brushed her hair back, 'I'm glad she's OK.'

'You don't have to go. She'll probably want to thank you.' Francesca felt awkward all of a sudden. She was aware it sounded as though she wanted her to stay. She attempted to cover it. 'I mean you can go if you want...'

Shay looked at her. She felt a little frightened at the intensity and intimacy they'd shared, not just tonight, but in their sessions as well. She'd seen a different side to Francesca because she hadn't done her usual teasing and pushing of her buttons. She'd felt and witnessed Francesca's vulnerability.

'It's probably best I go.' She could barely look at how raw and vulnerable Francesca was as she stood in front of her, it made her realise that this wasn't a game. Francesca had real feelings and emotions. She wasn't just some shrink to play cat and mouse with. 'Give Mia my best though.'

CHAPTER FORTY THREE

Mia had been moved to a ward to recover and she'd been fast asleep ever since. Francesca sat patiently, holding her hand, waiting for her to rouse. After a while Mia eventually opened her eyes.

'Mum...' Her voice was even huskier than before. The tube that had been put down her throat, to empty her stomach, had scratched it slightly. 'I'm so sorry. I was stupid. I was just so mad at everyone and...'

Francesca took her hand to try and calm her down. 'No. I'm sorry, more than you could ever know. I wasn't there for you. I should have seen the signs. I'm a psychologist for god's sake, and I should have known you weren't coping, but I was too wrapped up in work, trying to ignore what's...' She didn't want to go into what was going on for her. She wanted to be there, in the moment, with Mia. 'I could have handled everything better.'

'Ignoring stuff doesn't make it go away.'

'Careful, you sound like me talking to one of my clients!' They both grinned at one another. Mia squeezed Francesca's hand and carried on the joke.

'Maybe I should study psychology! Grandma would be pleased with that!'

Francesca laughed as she stroked Mia's hair. She looked into her daughter's eyes, overwhelmed with love for her. 'I want to talk like this, like we used to. Why don't we talk anymore?'

'You started working more and more...' Mia could see the hurt on Francesca's face from her comment, she knew it might upset her, but now, more than ever, seemed to be the best time to be honest about how she felt. 'And my hormones happened!' Mia knew she had to take some responsibility for their change in relationship. She was well aware she hadn't been the easiest person to be around recently.

CHAPTER FORTY FOUR

Francesca stayed with Mia, at the hospital until around 4.30am.

She drove home and went straight to bed, exhausted by the roller coaster of events. As soon as her head hit the pillow she fell into a deep sleep, so deep that she didn't realise she was dreaming.

She got out of bed and walked towards her en-suite shower. She switched the shower on and let the water run for a bit, so the water would be hot on her skin and achy muscles.

The room began to fill up with steam. She got undressed and stepped in to the shower, and stood under the gushing water, letting it soothe her tension. She tilted her head up and ran her fingers through her wet hair. As she began to wash away the stress of the day she heard the shower door open behind her. Garth appeared and joined her. He stepped forward under the water. Francesca acted as though she'd expected him, as he began to slowly kiss across the top of her shoulder.

Liking the sensation, Francesca leaned back into his body and pressed against his skin. He moved his mouth onto her neck and slowly kissed along the side of it. She groaned as he reached her ear lobe.

Aroused, Francesca turned to kiss him, but as she did she realised it was Shay not Garth. She hesitated. Staring at Shay, who was hungry to kiss her and focused on her lips, Francesca leaned in and softly kissed her. Almost instantly her body responded to Shay's as a wave of excitement and desire shot through her. She lifted her head up and moaned out loud, as if it was exhausting keeping the energy she felt in her body.

Shay placed her hand loosely around Francesca's throat, so she could angle it up to the right. She kissed along her neckline and was about to move her hands and mouth onto her breast when Francesca heard a distant noise in the background.

'What's that noise?' She couldn't hear properly over the sound of the running water.

Shay was more interested in carrying on kissing her. 'I don't care...' She whispered in Francesca's ear.

BEEP...BEEP...BEEP.

Francesca woke up startled by the beeping of her alarm clock. She sat up in bed and switched the alarm off realising the sound must have transferred into her dream. She lay back down and slammed her head on her pillow. She stared at her bedroom ceiling, replaying the dream and the response her body had to Shay's. She could still feel it in her body. 'Fuck!'

Later in the morning, anxious, and not being able to clear her head of thoughts about Shay, Francesca panicked and phoned Garth to arrange a lunch date.

Exhausted from the few hours' sleep she'd had Francesca slowly drove into town to meet Garth. She found it hard to control her thoughts during lunch. All she could think about was Shay at the hospital, how supportive she'd been and the times they had accidently touched...

'So how's your sandwich?' Garth waited for her response, oblivious, to what was going through her head. 'Francesca, where are you? You seem miles away today.'

The sound of a plate being dropped, by one of the waitresses, brought her back into the room. 'No, yes. It's good, thank you... Thank you for agreeing to meet up with me this afternoon. I haven't been sleeping well lately, so I might not be good company.' She knew she would begin to warble at him if she didn't stop. 'It's nice to get out for lunch!'

'It's my pleasure!' Garth took a bite out of his sandwich and stared at Francesca. He swallowed his mouthful and took a sip of water. 'How would you like to go out with me for dinner on Friday? This time I promise we'll skip the crap movie!'

Francesca thought about kissing Shay in the dream again, and tried to reframe it as Garth in her head. It felt more comfortable and realistic that way. 'That sounds good. Where do you have in mind?'

CHAPTER FORTY
FIVE

Jamie felt sick as he stood in front of the front door, on the doorstep. He gripped his fist and knocked. It didn't take long for the door to be answered.

'Son!' Richard was shocked to see his son standing outside his house. It was the last place he had expected to see him after such a long time. Jamie looked at his father. He thought he looked younger than his fifty three years, he felt a bit resentful that the years had obviously been kind to him. Richard stood there waiting for Jamie to say something but he didn't, he just stared. 'I didn't expect to see you here, come in... come in.'

He showed him through to the living room. Jamie noted that the décor and style of the house seemed quite upper class, it must have cost a good amount of money, he thought. It was completely different, and a world away, from what Jamie had grown up in. He wondered if it was his father's money or that of the woman he'd married.

Not wanting to take a seat, Jamie remained standing. The room was full of photos of Richard and his wife looking happy together. 'You're still married then?' Jamie didn't even try to hide his bitterness at his father's new life.

Richard ignored his tone. He understood, and expected, he probably wouldn't be pleased for him. 'Yes, five years now. Janet is the best thing that's ever happened to me.' The declaration triggered Jamie's insecurity of never feeling good enough for him.

'I was, and never will be good enough for you, will I?'

'No, son. Sorry, that's not what I mean.' He regretted not thinking about what he'd said since he didn't want to upset Jamie even more. Jamie said nothing and looked at him in amazement.

'What is it?' Richard wondered what he had said now. Was it calling him son? Was it too soon, he wondered?

Jamie got over his initial shock and found his voice to answer. 'I think that's the first time I've ever heard you apologise. You always told me a man should never apologise...'

Richard was glad and relieved he hadn't offended him again. 'I'm a different person now. I've changed. I'm not that person anymore... I know I don't deserve your forgiveness, but can you forgive me son?'

It felt strange hearing him call him son again. He hadn't heard it for so long and he hated the fact that he liked it, that he'd missed it. 'Forgive you for what?' Jamie tested him to see what he would admit to or what he thought he needed forgiveness for.

'For not being there for you.'

Jamie waited for the rest, but Richard didn't say anything else. 'Is that it? Is that all you think you need forgiveness for?' He was annoyed and couldn't help but raise his voice. 'How about when you came home drunk, abusive and oh, how about the times you hit me?'

Richard found it uncomfortable hearing about, and being reminded, of how he used to treat him. He tried to explain himself and his behaviour. 'I did that because I had to, for your own good, to protect you...'

Jamie couldn't believe the words coming out of his father's mouth. He'd heard enough. He went to leave, but stopped and turned in the doorway, fed up with carrying so much anger around. He turned to face his father. 'You haven't changed one bit! I'm so foolish! I came here to... My therapist suggested asking you to join me in therapy so I don't have to feel like this anymore. So I can move on from my childhood and be the best father I can for my baby, so I'm not like you were!' He checked Richard up and down. 'Now I see there's no point because you haven't changed a bit! You're in just as much denial as you were when I was a kid. You don't hit your child to protect them!' He slammed the living room door and then the front door behind him.

He was still angry and full of rage when he arrived home. As he entered he tripped over a pair of Maggie's shoes which she'd left in the corridor. 'How many times Maggie!'

Maggie popped her head around the corner, having heard him. 'What? You've only just come through the door and you're grumpy with me already?'

'How many times have I told you not to leave your shoes here? Put them under the stairs...' He grabbed them from the floor and violently chucked them under the stairs.

Maggie, fed up with Jamie's attitude, picked them up and began to put them on. 'Do you know what Jamie? I'm leaving! If I had known being pregnant would turn you into this horrible, grumpy, violent person, I would have...'

'Don't call me violent! I'm not violent...' Distraught at her choice of words he broke down crying. 'Please don't call me...'

Maggie was shocked to see how upset he was. She knew the way he'd been acting was out of character, but for him to be this distraught worried her. She moved over towards him and held him. His body went completely defenceless in her arms.

'I'm not like him. I'm not, I can't be...'

She wasn't sure who he was talking about. 'Like who Jamie? Talk to me, tell me what's going on with you?' She held his face in her hand, to try and get him to look at her.

'My father, I can't be like him...'

Maggie gave him a few minutes to calm down before she led him into the living room and sat down next to him, on the sofa, gripping his hand tightly. She waited patiently for him to start speaking again.

'When he was drunk, he didn't know how hard he was hitting...' He wanted, and was ready, to tell her everything. 'Once he hit me so hard I think he broke one of my ribs. I was in agony for weeks but never told anyone.' Maggie squeezed his hand. 'He just didn't know when to stop.'

'Why didn't you tell me?'

'I couldn't. I was ashamed, in denial...' He paused and breathed out. 'Just like him. I'm angry at him for doing something I'm doing myself! What if I'm like him in more ways? What if when the baby comes I... I...'

Maggie wiped away a tear from her cheek. She couldn't bear to see him in this much pain. She took his face between her hands again. 'Now, you look at me, Jamie Malin! You are nothing like that! You are going to be the best father to our baby!'

'You can't know that Maggie. How can you know that? Look how I've been recently...'

'I know it because you're a good person.'

Jamie moved her hands away from his face and got up to walk across to the other side of the room 'I feel like I'm falling apart. Seeing him today...'

'You've seen him?'

'Dr Francesca suggested it.'

Maggie didn't understand. 'Who's Dr Francesca?'

'She's the therapist I've been seeing. I was going to tell you but I wasn't quite ready...'

'So that's where you've been going and who you've been talking to on the phone?' She was relieved he hadn't been cheating on her for all this time. She got up from the sofa and walked over to him and kissed him on the lips.

He looked at her lovingly. 'I'm sorry I lied to you...'

Maggie could see the shame on his face. She kissed him again, more passionately. 'You don't think I'm less of a man for talking to someone?'

She gave him a long look and tried to answer his question with another kiss, but he still looked at her waiting for a verbal answer. 'I think you're more of a man for talking to someone! It's brave, having the guts to face your past pain, so you can be the best version of yourself for your family.' Jamie kissed her softly and leant his head on her shoulder. 'Shall we go upstairs?' Maggie asked.

When In the bedroom they slowly and attentively took each other's clothes off, one item at a time. Lying on the bed next to Maggie, Jamie ran his mouth down her body, softly touching her skin with his lips. He kissed every inch of her body and then stopped at her swollen, pregnant belly.

'How can I love and want someone so much that I haven't even met yet?'

Maggie beamed at him with joy, she brought his face back up towards hers and kissed him deeply. They made love to one another gently and slowly, for the first time in years, Jamie felt he'd had a weight lifted from his shoulders, knowing he'd been so honest with the woman he loved and the mother of his child. There was no longer a secret between them to push them apart.

CHAPTER FORTY SIX

Francis had been in the supermarket, picking up everything she needed for her weekly shop when she realised she had forgotten to get fresh bread. She returned to the bakery section to look for her favourite crusty, olive bread, which was baked, specially, in store. There was none on the shelf so she went to the cake isle to see if a member of staff was available, but panicked when she saw Chris with another woman, looking at the cupcakes. She froze as she watched him put his hand, affectionately, on her back. She didn't recognise her but could tell she was young and attractive. Francis noticed that she had an air of confidence about her that she could only ever dream of.

She saw Chris move and tried to turn away before he spotted her but, just at that moment, a member of staff approached her to ask if she needed any assistance. She tried to send him away with a 'no thank you' but, by then, it was too late.

'Francis?' Chris called. Francis acted as if she hadn't heard him and turned to walk the other way. 'Francis!' He shouted louder.

She couldn't pretend any longer and, awkwardly, turned around and peered in his direction. 'Chris? Oh hi! Fancy seeing you here!'

As Chris walked towards her she could feel her nerves heighten, she became conscious of how she looked.

'It's been a while.' He gave her a warm, calm smile which made her realise how much she'd actually missed him.

'It's been too long!' she replied.

The tension between them hadn't lessened with absence and there was a silence between them, as neither one of them knew what to say next. The attractive woman, with Chris, caught up with them and held her hand out towards Francis.

'Hi, I'm Kathy. Nice to meet you.'

Francis shook her hand, unnerved by how beautiful she was. 'Hello I'm Francis.' It became awkward very quickly between the three of them. 'I eh, better be off. I'm on a schedule. It was nice to see you again Chris...' She couldn't bring herself to look him in the eye. 'And nice to meet you Kathy. Excuse me.' She pushed her trolley away from them, not caring if she didn't have any bread for the week. She just wanted to get out of there. She paid for her food as fast as possible, since the last thing Francis wanted was to meet them again at the checkout, and headed back to the car park. As she put the last couple of bags in the boot she heard Chris's voice again.

'Do you have to run off so quickly?' It startled her slightly since she wasn't expecting him to follow her out into the car park. 'I'm not contagious or anything!' He grinned, trying to keep it light and get a response from her, but she just continued to load the car. Francis didn't want to stay any longer than she had to and see his face.

'Sorry Chris, I'm in a rush!' She prayed he would get the hint but he took a step closer to her so she had to look at him.

'Meet me for a coffee then, to catch up?'

She looked up at him 'No, I can't.'

'It would mean a lot to me.'

She felt torn. She hadn't forgotten how much he'd done for her in her days of need. Even though she had convinced and promised herself, if she ever saw him again, she wouldn't agree to meet with him, she found herself saying, 'OK.'

Francesca had been listening, intently, to Francis, quite excited about the fact she had bumped into Chris again. 'So when are you meeting him?'

'Friday. I'm meeting him for coffee at Yani's...'

Francesca flinched hearing the restaurant's name. She'd done her best over the past few days to try and forget about Shay. The only time she wanted to be thinking about her was when they were in a session together, and that was it.

'What? You don't think I should?' Francis paused. 'It's just you flinched when I said it.'

'Did I?' Francesca felt slightly embarrassed and tried to pretend it was nothing. 'I think this could be really good for you. I don't know if you're aware of this but every time you talk about Chris your face lights up and you smile!' Francis looked down and blushed.

Francesca continued, 'Maybe now it's time to move on? I understand how your daughter feels about the whole relationship and yes, maybe the timing wasn't the best, but she needs to try and move on too. You both do. You deserve to be happy Francis, and love, have a relationship with whoever you want to. No matter what other people think or say.'

She thought about it. 'I don't think it could get any worse with my daughter at the moment.' She still hadn't spoken to her since their argument. 'But with Chris... I've missed my opportunity. I've lost him.'

'You don't know that. Why would he ask you for coffee if he wasn't still interested?'

'He has another woman now, Kathy. They looked close. She was gorgeous and younger than me. Why would he be interested in me when he could be with someone like her?'

CHAPTER FORTY
SEVEN

To kill time between appointments Francesca browsed the local shops in town. She picked up a bar of chocolate and a magazine for Julie and walked back to her office building. She felt nervous walking up the stairs to the reception entrance. She anticipated Shay being in the waiting room and they hadn't seen each other since the hospital. Francesca had done her best to block that episode out but it was all rushing back now.

She reached the reception entrance and opened the door. Julie was away from her desk so she checked the waiting room, it was empty, Shay wasn't there yet. Francesca heard the toilet flush and Julie strolled out from the restroom.

'Is Shay not here yet?'

Julie jumped a little, not expecting Francesca to be waiting for her. 'Nope, not yet.' She walked back behind her desk and picked up a pile of messages she'd taken for

Francesca while she was out. 'Here are all the messages that came in.' as Julie handed them over to her one of the pieces of paper flew off and dropped to the floor. Francesca bent to pick it up just as Shay walked through the door. She was greeted with Francesca's bottom, pert and tight, in her pencil skirt. Shay grinned and lifted her eyebrows, pleased.

'That's a nice welcome!'

Julie couldn't help but laugh at Shay's comment.

Francesca stood back up unimpressed. She looked at Julie. 'Don't encourage her!' She made sure her skirt was straight and began to walk towards her office.

Shay followed aware that, since she'd entered, Francesca hadn't really looked at her.

Francesca placed the pile of messages on her desk and turned around and purposely leant against it, rather than sit in her usual chair straight away. She wanted to create more space between them.

'So did you miss me?' Shay slumped down on the sofa and looked up at her with a cheeky smile.

'Can we be serious for a minute? We have one more session together after today and I want to talk some more, to find out a bit more about you.' She looked at Shay's face and suspected she still wasn't taking her seriously. 'If I'm going to clear your case with the judge...'

'Is that a threat?' Shay could tell Francesca wasn't in a good mood, she became more serious and matched her temperament. 'If you want to know more about me, then first, shouldn't we talk about what happened at the hospital?'

Assuming that she was talking about what happened between them in the waiting room, Francesca decided to evade the subject. 'Nothing happened, Shay.'

'Yes it did... Mia looked pretty rough to me, How is she?'

Francesca breathed out, relieved that that was what she was actually talking about. 'She is doing OK, thank you.' She glanced over at Shay, her mood a little more humble. 'Thank you for what you did, helping her...'

Shay didn't say anything. She just stared at her in the way that always made Francesca nervous. She tightened her body again, knowing Shay was trying to figure her out. 'Now, can we get back to you?'

Shay was confused by the way Francesca was behaving, the back and forth, the hotness and coldness towards her. She thought they'd got past the cat and mouse antics. 'If that's what you want to do...' It felt as though Francesca was treating her like a stranger.

Francesca nodded her head. 'That's what I want to do.' She walked over to her chair and sat down to listen to Shay talk.

TEN YEARS EARLIER.

Shay sat at the table eating dinner with her mother. The atmosphere was tense because her father was late and his food was going cold. It was the fourth time that week he had arrived late from work.

'Pass me the bottle...' Her mother gestured to the bottle of white wine on Shay's side of the table. 'I'm not going to ruin it by letting it go warm, waiting for him.'

Reluctantly, Shay passed the bottle to her mother and watched her fill her third glass up to the top of the rim and take a sip.

'Please don't drink as much tonight. You know you always feel worse for it in the morning.' Shay was always the one to help her mum with her hangovers. She'd done it a few times already this week and didn't want to have to do it again in the morning.

'I'll be fine darling. Don't worry about it.'

By nine o'clock, Sara had drunk the whole bottle and opened another one. She ignored Shay's pleas and kept on drinking.

By the time her father came home, three hours late, Sara was out cold on the sofa. Shay was in the kitchen washing up the dinner plates when he walked in, having seen and walked past Sara. Shay knew he had seen the state she was in, but he hadn't say anything to her. He didn't ask what had happened. It was as if he'd expected Sara to be drunk and out of it by the time he got home, like it was normal.

'Where have you been? We waited the whole night for you. You said you'd be home for dinner tonight.' Shay was angry and tired, 'You can't keep just leaving me with her. She needs help dad.'

'I got caught up at work...'

She scoffed at his flimsy excuse. 'Caught up in someone else's sheets more like!'

'What did you say to me?' He said angrily.

'Nothing.' She couldn't be bothered to have an argument, but he didn't let it go.

'Yes you did. Come on. Say it to my face!'

Shay slammed the dinner plate she was washing into the sink and turned to face him. 'Fine! I said you were probably caught up in someone else's sheets, as in fucking another woman! Because that's what you do, isn't it dad? Oui? You chase women, and mum gets pissed. And do you know what? None of it is going to change the fact that Tommy's dead...'

He slapped her hard, across the cheek, and pointed his finger in her face. 'I'm your father. You do not speak to me like that!'

In shock, she put her hand to her cheek. 'You might as well not be my father. I barely see you and when I do, you're never really there anyway, you fade off somewhere...'

'That's not true!'

'Really? What books am I into dad? What movies do I watch? Do I like sports?' He didn't know what to say, what to answer. 'You're not there for me dad! You weren't there for Tommy and you, sure as hell, aren't here for mum now!' She dropped her hand from her burning cheek.

'If that's how you feel, you can get out... out of my house!'

Shay stared at him and saw how broken and in denial he was. She'd come to resent him over the past few years because of it. 'Give me a few hours and I'll be out of your way.'

It took her an hour or so to pack the belongings she wanted to take. As she packed her last item Sara *stumbled in desperate and erratic, having heard from her husband Shay was leaving.*

'Shay you can't leave me! I can't cope without you.'

Shay looked at her and started to cry. Her heart felt like it was being pulled apart. She knew she had to stay strong, the three of them together had become toxic and staying would do nothing but make it worse. 'You can't cope 'with' me mum. I can't do this anymore. I'm angry all the time... Dad's not here and you're... you're pissed most of the time.' She went to walk past Sara to leave but Sara took hold of her arm and clung onto it like a child.

'Please don't. I need you... I can't lose you as well.'

Shay could barely speak through her tears and the pain in her chest. She couldn't look at her mother's face. 'You don't need me mum... you need help!'

It was silent in Francesca's office after Shay finished speaking. Francesca was moved by the amount of courage it must have taken her to leave. 'Did your mother get help?'

Shay combed her hair back before she answered. '*Oui*. My Uncle George arranged for her to go to rehab after my dad left and started a new family. He went abroad. Acted like we didn't exist, which was his way of moving on.'

'What about your mum did she stay in contact?'

'We tried but it just became too hard. All we did was remind each other of the accident and losing Tommy. When we met up, after she'd been one year sober, I knew something wasn't quite right. I didn't hear from her again until three months later. She was back in rehab... seeing me had triggered her to drink again.'

Francesca could sense she was blaming herself for her mother's relapse. 'That must have been tough.'

'It would have been tougher seeing her, knowing I was setting her back. I haven't had contact with her for ten years...' She paused as she thought about how broken her immediate family was. 'Do you know what scares me the most? It's that I'll be alone. I don't let people get close because I'm afraid to lose them. I'm empty... I'm here, but I'm not here.' She let a deep breath out and gasped. 'Fuck! It feels so raw, so hard, feeling this vulnerable...' Tears began to fall silently down her cheeks.

Francesca leant forward in her chair to encourage Shay to carry on, but she couldn't. She couldn't get any more words out. Francesca went to touch her leg but then hesitated. She looked at Shay, who was staring down at the floor. 'You're not the only one who finds it hard, letting people in, feeling vulnerable. It can be a scary, overwhelming feeling...'

Shay felt that she couldn't breathe. All she could feel was an overwhelming sense of grief rising up in her. She stood up, abruptly, and walked behind the back of the sofa to find some space from Francesca and from her own feelings. 'I'm fine.'

'You don't look fine.' Francesca replied.

'That's because I have to come in here and dredged everything up that I've tried to put behind me.' She felt her anger rise in her stomach. 'All because of some stupid assault charge!'

Francesca could see the tension and stress building up in her body language and movements. Worried Shay might start hitting the wall again, she got up and walked over to her. 'It's OK to feel what you're feeling Shay.' She slowly got closer, still making sure Shay felt she had her space. 'Tell me what you're feeling right now. Express it. What's going on inside you?'

Shay clenched her fists as she tried to resist the emotions coming up in her. She felt like a caged animal that wanted to escape.

Francesca tried again. 'You need to let this stuff out...the hurt, the pain, the anger.' She moved closer again and attempted to get Shay to look at her. 'I would be angry if I was you...'

'Don't...' Struggling to keep it together, Shay turned her body away from Francesca. She faced the wall with her fists still clenched.

Francesca slowly moved another step closer and stood behind Shay, within touching distance. She lowered her voice gently. 'Don't what? Validate your feelings?'

Shay pressed her fist against the wall so hard that her knuckles began to go white. She wanted to punch it and release the feeling she had stuck inside her. She resisted and leant her forehead against the wall instead. She tried to stop the tears, building up behind her eyes, from falling. 'I can't... I can't... You don't want to see my pain...' She clenched her jaw. 'Nobody wants to see a person's pain.'

Francesca felt a strong wave of emotion go through her own body. She stepped to the side of Shay so she could see the side of her face and get her attention. 'I do! I want to see it!'

Francesca meant it. She reached out to touch Shay's arm, but stopped herself. 'I want you to be able to live your life, without walking around with this... this weight on your shoulders.'

Shay turned around and pressed her back against the wall, she slowly slid her body down it, until she hit the floor. She hung her head in her hands and shook it from side to side. 'I can't let it go! I've held onto it for too long. If I let go of the pain, then I'm letting go of him.'

Francesca felt overwhelmed by both Shay's emotions and her own. She felt unable to pull away. 'The pain you feel and the relationship you had with Tommy are two completely different things. You letting the pain go isn't letting him go or forgetting him... You're just letting go of the strong negative emotions you have around his death.' She squatted down next to her and sat on the floor but Shay still wouldn't look at her. 'You need to let those emotions go, otherwise they will eat you up from the inside...'

Shay shook her head again trying not to let Francesca's words in. 'It was my fault! Tommy shouldn't have been in the front... It was my seat... On any other day it would have been me...' She choked her last words out. 'It should have been me...' She began to sob. This time Francesca didn't hesitate she made contact and put her hand on Shay's forearm.

'I want you to listen to me. Tommy's death was not your fault.' Her voice began to break with emotion. 'Nobody could have known what was going to happen. That's the thing about life. We just don't know what's going to happen or how it's going to happen.'

Shay turned her head and looked at her. She had the feeling that Francesca wasn't just speaking to her, but to herself as well, she was surprised to see tears forming behind Francesca's eyes.

'For most of my life, my mother, she suffered with bi-polar. When I was eighteen, I left home to go to university and, I know, my mother struggled with the change. I was her only child, the one thing stable in her life, but I knew I had to, I wanted to go out into the world and live my own life. After my first year of university she begged me not to go back, but I did...' She could feel her grief hit the back of her throat. 'I went home the next weekend to find the house empty. Her car was still parked outside and I was confused as to where she had gone.' Francesca paused. 'I found her in the bath, unconscious. She'd taken all her medication with a bottle of whisky. I pulled her out of the water and tried to give her mouth to mouth. All I remember was how cold she was... she was gone. I always thought, for a long time, if I hadn't left, if I had listened to what...' Francesca couldn't finish her sentence. She was too overcome by emotion.

Shay felt she knew what she was trying to say, what she was feeling. She took Francesca's hand in her own and held it. 'I'm sorry you had to go through that.'

It was the first time anyone had said that to her. She didn't talk about what had happened anymore, at the time, the people around her had either ignored her, not knowing what to say, or had simply said that they were sorry for her loss. Francesca leant back against the wall and sighed deeply. They both sat on the floor, next to one another, holding hands in silence for the rest of the session.

CHAPTER FORTY EIGHT

Jasmine walked through the park after school, as she did every day. There was hardly anyone about and she was deep in thought so she didn't see Bonnie and Denise walk up behind her. They had followed her from the school gates knowing she was heading for the park and ran to the side entrance, with the intention of cutting her off.

'They let you out of the druggy ward then?'

Jasmine knew it was Denise's voice straight away. She didn't turn to look at her but just carried on walking. 'I'm not taking drugs. Leave me alone and get a life!'

Denise began to taunt her. 'God you're angry! What's the matter? Need another hit of something?'

Annoyed, Jasmine stopped walking and turned to face her. She saw Bonnie by Denise's side and realised she was going to have to square up to both of them if things got nasty.

'You're right! I could hit something right now, your face!' Jasmine surprised herself by her words and the force of the fire in her belly that came with them.

Denise stared her in the face and leered at her. 'Are you threatening me?' She pushed up against her body which made Jasmine realise that, maybe, she shouldn't have been so cocky.

Mia entered the park just as Denise pushed Jasmine to the floor.

'Hey leave her alone!'

Denise and Bonnie backed off as Mia started running towards them. They knew Mia from school as one of the girls who was a couple years above them.

Jasmine stayed, sprawled, on the cold ground, her bag had opened and emptied as she'd fallen and all her belongings were scattered over the concrete path.

'We were just talking and she tripped.' Bonnie tried to lie and cover their tracks. She didn't know that Mia had seen what had happened.

'You pushed her! I saw you! Do you think I'm stupid? Get out of here!'

Both the girls rushed off since neither of them were willing to get into an altercation with an older girl from school.

Jasmine started to pick up her belongings and put them back in her bag. Mia bent down to help her and hesitated when she saw one of Jasmine's syringes on the floor. Jasmine looked at her and grabbed the syringe, tossing it back in her bag. 'I'm not taking drugs.' She felt defensive, as if she had to stand up for herself.

'It's none of my business.'

'I know it's not. I'm just telling you!'

Mia continued to help her gather the rest of her belongings. One of the last things she picked up was a book. She read the cover.

'You're a deep thinker then huh?' Mia held the book up so Jasmine knew what she was talking about. ''The meaning of life... That's some deep shit right?'

Jasmine took it from her and held it to her chest like a safety blanket. She got up and brushed the dirt from her trousers, flung her bag over her shoulder and began to walk the rest of the way home through the park.

Half way through she could sense Mia following her. 'Thanks for saving me and everything but you don't have to carry on walking with me.'

'I know, but you look pretty close to the end of that book. I was wondering if you've learnt the meaning of life and why it brings so much shit.'

Jasmine slowed down and let Mia catch up with her. 'It can be pretty shit, can't it?'

Mia gestured towards the café that was situated at the end of the park, where she'd been with Josh a couple of times, she knew it was good. 'So do you want to get a drink? We could see who's got the worst life?'

Jasmine hesitated. She wasn't sure. Mia tried her best pleading face to try and convince her.

It worked. 'OK, but I'm pretty sure I've got the worst life!'

Mia challenged her statement. 'Has your family fallen apart? Has your dad got a new girlfriend who everyone but you knew about? Oh, and did I mention he got her pregnant before my parents even split!'

'Is that all you've got? Try not even knowing your dad, and having to live with diabetes and depression!'

'Diabetes? Is that what the...'

Jasmine just nodded in acknowledgement.

Mia smiled softly. 'Maybe you will win then! Come on I'll buy you a drink.'

CHAPTER FORTY NINE

Shay had been on her evening shift for an hour, serving tables. She thought working would keep her occupied but she couldn't get her mind off Francesca.

'We didn't order chicken. I ordered the beef and my wife ordered the burger.'

Shay had completely messed the order up on the table she was supposed to be serving.

'I'm so sorry! I'll come back with the right order.' She picked the plates up and walked back into the kitchen.

Faith followed behind her knowing something was wrong. 'Dude what's up with you? That's for table four, not twelve!' She took the plates from Shay and left to give the food to the right table before it went cold.

At the end of the night the last customers paid their bill and left. Faith went over to the entrance door and locked it so no one else could walk in off the street. She flipped the open sign to closed and walked directly over to Shay, who was leaning on the bar, staring into space, deep in thought.

'Dude, you're doing it again!' Faith knew that look. 'Who is it?'

'Who's what?' Shay didn't want to talk about it.

'Who's the person you're totally crushing on so badly that you can't even concentrate!'

'No-one.'

Faith knew she was lying. She knew Shay too well. 'Yeah, that's why you've got your puppy dog eyes on! Come on spill.'

'Faith it's no-one. Just leave it alone!' She turned away from her and began wiping down the bar.

'Shit! You got it bad! Shay Bentley has been infiltrated!'

Shay kept her back to her, choosing to ignore her. 'Oh come on, I'm only messing with you!'

'I'm glad my personal life is such a source of entertainment for you!'

'Speaking of entertainment...' Faith completely changed track. 'Are you going to come with me and Frank to this music festival on Friday? It'll be a laugh!'

'No I can't, I've got my last session this Friday. I have to go otherwise she won't sign me off.'

'Oh! The sexy and mysterious Dr Francesca Draw! I thought you would have seduced her by now. Got her to sign you off already!

Shay straightened some beer mats and lined them up on the bar. 'Shut up Faith...'

Faith put two and two together from Shay's attitude and tone of voice. 'Oh my god, it's her isn't it? She's the one that's turned you into a pining puppy dog! Shay, she's like the worst person you could ever crush on! She's your therapist! Hello? What are you thinking?'

Shay walked away from the bar, over to one of the tables, to re-lay it. 'She won't be my therapist after Friday.'

Faith could see she was serious and she knew you couldn't talk Shay out of something, especially when it came to women and the thrill of the chase. 'Well I hope you know what you're doing.' She joined her at the table to help. 'Just be careful OK? I don't want to be consoling you and your broken heart.'

CHAPTER FIFTY

Francesca and Jasmine were in session. Francesca noticed that Jasmine's demeanour seemed a lot brighter than the last time they had met.

'Well, you seem a bit better than when I saw you last. It's nice to see!'

'Yeah, I guess today is a good day.'

'Tell me what you've been up to since I last saw you. Is there anything you've done that's contributed to you feeling brighter?'

'I'm taking my insulin properly. I'm taking it slowly, one meal at a time, so it doesn't feel so overwhelming.'

Francesca was more than pleased to hear it. 'That's great!' She made a note of it on her pad and drew a smiley face beside it.

'And I've made some new friends, I think?'

'Brilliant, tell me more!'

'Outside of school, I went to the cinema with them...'

2 DAYS EARLIER.

Jasmine and Mia had only just met outside the cinema. Jasmine was ready to go in but Mia stopped her.

'I hope you don't mind but I've invited someone else.'

Jasmine felt anxious at the thought of someone else joining them. She had pushed herself just to get there and felt like she barely knew Mia, someone else she didn't know, in a social setting, freaked her out even more.

'I don't know Mia. Just doing this, being here, is outside of my comfort zone. My social anxiety is bad enough as it is.'

'Don't worry. He's cool. He's into art and shit...' She nudged Jasmine to reassure her. 'He's another wannabe philosopher!'

Jasmine looked across the road to where Mia was staring. She saw Josh walking over towards them with a spring in his step.

'Hey ladies, are you ready for the best date of your lives?' He hugged Mia and offered his hand to Jasmine. 'Hi I'm Josh...' She shook his hand and he smiled at her. It made her relax a little more and it put her at ease knowing it was him. She'd seen him around school and he

seemed alright. 'Shall we go in then? I hate missing the film trailers!' Josh eagerly walked a head.

While they watched the trailers Jasmine went to the restroom, leaving Mia and Josh alone. He felt the most nervous he had ever been, alone with her.

'Sorry, I didn't ask if you wanted some popcorn... Shall I go and get some...'

'Er Josh, you do realise this isn't a date?' Mia had picked up on his nerves and saw it as an opportunity to tease him.

'Oh yeah, no I didn't mean...' He saw her smiling at him and playfully nudged her in the side.

After the movie had ended they headed for a popular milkshake bar that Josh had been to with a couple of his friends, a couple of weeks ago. Inside there was a chilled atmosphere with music playing in the background and only a few other people, so they more or less had the place to themselves.

'I just don't get it! How could you not like it?' Josh was talking about the film they had seen. 'Zombies taking over the earth, killing the human race off...'

'Zombies! Is that not reason enough!' Mia was less than impressed with the film. Spending an hour and a half watching people get eaten alive wasn't her idea of entertainment.

Josh looked over at Jasmine for some support. 'Come on, Jasmine, back me up here!'

'I thought it was OK actually...'

'See! Thank you...someone with taste!'

'What did you like about it?' Mia was intrigued.

'I don't know, there was just something symbolic about how the world was being taken over by zombies.' Jasmine had watched the film on a totally different level. It was more of a symbolic story for her. 'You know it's kind of what's happening now already, people turning into lifeless beings because they're working for the system we call society. How often is it that you see people actually walking around with life inside of them? And I mean living, not just surviving!'

Josh went quiet. He wasn't expecting such an in-depth reply. Mia smiled at her, she understood what she was saying and, in hindsight, Jasmine's analogy even made the film seem a bit better to her.

'Do you know what, Jasmine? You are so refreshing. You have a talent for calling bullshit out. You say how it is for you! I want to be around more people like you. You own your shit and speak your truth, your sadness, your pain. No mask, no pretence.'

Jasmine was a little embarrassed by the attention. 'No one ever said that about me before... They don't usually want to hear my 'bullshit.'

'Bullshit?' Josh piped up, impressed as well. 'I don't think its bullshit! Its bloody real shit! We need to talk about your theory some more but, first, who wants a shake?' He tugged his wallet out of his pocket. 'It's on me.'

Mia gave him her order. 'I'll have a chocolate shake please, extra thick.'

Jasmine stayed quiet and didn't say anything. He looked at her. 'Jasmine? What are you having?'

'I'll just have a water thanks.' She said it with a low voice as if she was ashamed.

'Come on have a shake with us! I'll even stretch to a large one!'

Mia noticed how uncomfortable Jasmine was with the pressure of having something other than water, she realised why.

'Josh, leave it, yeah. She just wants water!'

Josh put his hands up in surrender and skipped across the restaurant to order.

'Sorry, he doesn't know. I didn't think it was my place to tell him about your... about the...'

Jasmine lowered her head, feeling like a nuisance. 'Its fine I get it all the time. People think you're normal because you can't see it from the outside.'

'What are you saying? You are normal! Actually no, you're not, you're better than normal! You're a total bad ass that can inject themselves with a needle without even wincing!'

'I've never thought of it like that before!'

Mia leaned a little closer to her from across the table. 'I don't want to seem patronising or anything, I don't know what it's like being you, but you shouldn't be ashamed to tell people about your diabetes, or even that you have depression...' She spotted Josh walking back over with the shakes on a tray, so she stopped talking.

Josh placed the glasses on the table and noticed something was missing. 'Shit! I forgot your water!' He went to walk back but Jasmine stopped him.

'Actually Josh, forget it. I'll have a strawberry milkshake please... I'll just take some insulin with it.'

'Insulin?' He wasn't sure if he heard her right.

'It's the medication I have to take for my diabetes... I have type one diabetes.'

He looked at her. Jasmine dreaded what he was going to say next, now that he knew.

'I know what people take insulin for!' She was amazed at how blasé he was about it. 'What do you take? Novo rapid?' He could see the surprise on the girl's faces that he even knew what novo rapid was. 'Yep that's right ladies! Behind this hunk of a man is a medical genius!' He paused and puffed his chest out as he explained himself. 'What I mean is that one of my cousins has diabetes and we pretty much grew up together, so I know all about it! OK, so now we've got that out of the way I'll go order this shake!' He grinned at them and walked back over to the counter. It was a different assistant behind the counter, this time. Josh knew him as one of his oldest brother's friends, they started talking, catching up on how things were going since they'd last seen each other.

After about five minutes Mia glanced towards him wondering what was taking him so long.

'He likes you.' Jasmine had picked up on their subtle flirting all through the evening.

Mia blushed a little at her observation. 'No. I just think he's nice to everyone.' She'd been telling herself that for months so she didn't have to think about her own feelings towards him.

'No it's more than that... like you said, I don't bullshit. I call what I see and I see he likes you!'

Jasmine didn't mention any names when relaying her story so Francesca had no idea that one of her friends was her daughter Mia.

'So you felt comfortable and relaxed with them?' Francesca was glad to hear Jasmine had had a positive experience socialising.

'Yeah, I did. I feel freer being honest with them. They just accepted me. In fact, they didn't really even care.'

Confused, Francesca frowned. 'Why would they care?'

'Because people don't always understand diabetes. Like, some people still think if you have diabetes then it means you can't eat any sugar but you can. You just have to take insulin...'

'Maybe if you started talking about it more, explained it to people more, people would learn!'

Jasmine smiled.

'What?'

'That sounded exactly like the kind of thing my grandpa would have said to me!'

CHAPTER FIFTY ONE

Francesca had finished with her clients and had left her office door open. She could hear Julie speaking to someone on the phone. 'Hello, how can I help you?' There was a short pause. 'Please could you hold the line.' Francesca waited for her office phone to ring and picked it up.

'Oh... Hello...' She had picked the phone up quicker than Julie had anticipated, it slightly shocked her. 'It's Judge Harmen on the phone.'

Francesca was surprised he was ringing her so late. 'Did he say what it was regarding?'

'Shay Bentley.'

Her stomach dropped, hearing Shay's name. 'Put him through...' She waited on the line while Julie transferred the call.

'Hello?'

'Hello Judge Harmen. How can I help you?' She didn't know why but she was nervous, afraid of what he was calling about.

'Hello Dr Draw. I was wondering if you could come in tomorrow, to my office, to talk about Shay Bentley's case.'

Francesca wasn't due to review Shay's case until after Friday, so she hadn't yet done her final notes on it. If she went in tomorrow she would have to rush and do a last minute sign off.

'Is there a problem? Has something happened?' She wanted to know why it was so urgent all of a sudden.

'I'd rather not go into detail over the phone but something has come up. Can you make it to my office for tomorrow morning, 10.30?'

Francesca quickly scanned her diary. 'Yes, sure. No problem. I'll see you then.' She put the phone down, hoping that Shay hadn't got herself into some kind of trouble again.

Francesca made sure she was early for the appointment with Judge Harmen. She sat, tapping her foot, waiting to see what was going on.

'Thank you for coming in on such short notice.' He was behind his desk looking through Shay's file.

'It's no problem.' She couldn't take it anymore. 'What's going on? Is Shay in some kind of trouble?'

'No. It's nothing like that. Nothing to worry about...' Francesca relaxed a bit, but not fully. 'It's just that I'm going in for an operation next week so I'm trying to clear as much paperwork as possible beforehand. I came across Miss Bentley's case and as it's her first offence and she's unlikely to offend again, I thought we could review her a little early? Unless you tell me otherwise that is. How has she responded with therapy?'

'Well, we do have one more session together, but I would say she's responded well. We've spoken a lot about her past and why she hit the gentleman on the night out.' She paused and thought about the correlation between the police officer holding Shay back and how the man in the club had held on to her. 'To be honest Judge Harmen, I would have done the same thing in her situation...'

He was intrigued by her statement. 'Oh? Really?'

Francesca explained her reasoning. 'She was physically and emotionally triggered. When we get triggered in that way, we tend to lash out, do crazy, irrational things. I'm not condoning what she did but I would be confident in saying I don't think anything like that would happen again. Shay's not a naturally violent person, in my opinion. I think she's actually quite sensitive. She had some issues from the past that she needed to work through, which we have. But, ultimately, I believe she was caught on a bad day at a bad moment. Plus, I think she would probably say having to have therapy with me is her lesson learnt!'

'So you're happy for me to sign her off then? A pass with flying colours?'

'Yes sir.'

'Please, call me Harry.' He took out the paperwork he needed to close Shay's case and signed it. He then passed it over his desk for Francesca to sign. 'I will let you inform Miss Bentley about the good news. Tell her from me, I don't want to see her in my court again!'

Francesca nodded as she put the pen to the paper to sign the document.

He continued. 'And by the sounds of it, if what you said was true, the last thing she'd want to do is be alone in a room with you again!'

Francesca slipped with the pen as she finished her signature.

Having no idea how close to home his comment was, Judge Harmen laughed softly at his own joke. 'Oh dear! Everything OK?'

'Yes fine! Just a slip of the hand.' The mention of her and Shay in a room alone together had almost tipped her over the edge. Francesca knew she only had to get through one more session and then they would be done.

CHAPTER FIFTY TWO

Francesca was in session with Jamie. After seeing his father he had called and asked for an emergency appointment.

'Thank you for seeing me at such short notice, I'm just feeling a bit wobbly and anxious...'

She could see he was unsettled. 'What's been happening?'

'I told Maggie I've been coming to see you.'

'How did she take it?'

'Great. She was relieved. She thought I'd been having an affair, or something, from all the secretiveness. I also told her about what happened in my childhood.'

'Well done Jamie that was a big step! I think it's important you've shared that with your partner. Maybe now she can help you through the healing process.'

Jamie bent forward and rested his elbows on his knees. 'She was so understanding and supportive. I felt a bit stupid for holding it back from her for so long, I should've trusted her.'

'It can be hard to trust someone with your deepest vulnerabilities...' She tried to focus as Shay ran through her mind. 'Jamie, I want to tell you, and acknowledge, that there is no shame or blame, at all, with what happened to you. You were a victim of abuse by a man who wasn't in his right mind.' She could see how uncomfortable her words made him.

He leant back and shifted position on the sofa. 'I can't be a victim. If I'm a victim how can I be a man?'

'Being a victim doesn't make you any less of a man. I want to make it clear that when I say 'victim' I mean a person who has been hurt or taken advantage of...' Francesca was aware it wasn't the first time he had referred to being a man. 'Who knows really what being a 'man' means anyway? What does it mean to you?'

He dropped his head slightly as if defeated. 'I don't know. I just know what being a man meant for my father. Not being beaten and not backing down. Staying strong and never ever being a victim.'

'I want you to think about that for when I see you next time. What being a man is for you and not what it is for your father.'

Jamie went quiet and thought about his father. 'I went to see him...' He paused. Francesca gave him the space and time to continue talking when he was ready.

He began twiddling his fingers. 'It wasn't for long. I went with the intention to ask him to come here, to maybe try and understand him a little... I ended up flipping out because he wouldn't own up to what he'd done. But he managed to tell me everything he did, he did for my own good!' Jamie saw Richard, in his head, as his father, when he was a child, and now. 'It was strange...

there was something different about him. He seemed more... settled. Part of me wanted to believe him when he said he'd changed but when he said that... I don't know, I just don't think I can trust him.'

Francesca was disappointed for Jamie. She had hoped his father would be more aware and take responsibility for his mistakes.

'It's understandable and justified that you feel you can't trust him. He broke your trust many times as a child.'

'When I was talking to Maggie about him and how he seemed, she thought I should give him another chance to explain himself, without flipping out! When she bumped into him in the supermarket he told her he was sober.'

'How do you feel about that?'

'I don't know. I thought I would say no, enough is enough, but he's my father. After everything he did, how he behaved towards me, there's still this little boy inside of me that just wants his dad... As much as I try not to, I still... love him.' Upset, he wiped a tear from his cheek.

CHAPTER FIFTY THREE

Janet had been keeping an eye on her husband, Richard, for most of the day. She could tell something was bothering him because he'd gone inward and distant. She wasn't going to grill him about what was going on, they had promised each other their marriage would be an honest, truthful one and if anything was bothering either of them it was their responsibility to address it with the other person and so far Richard had said nothing to her.

They were out in the afternoon, gardening, weeding and tidying the borders of their back garden. Richard was by the side of Janet breaking up the soil with a trawl when he stopped what he was doing.

'Jamie came around.' As soon as he'd said it he felt a relief. Janet was taken aback. She knew he would eventually tell her what was bothering him, but she didn't expect it to be something as big as that.

'What? Richard! Why didn't you tell me?' She stopped what she was doing to listen to him.

'I was scared. I thought I wanted to see him, maybe try and be part of his life again, now that I'm not drinking. Ask for his forgiveness maybe, but when I saw him, all I could see was that little boy I used to tease, bully and... beat. What if it... I don't want to start drinking again.'

Janet took his hand to show support and to let him know she was there for him.

Emotional, Richard looked up and stared into her eyes. 'He wants to go back there, talk about it all but I don't want to. I don't want to be that man again.'

She brushed her hand over his cheek. 'What do you mean he wants to go back there?'

'He wants me to go into therapy with him, but I don't think I can talk about...' He started to break down thinking about everything he'd tried to put behind him, everything he thought he'd put behind him.

CHAPTER FIFTY FOUR

After a full day Francesca's last appointment was Shay. She saw her previous client out of her office, expecting to have a few minutes break, but Shay was early and already in the waiting room. She attempted to compose herself, knowing it was their last session together. All she had to do was stay assertive and in control. After today she could relax, there would be no more contact between the two of them.

Shay attempted to catch her eye, by smiling at her, but Francesca didn't look at her, or in her direction. Francesca walked over to Julie, to speak with her, but Julie got up from her desk before she got there. She picked up her bag and jacket.

'Where are you going?' Francesca felt anxious at the thought of Julie going and being left completely alone with Shay.

'You said I could knock off early today. It's my mum's birthday?' Julie knew she would completely forget. She saw the look on Francesca's face and turned back to put her bag and jacket back behind the reception desk. 'Don't worry I'll stay.'

Francesca heard the disappointment in Julie's voice. 'No, no it's fine. I just forgot it was today, if I'd known... Go see your mum and wish her a happy birthday from me.'

Julie beamed and walked past the waiting room to leave. She popped her head around to see Shay. They'd been talking while she was waiting for Francesca's appointment to finish.

'Behave yourself!' She jokingly teased her.

Shay gave her a cheeky smile and watched her leave. She got up and strolled into reception where Francesca was locking the front entrance door, slowly. She wanted a bit more time to gather her thoughts and ground herself before she turned to face Shay. She could already feel the tension building up in her body.

Standing in front of the reception desk, Shay heard the lock of the door. 'Are you that desperate for me not to leave?'

Francesca began to nervously play with her ear. She turned to look at Shay but didn't say anything.

Shay had expected her to at least grin at her joke. She picked up on Francesca's nervous energy. 'Are you alright? That was a joke!'

Francesca glanced down, attempting to flatten out the creases in her shirt and deflect answering the question. She looked back up at Shay feeling determined to face her and whatever came up in the session. 'Do you want to come on through?'

Shay followed her in to her office and took her seat as usual. Francesca sat down and, without realising, crossed her legs and arms straight away in defence. The atmosphere was tense.

Shay attempted to change the energy in the room to something a little lighter by teasing Francesca, in her usual way.

'You called me in early! What? Couldn't wait to see me?' She was trying to get her to smile but it hadn't worked. Shay thought their relationship had changed with what had happened between the two of them, what they'd been through together, but Francesca switched straight to professional mode, wanting to ignore the strong undertones that had been building up between them.

'So, I have good news for you. Your court hearing meeting came through early and I went to see Judge Harmen. Everything's signed...' She handed Shay the piece of paper with the court findings. Francesca looked at her. 'Congratulations, you're a free woman!'

Shay held the piece of paper in her hand but didn't look at it, she stayed silent, confused by the way Francesca was acting. 'I don't understand?'

Thinking Shay was referring to the court papers, Francesca leant forward to explain and talk her through what had been discussed at her meeting with the Judge. She scanned the piece of paper and went to point at the verdict written on it.

Shay was aware how close they were, she could smell her subtle perfume that had weakened through the day, she could feel the tension coming from Francesca's body. She stared at her, trying to figure her out, not the least bit interested, or focused, on what Francesca was saying.

'Judge Harmen wanted to asses you early... It explains everything here...'

Shay pulled the piece of paper away from Francesca so she didn't have any distraction, she placed it on the sofa next to her, out of sight.

'No, I understand that...'

Startled by Shay's actions, Francesca looked up at her. She hadn't realised how close she'd leaned in towards her, until they locked eyes. Shay waited for an explanation from her, but Francesca leant back and pulled away.

'What do you mean, then? What don't you understand?'

'You! You've totally gone cold on me...'

Francesca cut in to try and control the direction of the conversation and situation. 'I'm just trying to do my job, Shay...' She got up from her chair, moved towards her desk and leant back against the front of it. She crossed her arms again, this time, even more defensively. She glanced towards the floor. 'I'm required to explain your case findings to you so we can wrap up today and our sessions together.'

Shay was silent for a time.

'Is that all I am to you? Just some job to wrap up?'

Francesca looked at her, she could see the hurt on her face. She did her best not to be pulled in by it, or by her own emotions.

'It may sound a little harsh but... yes.' She tried to grasp for clarity, not just for Shay but for herself as well. 'You're my client. I am your therapist. We had a job to do together which we've completed. That's all it has ever been and can be.' She went to play with her ear but realised Shay would notice and know she was nervous, so she pulled her arms tighter to her tummy instead. 'Let's not lose objectivity here!'

Angry and hurt, Shay stood up.

'Fuck objectivity! You're making our time together sound like nothing, nothing! See this is what I was talking about and it's happening again!' She paced over to the other end of the room, away from Francesca, to try and get some head space.

'Nothing's happening here Shay!'

'Yes it is! This is what happens! I get close to someone. I let them in and open up, start to have feelings for them and then they leave me...'

Francesca stood up straight. 'Shay, we both knew these sessions would come to an end... If you're having feelings for me, maybe that's something we should talk about today?'

Shay didn't reply. She clenched her jaw in response to the thoughts rushing around her head.

Francesca tried to continue. 'You know, it's quite common in therapy, when two people are working quite close and intimately together, that a client can start to...'

'Don't you dare!' Shay moved over towards her. 'Do you know how patronizing you sound right now?'

Francesca panicked a little with Shay physically closing the gap between them. Shay noticed her reaction from her movement and stopped where she was, near the middle of the room.

'What are you so afraid of? Is it because you can't hide around me? Or because you can't convince yourself you're not attracted to me?'

Francesca, agitated, raised her voice a little. 'I'm not afraid of anything! There's nothing for me to be afraid of... I'm just trying to have clear boundaries with you, so we don't get confused...'

Shay took a few more steps towards her. 'That's a joke! Where were the boundaries when we were at the hospital?'

Francesca felt caught out by her. She knew she had a point but couldn't think clearly with Shay standing only a few metres away. She felt vulnerable being so close to her so she moved around to the back of her desk and picked up some files, acting as though her desk needed tidying. She lowered her voice again. 'Look, that wasn't great on my part. I admit that. It shouldn't have happened and I'm sorry because it was obviously confusing for you...'

'Confusing?' Shay moved to the front of the desk and leaned on it, towards Francesca. 'What's confusing is, the day I met you, there was a blatant attraction between us, but I'm the only one admitting to it. You can't hide behind therapist role here, not on this one, Francesca.'

Francesca felt frustrated that she wouldn't back down.

'It's Dr Francesca! And I'm not hiding behind anything...' She heard the wobble in her voice. 'You can think what you like!'

Before Francesca could move, Shay, fed up with her denial, quickly shuffled around the desk. She grabbed Francesca and pulled her body into hers. Pressed against

Shay, the adrenaline in Francesca's body kicked in and made her chest pump more prominently than usual. She knew she should push herself away from her, but something stopped her.

Shay stared directly into her eyes.

'I can't think what I want... because all I can think about is you!' She slowly moved her mouth closer to Francesca's.

Francesca attempted to make one last, breathless, verbal protest. 'Shay, please. Don't do this!'

Shay didn't move away but continued to hoover her lips close to Francesca's, so close she was almost speaking into her mouth. 'Say it. Tell me you don't want me to kiss you and I won't.'

Francesca struggled, but she managed to get her voice to betray her body. 'I don't want you to kiss me...'

Shay immediately let go of her, breaking contact and relieving a bit of the intensity between them. She stood back and looked at Francesca.

'You won't see me again...' Shay went to leave, to walk out. 'Thanks for all your help Doc!' she said sarcastically.

Francesca couldn't do anything but watch, frozen to the spot, as Shay left, slamming the door behind her and leaving her alone in the room. It seemed so still and quiet to her now. As if a hurricane had come in, shaken her up and then left. She didn't know what to do. Her mind was racing, trying to work out what had just happened. In shock, and slightly dazed, she glanced around her office. She noticed the picture, on the wall by the door, had tilted again. Assuming it was from Shay slamming the door on her way out she walked over to it to straighten it. As she touched the frame Shay opened the door and walked past her, back into the room.

'I'll be out of your way. I just need this...' She walked over to the sofa and picked up her court findings. She didn't even look up at Francesca as she walked back past her.

In the short moment Shay passed, Francesca ignored her head and gave in to her body. She impulsively reached her hand out and grabbed Shay's wrist. She tugged her towards her body and glanced down at her lips. She hurriedly, but softly, pressed her mouth against Shay's. After a few seconds Francesca pulled back on the pressure of her lips slightly, so they were able to open and part their mouths to kiss more freely.

They both took their time working out each other's movements, rhythm and technique. Within about a minute of kissing one another they came to a natural pause and gazed at each other. Francesca attempted to catch her breath and work out what exactly they were doing, but Shay didn't let her, she kissed her again, this time harder and more hungrily. She moved and guided Francesca up against the office wall. Francesca groaned as she hit the cold, hard wall. She could sense the tension in her body turn into heat. It rushed around her body and she completely gave in to it.

CHAPTER FIFTY FIVE

Chris had been waiting at Café Rouge for fifteen minutes. It was quiet and he'd found a nice private table in the corner.

As soon as Francis came through the door he was hit by relief that she had turned up, but he was also nervous. Francis spotted him as soon as she entered and tried her best to hide her anxiety as she made her way over to his table.

'Sorry I'm so late but my car wouldn't start, I had to get a bus!'

'I thought you had stood me up...changed your mind!' He went quiet as he watched Francis take her seat. 'It feels strange to meet here again. It's been a while...' He was trying to make conversation to fill the silence between them.

'It shouldn't be weird. We're friends aren't we? Friends should be able to meet up without feeling weird.' Francis wanted to be as clear as possible with him from the start that she wasn't expecting anything more than friends between them, but stating it didn't make their meeting any less awkward.

'Is that really how you see me, as just a friend? Is that all?'

She looked up into his eyes for the first time. His eyes were still as soft and gentle as she remembered them when he'd scanned every part of her naked body.

'Yes. Everything that happened between us, I want to just move on from, OK? You've moved on so let me move on too. It was all just a mistake...' She felt herself getting flustered and rushing her words. She didn't understand why he wanted to bring all that had happened between them up again.

'I don't see it as a mistake... and I haven't moved on.'

Francis was a little confused. 'You seemed pretty close with your girlfriend. Surely that constitutes as moving on?'

'Girlfriend?' Chris scrunched his eyebrows, not knowing what she was talking about. 'I don't have a girlfriend, as far as I know, any way!'

'The woman in the supermarket? Kathy was it?'

He laughed gently when the penny dropped. 'Francis, Kathy is my little sister! I don't know what you think you saw but...' He stopped, deciding her knowing Kathy was his sister was explanation enough. He leaned in towards her. 'I'm not seeing anyone. I haven't seen any one since...'

Francis held his gaze, she felt herself begin to slowly lean into him, but then her mobile rang. She found her mobile in her handbag and looked down at the screen. She was surprised to see Hilary's name on the screen.

'Hilary? Hello...'

'Mum, please...' Hilary's voice was erratic. Francis could tell she was upset. 'I need you! It's Henry. He's been in an accident. Mum I can't take it...'

'Whoa, whoa, Hilary darling try to calm down. Where are you?'

'I'm at the hospital. I can't get hold of James. He's at work...'

'I'll be there as soon as possible, OK? Just try to keep calm.' She put the phone down and glanced at Chris who was anxious to know what was going on.

She got up to leave. 'I'm sorry Chris but I have to go. My daughter needs me.'

He could see the panic on her face and stood up. 'Is there anything I can do? What's going on?'

'My grandson has been in an accident and my daughters at the hospital with him.'

Chris grabbed his car keys off the table. 'Let me drive you to the hospital!'

'No it's fine. I can manage. I'll get the bus.' She knew it would probably take her twice as long that way, but she didn't want to ask anything more of him.

'Francis don't be ridiculous, I'm taking you!'

Chris drove her straight to the hospital, Francis, leaving Chris following behind her, rushed directly into the accident and emergency department to find Hilary sitting in the children's waiting room, which was off to the side of the main waiting area.

'Hilary...' Francis instinctively grabbed and hugged her daughter who looked in shock and was pale as a ghost.

'How is he? Where is he?'

Hilary was almost too emotionally drained to stand up so she held on to her mother.

'Mum, I'm so worried! James still isn't picking up and Zach's still at school. I'm all alone and...' She stopped when she saw Chris hanging by the department entrance door. 'What's he doing here?'

'He brought me here. My car broke down.'

As Chris walked towards them, Francis held her breath, uncertain how Hilary would greet him and what she was going to say. Different scenarios flashed through her head. Was she going to tell him he has no right to be here, or tell her how disgusting she was for thinking it was OK to bring him here?   As Chris got nearer he approached cautiously, not confident, either, in how Hilary was going to react.

Hilary just looked at him.

'Thank you.' She gave him a warm smile, grateful to him for getting her mother here so quickly. Chris smiled back at her, relieved, and gave her a reassuring nod.

Francis breathed out, witnessing their interaction, as it came back to her why they were at the hospital in the first place.

'Hilary, darling, what happened?'

Hilary was giving her four year old son Henry a bath. He was off school with a bad case of chicken pox and had been itching like mad, so she'd decided to run him a camomile bath, to try and soothe his agitation and to stop him from itching so much. She didn't want him to pick off all the scabs and be left with scars later.

She placed him in the bath and sat by the side, on the bathroom floor. She watched as he played with his toys, when she heard the phone ringing downstairs. Hilary hesitated whether to answer it or not, she was expecting an important call from work.

'Mummy the phone's ringing. Bring bring, bring bring...' Henry giggled as he poured the bath water over his belly with a plastic cup.

The phone kept ringing over and over as if whoever it was knew someone was home. She decided to answer it.

'Mummy's just going to get that. I will be really quick OK?'

'OK.' Henry carried on splashing and giggling in the bath water. He was now so immersed in his bath he'd forgotten about scratching his scabs.

Hilary ran down stairs to the phone. By the time she got there she half expected the person to have rung off. She picked it up.

'Hello?' She could hear Henry giggling and splashing in the background as a man on the other end spoke.

'Hello madam, how are you today?' Straight away Hilary got the feeling it was a nuisance caller. 'Can I ask what insurance company you're with please madam?'

'No you can't. I've told you before I'm not interested and I'm busy. Please don't call me again.'

'No, please madam, we can save you lots of money on your bills if you switch to us. Let me just run through our details quickly. It will only take a second.'

Hilary was about to answer when she became aware that she couldn't hear Henry splashing or giggling anymore. She moved the phone and pressed it against her cheek.

'Henry!' She shouted up to him. 'Henry, are you OK? Answer mummy...' she didn't hear any reply. A wave of dread hit her. She dropped the phone on the floor and rushed up the stairs towards the bathroom.

She turned the corner on the landing and entered the bathroom to discover Henry, face down, in the bath water. She grabbed him, pulled him out of the water and onto the bathroom floor. His lips looked like they were turning a light shade of blue. She tried to stir him by tapping the side of his face but he was unresponsive.

She began CPR on his small, wet body. 'Henry! Henry... Oh god...'

'I wasn't gone for long... he was fine... I don't know what happened... I ...'

Francis grabbed her daughter again and held her as she stroked her hair to try and calm her down. 'It's OK. This isn't your fault. Something must have happened. What have the doctors said?'

'They haven't been back to see me...' She began to weep, 'It's been too long mum. Something must be wrong...'

Francis squeezed her tighter and peered at Chris over her shoulder. He felt helpless and was unsure that, if he did think of something, it might be seen as intruding, which was the last thing he wanted.

'Do you want me to go? I don't want to be in the way...'

Before he finished a nurse wearing a colourful child friendly tabard entered.

'You can come through. Don't worry he's OK.'

'But he wasn't breathing!' Hilary couldn't believe what the nurse was saying. She'd thought the worse when she'd pulled him out of the water.

The nurse smiled softly. 'Well, thanks to your CPR and the doctor's hard work, he is now!'

She showed them to Henry's bed, and explained what the doctor and nurses had done. Feeling it was the right thing to do Chris held back in the waiting room and didn't follow them in.

When Hilary and Francis saw Henry lying in bed he was tired but awake. They went straight to him and Hilary hugged him, not wanting to let him go. Francis took his little hand, covered in spots and scabs, and sat down next to his bed. He was pleased to see his nana, after what seemed like ages to him.

'Nana my throat hurts!'

Comforted, hearing his little high pitched voice, Francis squeezed his hand and brushed his hair away from his forehead.

'That's because they had to put a special magic tube down your throat to help you breathe.'

'Really?' He was amazed and couldn't believe it, 'I've had a tube down my throat? I didn't see or feel it!'

'That's because you were asleep honey. It was a big one apparently, so the doctor says. Wait until Zach and daddy find out. They'll be impressed!'

Henry beamed. He couldn't wait to see his big brother and boast about it, he felt like a magician having a tube put down his throat.

As Francis and Henry spoke, Hilary spotted one of the doctors walk by the room.

'Mum, can you sit with him while I...'

'Of course.'

Hilary left Francis with her son and hurried out into the corridor. 'Doctor! Excuse me...' The doctor stopped in her tracks and turned to look in the direction of the voice. 'Sorry to bother you, but what's going on? Do you know what happened?'

'Mrs Digby I presume?'

The doctor was younger than she'd expected. 'Yes, sorry. Henry's mother. I brought him in.'

'I was going to come and see you next...' She gave Hilary a reassuring smile. 'Your son is going to be OK but we believe he may have had an epileptic fit of sorts, which is what caused him to fall unconscious. We can't be sure though, I'm afraid. The fact he has chicken pox at the moment, as well, blurs our investigations slightly.'

'So what are you saying? He has epilepsy? Does that mean he'll have more fits?'

'No. Not necessarily. Some children have fits, grow out of them and then they stop. It's just something that can happen to some children, even adults, and we don't know why.' The doctor's beeper, on the rim of her waist band, went off. She peered down at it. 'I'm sorry Mrs Digby, but I have to take this. I will come and find you later so we can speak some more.'

Hilary walked back to Henry's bed and sat with Francis, by his side. They chatted for over an hour with Henry asking most of the questions, wanting to know what toys he could get for being such a brave boy.

Hilary got up to stretch her legs and get them all a hot drink from the vending machine. As she passed the waiting area she was surprised to see that Chris was still there.

'You've been waiting all this time?' She glanced down at her watch. 'It's been hours! If I had known you were still here...'

Chris stood up, concerned about Henry and Hilary could see the worry on his face.

'How is he? Is he OK? If there is anything I can do?' He was completely flustered but Hilary felt calm. She glimpsed the kindness and warmth in his eyes and realised immediately what her mother saw in him.

'He's OK thank you. The doctor said he had some type of seizure but they can't really be sure.'

Chris felt a little less agitated hearing he was all right, that it wasn't bad news.

'I used to have seizures when I was a teenager. I grew out of them eventually. I think it was around sixteen...'

'That's what the doctor said might happen.' She felt as though she was talking to an old friend. She hadn't expected to get over what had happened between him and her mother, but meeting him now, maybe she thought she could, eventually.

They both went quiet. It was as if he could hear what she was thinking.

'I'm sorry about what happened with your mum and I... It wasn't how either of us wanted it to go. Please don't blame her. It was my fault, I pursued her. I care about your mother a lot...' He realised he had started to ramble a bit. Now, probably wasn't the time he thought. 'Sorry, I'm blathering! I do that when I'm nervous...' He touched Hilary's arm, lightly, in a supportive way. 'I'll go and leave you to it, now that I know he's safe... but honestly if there's anything I can do for you, please let me know.' He turned away from her to leave.

'You could give my mum a lift back home! Make sure she gets back safely.' It was a peace offering to him, so he knew she didn't hate him.

He grinned and turned back to face her. 'Of course. I can do that.'

CHAPTER FIFTY SIX

Francesca and Jasmine had been in session for around ten minutes or so. Jasmine was having a good day, so far, and felt quite bright. Since she'd been in the room with Francesca she'd noticed she wasn't her usual self. She seemed, different, somehow.

'Are you OK?' Jasmine asked.

Francesca hadn't been able to stop thinking about her kiss with Shay since it had happened. She felt completely out of control with what she'd done. She hadn't seen or spoken to Shay and it made her feel on edge.

'Yes, thank you.' She could see the way Jasmine was looking at her, as if she didn't believe her and as if she knew what she'd done. She tried to sound as casual as possible 'Why do you ask?'

Jasmine took her time to study her again, she tried to put her finger on what it was that was different about her. 'I don't know. You just seem different.'

In her mind Francesca saw herself with Shay, in her office, pressed up against the wall, with Shay's mouth on hers. She could hear the sound of her own groaning in her head...

'I'm just tired...' She pushed the memory away. 'Anyway where were we? You were talking about your insulin?'

'I haven't missed an injection!'

'That's great! What about your mood? How do you feel in yourself?'

'Most days I'm still up and down. I have my moments of what's the point? What am I doing?' She put her hands to her chest. 'It's like I get this feeling of heaviness on my chest, an empty void.'

Francesca wanted to reassure her. 'It probably won't change overnight, as much as I would like to tell you it does. It's a process you have to work through and around until you start to feel better again.'

Jasmine looked at her and wondered. 'Do you think depression can disappear altogether? Or do you think it stays with the person for the rest of their life?'

'That's a good question.' Francesca paused to think about it. 'In my experience, it's different for everyone. Some people have the good fortune of never experiencing it again. I've know people who've only had it once in their lifetime and it was a short bout but some people experience it, second hand, through a friend or family member, and others as a constant cycle and they just have to be more cautious with how they live their lives...not to overdo it or run themselves into the ground and be aware of their triggers.'

'Where do you think it comes from? I mean what do you think causes it?'

'I believe, for some people, it's a chemical imbalance in the brain but for others its grief, trauma, loss, internalised anger, circumstances... lots of things.'

Jasmine sat, quietly, contemplating what Francesca had said. She thought about her own depression.

'It's weird you know. I have these patches of going into a deep, dark despair, and I feel like I'm never going to get out of it or come through, and then all of a sudden, one day, it feels a little easier. A moment of hope helps me to see past it... but just as quickly, a moment of sadness can throw me back into the darkness again. It just feels so out of my reach and control, the way I feel sometimes...'

Francesca related to not being able to control her feelings as she tried to push the image of Shay out of her mind again. 'Have you ever been offered anti-depressants to help cope with your ups and downs?'

'I took anti-depressants for a year when I was thirteen. I didn't get on with them. I couldn't feel any emotion at all, so I came off them. I'd rather feel like this than feel nothing at all.'

Francesca jotted her reply down on her notes. 'Did you tell your doctor about your experience?'

Jasmine lied. 'Yes.'

'What did he say?'

'He said it was my choice whether I took them or not.'

Francesca frowned, wondering why he hadn't pursued any other possibilities with her.

'He didn't offer you an alternative...a different tablet?'

'Nope. 'Jasmine was eager for the subject to change, she didn't like lying to her, but Francesca wanted to make sure she was covering all the possibilities with her.

'Would you consider taking a different anti-depressant? I know there's a lot of stigma around taking tablets, some people do experience the side effects you've described, but I've also seen a lot of people respond really well with trying something different.'

Jasmine stared down at her feet. 'I don't know. Can I think about it?'

' Of course, there's no pressure. This is your decision. You're the only one who can know if something helps or hinders you and there's no rush.'

Debra picked Jasmine up after her session and drove her back home. She dropped her car keys on the table and headed for the cupboard with the medicines in.

'God I've got such a headache. I don't think I've drunk enough water today...' She searched through but couldn't find any Paracetamol. 'I thought we had some? Jasmine have you seen the Paracetamol?'

Jasmine dropped her school bag by the kitchen table and got a yogurt out of the fridge.

'No. I think they all got used.'

Debra checked the cupboard once more to make sure they hadn't been pushed to the back. 'But I'm sure I only just bought a new box. Surely they haven't all gone?'

'I had bad period pains again, sorry.' She ate a couple of mouthfuls of her yogurt. 'Do you want me to go to the shops and get another box?'

Debra closed the cupboard door and turned to look at her daughter. 'No, don't worry I'll manage. Tell me next time, though, so we don't get caught short again.'

Jasmine finished her yogurt and went upstairs to her bedroom for a rest while Debra began to start getting dinner.

When Paul arrived home from school he strolled in to the kitchen and hugged his mum hello.

'How did you get on today?' she asked.

'It was great, I really enjoyed it! I did a science experiment with litmus paper. Sir said I was really good at doing the testing.'

She smiled as his excitement. 'I wish your sister was half as interested in school as you were!'

Paul took a seat at the kitchen table and got his books out to do his homework. He really wanted to make something of himself and do well in school. He believed, if he did, he could look after his mum and sister, be the man of the house.

He finished his maths homework first then went on to English, his favourite subject. He completed that twice as fast as his maths.

'Mum, can you check it for me please?'

Debra picked up his books and swapped them with a plate of pasta. 'I will later sweetheart but it's dinner time now.' She walked to the bottom of the stairs and shouted. 'Jasmine, tea's up!' She didn't hear any reply or response. 'Jasmine?'

Jasmine was lying on her bed listening to music, through her headphones, in the dark. The track she was listening to finished and she stared up at the ceiling, in silence, waiting for the next song to start when she heard something. She pulled her headphones off to check she wasn't hearing things.

'Jasmine!' it was her mum's voice calling her.

'Coming!' She walked over to her desk, wrapping the headphone wire around her mp3 player and opened the top draw to put it away, safely, out of sight. She opened the second draw, to check that her secret stash of tablets was still there, including all the Paracetamol she'd taken. They were all there, stuffed at the back of the draw. She closed the draw and went downstairs.

As she walked passed Paul, who was still sat at the kitchen table eating, she scuffed his hair up with her hand. He turned and smiled at her. Debra watched her take a seat at the table. Not wanting to say anything to her, Jasmine didn't make eye contact.

'Everything OK?'

'Yep, fine mum.' Jasmine quickly ate her plate of pasta and then asked to be excused. After dinner, she headed straight up to her bedroom to go to bed.

CHAPTER FIFTY SEVEN

Garth had called Francesca at work, earlier in the afternoon, to ask if she was still up for Thai food that night. Francesca had totally forgotten she'd agreed to go out with him again, but after what had happened between her and Shay, it didn't seem like a bad idea.

They met up in town at nine thirty after they'd both finished work. Francesca held his arm as they walked down the street, towards the middle of town, where the Thai restaurant was.

'It's cold tonight...' She was trying to fill the silence between them but Garth took it as a hint that she wanted him to put his arm around her. He placed his arm over her shoulders and pulled her into his chest. Francesca didn't mind it. He was a lot warmer than she was and she liked the smell of his aftershave, but really, if she was honest with herself, she was trying to convince herself that she was attracted to him.

'We're nearly there. It's just around the corner.'

Francesca was confused by the direction in which he was leading her.

'I thought we were going to the Thai place?'

'We were, I tried getting us a table but they were fully booked. Somebody was having a surprise 50th birthday party.'

'Where are we going then?'

'I booked a table at Yani's. They had a last minute cancelation and I managed to get us in.'

Francesca shuddered and stiffened at the thought of having to walk into the restaurant on a date with Garth. She couldn't think of anything worse, especially if Shay ended up serving them.

Garth noticed the sudden tension in her body. 'Are you OK? What's the matter?'

'Yeah I'm... just cold still, that's all.'

He pulled her in closer to his body and squeezed the top of her arm gently.

'Can we go somewhere else for tonight?'

'Why? Is it not good food there or something?' Garth was a little confused.

'No the food's great. It's just...' Yani's was the last place she wanted to be.

Garth interrupted her. 'I've been wanting to go for ages and the guys at work have been raving about it!'

She looked up at him suspiciously. 'What, like they did the movie?'

'Point taken, but this time they were serious. Come on, it will be fun. Besides I doubt we're going to find anywhere else to eat tonight at such late notice.'

'Fish and chips?' It was Francesca's last ditch attempt to get out of eating at Yani's.

Yani's restaurant was busy but, because of the candle lit tables and quiet music playing in the background, the atmosphere was still relaxed and romantic. Garth held the door for Francesca and they waited to be seated.

Francesca scanned the room quickly, seeing if Shay was working. She noticed a few members of staff waiting tables but couldn't see Shay. She breathed out and began to relax a little bit more, knowing she wasn't there.

Garth stepped forward as Faith approached them by the door. 'Hi! I booked a table for two.'

'What's the name please?'

'Garth Lowe.'

Faith scanned through the booking's book and saw his name, she ticked it off and led them over to a private booth table.

She handed them both a menu and went straight into her habitual introduction.

'I'll be your waitress for this evening. The specials are up on the board over there...' She pointed behind the bar, where there was a chalk board. 'I'll give you a few minutes to decide what you're having and I'll come back and take your food order. Can I get you any drinks in the mean time?'

Garth gave his order first. 'I'll have a cider please.'

Francesca ordered the wine she'd tried last time and shared with Laura.

'I'd like a glass of your house red, please.'

'No problem.' Faith wrote her order down and left.

CHAPTER FIFTY EIGHT

Yani's kitchen was hot, stuffy and busy with trying to complete and serve the food orders that were rushing in. Shay was sorting out some of the bills from the food distributer who usually supplied them with steak. They had accused them of not paying for the last order, so George had asked her to sort it out during her shift and see if she could find the receipt, to prove they had paid it.

After serving Garth and Francesca their drinks, Faith walked into the kitchen. 'That's the last table in for tonight!'

'I'll be home before you then, if that's your last table just now!' Shay teased her. She knew how exhausted Faith was from working most of the day.

'Yeah, OK, you don't have to rub it in! Anyway, I thought you had some bill to sort out?'

'I've done it.' She put the receipt she needed into an envelope and put it in her pocket, to give to George tomorrow. 'All sorted!' She was pleased with herself, she'd thought it was going to take her most of the night to track it down among all the other receipts and paperwork. 'You didn't happen to see if table twelve had finished on your way through, did you?'

Faith had automatically noticed Shay's table as she'd walked past, towards the kitchen. 'Yeah, they were still eating their mains, so you might as well take your break.'

Garth took a sip of his cider whilst Francesca was trying to convince herself she liked him more than she actually did, and that she wouldn't find anyone much better than him. OK, he was a bit drippy she thought but...

'So how's your daughter doing with her exams?' He interrupted her evaluation of him.

'She's nearly finished them. It will be a relief when she does. There's quite a lot of stress in the house at the moment.' She picked up her glass and sipped her wine. 'I've promised her a party to celebrate afterwards.'

'Does she know what she wants to do after school?'

'We haven't really discussed it yet but I wouldn't be surprised if she does something to do with performing arts. Her dad would prefer her to have a job and stability...'

'What would you prefer?'

Before she could answer Faith interrupted they conversation by walking back over to their table.

'Are you guys ready to order?'

'I think so. Can I have the steak, rare, with chips please?'

'Yep sure...' She wrote it down and then looked over at Francesca. 'Madam, what can I get you?'

'I'll have the special please.'

'No problem. Good choice!' She gave Francesca a smile and walked off to put the order through to the kitchen.

Their meals arrived fifteen minutes later. Francesca hadn't eaten much at lunchtime and was starving. Garth was still eating by the time she had finished her whole meal.

'Excuse me, I need the ladies room.' She wiped her mouth with her napkin and stood up to walk to the rest rooms.

The ladies' room was a large and modern space, each cubicle had a separate door, for extra privacy. The lighting was atmospheric and the music from the restaurant was playing through, quietly, in the background. As Francesca walked in to the room Shay appeared from one of the cubicles. They both froze with surprise when they saw each other. Shay recovered quicker, she glanced around to make sure the other cubicles were empty.

'You're not taking my calls' Why?'

Francesca stared down at the ground as she tried to walk past her. 'We can't do this here, Shay...'

Shay stepped in front of her so she couldn't pass.

'You kissed me Francesca!' The words echoed around the empty room.

Francesca looked at her, wanting to give her an excuse for what had happened that day, but she couldn't get her words out. They just stood facing one another.

Shay could feel the pull in her body towards Francesca, she went to kiss her, when another customer from the restaurant entered. Francesca took a step back away from Shay so the woman could get past.

Shay knew Francesca, definitely, wouldn't want to talk now they had company, she watched as Francesca left.

Francesca went back to her table, nervous and aware that Shay would soon come out of the restrooms and she wouldn't be able to hide from her.

'That was quick!' Garth was just finishing his steak, he was surprised to see her back so soon.

Francesca lied to him. 'All the cubicles were busy.' She glanced over to see if Shay had come out yet and saw that she had gone behind the bar, from where she could see Francesca and Garth's table.

Francesca looked away from her and tried her best to concentrate on Garth. She wanted to make sure it looked as if she was having a great time with him, and the fact that Shay was there didn't bother her.

Shay clenched her jaw as she watched them from across the room. She saw Faith walk over to their table and start talking to them. She wondered what they were talking about when, out of the corner of her eye, she noticed a customer on a nearby table trying to get her attention. Shay didn't realise what he wanted until he held up his credit card. She picked up the card machine and walked over to the table, which only a few metres away from Francesca's.

Shay made sure she had her back to Francesca as she sorted out his bill. She was trying to listen to their conversation without making it obvious. She could hear

Faith taking their dessert order but neither of them could decide what to choose.

'I can recommend the chocolate mousse, if you can't decide.'

'We can always go back to mine for dessert!'

Francesca could tell Shay had heard Garth's joke, by the change in her body language. Maybe going home with Garth would help her get her feelings and priorities on track, she thought. She couldn't handle the strong gravitation towards Shay, or the intensity between them when they saw one another. She needed and wanted Shay to back off.

'OK, let's go back to yours then!' Francesca said it louder on purpose, knowing Shay could hear.

Garth nearly choked on the cider he was sipping. He had said it as a joke.

'OK. Right, OK.' He tried to keep calm. He hadn't planned or expected the night to go in the direction it seemed to be going, he was unprepared.

Francesca peered over in the direction of Shay who stomped off.

'That's decided then! Let me know when you're ready for the bill.' Faith left them to it.

Garth smiled at Francesca and attempted another joke.

'You don't even want to know what I have for dessert?'

'No, I just want to get out of here!'

Garth insisted on paying for the whole bill before they headed off to his house.

Shay had stayed away in the kitchen, not prepared to see them together for any longer than she had to.

Francesca and Garth barely got over Garth's front door step before Francesca pounced on him. She kissed him hard and roughly with a kind of desperation. Hurriedly pulling at his buttons, she began to try and take his shirt off. Garth grabbed hold of her hands to slow her down.

'Whoa, slow down. What's the rush?'

Francesca tried to kiss him again but he pulled his face away.

'What? Don't you want me?' she asked, confused by his withdrawal.

'Of course I want you...' He didn't know what he was thinking. An attractive, sexy woman who was, obviously, desperate to have sex with him and he was trying to slow things down! He kissed her and began tugging at her clothes.

Francesca kissed him back hoping the harder she kissed him the quicker she would forget about Shay. Garth took her by the hand and guided her up the stairs to his bedroom. He helped to undress her and then took his own clothes off.

Lying down on the bed, naked, Garth slowly moved on top of her. She could feel his erection and excitement against her leg and wondered why she wasn't more excited herself. He stopped kissing her and leant over to his bedside draw to take out a condom and looked at Francesca for approval. She nodded her head and he tore the wrapper off and put it on. Francesca opened her legs slightly so he could position himself and penetrate her. His lovemaking was rougher and faster than she'd expected. He tried to slow himself down but he was too aroused and orgasmed before Francesca had even had the chance to warm up. He let out a short grunt and rolled off to the side of her.

Lying beside her, he started to kiss and caresses her arm. She could hear his heavy breathing directly in her ear as he tried to catch his breath.

She stared up at the ceiling, wondering what she had just done. It was like something had taken over her.

Garth broke her trail of thought whispering in her ear. 'Was that OK?'

She turned her head to look at him and was met with his face, close to hers, staring directly at her. She didn't know what to say so she lied and told him what she would always tell David after sex.

'Yeah, it was nice...'

Garth grinned at her answer, completely oblivious. He could still feel the pleasure of his release running around his body.

A feeling of dread, panic and regret hit Francesca. She got out of his bed and began to get dressed.

'I'm sorry Garth but I need to get back.' She was dressed and out of his bedroom before he could even get out of the bed to kiss her goodbye. He ran to the top of the landing, with the bed sheet wrapped around him, to watch her leave.

'Call me!' he shouted after her.

Francesca didn't even turn around to look at him, she left as quickly as she could.

CHAPTER FIFTY NINE

Shay was still fuming after seeing Francesca at the restaurant, knowing where she was going after and what they were probably going to do. She decided the only way to get over it was to get drunk and get off with someone else, like Francesca had. If Francesca could do it, so could she.

She headed for Club Juice and hit the bar as soon as she got there. Ordering two shots and downing them one after the other she listened to the music booming in the background.

After about five minutes, Shay hit the dance floor. She gradually moved herself towards the middle so she could be in amongst the crowd, with all the hot, sweaty bodies. She'd only been dancing by herself for about five minutes when a man, she'd seen at the club a couple of times before, approached her from the side. She smiled at him and encouraged him to move up behind her. She teased him and pushed her bottom into his groin as they danced together for the next few songs.

Twenty minutes later Shay was kissing him up against the wall in the club. The alcohol had hit her empty stomach and she was in a numb bubble. She wanted gratification and to forget Francesca, so she could move on. Sex was her usual way of getting over someone. She would always tell Faith 'get drunk and get under someone to get over someone.' But as his hand started to wander up her top and then back down towards her scar she pulled back.

'I'm sorry. I can't do this.'

'Why not?' He tried to carry on kissing her but Shay didn't let him and pulled away. 'What's the deal with you?'

'I like someone else. This isn't right.' She couldn't believe she was admitting to him, or herself, that she actually liked someone. That wasn't what usually happened. They usually got hung up on her, not the other way around. She was always the one who stayed safe and made sure she never had any real strong feelings that would get her into trouble.

The guy looked at her wondering if there was some leeway. No-body went from hot to cold that quickly, he thought.

'I won't tell! I don't mind being used for one night!'

Usually Shay didn't mind either, but something had changed for her.

He tried to kiss her again but she blocked his mouth with her hand.

'I can't believe I'm saying this, but I do!'

CHAPTER SIXTY

Jamie had been to the hospital with Maggie for her second scan, before seeing Francesca in session.

'So we're having a baby girl! I can't believe it!'

'Congrats!' Francesca was really pleased for him. 'How did it feel being at the scan?'

'Like I was about to explode! I had so many emotions going on at once. All these thoughts were spinning around my head.'

'What kind of thoughts?'

Jamie had the biggest grin on his face. 'At first I was completely overwhelmed with joy and cried when they told us, but now...' His smile disappeared as he thought about it. 'It's, what if the baby isn't OK? Can I do this? Do I deserve to feel this happy and this much love...'

'What makes you think that? We all deserve to be loved and feel loved.'

Jamie breathed out. 'It's just something I felt as a child. I started believing I didn't deserve to be loved and the idea that I wasn't lovable kind of stuck with me. I believed there must have been something wrong with me and that's why he treated me the way he did...'

'Jamie, everything your father did to you was nothing to do with who you are as a person...what you deserve and don't deserve. It has everything to do with your father's own pain, that he couldn't deal with, and so he projected it on to you. Do you understand? None of it was your fault.'

He didn't believe her. He couldn't. He felt too responsible.

'But what if I had just been a bit better behaved...hadn't provoked him so much, talked back to him? Maybe I was partially to blame...'

Francesca moved forward in her chair and made sure he was looking at her, so he could hear and take in what she was saying.

'You were a child, Jamie. You shouldn't feel any guilt or responsibility for what happened because you were the vulnerable one in the relationship and your father was the adult. He should have been the one to know better, not you.'

'But he was drunk, intoxicated. I was more with it than he was.'

'That's no excuse. He...' A knock at the door interrupted her. She looked towards it surprised to see Julie slowly opening it.

Knowing it wouldn't be for him, Jamie didn't bother to look around to see who it was.

'Sorry Dr Francesca...' Francesca knew it must be important because Julie rarely referred to her as Doctor. 'I think you should know there's a man waiting in reception. He says it's important he speak with you.'

'Who is it?' She wondered if it was Judge Harmen. Maybe Shay had done something stupid after seeing her leave with Garth.

'He says his name is Richard Farrow.'

Francesca was confused. She'd never heard the name before. 'I don't know any Richard Farrow.'

Jamie turned to look at Julie. 'I do...' He turned back around and looked at Francesca. 'He's my father.'

The energy in the room had become awkward since Richard had taken a seat on the sofa, next to Jamie. Francesca wasn't prepared or expecting him to join them, but Jamie had insisted he might as well since he was there.

Francesca felt a little flustered as she tried to regroup. 'Sorry, I wasn't expecting you today Mr Farrow.'

'My wife, Janet, convinced me to come. She told me...' He turned towards Jamie, 'She told me you deserve to know the whole truth, and she's right.'

Jamie stared quietly at his father. He still couldn't believe he was there.

Francesca was concerned for him. She wasn't sure if Jamie was ready, they hadn't spoken about Richard joining them, recently. She checked in with him again to make sure he was OK.

'Jamie, are you OK with this...with your father being here today?'

'Yes.' He nodded as he said it.

'I'm sorry son. I apologise... for all the things I did to you. For hitting you, for blaming everything on you, being drunk and abusive all the time... but I promise you, I did it because I thought I was protecting you and now I see that I wasn't. I did the opposite.' Richard couldn't get his apology out soon enough.

Richard wasn't what Francesca had expected. He seemed like a totally different man to the image she'd created of him in her head.

'What made you think hitting him was protecting him? What were you trying to protect him from?' She was intrigued to know his reasoning and answer.

'He needed protecting from...' he paused...'from me.'

50 YEARS EARLIER.

Richard walked to the local shop as fast as his little eight year old legs could carry him. He pushed the door open to see the familiar face of Gary, the shopkeeper, standing behind the till.

'Hello Ritchie. Is your mum out of milk again?'

'No, Mr Gary, it's my pa. He said you'd have a bottle of wispy for him.'

Richard was pleased as punch at himself for making the walk to the shop on his own. He had always been scared at the thought of having to walk all that way alone, but the thought of coming home empty handed to his father scared him more.

'Wispy?' Gary didn't understand what he meant. 'Ah, you mean whisky?'

'Yes whisky!'

'I've told your father before not to send you for his drink. It's illegal for me to sell alcohol to a child.'

'He knows that, Mr Gary, and he told me to tell you it won't happen again, that this is the last time.'

Gary hesitated. He didn't want to lose his shop or his licence, but he knew how Kurt Farrow could kick up a fuss.

'Please, Mr Gary, just today...' Richard began pleading with him. 'He has friends over and he won't like it if I don't come back with his bottle...'

Gary had heard that the boy's father could be aggressive to his children and his wife, who had come in his shop a few times with a black eye. He didn't want to be the catalyst for more violence or arguments.

'OK, but only because it's you, Ritchie, and this definitely is the last time. You tell your father that, OK?' He turned around to the bottles of alcohol he kept behind the counter and got a large bottle of whisky down.

Richard took the bottle and handed him the note his father had given him to pay for it. As Gary took the money from him, he felt sorry for him, so he leaned across the counter and picked up a chocolate bar and handed it to him. 'Here lad, take this for your walk back. My treat!'

Richard's face lit up. He rarely had chocolate, since they never had enough money for treats.

'Thank you Mr Gary!'

'I knew he felt sorry for me. Everybody did...for the whole family. They knew what my father was like. A useless drunk that cared about no one but himself...'

Jamie's ears pricked up at his father statement. 'Sounds familiar!'

Richard ignored him. He knew he was right but he couldn't do anything about it now. All he could do was explain.

'Half the men in the village wanted to wring his neck. He had slept with most of their wives at the end, or during a drunken night out. When I got back home, late that afternoon, he and his friends had started drinking already. They were through the first couple of bottles that his mates had brought round.'

50 YEARS EARLIER (THE SAME DAY).

Richard entered his house through the front door. His house was small and in a rough, poor area where un-employment was high and drugs were a big issue. They, as a family, had lived in the street all his life, it was all he had ever known. As he walked over the doorstep he could already hear his father and his friends, drunk, rowdy, and being vulgar with one another in the living room. Larry, one of his father's friends, who had known Richard since he was a baby and was always at the house most Friday nights drinking, saw Richard enter.

'Here you are Kurt, your boy's back with the booze!' Larry stumbled over to him and snatched the bottle from him. He was too drunk to know his own

strength and hurt Richard when he ruffled his hair. 'Good lad!'

Kurt wasn't so pleased with his son, he waltzed over and walloped him around the back of his head. 'What took you so long boy?'

'I only have little legs, dad, so it takes me longer!' He regretted saying it as soon as it had come out of his mouth.

'Are you being smart with me? I've told you what happens when you try and be clever with me!'

Richard panicked. He didn't know what his father would do next and he could see he was agitated. 'No daddy, I'm telling the truth!'

Kurt just stared at him. He enjoyed seeing the fear and panic on his son's face.

'Well? Have you got something for me?'

Richard was confused. Larry had already taken the bottle and he hadn't asked him for anything else.

Kurt towered over him. 'My change, boy! I gave you a ten pound note.' He glugged the bottle of beer in his hand as Richard scrambled around in his pockets. He pulled out the change but, as he did, the chocolate wrapper fell out onto the floor.

Kurt counted the change. Being so drunk he miscounted and thought Richard was short changing him. He became more aggressive and threatening. 'Where's the rest?'

'That's all he gave me! I promise!'

Kurt glared down at him, he noticed the chocolate wrapper on the floor by Richard's foot. He grabbed Richard by the shirt and yanked him closer so that he *could see his face better. He spotted some melted chocolate around his son's lips.*

'You bloody bought chocolate with my change, didn't you?' It wasn't a question but a statement. Kurt slapped him hard across the face for lying to him.

Richard held his stinging cheek and began to cry.

Kevin, another one of Kurt's friends, saw how hard he'd hit him. 'Ease up on him Kurtie. He's only a kid!'

Kurt shouted at his friend. 'He's my kid, so keep out of it. He has to learn! Someone has to teach him. It's good for him. I'm making him into a man...' He stared at his son. 'Scram boy! It's your bedtime but you'll pay for this later!'

Richard ran up the stairs as fast as he could, knowing he probably wouldn't get any sleep. He knew he would be in for a beating later. It didn't matter whether he was telling the truth or not, once his father had something in his head, that was it.

At half past eleven in the evening, Kurt and his friends were still drinking and chatting, with the television blaring out in the background.

'So come on Kurt, spill! What woman will you have in your bed this week, apart from your wife of course?'

Kurt knew Gavin was teasing him. He hadn't known him for long and knew he, obviously, needed to put him in his place. No-one goaded him like that, even if it was just for a laugh.

'Oh, she's useless...' He raised his eyebrows, 'but your wife on the other hand...?'

They all laughed except for Gavin, his face turned to steel.

Kevin could see that he was angry and not impressed with Kurt referring to his wife like that. He tried to reassure him and kill the animosity in the air.

'Come on mate, he's only joking!' He thumped Gavin hard on the back to try and perk him up.

Gavin watched Kurt change the channel on the television as he muttered to Kevin under his breath. 'You wouldn't be laughing if he said that about your wife!'

'That's why I don't have a wife, mate!' Kevin nudged and smiled at him. 'Drink up and enjoy yourself!'

Kurt left the television on a quiz programme and walked over to the sofa where he was handed another glass of whisky by Larry.

'Where's your wife tonight? She's usually down here running after you!'

'She's gone to her sister's, She's about to blow and Jenny wanted to be there for the birth.' He downed the whisky in one. 'I'm not complaining because it gets her out of my hair.' Kurt pulled out his packet of cigarettes and took one out. He placed it between his lips and Larry lit it for him, he didn't even have to ask.

'You'll be stuck tonight then?'

Kurt took a puff and pulled the cigarette out of his mouth, blowing the smoke directly in Larry's face.

'What do you mean?'

'For a woman!' He attempted to waft the smoke out of his way. 'You know what you're like when you've had a drink or two. You become a randy bastard!'

'Well I guess I'll have to please myself tonight, so to speak!'

Larry held his drink up in the air. 'Cheers to that!'

By one in the morning everyone, apart from Kurt, had passed out, drunk, on the floor. Obliterated, but still able to walk, he stumbled up the stairs to go to bed. He reached his bedroom door and went to open it when he noticed Richard's bedroom door was slightly open. He crept across the landing and slowly pushed the door open. The light from the landing shone through on to Richard's bed and woke him up. Kurt entered the room and moved to the side of his son's bed, all six foot of him stood over him.

'Pa?' Richard was still half asleep and dazed, but his body still tensed up automatically, prepared for a thump from his father.

'What have you got for me, boy?'

Richard could smell the stench of alcohol on his breath as his father slurred his words.

'I gave you the change Pa...'

'I wasn't talking about the change...' He slowly pulled down the zipper on his pants.

Jamie didn't know what he was more shocked at, his father's story or seeing how, for the first time, vulnerable and upset his father was. He had never seen him like that before.

'What did he do to you, dad?'

Out of shame, Richard couldn't look at his son as he answered.

'It was the first time he touched me, sexually, but it wasn't the last... he would get drunk as usual, wait for my mother to go to bed, then he would come into my room and...' He couldn't bring himself to say it.

'How long did this go on for?' Francesca was shocked. She had suspected that something must have happened to him, as a child, for him to hit out at Jamie the way he had, but she hadn't imagined something as serious and upsetting as sexual abuse by his own father.

'Not that long, really. About a year. He died the following June.'

'How did he die? Neither you nor mum ever told me. Was he drunk?' Jamie, secretly, hoped it was a slow painful death, after hearing about what he had done.

'No, he wasn't drunk...'

50 YEARS EARLIER (JUNE)

Kurt was sat in the living room watching television. Richard was sitting next to him, too petrified to move. He didn't want to annoy or agitate his father in any way. His tension was broken by a violent pounding on the front door.

'Kurt! You fucking scoundrel!' The voice boomed through the door. 'Come out here and face me like a man!'

Richard recognised the voice but couldn't place it. He got up and went towards the front door, to see who it was.

'Boy, what are you doing? Get away from that door! If you open that, I'm a dead man!'

He had never seen his father, the man who he hated so much, look so worried.

'Why, what did you do?'

The door vibrated. It was being hit so hard.

'Don't you dare question me boy! Just do as you're told, you hear?' Kurt got up from the sofa to give Richard a physical warning. Richard flinched, afraid of him, and moved closer to the front door as a way of protection. Kurt backed off straight away, realising now wasn't a good time to threaten him.

'Come on Kurt! You fuck my wife, you fuck with me!'

Richard realised whose voice it was. It was Gavin's. He put his hand on the front door handle and glared at his father.

'Son... don't...'

Within seconds Richard let the latch off the door and pushed the handle down. Gavin rushed into the house.

'You bastard! You'll pay for what you did...' He ran over to him and punched Kurt squarely on the jaw, knocking him to the floor. Blinded by rage, he repeatedly kicked him over and over again. After more than a few blows he realised Richard was standing there, watching. 'You won't want to see this lad! Go upstairs.'

'I knew he would kill him and I still let him in. I took it as my opportunity to be free of him... and the abuse.'

The room was silent.

Francesca spoke softly. 'I'm sorry Mr Farrow. Nobody deserves to go through something like that.'

Richard didn't really hear her comment, he was still caught up in his memory of that day.

'I tried to numb the sounds, but I could hear them over and over again. My father being beaten to death. At any time I could have asked him to stop, gone for help, but I didn't...' He changed direction. 'I was twelve when I had my first drink. The feeling it gave me... helped me to forget, to avoid. I wanted to carry on forgetting.'

It was exactly what Jamie had tried to do, forget and avoid his own childhood. 'If you knew what it was like to be beaten by a drunk, why did you do the same to me?' He had tears in his eyes. He didn't understand but he wanted to.

Richard swallowed the lump in his throat before he answered. 'I heard that children who are sexually abused can go on to abuse their own children. I never wanted to take that risk, so I always kept you at a distance... I beat you back... I tried to make sure you hated me and would never want to be close to me.'

Jamie dropped his head and began to sob. 'I thought for years it was something I had done. That's why you couldn't love me...why when you were drunk you used to look at me with such disgust...'

Richard took his son's hand and squeezed it. 'That's only because you reminded me so much of myself as a little boy. Under all the shit that was going on, I always loved you, more than I could even cope with. I'm sorry son, please forgive me.'

Jamie pulled his hand away, confused by all the thoughts rushing around his head. 'I want to believe that you love me, I do...' He became too upset to finish his sentence and Richard could do nothing to soothe him.

'Mr Farrow, have you ever had help for what happened to you?'

He looked at Francesca and let out a deep sigh. 'I got help when I met Janet. She took me to AA, made sure I stuck with the steps and the therapy. It was one of the most difficult things I ever did. That's why I'm so proud of Jamie to be able to do this...' He turned back to look at his son, but Jamie still wouldn't look up at him. 'I didn't want to come into a place like this and address my memories and feelings again. I wanted to put them behind me. Janet said if it was affecting me that much, the thought of talking about it again, that maybe it still wasn't all behind me. That's a truth, and possibility, I need to face, so here I am.'

'It can be hard to face the truth of our feelings.' Francesca tried to convince herself she was only saying that for Richard to hear and not herself.

'This is what I want to do dad...' Jamie managed to look up at his father. He felt ready to face him. 'I want to put my past behind me. Deal with it, not deny it or try to drink it away! I want to be there for my daughter. I don't want to carry on our messed up family pathology.'

'Your daughter? You're having a girl?'

'Yes.'

'Son, that's great! Congratulations!' He was genuinely pleased for him. He became nervous and unsure.

'I know it's a lot to ask... I'm sober now... I would like to try and have contact with you...I mean only if you want to? I don't want to rush you... I'll understand if you say no. It would all be on your terms...'

Jamie didn't answer him, he just sat silently, thinking about how to answer.

Francesca was aware of how fast the pace of everything was going, she didn't want Jamie to become overwhelmed or feel rushed into making a decision.

'How long have you been sober for Mr Farrow?'

'Nine years, no relapses.' Jamie looked at his father in surprise. 'I'm changed Jamie and I know I can never make up for what I did, what I missed with you, but I would like to live the rest of my life trying...' Full of emotion, he turned his body to face Jamie properly. 'I'm so sorry son. I know that's not enough. I know...' He wiped away a tear from his cheek not knowing what else he could say or do.

There was a pause before Jamie said anything. 'I would like that...to try. I can't promise anything, but... we could try...' He could see how different his father was. It was as though he was looking at a completely different person, compared to the man he knew as a child.

Richard placed his hand over Jamie's and squeezed it. 'You don't need to promise me anything Jamie. I just appreciate, more than you know, that you're even speaking to me.'

CHAPTER SIXTY ONE

Mia finished her maths exam. She packed up her things, left the exam room and walked down the school corridor, relieved to have got it out of the way.

'Only three more to go!' Josh had seen her leave and chased after her.

'Three what?' Her head was so in the clouds that she didn't know what he was talking about.

'Exams! Then we're done...school life over!'

'I thought you were going to university?'

'True! But that's different.' He calmed down a bit and walked alongside her. 'Have you decided what you're going to do yet?'

It was the last thing on Mia's mind. All she wanted to do was complete her exams, finish school for good and then maybe experience a bit of the real world.

'I haven't decided. I've got ideas, but I'm not sure.'

'Share and grow!'

She trusted him enough to tell him. 'I would like to study theatre... but I could take a job at my dad's accounts place to get some proper training.'

Josh could tell she wasn't as excited about the latter prospect.

'Have you even spoken to him yet? Would you really want a job with your dad after...' He felt awkward bringing up her father's cheating, so diverted. 'You'd be great in the theatre!'

Mia stopped and looked at him. 'How would you know?'

'OK, this is a little embarrassing... I was kind of stalking you, a little, after seeing you in the school play. I couldn't help it because you stood out. You were miles better than everyone else.'

Mia didn't know who was blushing most, her or Josh.

'You noticed me?'

'Of course! I always notice you.' Josh grinned.

They walked to the school canteen where they had lunch together.

After school had finished Mia met up with Jasmine, outside, by the gates.

'How did your exams go?'

'OK, I think?'

Jasmine could see the worry on Mia's face. 'You know exams are made into a really big deal but, ultimately, they can't teach you about life or experience. It's just results based for a system the government uses. It has no reflection on you or what you can achieve in your life.'

Mia smiled at her. 'Have you ever thought about running for school council?'

Jasmine scoffed. 'Who, me? Are you kidding?'

CHAPTER SIXTY TWO

Francesca was at work, in the kitchenette, which was directly off the reception area. She was filling her glass with tap water, she'd barely drunk anything all day and could feel the start of a headache. As she put her lips to the rim of the glass Julie popped her head around the door.

'Your four o'clock is here.'

'Thank you.' Francesca quickly glugged the water and walked into reception to greet Francis. They said their hello's and headed for her office where they took their usual seats.

'We haven't seen each other for a while.' Francesca could feel the cold water trying to settle in her stomach.

'Yes, sorry. I've been a bit sporadic with our appointments, my grandson hasn't been well.'

'I'm sorry to hear that. Is he OK now?'

'I hope so. He had a seizure, the doctors are querying epilepsy but it could have just been a one off, only time will tell. Chris had a couple of them when he was a kid but he grew out of them so, fingers crossed, the same happens to Henry.'

'Chris?' Francesca was surprised to hear Chris's name come up. 'He's back in the picture then?'

'Yes. We're, eh... seeing each other. Seeing how it goes.'

Francesca was pleased for her, but wondered if her daughter knew and how she had taken it.

'Does your daughter know you're seeing him again?'

Francis could feel herself blush a little. 'Yes, actually it was her who bumped our heads together!'

FOUR DAYS AFTER HENRY'S ACCIDENT.

Francis was sitting at her kitchen table contemplating whether to ring Chris, to thank him again for taking her to and from the hospital. Her indecision was interrupted when her phone rang. It was Chris.

'Hi, Francis. How are you?'

'I'm tired but OK thank you, relieved...' They hadn't spoken or seen each other since the journey home from the hospital and, for Francis, it felt like it had done nothing but create more tension and awkwardness between them.

'How is he? Is he still in hospital?'

'No, they let him out yesterday. I'm going over to see him today.'

'Have you got your car back?'

'Nope, the garage said it was a bigger job than they first thought.'

'You know that means that it will cost more than they thought, as well!'

She laughed at his teasing. 'Oh don't! I'm dreading the bill already!'

They both paused and the line went quiet between them.

'Let me take you to see Henry.' Chris knew he was on uncertain ground with her still, but he wanted to meet with her so he knew where they stood. 'We never got to finish our chat. I won't come in or anything. I'll just drop you off. Maybe we could talk on the way over.'

'Actually, Hilary may want to see you, she told me she wanted to thank you.'

'Thank me? She already did, at the hospital.'

'Maybe she forgot?'

He asked again, to be clear. 'So, can I pick you up then?'

Chris drove over to her house. Their greeting had been a bit stiff and bumbling, Chris hadn't been sure whether to kiss Francis on the cheek or not, in the end, he decided not to.

They'd been driving for about five minutes, heading towards Hilary's, he was trying to concentrate on taking the right route, but he was finding it challenging when he was so close to Francis and her perfume was filling up his car.

'I take the next left, right?'

Francis felt nervous and couldn't really focus either. She just wanted to get to Hilary's and not be sharing a small, intimate space in the car with him.

'Not the next right, the next left.'

'That's what I said. I said take the next left, right!'

'Oh, I only heard the word right and thought you meant turn right...'

They both giggled at the confusion. Chris turned left and glanced at Francis quickly.

'I've missed this! Your laugh...your company...' He gently put his hand on her leg. It felt right for him, but his touch was too much for Francis to take.

'Chris, we can't... after what happened last time... and nearly losing Henry...' She became emotional. 'I can't risk losing my family again...'

Chris took his hand away, not wanting to upset her even more. She saw the disappointment on his face and felt guilty.

'I'm sorry. I do care about you...a lot. If things were different...'

'It's OK Francis. I understand and I don't want to push you into anything. I just want you to know where I stand.'

She didn't know what to say to him. She just knew she was relieved when they approached Hilary's house.

'It's just over there.'

He drove up outside, they silently got out and walked towards the house. Francis knocked on the front door whilst Chris hung back behind her. He stood in the pathway, not quite convinced Hilary would want to see him.

Hilary opened the door. Pleased to see Francis, she gave her mum a warm, tight hug.

'How are you?' She let Francis go.

'Oh it's been chaos! Henry is still off school and running around the place like nothing ever happened!'

'That's kids! They're resilient alright!'

Hilary heard Henry screaming in the background and was worried he was going to get himself into trouble.

'Come on in.'

As Francis entered, Henry spotted her straight away.

'Nanny!' He took her by the hand and dragged her off through the house and into the back garden to play. Hilary watched them and then looked back at Chris. She motioned for him to come in, using just her head, but Chris wasn't sure, he thought she was only inviting him in out of polite awkwardness. He saved her the bother.

'It's OK. I actually, probably, should go...' He stepped back and began to walk away, back down the path.

'If you think you're escaping the mad house you've got another thing coming!' He turned around to see Hilary grinning at him. 'Come on! I've just put the kettle on and we've got cake!'

They had been at Hilary's house for over an hour. Francis and Hilary had sat at the kitchen's breakfast bar watching Chris playing with the boys in the garden. Zach had come home from school and warmed to Chris straight away. They were laughing, climbing and jumping all over *him as he tried to tickle them. Hilary smiled at the joy on her son's faces.*

'He seems nice, Chris. I can see what you like about him.'

It sounded strange for Francis to hear Hilary saying something like that. 'Hilary, there's nothing going on between us and I've made it clear it's not going to work.'

'Why wouldn't it work? You like him don't you? He likes you!'

'I don't want to upset you...'

'It's OK mum, I'm over it... I never told you this but dad, before he died, when he was himself, he asked me not to be mad if you found someone and moved on. He wanted you to be with someone, not alone and I... well I was in denial about his diagnosis. I didn't want to hear it.' Francis could feel herself getting emotional hearing Jack's wishes. 'I wasn't there for you when dad was sick and you needed someone to lean on. Anyone would, with the pressure and stress of looking after someone so ill. I wasn't there...' Hilary took a deep breath out. 'I guess what I'm trying to say is, I understand why you would turn to someone like him.' Her eyes began to water, she looked at her mum and leaned forward to take her hand. 'It would upset me more if you were alone because of me. You should go for it. He seems lovely and he cares about you. Plus, it's not every day you meet a toy boy!' They both laughed and Francis blushed a little as Chris walked in from the garden. The boys followed behind him, trying to drag him back out to play some more. He smiled at Francis and Hilary as he waited for them to finish laughing.

'I better go now. Thank you for the cup of tea and cake.' Zach and Henry each grabbed hold of his legs and he looked down at them and grinned. 'I think you boys have helped me burn it off!'

Henry tugged on his T-shirt, stretching it to the maximum. 'Do you have to go? I haven't shown you my bike yet!

'Come on boys, let Chris go. He's probably got somewhere to be.' Hilary stood up from the table and ushered them away from him. 'If you behave yourselves, you never know, he might come around again on another day?' Zach and Henry grinned from ear to ear with excitement. Chris glanced at Francis for a long moment. She said nothing, he took her silence as a sign to leave. He gave her an understanding but slightly disappointed smile.

'You take care of yourself. I'll see myself out.'

Hilary walked across to the snack cupboard to get something for the boys to eat. She didn't say anything to Francis, she just watched her and waited to see what she'd do, whether she would go after Chris.

'What?' Francis could feel her daughter watching her.

Hilary smirked at her. 'Well aren't you going to kiss him goodbye!' The boys giggled at the thought of their nana kissing someone.

Chris walked back down the pathway and reached his car. He opened the driver's door feeling disheartened. He'd hoped to speak more with Francis and change her mind about their relationship.

'Chris, wait! Hang on a second!'

He turned to see Francis rushing towards him.

'Did you leave something in the car?'

'No, I just wanted to... to...'

*'What is it Francis? Are you OK?' He was worried,
she looked flushed.*

*'Yes. I just wanted to do this...' She grabbed him by
the neck and kissed him passionately.*

*After a few seconds Chris pulled away confused. 'I
thought you said...'*

'Forget what I said! I've changed my mind!'

*He beamed at her as he leaned in for another kiss.
Knowing she had Hilary's blessing, Francis kissed him
again, this time, there was no guilt.*

Francesca was impressed with Francis' bravery. 'Wow,
well done! So you just went for it?'

'Yep, and we can't keep our hands off one another!
We just couldn't deny it any longer!'

'What do you think you were denying?'

'The chemistry, you know, when you're near
someone and it's like you can't breathe and their body is
like a magnet to yours... I can't resist him. When we are...'
She thought she was getting a bit too carried away. 'Sorry,
I'm going on. You don't want to hear about my love life!'

'I don't mind. I'm here to listen.' Francesca was
fine up until the body being like a magnet comment, it
made her think of Shay and the way she felt when she was
with her.

'That's something I wanted to talk to you about. I
think I'm ready to stop coming to see you.'

'That's fine!' Francesca could tell Francis felt a bit guilty saying it, as if she was worried she was going to take it personally. 'That's always the aim in therapy. It means our work is done!'

'I just feel so much better and less guilty about... I'm not over Jack's death, and maybe I never will be, but I'm ready to try and move forward.'

'I'm really pleased for you Francis. I'm happy to hear you want to move on. It's a big part of the healing process. I wish you all the best, sincerely.'

Francis got up to leave. She waited for Francesca to stand so she could hug her. She was grateful for their time together and her support.

CHAPTER SIXTY THREE

Francesca was at her desk. It was the end of her working day and she began to check through her paperwork and schedule for tomorrow, unaware that Shay had entered the building and walked up the stairs into reception. She'd opened the door to find Julie wasn't at her desk and, as she couldn't see her anywhere, strolled straight through to Francesca's office.

Before she entered she took a deep breath out to try and centre herself. She knocked lightly on the door.

'Come in.' Francesca answered but didn't look up, she just assumed it was Julie.

Shay quietly walked in and shut the door behind her. She said nothing and waited for Francesca to look up.

'Shay!' She was surprised, and shocked to see her and went straight on the defence. 'What are you doing? I could have been with a client!'

'That's why I knocked! Besides, it's late, so you wouldn't have a client at this time...' Shay raised her eyebrows in animation, 'or maybe you would!'

Francesca knew she was insinuating that she would see her later. She got up from behind her desk and took a few steps towards the middle of the room.

'You need to leave!'

'No, you need to see me!'

'Our sessions have finished, Shay. Our talking has finished!'

'I thought therapy was supposed to make you feel better?' She wasn't going to leave Francesca's office until she'd had her say. 'I feel angrier... even more messed up than before I started seeing you...' She took another deep breath to try and calm her racing heart, which she could hear thumping in her ears. Francesca didn't say anything or make any movement, so Shay carried on. 'What do I need to do to get you to talk to me? Assault someone again?'

'Don't be stupid...'

'Then talk to me Francesca, because I don't think I'm the only one struggling with their feelings here...' She moved towards her.

Francesca panicked as Shay walked over towards her.

'It will pass...' Her comment made Shay stop where she was. 'Whatever it is you're feeling for me, just give it time, some space and you'll get bored and find someone else to chase...'

'Is that what you think? That this is just about the chase for me?' Shay couldn't hide the hurt from her voice.

'Well isn't that what you do? Chase women, sleep with them and then leave them?'

Shay didn't answer. She just looked at her and clamped her jaw, angrily.

'Did you sleep with him?'

'Who?' Francesca knew she was asking about Garth.

'You know who! That guy you were with at Yani's.'

'That's none of your business...'

With both of their emotions running high, the tension escalated between them. Shay began to pace the room trying to fight off images of Francesca with Garth.

'Right, sure...' She whispered sarcastically to herself. Angry and frustrated she stopped pacing and looked back up at Francesca. 'Was he good? Was he worth it?' She moved a few more steps closer towards her. 'Did fucking him help you get me out of your head?'

Livid, Francesca took a step towards her. 'Get out!'

Shay wasn't willing and didn't want to back down, she moved closer towards her again. Francesca backed away until she bumped into the back of the sofa. Shay stepped right up into her space and pressed her body against her. She could feel Francesca respond.

'No, it didn't work, did it? You can't stop thinking about me, just as much as I can't stop thinking about you.' She leaned forward, her mouth hovering over Francesca's ear. 'Admit it, you want me...'

Francesca felt like her body was about to melt into Shay's, she couldn't deny that she wanted her, but before she gave in someone knocked on the office door, interrupting them. Shay moved away from her as Julie opened the door gently and carefully, her hands full with two cups of hot tea. She was surprised to see Shay in the office.

'Oh! Hello Shay! I didn't see you come in. Sorry, I didn't realise you had an appointment.'

'I don't.' Shay's voice was flat.

Julie picked up the tension between them. 'Well, I've made you a cup of tea anyway... Shay do you want one?'

Francesca jumped in before she could answer. She felt Julie had saved her from making another big mistake. 'Shay was just leaving.'

Shay glared at her, annoyed, as she turned and walked out the office, giving Julie a quick, forced smile.

Julie stood there with the hot cups of tea in her hands. 'What was that about?'

Francesca stepped forward and carefully took a cup from her. 'Nothing. It was just something about her case that didn't go how she'd imagined.'

'Was that why she seemed so upset?'

Francesca lied. 'Yes.'

CHAPTER SIXTY FOUR

When Jasmine walked into Francesca's office she could tell straight away that Jasmine wasn't in a good place. She let her sit and settle before she said anything.

'Not a good week then?'

Jasmine sighed as her body slumped. She rested her head on the top of the sofa and stared up at the ceiling. 'Do you know the shittiest thing about living with this cloud over my head? I feel utterly helpless, abandoned by the world, detached even. I know that very few people understand how hard or painful life can be for me and others like me... There's nothing that feels more isolating or lonely than when you're trying to explain to someone how you feel, that you can't help it and they just look at you, in disbelief, thinking why can't you just get up and get on with it?' Tears slowly and silently fell down her face, she dropped her head down. 'People have actually asked my mum 'do you think Jasmine is just making it up?' and 'Oh she's just doing it for attention!' She went quiet.

'How long have you been feeling like this?' Francesca was concerned about her. 'I know you've been up and down since you've been coming here, but I've never seen you this low.' She had hoped that Jasmine had had another good week, if not good then at least steady or stable, but she could see she'd gone downhill dramatically.

'I don't know. It's just crept up on me.' Jasmine squeezed her eyes shut to try and stop her tears. 'I'm sorry. I can't do anything about it...'

'Jasmine please, you don't ever need to apologize for how you're feeling.' Francesca was overcome by her own emotions. She cared about her and hated the fact that she couldn't give her a magic wand to fix it all. 'A lot of people don't realize that depression is an illness and not a choice. It's not a cold that passes in a few days, and I wouldn't wish it on anyone. If people knew how it felt they would think twice before shrugging it off as no big deal. I know it seems pointless saying it and you've probably heard it a hundred times, but I promise you, Jasmine...' She could feel her eyes begin to sting, 'these feelings you're having and what you're going through right now, they will pass and you will feel better...'

'You can't know that!'

'I can, and I do!' Francesca's voice shook. 'In my twenties I went through depression. It took me years but I got through it, I'm not quite sure how, but I'm here now...'

'Maybe I'm not as strong as you. I'm fed up with trying to survive... to push on and keep going...'

Francesca moved to the edge of her seat and grabbed hold of Jasmine's hand. 'You are strong, stronger than you can even imagine. We all are. You're stronger than me...' She squeezed her hand again. 'Look at you! You don't lie to yourself about your feelings. You live with honesty and authenticity. It takes a whole lot of strength, when you feel the way you do, just to get out of bed every morning. I know it may not feel like it but you're doing so well... so well. I wish you could see that!' Jasmine was surprised by Francesca's strong emotional response, it brought her round a bit, seeing someone she didn't really know who cared about her. 'Will you promise me, if ever you feel this upset and low again, you will phone and come and see me sooner? Don't leave it for so long.' She got up to get a piece of paper from her desk. 'Let me give you my mobile number. You can call me anytime...' She wrote her number down knowing it was against all the rules, and passed it to her. 'You're not alone in this, you know.'

Jasmine stared down at the piece of paper in her hand. 'Thank you'

CHAPTER SIXTY FIVE

Josh had given Mia a lift home from school, in his car. He pulled up outside her house, as he stopped the engine a silence came over them, neither of them said anything. Josh started fiddling with his fingers. It was his nervous habit he did. Mia knew he had something to say to her so she waited.

'Can we talk about what happened the night you ended up in hospital?'

'There's nothing to talk about...' She wanted to just put it behind her, she felt guilty about the way she'd spoken to him and treated him that night.

'I shouldn't have let you go with them...'

'Josh, I treated you like an arsehole that night! I deserved everything I got. It wasn't your fault.'

He'd been worried about what might have happened to her if she hadn't been taken to hospital. 'You didn't deserve what happened to you...'

'I'm over it so can we talk about something else? Have you seen or heard from Jasmine recently?'

Josh had known Mia long enough to know when not to push something with her, so he dropped the subject and answered her question.

'No.'

'I'm worried about her, when I last saw her, she...' Mia couldn't put her finger on it.

'What?'

'I don't know. I just got the feeling something wasn't quite right with her. She seemed a bit withdrawn.'

'Did you ask her how she was? Maybe she was just having a bad day or maybe her sugar levels were up. My cousin goes strange when his are!' He could see she wasn't convinced and was really concerned about Jasmine. 'I'm sure she's fine, Mia. You know Jasmine doesn't beat about the bush. She would tell you if she wasn't OK.'

Mia opened the car door and got out. She walked towards her house and waved goodbye to Josh, from her front door. Josh waved back and tried to give her a reassuring smile. He pulled away slowly.

Mia convinced herself Josh was right. Jasmine didn't beat about the bush. She was always honest with how she felt and what she was experiencing. She stepped through the front door and went straight to the living room to slump on the sofa and rest.

'Hey, sis!' Mark had beaten her to it and was already sitting there waiting for her.

'Mark!' Mia screamed and ran over to him, to hug him. 'When did you get back? You didn't tell me you were coming home!'

'Surprise! I thought as I can't make it to your exams party I'd come down before, to hang out and celebrate!'

They chatted and caught up with what was going on with their lives, what their friends were up to and about a new Netflix series that Mia wanted Mark to watch. After about twenty minutes Mia took him into her bedroom so she could show him the outfit options she had for the party. It wasn't really his thing but he was willing to tolerate it, so he could spend as much time with her as possible.

'So what are you doing? Where are you having it and who is coming?' He tried to pretend to be one of her girlfriends asking all the right questions, in a silly voice.

'Hah, hah!' Mia walked over to her wardrobe. 'I've got to decide what I'm going to wear first... priorities!' She went through her clothes trying to visualise what she would look good in. Mark took a seat on her bed, assuming, he was about to be shown at least half of her wardrobe.

Mia stopped when she came across Shay's jacket hanging up. It had got lost between her old dressing gown and a dress. She pulled it out and turned to Mark.

'Shit! I never gave this back.'

'Whose is it?'

'You know the waitress at Yani's? It's hers. She gave it to me the night I got... when I went to hospital.'

He laughed. 'Another epic tale of yours I missed!'

Mia stared at the jacket again. 'I need to get this back to her.'

Mark looked at her. He wanted to talk to her about the phone call they'd had, when she was upset finding out about their father cheating and the baby. He hadn't felt like the right moment had come until now.

'What?' She could sense him staring at her.

'Mia. About what happened with the whole dad situation...'

'Forget about it, I know you were just trying to protect me, trying to play the big brother card.'

'I was but, it didn't work. I don't want anything to ever come between us.' He got up from the bed and went across the room to hug her again. As he squeezed her he realised how much he'd missed her. As much as he liked to tease her, she was still his little sister and always would be.

Mia playfully pushed him off. 'Alright don't get all soppy on me!' She smiled.

'Have you heard from him?' Mark's voice was more serious and lower when he asked the question.

'No. He's on some business trip at the moment, apparently.'

'So he's going to miss the party as well then?'

'Yep. The way I feel towards him at the moment, it's probably a good thing he's not coming.' She had secretly hoped her father would have apologised to her and tried to make amends, but he hadn't even tried to contact her.

Francesca got home from work and was surprised, but pleased, to see Mark. They settled down in the living room together, Francesca smiled to herself, she loved it when the three of them were in the same room, back together again.

'So, are you organizing this 'epic' party mum?'

'No.'

'No?' Mia was confused by her answer, she'd thought her mum was organising it all.

'Who is then?'

'Laura has been sorting it out for me as I've been so busy at work.' She took a sip of the tea that Mark had made for her. She knew Mia wasn't going to like the idea of Laura being in charge of her party and was half trying to hide behind the mug.

'Mum! You know what Laura's like!' Mia was horrified. 'She's sex obsessed! It's going to be a penis and boobies theme if she organises it! Remember her fortieth birthday party? It was more like an Ann Summers party than a birthday party!'

'That was different darling. It won't be anything like that. Don't worry. I talked it through with her.' Francesca was actually a little worried herself, if she was honest. She knew how eccentric and carried away Laura could be when it came to parties. Mark found the whole revelation hilarious, he peered across the room at Mia.

'You're so going to end up with a sex education party!'

'I'm glad you find my embarrassment funny. Like, my whole school year is going to be coming!' She playfully threw a cushion from one of the sofas at him. The zip on the cover hit his watch and made a noise.

'Hey watch my watch! This thing cost me a whole month's wages!' He looked down at it to check it wasn't damaged. It wasn't, but he noticed the time. It was already six o'clock. 'Hey Mia, we better go to Yani's before it gets packed with hungry customers!'

Francesca felt strange hearing the name of the restaurant coming out of his mouth.

'Yani's? Why do you need to go there?' It was hard for her to even say the name.

'I forgot to give Shay back the jacket she lent me.'

It felt even stranger for Francesca to hear Mia saying Shay's name so casually, as if they were friends.

'She lent you a jacket?' It was the first Francesca had heard of it.

'When she took me to A&E.'

'Mia! That was ages ago!'

'Chill mum. I know. I just forgot, with everything going on...'

'Do you want me to take it back?' She offered without even thinking it through properly. 'You guys can chill here and I'll drop it off and pick us up some take out on the way back?'

'That sounds good to me!' Mia was pleased that she didn't have to get dressed and go out to drop the jacket off, she ran up the stairs to fetch it.

There were only a couple of customers in by the time Francesca got to Yani's. She'd taken her time, partly due to the drizzly rain but mainly because of her nerves. The whole time she was driving towards town, she fought thoughts of turning back and not going through with it. She attempted to rationalise the situation, it was only a jacket she was giving back. It was no big deal. She entered and walked straight to the bar where Faith was pouring drinks.

'Hi, excuse me?' She recognised Faith from her previous visit. Faith glanced up at her while still pouring a lemonade, so Francesca took it as a sign to continue. 'Is eh, Shay here?' She could hear the anxiety and nerves in her own voice.

Faith finished pouring the lemonade and placed it on a tray. 'That depends on who's asking!'

'Francesca. She'll know who I am. I just have something to give back to her...'

Faith picked up on Francesca's nervousness and wondered why she seemed so anxious. She looked up to study her properly, she thought she recognised her, but she couldn't be sure.

'Have you been here before? I know you, don't I? What did you say your name was again?'

'Francesca...'

Francesca saw the recognition on her face and assumed Faith remembered her from serving her. 'I think you served me before...' She had no idea Shay had spoken about her to Faith.

'Oh, so you're Francesca!' Faith smirked at her.

Francesca was confused by the way she said it. 'Yes, I'm Francesca...'

'Dr Francesca?'

'Yes...' Francesca was filled with a mixture of dread and embarrassment, she could tell, by Faith's face, that she knew who she was. Shay had obviously mentioned her but in what regard she didn't know and couldn't be sure. 'Is she here? Can I see her please?'

'Actually it's her day off today...' Faith tried to discreetly check Francesca out as she spoke with her. So this is the woman who's managed to catch and hold Shay's attention, she thought. 'She's at home, but I'll give you her address. It's only round the corner.'

Francesca didn't feel comfortable with just turning up on Shay. 'Don't worry! If it's all right I'd rather leave it here with you. It's just a jacket and I don't want to disturb her.'

'You'd be doing me a favour checking in on her. She had an accident...'

'Is she OK?' Francesca was more concerned than she wanted to be and was conscious that Faith knew it as well, by the tone of her voice.

'Don't worry. Nothing life threatening. She burnt her arm quite badly on the coffee machine so I sent her to A&E last night, but I haven't heard from her since.'

Francesca hesitated, wondering whether to check in on her or not. If Faith was that worried, surely she could just phone her, and, technically, Shay wasn't her responsibility any more.

'What's the address?'

'I'll write it down for you.' She moved to the back of the bar and scribbled Shay's address on the back of a bar mat. She smiled to herself and whispered out loud. 'I hope I'm doing the right thing... you owe me Shay!' She went back over to Francesca and handed it to her.

Francesca thanked her and left, leaving Faith wondering how Shay was going to react to 'the' Dr Francesca knocking at her door.

CHAPTER SIXTY SIX

Francesca arrived at Shay's ground floor flat, she'd arrived sooner than she'd thought, and wanted.

As she stood facing the door she became conscious of what she looked like. It was a breezy evening and she wondered if her hair looked a complete mess because of it. Regretting not having a small mirror, she did her best to smooth her hair down with her hands. She cleared her throat and rang the doorbell. She could hear it echo through the door as she waited. Shay didn't take long to answer.

'Francesca!' She was shocked to see her there and they stared at each other for a moment. It started raining again and Shay realised Francesca was getting wet standing outside.

'Do you want to come in?'

As Francesca entered she could feel the sweat on her hand, where she'd been holding onto Shay's jacket tighter and tighter with nerves. It felt strange for them to meet outside of the office and Yani's.

Shay shut the front door and turned to Francesca. 'You can go in properly you know, you don't have to stand in the hallway!'

The flat wasn't how Francesca had imagined. She'd thought it would be a messier, smaller place, but it looked tidy and clean and more grown up than she had imagined. She had big pieces of artwork on her walls and candles everywhere, which brought a soft light into the hallway. Francesca hadn't realised that the reality of being alone with Shay again would be so scary and un-nerving. It felt different being in Shay's space and not her own. All of a sudden panic, or common sense, she wasn't sure which one, hit Francesca and she tried to back out.

'I'm sorry, I shouldn't have come...' She stepped past Shay to get to the door, and went to turn the latch to open it, to leave, but she found herself stopping, realising how stupid she must look to Shay, just showing up out of the blue, and then leaving again without saying anything. 'The waitress where you work, Faith is it...?' She turned to face Shay. 'She said you had hurt yourself and she hadn't heard from you, so I was worried...' Francesca felt a lot calmer remembering she had a legitimate reason for being there. She held Shay's jacket out. 'From Mia. She's sorry it's so late, she just totally forgot...'

Shay didn't reply but stood still and stared at her. Francesca felt more awkward and tense, the longer she stood there, with her arm out holding the jacket. She gave Shay a pleading look to just take it from her and not say anything, but Shay walked, slowly, towards her. She reached out to take the jacket, as she did, Francesca saw the large burn on Shay's arm.

'Shit, Shay... let me see that!' She dropped the jacket on the floor and grabbed her arm.

Shay didn't even let her look at it, she pulled her arm away. 'It's nothing, don't worry.'

'It doesn't look like nothing...' Francesca stepped closer to her, to try and get a proper look. 'It looks nasty...' She went to reach for Shay's arm again.

'Please don't touch me!'

She could see Shay was serious so she backed off, dropping her arm back down by her side. 'Shouldn't you have it wrapped up or something? So it doesn't get infected?'

'The nurse at the hospital told me to try and leave it to the air for as long as possible.' She combed her hair back with her fingers. She wasn't sure how she felt about Francesca seeming to be so concerned about her, and her wellbeing, considering that last time they'd met, she hadn't even been willing to talk.

Francesca felt a little pang in her belly. She realised she'd missed seeing Shay, knowing how she was. 'How are you?'

Shay scoffed at her question, she felt patronized. 'Are you kidding me? You're really asking me that, right now, after what happened? You're not my therapist anymore. You made that very clear last time, remember?' She raised her voice a little, with annoyance. 'You don't have the right to ask me how I am anymore!'

'Shay, don't be like that...'

'Don't be like what? Hurt? Honest? How do you want me to be? Tell me!'

Francesca didn't know what to say, she was confused about what she actually wanted from Shay. 'I'm sorry, everything just... just got out of control...' Shay stood there, facing her, waiting for the rest of her excuse. Francesca took a deep breath in and continued. 'When I'm around you, you make me feel... completely out of control!'

'What's so bad about losing control?' She softened her voice and became a little less defensive. She could see Francesca was trying to be honest with her.

'Sometimes control feels like the only thing I have left in my life, especially when I'm with you. You make me feel...'

Shay took a step into her personal space and held her gaze. 'How do I make you feel?'

Francesca froze. She could feel the heat and attraction of her body towards Shay's. Slightly breathless, she lowered her voice. 'Like I can't move or breathe. I can't hide when I'm with you and that scares me, more than I want to admit.'

Shay could feel the desire coming from Francesca's body and played on it. 'I'm not going to chase you Francesca. If you want me, you make the first move.'

Francesca didn't move. She couldn't. Her head was over-riding her body. Shay knew Francesca wasn't going to do anything, she reached for the door latch and opened it slightly to let her out. Francesca put her hand out and pressed against the door, closing it again. Shay looked at her, a little surprised, wondering what she was going to do next. Francesca closed her eyes in an attempt to try and shut off her brain and its stories of denial. She re-opened them and slowly lifted her hand to Shay's cheek, she lightly brushed her thumb over her lips. Feeling the warmth and softness of them under her fingertip she moved her body forward and kissed her.

Shay pulled away after a couple of seconds to test her, see if she would back off, but Francesca just stared at Shay's mouth. Shay grabbed her around the back of her neck and kissed Francesca even harder. This time, it was Francesca who pushed Shay up against the wall.

Still kissing and exploring each other's mouths, Shay tried to guide Francesca to her bedroom. Neither of them wanted to pull their bodies apart as they stumbled in to it. They kissed passionately at the end of the bed. Shay peeled off Francesca's top and began to gently and slowly kiss the soft, warm skin on Francesca's stomach. Francesca groaned with the sensation and teasing of her lips on her skin. She could feel her body begin to tingle and heat up. Shay carried on kissing her stomach and then slowly moved down until she reached her waistband. She, leisurely, undid the button and zip of Francesca's trousers and crouched down to pull them down her legs. Hungry for Shay's mouth again Francesca pulled her back up and kissed her. As they kissed, Shay ran her fingertips up and down Francesca's back, gently scratching her skin with her nails. Francesca moaned, her body wanting more, she tugged Shay's T-shirt and quickly pulled it off, over her head.

'Ouch!' The material of her t-shirt had caught the burn on Shay's arm.

'Sorry, did I hurt you?'

She looked down to check her arm. 'You just hit my burn, that's all...' She felt it throb and sting but she felt she had more important things on her mind. 'Don't worry, I'll get over it!' She grinned and started kissing Francesca again. She gently bit and pulled on the bottom of her lip, when she let go of her lip, she pulled back and softly pressed her forehead against Francesca's. She gazed into her eyes.

'What?'

Shay breathed out slowly, trying to release the adrenaline rushing around her body. 'Nothing... I just feel a bit nervous...' She couldn't believe she was saying it. 'I really like you...'

Francesca smiled at her and gently kissed her. 'I'm nervous as well. I've never been with a woman before.'

'Never?' Shay moved her right hand down and around to Francesca's lower back, feeling a lot more confident. She pulled her body closer into hers and grinned. 'Well then, I better make your first time unforgettable!'

An hour and a half later Francesca rushed into her house with the Thai takeaway. Wrapped up with Shay, in her bed, she'd completely forgotten she had told Mark and Mia she would bring dinner back for them. It was only when Shay had asked if she was hungry that she'd remembered.

'Sorry, sorry. Friday night is always mayhem at the Thai. I forgot!'

'I'm not surprised it took so long...' Mark took the bags from her. 'How much did you get? It looks like your feeding the five hundred!'

'Have I gone overboard?'

'No, no, Mia and I have worked up an appetite on the PlayStation, waiting for you, so let's dig in!' He took the bags to the kitchen table where he'd already set up the cutlery and plates. Mia strolled in from the living room and took a seat at the table, next to Mark and opposite Francesca. 'Finally! I was about to pass out!' She peered at her mum. 'Why do you look so flushed and frazzled mum?'

'It gets hot and cramped in the take out waiting area.' She picked up one of the dishes to try and divert attention away from her. 'Who wants some Thai green curry?'

'Yes please!' Mia grabbed her favourite dish and piled it onto her plate. 'Did you remember to drop the jacket off?'

'Yes Mia, don't worry. I remembered.

CHAPTER SIXTY SEVEN

S hay arrived early at George and Kate's house. She was there to pick up the boys and take them to the park, something she tried to do every other Saturday when she wasn't working. She enjoyed having quality time with them and it gave George and Kate a break.

She strolled in, in a good mood, from her night before with Francesca, and entered their kitchen. George was at the table reading his newspaper.

'Morning!'

He lowered the newspaper and looked at her.

'Why are you so spritely today?' Straight away he was suspicious, normally she would walk in like a zombie, hung over, after having hit the town the previous night. Before Shay could answer Kate walked in and joined them. She greeted her with a hug.

'Hi Shay! How are you? I feel like we haven't seen you for ages!'

'Well maybe Uncle George would, if he actually came to work!' She teased him by nudging him in the back

'Oh, so you're a comedy genius this morning as well! How many times do I have to tell you, I work a lot behind the scenes! Don't I love?' He got no support from Kate, she just raised her eyebrows and smiled at Shay.

'I'm good thanks, I'm a free woman! The court hearing came through early.' She went across to the fridge and pulled out a cartoon of orange juice, she then got a glass out of the cupboard.

'Well done!' Kate was really pleased to hear her good news. 'So you survived the therapy then? The doctor was satisfied with the work you did together?'

With her back to them, Shay poured her orange juice and smiled at Kate's choice of words. 'Satisfied' was, absolutely, the word she would use to describe Francesca last night. She started going over images in her head of kissing Francesca's breasts, her hand between her legs and Francesca arching her back as she org... She remembered Kate had asked her a question and was waiting for her to answer. She turned around with the glass of juice in her hand.

'You could say that she made no complaints!' She joined them at the kitchen table. 'You were right. Therapy does have its perks!'

George hadn't said much, he was still trying to work out why Shay was so happy, whilst half trying to catch up on the sports' page as well. It naturally became quiet between the three of them as Shay took a few sips of her juice.

'Are the boys up?'

Kate scoffed. 'Are you kidding? They were up at seven! They're upstairs playing.'

'I'm going to take them to the park to feed the ducks and, maybe, get an ice cream. That's if the van is there!' She finished her juice and got up from the table, kissed Kate and George on the tops of their heads and ran upstairs. George dropped his paper down and looked at Kate.

'I think that therapy has done her more than good!' He glanced at his watch, 'For starters, she's actually here picking up the boys on time! When have you known Shay to ever be on time?'

CHAPTER SIXTY EIGHT

It was a beautiful, bright day and Francesca had agreed to meet Garth for a walk through the park. She wanted to tell him that their relationship wasn't working out for her, but hadn't yet found the courage. When they reached the park they entered at the side entrance. Garth spotted the ice cream van parked by the stream that ran along the back of the park.

'Hey! What about an ice cream? Do you fancy one?' He was oblivious as to how Francesca intended to end their meeting up and going out together, ice cream was about the only thing she fancied right now. Before she could answer him, he'd already started pacing towards the van like an excited child.

'OK, I guess we're getting an ice cream,' she muttered to herself as Garth rushed on ahead.

Before Garth reached the van he spotted Shay wrapping the boys' ice creams with a napkin to try and stop them dripping. Out of the corner of her eye, Shay saw him walking towards her and Francesca walking, quite a bit further behind him. She assumed they were on some romantic date and a strong wave of jealousy hit her. She wasn't sure if Francesca had seen her, she encouraged the boys to walk towards the stream and away from the van.

'Hi! Hello...' Garth had recognised her. Shay wasn't expecting him to talk to her, she thought he would just smile and walk on. 'You're the waitress from... Yani's, right?'

Excited to play with the ducks, the boys carried on towards the water. Shay made sure she could still see them as she spoke with Garth.

'Yeah, that's right.'

He grinned at her. 'That was the best steak I've had in a long time!'

'I wish I could take credit for that but the food is nothing to do with me!' She didn't mean to sound short but she had no interest in making polite conversation with him. It became awkward and quiet between them.

'Sorry, I just had to say that. I'll leave you to your day.' He turned around to check where Francesca was. She was walking towards him, still a bit behind. A queue was building up at the ice cream van so Garth beckoned to her. A couple of minutes later she had nearly caught up with him when she spotted Shay, she walked sheepishly towards her.

Before she said anything to her she checked to make sure that Garth was out of ear shot. He was at the back of the queue behind a few people. He turned around expecting Francesca to be closer and shouted over to her. 'What do you fancy, Cesca?'

'Just get me anything!' She yelled back and looked at Shay a little embarrassed, not just because of Garth, but because she hadn't seen her since they'd slept together. 'We're just on a walk...' She was worried about what Shay might be thinking.

'Cesca? I don't even call you that! You two must be getting close, *oui*?'

'It's not like that!'

'We slept together and now you're on a date with *him*?' She wasn't even sure, herself, if she was teasing Francesca or if she was actually, genuinely annoyed.

'Yes. No, no, that isn't what this is. Yes it's a date but it's an 'I don't want to date you anymore' date!'

Shay could tell she was telling the truth. She looked across to check on Garth, he was still waiting in line, closer to the van, chatting with the man in front of him. She turned back round to face Francesca and grinned at her. She knew her body was blocking Garth's view and he wouldn't be able to see anything if he looked over at them, so she moved in closer.

'Well, you better tell him soon because he seems pretty keen to me!' She hooked her finger over the top of Francesca's belt. 'How are you? Last time I saw you, you were...' She gently tried to pull her a bit closer but Francesca resisted, conscious Garth might see them.

'Shay!'

Shay smirked at her with a cheeky look in her eye. Francesca felt the pull and attraction towards her and knew, if they were alone there would be no way she would be able to resist her. Shay felt it as well, she leaned in close, as if she read Francesca's thoughts. Francesca put her hand out and pushed against her stomach.

'Shay! Garth is only over there!'

Confident Francesca wanted to kiss her, she playfully pushed against her hand and didn't back off fully. 'What? He's not looking...'

Francesca didn't say anything more, enjoying the need and tension between them. The moment was broken by Noah, who ran up to Shay, crying. He grabbed hold of the front of her leg. Shay and Francesca took a step back from one another, Shay looked down at Noah and brushed the top of his head softly.

'What's up *mon amour?*'

'My ice cream, it fell...' He could barely get his words out, he was so upset. 'The ducks took it away!'

Shay and Francesca both looked over to the water to see a duck pecking at Noah's ice cream. They both smiled as they watched Toby and Jordan trying to retrieve it.

Shay picked him up to try and calm him down. 'Don't worry. I can get you another one.' She kissed him tenderly on the cheek.

Francesca watched them, noting how close their relationship was. She felt that she'd witnessed another softer, vulnerable side to Shay that she'd never seen before. They had spoken about the boys during a couple of their sessions and she knew how much Shay loved them from how she spoke about them, but to see them together was even more special.

Garth joined them, holding two ice creams. Francesca had been so focused on Shay and Noah that she hadn't even noticed him walk towards them.

'Oh hello...' He passed a chocolate cone to Francesca and looked at Noah. Not sure of him, Noah shyly snuggled into Shay. 'Who's this then?'

'This is my cousin, Noah, and those munchkins over there are his brothers, Jordan and Toby, right?' She playfully nuzzled into Noah's neck, making him giggle.

'Right!' Noah shouted back, feeling proud of his brothers.

'Hi, Noah.' Garth attempted to make eye contact with him but Noah was having none of it and turned away from him, clinging tightly to Shay's neck.

Francesca playfully shook Noah's foot as it dangled down.

'He dropped his ice cream...' He liked her playing with his foot and smiled at her. Francesca gave him a wide grin. 'Here, you can have mine if you want?' She offered Noah her chocolate ice cream, he took it from her straight away. 'It's a special one that tastes twice as nice as the one the ducks have!'

Shay put him back down on the ground. *'Qu'est-ce que tu dis?'*

He looked up at Francesca with the ice cream in his little hand. 'Thank you.'

'Good boy.' He peered up at Shay again. She knew it was his 'can I go now look', so she gave him a nod of agreement. He ran back over to his brothers, excited to show them his new ice cream.

'Well, I better let you two get back to your date. I wouldn't want to spoil it by becoming the third wheel!' She couldn't resist teasing.

'Right, well, it was nice meeting you again...' Garth didn't pick up on Shay's sarcasm, or the look Francesca and Shay gave one another. 'Hopefully we'll be back for another dinner sometime soon.'

'Oh I hope so!' She stared at Francesca and teased her again. 'You should come on your next date and ask for me. I'll be happy to serve you both!'

Garth smiled a goodbye and began to walk away.

Shay gave Francesca a cheeky wink as she walked past. Francesca replied with a 'you just wait' look back.

CHAPTER SIXTY NINE

Jasmine had been playing netball for the past ten minutes. It was the trials for the school team and she enjoyed the game, so Debra had convinced her to have a go. Jasmine wasn't going to take it too seriously, she just wanted to see if she could make the team. She wasn't expecting Denise and Bonnie to be there, if she'd known, she probably wouldn't have shown up. She did her best to stay out of their way but they'd been playing rough with her whenever the teacher wasn't looking. .Jasmine thought she could handle it, that they wouldn't try anything in front of a teacher at school.

The ball was down the other side of the court and the teacher had his back to her. Everyone's attention was on the team about to score when Denise, who was behind her, shoved her hard in the back. Jasmine fell to the ground and looked up at Denise.

'What did you do that for?' Her knee was stinging and had a deep gash on it that had started to bleed.

'No reason really!' Denise grinned. 'I just don't like weirdos like you.'

The team with the ball scored, the teacher blew his whistle. He turned and noticed Jasmine on the floor and jogged over to her.

'Jasmine are you OK? What happened?'

Denise stared her down so she wouldn't dare say anything.

'Nothing sir. I think I must have just tripped but I'm OK.'

'She's clumsy sir!' Denise helped her up, making it look like they were friends. Their teacher looked down at Jasmine's knee.

'Right, well, that graze looks nasty. Go and see the nurse to have it cleaned up a bit.'

'Yes sir.' She began to walk away, back towards the school building and, as she turned around, she saw Denise and Bonnie huddled together and giggling, watching her leave. She knew she had no chance of making the team now.

A couple of hours later Jasmine got home from school. She ran straight up to her bedroom and curled up on her bed in the dark. About an hour later her mum called up the stairs.

'Jasmine! Paul! Dinners ready!'

Jasmine put the hood up on her sweatshirt and headed downstairs into the kitchen. Debra and Paul were at the table, already eating.

'Are you OK Jasmine?'

She knew she didn't look good. 'I'm fine mum. I'm just feeling a bit rough at the moment, that's all.'

'Do you need to go and see Dr Fran...?'

'No mum! It will pass. I'm just tired.'

'Are you taking your insulin?'

It was the worst thing Debra could have asked her, she answered, annoyed. 'Yes!'

Paul didn't like it when they fell out with one another, he tried to break some of the tension building between them.

'We can play on my bike after dinner if you want? That always makes me feel better. It cheers me up!'

Paul's sweetness calmed Jasmine down a bit, she knew he was trying to help. She ruffled his hair. 'Cheers bro! I might just do that.'

As she took her seat at the table Debra noticed the plaster on her knee.

'What did you do to your knee?'

'Nothing, I just fell in gym class.' Debra had forgotten about the netball trials and Jasmine didn't want to remind her. She knew it would only lead to more questions.

'Is it nasty?'

'It's not too bad. The school nurse cleaned it up for me.'

'Well, keep an eye on it because you don't want to get it infected. You know it takes you longer to heal, especially when your sugar levels are high.'

Jasmine had had enough of her mum reminding her she was different, she got up from the table.

'Jazz! Where are you going? Your dinners...'

'I'm not hungry!'

She stomped up the stairs to her bedroom and went straight over to her desk. She opened the draw and stared at her stash of tablets. She contemplated whether now was the moment to take them all, to end the pain she felt. She slammed the draw shut and burst into tears. She climbed back into her bed and pulled the covers over her head, wanting to block the world out.

CHAPTER SEVENTY

Francesca was in session with Jamie.

'How are Maggie and the baby?'

'She's doing great thank you. They both are.'

'Have you been in touch with your father again? Have you seen him?'

'I have actually. I saw him yesterday.'

Francesca made a note of it on her pad and looked back up at Jamie. 'And? How did it go? How did you feel?'

He flicked a bit of fluff off his trouser leg. 'I feel a bit more positive and hopeful about our relationship...' Francesca was pleased for him. 'I told him I couldn't let him one hundred per cent back into my life, that I needed time to be able to do that. I need to know I can trust him before that.'

'That sounds very reasonable to me.' She didn't want him to feel ashamed or guilty with his boundaries towards his father.

'We chatted for hours and hours, into the night, the other day going over everything. He really listened to me and I felt he was taking in everything I was saying.' He paused. 'He even told me a bit more about himself, stuff I had always wondered about as a child. How he met mum...where he grew up. I even met Janet his wife, she's absolutely lovely. I felt so comfortable and welcomed by her.'

Francesca softly smiled at him, relieved it had gone so well. 'Do you have plans to see him again?'

'Yes. Tomorrow night. We're going to go out for dinner so he and Maggie can officially meet and get to know each other a bit better.'

Francesca saw how content and calm Jamie was. To her, he seemed like a totally different person with a weight lifted from his shoulders. She took a moment to wonder how, and if, she could help him from here.

'How do you feel about our sessions together? Do you feel you want to continue with them or...?'

Jamie had felt awkward about bringing the conversation up, he was pleased she'd asked first. 'I think I'm OK to stop coming. I can see you again if I need to though, right?'

'Absolutely. Anytime!'

'Can I leave it open to come and see you if I need to, just in case, hopefully, it won't be necessary!'

She nodded in agreement, the room fell quiet between them as Jamie contemplated his new relationship with his father.

'I really believe he has changed. I know it hasn't been long, him being back in my life, but there's something different... something behind his eyes, the way he is, he's different.'

'I'm really pleased for you and your father. It's a big step you're taking, forgiving him. I genuinely do hope it works out for you and, of course, with the baby! Do you have a name yet?'

'No. Not yet, we haven't decided. I don't think we will be able to until we meet her.'

It was the end of Francesca's working day. She walked out of her office into reception to chat with Julie, who was getting her things together ready to leave.

'Is it OK if I take off now? I've got a date tonight and I want to pamper and preen myself a bit beforehand.'

'A date?' Francesca was a little surprised. Julie hadn't dated anyone, as far as she knew, since her husband Harry had passed away eight years ago. 'I didn't know you were dating! How come you didn't tell me?'

Julie felt her face flush a bit. 'It's early days yet and there's not much to tell really.'

Francesca could tell she didn't want to divulge any more information but she couldn't resist asking. 'Anyone I know?'

'Er...no. I don't think so.' She was hesitant, but not enough for Francesca to pick up on it.

'Go on then! Off you go! Go on and enjoy yourself!'

'Don't stay too late tonight will you?' She picked up her bag and keys. 'Tomorrow we need to sort out this air conditioning. It's too hot to carry on like this!' The temperature had been boiling in the office because the air conditioning had broken and they'd had to manage with the windows wide open to let a bit of a breeze in. Francesca could feel the stickiness and dampness on her skin from perspiring for most of the day. She waited for Julie to leave before she got a large bottle of water from the fridge and took it to her desk. She picked up Jamie's notes and walked over to her cabinet knowing, hopefully, she wouldn't need them back out any time soon. As she walked back to her desk she stopped in front of it and stared at the amount of paperwork that had accumulated on it. Too busy in her own thoughts, she didn't hear Shay enter from behind her.

Shay quietly sneaked up on her, she wrapped her arms around her waist. Surprised, Francesca jumped a little so Shay whispered in her ear.

'It's OK. It's only me...' Recognising her voice, Francesca immediately relaxed. She let her body lean back into Shay's. Shay gently kissed the side of her neck. She could taste the salt on her skin and feel the heat from her body. She put her mouth to Francesca's ear again. 'Did you think it was someone else like... Garth, is it?' She couldn't help but laugh at her own joke.

Francesca, playfully, pushed her off and turned to face her. 'That's not funny, Shay! Nor was what you did at the park!'

Shay, still grinning, grabbed the bottom of Francesca's shirt and used it to pull her towards her. 'I thought it was pretty funny! At least, it was from where I was standing!' She kissed Francesca on the lips, confident she could get her to forgive her, she pulled Francesca's shirt up, out of her skirt and held it up. She crouched down and gently caressed the skin on Francesca's stomach with her lips, she slowly moved around to Francesca's right hip.

Francesca gasped for breath. 'Wait! No. Not here...'

Shay stopped, stood up, and looked at Francesca, who didn't say anything, so Shay started kissing her neck again

Sha...' She couldn't get her words out as Shay nibbled on her ear.

'Why not here?' She teased.

'Because...this is my work place...'

Shay moved to Francesca's mouth and brushed her lips over hers, teasing her, daring her to kiss her back. 'That didn't stop you before... when you kissed me!'

A little offended, Francesca jerked her head back and looked at Shay to say something, but she couldn't stand not being touched or kissed by her. She gave in, leaned forward and kissed her again.

CHAPTER SEVENTY ONE

Francesca drove over to Laura's house to discuss Mia's party plans. She trusted Laura to organise everything appropriately but Mia still wasn't convinced, so Francesca had told her she'd go over and check things out with her. Laura had spread all her ideas for the party over her kitchen table. It looked like a huge professional picture board, Francesca was amazed by how much effort and planning she had put into it.

'So, I've managed to hire a club, you know, the one on the corner?' Laura handed her their business card.

Francesca looked at it. 'Juice?'

'They said they could close the bar off and have a make-shift one to sell non- alcoholic drinks. I asked them to close off the private booth area as well because the last thing we want is randy, horny teenagers alone in private...'

Francesca spotted the price list on the table and leant over to pick it up. As the weather was still warm she'd put on a light, loose top, the neck line fell down lower as she leaned and grabbed the list.

'Speaking of randy and horny, how did you get that hickey?'

Francesca thought she must have mis-heard her. 'What?'

Laura glared at her. 'You know what!'

'I don't have a hickey...' Francesca panicked. 'Do I?' She rushed over to the mirror and saw a small red mark just underneath her collar bone, near her shoulder. 'Shit!' She tried to rub at it, as if it would make it disappear. 'What if Mia's seen it...'

'Never mind Mia love, spill! How was he?' She hadn't told Laura about how she and Shay's relationship had escalated, so Laura had assumed it was Garth who had left his mark.

'Who?' She was still hopelessly trying to rub the hickey away.

'Err, Garth! Unless there's something you're not telling me! You're not seeing David again are you?' She had started off joking but became serious with the thought of Francesca getting back with him.

Francesca stopped rubbing her skin and looked at her. 'Laura! This is not from having sex with David!'

Laura put her hands up in the air as if surrendering. 'OK, I was just checking.'

Francesca turned away from the mirror. Laura thought she'd made the love bite look worse and more obvious since the skin around it had gone even redder. Francesca looked at her friend.

'Or Garth!'

Laura's jaw almost dropped to the floor. 'OK, now you have my full attention! Tell me all?'

'I can't.' She smiled a little at the thought of Shay.

'It's the girl from the restaurant, isn't it?'

'Fuck, Laura! How do you do that? Humour me, at least, and pretend you don't know! Is it that obvious?'

'That day, in the restaurant, the two of you were more or less dribbling over each other...' She grinned and raised her eyebrows. 'You dirty dog!'

Francesca began to panic again. It made it even more real that someone else knew about the two of them. She couldn't believe what she'd done.

'Don't! I know it's not right... Fuck!' The realisation hit her, stronger this time. 'I should stop. I'm going to...'

'What? No, I meant dirty dog in a good way! It's about time someone blew your mind in bed, and a woman sure knows how to!'

There was something about the way Laura said it. 'You've been with a woman?'

'Please Francesca! Are you trying to insult me right now? I'm a sex psychologist and I did plenty of research in college!'

Francesca couldn't help but laugh, she blushed, remembering how Shay made her body feel.

Laura stared smiling at her. She knew that look. 'It's good, right, the sex?'

Francesca picked her top up and pulled it over her head to cover her face. She felt her cheeks heat up and turn red. 'It's better than good!' she mumbled.

'Look at you all bashful! Miss 'I can live without sex!''

CHAPTER SEVENTY TWO

Mia and Josh had sat their last exam, she couldn't believe the relief she felt knowing everything was now out of her hands, that she couldn't do anymore even if she wanted to. She waited in the corridor for Josh to finish his biology exam, knowing he wouldn't be long. He came out of the exam room about fifteen minutes later, gave Mia a congratulatory hug and offered to drive her home.

He drove slower than usual and she could tell he was nervous. His behaviour didn't make sense to her, she thought he would be less nervous now he'd finished his exams as well.

Josh pulled up outside her house and stopped in his usual spot. He turned the engine off and stared forward, out of the windscreen. He took a couple of deep, loud breaths and turned in his seat to face Mia.

'So, can I give you my present for finishing your exams? Well our exams really...it's for both of us.'

'Josh! I thought we said we weren't going to buy each other anything.' They had spoken a couple of times about the idea of buying a present for one another, but had decided it would be better to save their money to do something together later in the year.

'Technically I haven't bought it.' He rubbed his sweaty palms on the top of his trousers. 'This gift is free.'

Mia was intrigued with what he'd got for her. 'What is it?'

He smiled and beamed at her. 'You want it?'

'Yes...' She just about got the word out of her mouth when he leant over and kissed her on the lips.

'Did you like it?' She didn't say anything but responded by kissing him back.

They kissed for a while in his car until Josh managed to pull himself away from her. He didn't want to ruin anything by getting too eager or going too far. The last thing he wanted to do was upset her.

'I've been waiting ages to do that!' he grinned.

Mia smiled at him and got out of the car. She entered her house, excited, and practically skipped up the stairs to her bedroom. She shut the door, got her mobile out and phoned Jasmine. It took Jasmine awhile to answer.

'Hey, how are you?'

'I'm OK.' Her voice was low and rough, Mia could tell she wasn't OK.

She tried to lower the excitement in her own voice. 'Are you sure? I haven't heard from you in a while and you haven't replied to my messages.'

Jasmine tried to reassure her. 'Sorry, I just didn't have any credit on my phone. Honestly though, I'm fine...just tired...' She attempted to sound a bit more upbeat. 'What have you been up to?'

'I took my last exam today, so I'm done! Josh dropped me off home afterwards...' She paused to see if Jasmine said anything, but she didn't.

'He kissed me! We kissed!' She couldn't hold her excitement back any longer but, still, Jasmine didn't say anything.

'Jasmine are you there?'

'Yeah, I'm here. I'm really pleased you two have finally got it together...' She wasn't really in the mood to talk, it was hard for her to congratulate her. She cleared her throat. 'Listen Mia, I've got to go, OK? My mum's calling me.' It was a lie that she knew wouldn't hurt Mia's feelings.

'OK, do you think you'll be able to come to my party? It would mean the world to me if you could.'

Jasmine wanted to say 'no', but she knew how much and how long Mia had been building up to it. 'I'll think about it.'

While Mia had been talking to Jasmine, Francesca was in the kitchen, home from work early, to cook dinner. She was by the oven when her mobile beeped with a text alert. She walked over to the kitchen unit where she'd left it. It was a message from Shay.

'WHEN CAN I SEE YOU AGAIN? XXX'

She smiled as her fingers work. 'YOU'VE ONLY JUST SEEN ME! X'

It didn't take long for Shay to reply. 'I KNOW, BUT I WANT TO SEE YOU AGAIN....'

Before Francesca could text back Shay had already sent another message.

'I WANT TO TOUCH YOU AGAIN... TASTE YOU AGAIN...'

Francesca blushed as her phone went off again.

'I WANT TO MAKE YOU...'

'Mum?' Francesca jumped and nearly dropped the phone on the floor. She hadn't heard Mia come down the stairs and into the kitchen. She pretended to clear her throat

'Yes, sweetheart?'

'When's dinner going to be ready? Do I have time for a shower before?'

Francesca looked at her watch, trying to stay calm and not turn red. 'Erm, I'd say about...ten minutes?'

'Cool. Are you OK?'

'Yes, I'm fine. Why do you ask?'

'You've gone all red...'

She started playing with her ear and turned to check the food on the stove, to deflect Mia's attention. 'It's hot in here, that's all, with the oven and stove on.'

CHAPTER SEVENTY THREE

Francesca had taken a breather between clients and headed for one of her usual haunts, Bluebells Bookstore. She'd been browsing for about five minutes in the non-fiction section, when she heard a voice behind her.

'Hello doctor!' It was a voice she thought, and hoped, she would never hear again... Roger's. She braced herself and turned around to greet him. Roger, unexpectedly, gave her a hug. It was one of the most stiff, awkward hugs she'd ever experienced.

'Roger! It's nice to see you.'

'I'm sure it is nice to see me.' He hadn't changed.

'Wow! OK!' she mumbled to herself. 'How are you? Still with Penelope?'

'No, we split. She just wasn't right for me, you know how it is.'

Francesca wasn't surprised to hear it. If she could only stand him for an hour, once a week, what hope would someone have being married to him?

'I'm sorry to hear that.' She lied.

Roger picked up one of the books from the shelf and had a quick flick through it.

'Onwards and upwards...' He put the book back, disinterested. 'I'm seeing someone else now anyway. It's still new but she's keeping my interest so far...'

Francesca wasn't interested in hearing about his next victim so tried to end the conversation before, knowing what he was like, he would turn their chance meeting into a therapy session.

'I'm sorry Roger but I have to go...' She made sure he saw her look down at her watch. 'I have an appointment soon.'

'That's great I'll walk with you.' It didn't have the desired effect. 'I'm going that way anyway.'

It was an awkward five minute walk back to her office with Roger talking about how much he'd changed into a better version of himself, thanks to the new woman in his life.

When they reached Francesca's building it wasn't soon enough for her but, to her dismay, Roger didn't leave. Instead he opened the door for her and gestured for her to go in first.

'You see, I now know it's polite to hold the door for a lady!' He was trying to prove he'd changed and knew how to treat a woman. Francesca was amazed since manners were never one of his strong points. He followed her up to the entrance of the reception area and held the door open for her again. It felt awkward because she hadn't expected him to walk her up to her office.

'Well, thank you Roger. I think I know where I'm going from here!' she said, in a patronising way, he didn't pick up on it and nodded his head. He began to close the glass door when he spotted Julie coming out from one of the side rooms. Julie noticed him when she looked towards Francesca.

'Roger! I didn't know you would be here!' She seemed a little flustered seeing him. Her behaviour confused Francesca.

'Yes, it was Francesca's good fortune to run into me and I was a gentleman and escorted her back.'

'That's very kind of you.' Julie blushed.

Francesca frowned, puzzled by their behaviour towards one another.

'So doctor, I will say good day to you.' He looked across at Julie. 'Are we still on for next week? I've booked the restaurant for seven.'

'Yes, I'm looking forward to it!' He gave Julie a smile and walked out.

Francesca stared at Julie.

Julie could sense her confusion. 'What?'

'You have got to be kidding me! You and Roger, dating?'

Julie moved behind her desk. 'What? I told you he's always been lovely and polite to me...'

'Roger?' She had to keep repeating his name, for it to sink in. 'That's who you've been dating...leaving work early for?'

'Yes.' Julie said it so calmly that Francesca didn't really know what to say so she headed to her office to prepare for her next client and to try and get her head round the news.

Near the end of the day Francesca and Julie had a cup of tea in the kitchenette. They hadn't really spoken between clients and there was an awkward silence between them. Julie couldn't take it anymore.

'Come on then, out with it!' She could see Francesca was dying to ask her questions.

'What? No, if you want to go out with Roger I'm happy for you, I wish you the best... the very best!' She covered her grin by taking another sip of her tea but couldn't hide the sarcasm in her voice.

'Oh, come on, if you met someone at work that you got on well with, don't tell me you wouldn't give it a try?' The question hit a little too close to home and wiped the grin off Francesca's face. 'I mean if you could, if it was appropriate?' Julie realised it was a pointless question so she changed the subject. 'So how's Mia enjoying her freedom after finishing her exams? I bet she's looking forward to the summer now?'

'Yes, it's been great! She's so much more relaxed now. It's her party tonight. I can't believe how quickly it's come around!' She took another sip of her tea and looked at Julie. 'Roger, though? Really?' She still couldn't quite believe it.

'Oh, shut up!' Julie walked away from her to get a biscuit to dunk in her tea.

CHAPTER SEVENTY FOUR

Francesca got home early to find Mia panicking about her outfit for the party. She tried to reassure her and tell her that she looked beautiful, but Mia didn't feel it. She ran back upstairs and disappeared into her bedroom.

Francesca knocked on her door an hour later.

'Mia, come on! Josh has been waiting outside for ages with his engine running. You'll burn up all his petrol!'

Mia shouted back through the door. 'I'm ready. I'm ready!'

Francesca could still hear her rummaging around until, finally, she opened her bedroom door.

'How do I look?' She stood in front of Francesca with a perfectly fitted red dress on.

'You look gorgeous darling. Now go and have some fun!'

'Aren't you coming with us?'

'I'm going to come later. I'll make my own way there. I didn't want to cramp your style by showing up in the same car!'

'Good point!'

'Besides, you're probably going to want to party hard and stay late. I'll show my face and then leave...' She saw Mia's face light up with the thought of a parent free party, Francesca continued, 'on the condition that I can trust you?'

'Of course mum!' She kissed Francesca on the cheek and ran down the stairs in her bare feet. She stopped by the front door to put her shoes on and left, excited.

Francesca was left in peace. She decided to take the opportunity to clean the house up a bit. She did some vacuuming and dusting and even attempted to clean out the fridge but, staring into it, she lost all motivation, so instead of picking up the cleaning products she picked up her bottle of wine and made her way into the living room.

She sat on the sofa and pulled her mobile phone from her pocket. She glared at the screen and hesitated as she went into her contacts and scrolled through until she found Shay's number, she pressed call.

'Hello?' Shay picked up after about four rings.

'Hi, how are you?' Francesca's tummy tingled just hearing her voice, she felt stupid for asking such a dull question.

'You never replied to my texts!' She wasn't mad but intrigued as to why Francesca hadn't replied.

'I couldn't. Mia walked in and I've been busy at work.'

'*Oui?* I've never heard that excuse before!'

'Really, honestly, I have...' She wanted Shay to believe her, she lowered her voice a bit. 'You can tell me again, what you want to do to me, in person... I've got half an hour until I go out.'

'Where are you going?'

'I need to show my face at Mia's exam party. Nobody's here so you could come over.'

Shay knew she must have been desperate to see her because she'd never invited her round to her house before.

'I would love to, really love to, but my friend just phoned and she's having some sound issues at a gig. I said I would go over and help her with it.'

'Oh, OK.' Shay could hear the disappointment in Francesca's voice, she liked it. It felt like Francesca was the one chasing her, for a change.

CHAPTER SEVENTY FIVE

Club Juice was packed full of noisy teenagers from Mia's school. The party had already been going for an hour or so and the air was full of hormones, sweat and body odour. The dance floor was packed and everybody was enjoying themselves.

Laura had done a good job with the decorations. The place was lit by lots of soft mood lights and the music was pumping. Mia and Josh were dancing together when she spotted Laura standing at the side of the room. She shouted, over the music, into Josh's ear.

'I'll be right back!' She shuffled through the crowd, over to Laura, and gave her a big hug.

'Thank you so much Laura! This whole thing is great and... no Willy balloons!'

'No! I tried but they'd sold out!' They smiled at one another. 'I'm glad you're having a good time. I'm sorry to say this, but I'm going to have to go home. I think the lights and music have got the best of me and my head hurts. Will you tell your mum I'll see her another time?'

'Sure, she should be here soon.'

'Maybe I'll try and hold out for a bit then.' Laura stayed for another twenty minutes but Francesca still hadn't appeared, so she decided to go. Shortly after, Francesca arrived. She scanned the room and found Mia at the bar, walked over and tapped her on the shoulder.

'You're here! You literally just missed Laura. She went home with a headache! She said to say she'll be OK so don't worry.'

Francesca nodded and took a look around the club. 'So how's it going so far?'

'It's awesome! Apparently there was a sound issue but I didn't notice anything, so maybe Shay's fixed it?'

'Shay's here?' Francesca didn't do very well with hiding her surprise

'Yeah.' Before Francesca could ask anything more one of Mia's friends motioned over to her. 'Look, I'm going to love you and leave you, OK?'

'OK, but Mia, I'm not going to stay long. I'm tired, and I think I'm about twenty years too old for a party like this!' She squinted at the lights flashing from the DJ's booth. 'I'm not surprised Laura went home with a headache!'

'Cool mum, that's fine. I'll see you tomorrow.' She left Francesca and went over to her friend.

Francesca made her way through the sea of teenagers towards the DJ's booth at the back of the club. As she got closer she saw Shay who was with the DJ, leaning close to her to speak in her ear. She saw the DJ put her hand on Shay's lower back and laugh at whatever she had said. She was jealous of how comfortable they looked together. Francesca decided she liked everything about the party Laura had organised, but not the DJ she'd chosen. She was walking over to the side of the room for some space when Shay spotted her in the crowd. She smiled, pleased to see her, and followed her. It was a lot less cramped there, but was still noisy from the music.

Shay leaned into Francesca's ear. 'I didn't know the gig was Mia's!'

'What was the problem with the sound?' She didn't match Shay's excitement to see her, she sounded flat.

'There wasn't one!' Shay paused, fed up with shouting over the music. She slowly leaned into Francesca's ear again. 'Follow me...' She walked over to one of the private booths that had been closed off. Francesca followed her, trying to control the bad mood she could feel creeping on.

Shay knew the code to the booth door. The club manager hadn't changed it since she'd worked there. She typed in the numbers 3672 and entered, holding the door open for Francesca, shutting it behind them. It made the music in the main room a lot quieter, they could hear each other speak without shouting. Shay sauntered over to Francesca and tried to kiss her but Francesca moved away. She still wasn't over the interaction between Shay and the DJ but she tried not to let it show.

'What were you saying about the sound?'

'Turns out there wasn't a problem. Freya's headphones weren't working with the sound that was all...' She tried to make contact with Francesca lips.

'Freya?' Francesca put her hand on Shay's stomach to keep her back. 'Is she a friend?'

'Yes, we go way back, from when I used to DJ here.' She pushed against Francesca's hand and managed to reach her lips, to kiss her quickly.

Francesca pushed against her stomach again. 'Did you sleep with her?'

Realising what was bugging Francesca, she backed off and smirked at her.

'You're jealous!'

'No, I'm not jealous!' She knew she sounded like Mia when she tried to deny something that was true.

'I haven't slept with her. She's like my little sister, I wouldn't...' She began to tease Francesca, playing with the bottom of her top. She playfully tried to pull her towards her. 'I do find it sexy though.'

'What?' Francesca desperately wanted to just give in to her, she knew that the way she was acting was stupid, but part of her liked the attention. She could tell by Shay's face she was telling the truth about this Freya woman.

'When you're jealous!' Shay tugged her shirt, sharply, and pulled Francesca against her. Their bodies bumped against one another and they started kissing. Shay's hands wandered all over Francesca's body and stopped, suddenly, between her thighs, it left Francesca breathless. Shay stared into her eyes and smiled. Francesca moved forward a few times to try and kiss her but Shay pulled back every time, teasing her. 'I love that you booty called me!'

Francesca, a little embarrassed, light heartedly pushed her away. 'I did not phone you for a booty call!'

Shay grinned and moved back in, closer to her body again. 'Oh yeah, what else would we have done in half an hour at your house?'

Francesca bit the bottom of her lip, trying to think of a valid answer, she couldn't. She moved forward and kissed Shay again. Soon things became passionate between them, Shay wanted to take in, and touch, the whole of Francesca's body and Francesca wanted to let her. Shay breathlessly whispered into her ear whilst trying to fit in as many kisses as she could down her neck.

'Come back to mine? I'm done here now.' Francesca groaned as Shay put her hand up her top and gently squeezed her breast.

Within twenty minutes they had driven over to Shay's flat. She started where she'd left off and they began kissing again. She took Francesca's top off and kissed her, moving down to her neck and above the top of her collar bone. Francesca's body was excited and aroused with anticipation. She breathed heavily into Shay's ear and grabbed on to Shay's t-shirt. She attempted to pull her body in closer by thrusting her pelvis against her, she was desperate for Shay to touch her. They were as close as they could get, Shay ran her lips across her shoulder, she could read Francesca's signal, she knew what she wanted her to do, but she teased her and made her wait.

'I can only stay an hour!' Francesca whispered between her rapid breaths.

It was the last thing Shay wanted to hear and it changed the mood in the room completely. She stopped kissing her and looked at her. Francesca hooked her finger under Shay's belt buckle and tried to undo it with one hand.

'That doesn't mean you have to stop!' She kissed her, but Shay wasn't in the mood anymore. She stepped back, away from Francesca.

Francesca saw the look on her face. 'What's the matter?'

Shay went quiet before she said what she was thinking. 'What is this for you?'

Francesca was confused by the question and by the change of mood.

'What do you mean?'

Shay took her time as she pulled her hair back out of her face. 'I mean for me, I want this... between us. I don't want to be sneaking off hiding, an hour here, half an hour there. I want more than that with you.'

'Shay listen, I like you...'

Shay could tell by her tone what was coming, she turned away from Francesca, upset, feeling burnt.

'You like me, I get it...' She locked her jaw with frustration, she didn't want to make a fool of herself, admitting her feelings.

'You've taken me by surprise...'

Shay turned back to face her. She decided if Francesca was going to bottle out of this then she, at least, should do it to her face.

'Obviously, I'm attracted to you... but I have a family I'm responsible for, who rely on me, I can't be...' She knew it was a cop out, it wasn't as though Mia and Mark were little kids anymore. They had lives of their own now, more or less. 'I'm going through a divorce...'

Shay knew she was being evasive, she took a step towards her. 'And?'

'You're twenty four!' It came out of Francesca's mouth in desperation.

'Wow! You're going there...' It felt like a punch to Shay's stomach.

'Yes I am! In reality I don't know how you and I would, or could even work! My rational mind...'

Shay cut in angrily. 'Fuck your rational mind! I'm asking you right now, what is it you feel for me?'

Francesca struggled with the intensity of the situation.

'Shay, we came together, probably through mutual pain. We both feel a connect...'

'*Merde!* Can you hear yourself? You're doing it again! Instead of answering my question, honestly, you start giving me shrink explanations!' Frustrated, she gripped onto her hair and combed it back again with both of her hands. 'Stop thinking and be real with me, now, in this moment!' She stepped towards Francesca wanting to touch her, hold her.

'I am being real with you!' Francesca couldn't help but back off. It was too much for her to take. She stared at Shay who was frozen by her words. She knew what she was doing would hurt her deeply.

Shay lowered her voice and gritted her teeth. 'I think you should go then.'

A silence fell between them as they stared at one another. A few seconds passed, Francesca bent down and picked her top up from the floor. She turned to leave, her eyes stinging with tears, she wanted to hold them back until she was away from Shay.

Shay stood there, her own eyes stinging, as she watched Francesca walk out. Their night together had

started with so much promise and it had come to a bad
end.

CHAPTER SEVENTY SIX

Jasmine was curled up on her bed in her dark, stuffy room. Debra was worried about her, she hadn't seen her all day. She walked upstairs and knocked softly on her daughter's bedroom door. She entered before Jasmine answered and walked over to her bed using the light coming through from the landing. Debra sat on the edge of the bed and felt for her body with her hand. She stopped and rested it on what she thought was Jasmine's back.

'I'm worried about you, Jasmine.' Jasmine didn't move or say anything. 'Do you think you should go and see Dr Sims again, talk about going on some tablets? You haven't seen him since starting with Dr Francesca, maybe...'

'I'm fine, really!' She jumped up out of bed. 'Stop worrying about me mum...' She put her shoes on and began to tie her laces.

'Where are you going?'

Jasmine hadn't planned on going, but she'd figured she'd rather go to Mia's party than stay at home, under her mums watch.

'Mia, one of my friends at school has a party tonight, it's only nine thirty, so is it all right if I go? I won't come back late.'

'That's great darling! You've made a friend. Why didn't you tell me?'

'It's no big deal, mum. So can I go?'

Debra was so pleased to know she had managed to make a friend at school. 'Sure, but be back by eleven, OK?'

Jasmine left, relieved she didn't have to talk with her anymore.

CHAPTER SEVENTY SEVEN

Mia was still enjoying herself, dancing through the night. She walked over to the bar with Josh to get a drink. Josh bought two lemonades with ice and they stood watching everyone else dance. Mia had taken a few sips when she spotted Denise dancing with a boy. She couldn't believe her eyes.

'Who let *her* in?'

'Who?' Josh couldn't see who she was talking about.

'Denise Reese.'

He looked in the direction Mia was staring and saw Denise, dancing with one of his friends, Adam.

'I don't know, maybe she got in with Adam? They've been hooking up lately.'

'Really? Why didn't you tell me? He's such a nice guy and she's such a... bitch!'

'Each to their own...' He took her hand, partly because he wanted to and partly to stop her from going over to Denise and starting something. 'Speaking of hooking up...' Josh kissed her softly on the lips.

'Don't get a head of yourself!'

'No, I didn't mean hooking up as in... I meant...'

Mia smiled and kissed him. 'Josh, I'm teasing you!'

He smiled back at her, relieved, and started to kiss her again.

While Josh went to the restroom, Mia stayed by the bar. She spotted Jasmine, with her hoodie over her head, walking round the edge of the dance floor. Excited, she rushed over to her and hugged her. It took Jasmine by surprise she hadn't noticed Mia approaching her.

'Jasmine, I'm so glad you could make it! Where have you been?'

'I've just been resting, chilling...' Jasmine glanced round the room and tried to take in everything and everyone. 'I'm sorry I couldn't come earlier and I'm sorry I didn't exactly dress up...'

Mia wanted to put her at ease. She was just so pleased to see her.

'Don't worry about it, forget it! You'll probably be the most comfortable one here! I'm just so glad you came...' From the corner of her eye she noticed Josh coming out of the rest rooms. 'Come and say hello to Josh...'

'I will in a bit, I'm just going to get a drink...' She was nervous and her mouth had become so dry that it was becoming hard to speak. 'Where are you hanging out?'

Mia pointed to the corner of the room where a few tables and chairs were set up.

'Just over there.'

Jasmine left Mia and headed towards the bar. She had to take her hood down, it was too hot to have it over her head. As she approached the bar a couple of boys were mucking around, shoving each other pretending to be in a mosh pit. One of the boys pushed the other so hard he lost his balance and bumped into Jasmine who was caught off guard. She lost her footing and bumped into someone standing by the bar. It was Adam, who was waiting for a drink.

'Shit, sorry! I didn't hurt you did I?' Their eyes met in the dim lighting, he gave her a sweet smile and helped her find her feet properly. She felt a weird sensation come over her face, she realised she was smiling at him.

'No worries, you didn't hurt me!'

He was still holding onto her arm, she felt the heat of his hand through her sleeve.

'I've seen you around at school. It's Jasmine, right?'

She couldn't believe he knew who she was, let alone her name but, before she could answer, one of the servers behind the bar interrupted them.

'Yes mate? What can I get you?'

Adam let go of her and turned to the barman. 'Hi...'

Jasmine felt a sense of disappointment. She wanted him to speak with her some more. She went to move away when he turned back a round and looked at her.

'Can I get you a drink?'

'Yes, thanks, just a water please.' She couldn't believe it.

Adam smiled at her again. 'Cheap date, huh?'

Jasmine couldn't help but grin as he ordered her drink. Adam turned around with a drink in each hand, sooner than she'd imagined, and caught her smiling. He passed the plastic cup of water to her.

'Thanks.'

'You're welcome.' He smiled at her. 'I'll see you around, Jasmine!'

She watched him walk over to his group of friends and start chatting. Jasmine noticed that she felt something she hadn't felt in a long time, happy and excited. She downed the water at the bar and left the empty cup. She glanced over to Adam's group and then checked that Mia and Josh were still at their table. She intended to go over and sit with them when she realised she needed the restroom first.

As she came out of the toilet cubicle, before she walked back into the main room, she checked herself in one of the mirrors, conscious of what she looked like. If Adam saw her again she wanted to look the best she could, even though she was the only one at the party wearing a hoodie, t -shirt and jeans. As she walked back to meet up with Mia and Josh she saw Denise walking towards her, she dropped her head down hoping she wouldn't spot her.

'Did you think I didn't see you?' Denise hissed.

'Excuse me?' Jasmine tried to walk past her, not wanting any confrontation, but Denise stepped in front of her and blocked her path.

'You, flirting with Adam. Keep your hands off my boyfriend!' She moved up close to Jasmine's face.

Jasmine kept her eyes down towards the floor. 'We were just talking...' She knew after she'd said it that she shouldn't have. Denise always had to have the last say. She stared at Jasmine and laughed, loudly, in her face.

'Like you'd have a chance with him anyway! Look at you! Can you not even make an effort to dress up?' Jasmine felt her looking up and down her body, she felt uncomfortable and ashamed, as the little self-esteem she had, plummeted. She believed Denise's comments and wanted the floor to swallow her up. Denise backed away a bit, giving her a bit more room. Jasmine took it as an opportunity to leave. As Jasmine went to walk past her, Denise stuck her foot out, Jasmine went flying onto the hard, cold floor. She stayed there, in shock, all she could hear ringing in her head was laughter. She peered up and saw Denise and a group of her friends, looking down at her, laughing, she felt like the smallest person in the world.

Mia rushed over to see what the commotion was, why people were gathered around near the restroom entrance. She pushed through the crowd and saw Jasmine, sprawled, on the floor.

'Jasmine! Jasmine, are you OK?' She bent down to help her up.

'I'm fine...' She didn't want to make more of a scene so didn't take Mia's help, she got up by herself.

Mia stood back up and glared across to Denise, who was smiling.

'She should watch where she's stepping!'

'Back off Denise...' Mia was furious with her. She didn't need to ask what had really happened, she knew straight away Denise would be involved. 'In fact, get out! Leave my party!'

She went to check Jasmine was OK but she shrugged Mia off. 'No, it's fine Mi. I've had enough anyway.' Jasmine walked away from them and left trying to hold her tears in.

CHAPTER SEVENTY EIGHT

The next morning, after her party, Mia tried to phone Jasmine to see how she was, but Jasmine didn't pick up. She tried a couple more times then gave up. As she walked downstairs she could smell cooking wafting through from the kitchen. Francesca was making pancakes for breakfast.

Francesca smiled as Mia walked in. 'So how was last night? I heard you come in around one.'

Mia took a seat. 'Yeah, Josh dropped me off...' She thought back to what had happened last night. 'It was good. Denise nearly ruined it, but I didn't let her. I wouldn't give her the pleasure!'

'Who's Denise?'

'She's just a girl that goes to my school. I don't know how she got in... I don't want to waste my breath talking about her. She's not worth it. She's just one of those girls who likes to make trouble.'

Francesca, still listening, got a plate out of the cupboard and served her up a hot pancake, straight from the pan.

'Thanks...' Mia took a mouthful. 'Delicious! How was your night?' She took another bite and looked up at Francesca as she chewed it.

'I ended up going to bed early.' Francesca poured some more batter into the pan. She hadn't stopped thinking about what had happened between her and Shay last night.

'Thanks for the party and everything else you do for me, mum...' Surprised, Francesca turned around to face Mia. 'I know I don't always say it, or show it, but I am grateful.'

Mia got up and walked over to Francesca to hug her. She was a little taken aback.

'What's this all about?' She tried to work out why, all of a sudden, Mia had come out with such a thing. 'Has your dad not been in touch?'

Mia pretended to be offended, even though her mum was spot on. 'I just wanted to hug you! Is that a crime?' She let go of Francesca and went back to her pancake. 'And no, he hasn't been in touch. I thought, at least, he would try and make an effort to contact me, especially after being in hospital and finishing my exams.'

Francesca sighed, disappointed. 'I'm sorry. I wish he would get his act together for you and for Mark.'

CHAPTER SEVENTY NINE

I t was getting late and Shay was working an evening shift at Yani's with Faith. She was still upset and moody over the argument she'd had with Francesca. She hadn't heard anything from her since she'd walked out of her flat.

'Can you take table four's drinks order for me please?'

Shay was so far away in thought she hadn't even seen Faith join her behind the bar.

'Yeah.' She half-heartedly strolled over to table four, to help Faith out.

The end of the night soon came, Shay wiped the bar down as Faith began to reset the tables. She was still staring into space, mulling over what had happened with Francesca.

'Can you pass me a table cloth please?'

Shay picked up a clean cloth and, instead of passing it to Faith, threw it at her.

'What's up with you grumpy? Got out of the wrong side of the bed again?' Shay kept quiet and didn't answer her. 'You've been like this for the last couple of days, you're scaring the customers off!' Faith was hoping the comment would make Shay smile but it didn't.

'I'm fine.'

'Evidently!' She wanted to know what Shay's problem was. 'What? Is the honeymoon period over with the doctor?'

'Something like that.' Shay mumbled.

Faith was silent for a while. She could see Shay was upset and struggling. 'You're probably better off without her if she makes you feel this bad! Forget her!'

'I wish I could but she's under my skin!' She dropped the cloth she'd been using to wipe the same spot on the bar for the past five minutes. 'This doesn't usually happen to me... I don't let it.'

'What happened with you and her?'

She went over to help Faith set the next table up for tomorrow's lunch service.

'She's confused... she dropped the whole age difference thing. Why does age have to even matter?'

Faith kept her answer simple. 'It doesn't.'

'Exactly! Thank you.' Shay passed Faith some clean napkins.

'So, what? You're mad at her for that? That's what this mood is about?'

'No, I'm mad at her because she doesn't know what she wants. I don't want to be kept dangling, wondering if she wants me or not... my feelings are getting stronger for her... If she's just going to leave me high and dry, I'd rather stop it now.'

Faith began to place the cutlery either side of the place mats.

'What makes you think she'll leave you high and dry?'

'Because she shuts down and walks away whenever feelings get involved. That's how she copes with what she's feeling...or she goes into therapist mode.' She passed Faith the salt and pepper.

'Takes one to know one!'

She hesitated and looked at Faith. 'What's that supposed to mean?'

Faith smiled at her. 'Shay, you're practically talking about yourself, minus the therapist bit. When we dated, if I can call it that, that's what you did. I told you I had feelings for you and you totally shut down and called it off. The next thing I knew you were fucking some student!'

Shay hadn't realised that was what she'd done. It was just a fling for her, she hadn't realised that Faith had had feelings for her. She thought back to that time and felt guilty about the way she'd treated her, she was a good friend and didn't like the idea of her hurting her like that. 'I'm sorry Faith. I didn't mean to hurt you or...'

'No, you never do Shay!' She didn't say it in a nasty way. She grabbed the remaining cutlery out of Shay's hand and started laying the next table. 'Don't worry because, by the way, I'm totally over you now. It was years ago. But surely you, of all people, should be able to understand why she's doing it. Give her a chance. She's probably one of those women who's never even see another woman as an option. You've probably come along and turned her whole world and perception upside down!'

CHAPTER EIGHTY

'It's from Mia as well...' Francesca handed Laura a present. They were at their usual table in the café Laura loved to go to for the chocolate cake. 'To say thank you for all your hard work planning the party.'

'It was pretty epic wasn't it?' Laura took the small package and tore into the paper to open it. It was a mini vibrator. 'Very funny! One to add to my collection! I would offer it back to you but you probably don't need it anymore, with your new...'

Francesca's mood changed, she'd been trying to forget about Shay. 'Can we not talk about her?'

Laura saw the look on her face, her reaction. 'Why not? What's happened?'

'It's over... whatever *it* was?' She took a sip of her tea and hoped Laura would stop staring at her, but she didn't. 'She asked me what we were doing and I said she was too young...' Francesca heard how condescending she must have sounded, repeating it to Laura. 'I have a family... she's a woman...' She took a deep breath out. 'What was I thinking, Laura?'

Laura responded to Francesca's first statement. 'I see. But why should that matter?'

'What?' Francesca was confused. 'Her age?'

'Both! Her age and that she's a woman. It's the twenty first century, Cesca, people are past age, gender, sexuality and, if they're not, they should catch up!' She was passionate when it came to subjects like equality and people being able to be themselves. Over the many years she'd worked she'd seen so many messed up and troubled people who couldn't accept themselves because other people had told them they were wrong. 'Love who you want to love, fuck who you want to fuck...'

'OK Laura, don't start!' She knew Laura was right but she saw customers in the cafe start to look over at them.

'What? I'm just saying it, because someone's got to!' Laura noticed people staring so she adjusted the volume of her voice. 'You don't fall in love with what a person has packed between their legs, you fall in love with their soul, their spirit, their heart, or whatever...' She paused and raised her eyebrows. 'Unless, their packing something pretty spectacular between their legs, like my Mike, then...'

'OK! I'll stop you there, before I get a description of Mike's member!' They both laughed at one another.

Laura became more serious as she looked at Francesca, she went into therapist mode.

'What is it you're really afraid of? It feels like you're grabbing for excuses. Why are you trying to sabotage it?'

'I'm not...' She went quiet for a moment and gave a long breath out. 'If I'm honest, I guess it scares me, the intensity of it.'

Laura knew there was more, something Francesca wasn't saying. 'And?'

'And... I was married to David for all those years. I didn't feel heard, supported, safe or wanted. With her I feel all those things and more already. It's so fast that it scares the shit out of me. It makes me want to run in the other direction and, well, I was her therapist for God's sake!'

'Granted, yes. It's not the best of ways to meet someone. Some people might say it's unethical but I believe in fate, reason, and connection. For whatever reason, you've met one another. Maybe, as a professional, I should warn you off but as a friend I would...' She wasn't sure if she was making herself clear to Francesca. 'I actually know a few therapists who have had relations with their clients. One of them even got married, I think they have two kids now. It does happen, Cesca, so don't blame yourself or beat yourself up.'

CHAPTER EIGHTY ONE

It was the first day back at school for Jasmine since the incident at Mia's party. She'd managed to convince her mum she had bad period pains and needed a couple of days off. She dreaded the day she would have to go back and face the people who had seen her splayed out on the floor.

She finished her math class, feeling it had gone well, so far, since nobody had said anything to her and she hadn't heard anyone gossiping about what had happened. As she entered the corridor on the way to her next lesson, she saw Denise, Bonnie, and a group of girls standing and chatting by the lockers. Her stomach sunk just at the sight of them. She knew she had to walk past them to get to class. It was Mrs Brown class, one of the few teachers in the school who she actually liked. She convinced and forced herself to walk past them and ignore them, no matter what they said or did.

'Jasmine!' Bonnie had clocked on to her straight away. 'I heard you had a nice 'trip' the other night and this time I don't mean you taking drugs!'

All Jasmine saw when she looked up at them was the whole group laughing at her. Denise pretended to re-enact her fall for them, it made the group laugh even louder.

Shame and embarrassment flooded through Jasmine's body, she felt completely exposed as she rushed past them, wanting to get as far away from them as possible. She only got a few metres down the corridor when, not looking where she was going because her head was down, she bumped into Adam. He looked at Denise and the group of girls pointing and laughing, he looked down at her, concerned, but all Jasmine saw in his eyes, was pity.

'Jasmine...'

Adam was the last person she wanted to see right now so she shrugged him off and ran out of the building. When she reached the school gates she couldn't hold it in anymore. She put her hand over her mouth as she let out a cry.

She ran all the way home with tears streaming down her face. When, eventually, she reached her front door, she fumbled in her bag for her set of keys, let herself in and ran straight upstairs to her bedroom. All she could see, in her head, were the people at the party, the girls at school laughing at her and the way Adam had stared at her. She went over to her desk and opened the tablet draw. Scooping them all into her bag, she wiped her eyes with her sleeve and left.

Jasmine waited at the bus station to get the bus to the beach. It was the one she and her grandpa would always go to. When she got to the beach she sat down on the damp sand and let out all the emotions she'd held in for so long. She wailed, screamed and cried. Jasmine watched the waves for a while and attempted to control her breathing, to calm down a little. She looked down at her bag and opened it, pulling out a pen and notepad. She began to write.

Dear family, I'm sorry...

She started crying harder. Tears fell on to the piece of paper, blurring the ink.

CHAPTER EIGHTY TWO

'Do you need to talk?'

Julie put a folder down on Francesca's desk and looked at her, confused. 'Talk?'

She grinned at Julie. 'I thought you might need to talk, after your date with Roger!'

'No, I don't need to talk!' She tried not to rise to Francesca's goading. 'If you must know, it was nice...he was nice...a true gentleman.'

Francesca nearly choked on her tea. 'Really? He didn't even insult you once?'

'No. He complimented me all through the meal.'

'Sounds like a changed man!'

'I don't know why you tease him so much, he always speaks so highly of you.'

Francesca scoffed, 'I bet he does! Probably nobody else can listen to him for more than hour...'

Julie peered over at her with a face of steal. Francesca could tell that she, for some reason, genuinely liked him, so she eased up with the teasing.

'I'm joking. I'm joking. I'm pleased for you, it's nice to see you this happy, honestly!'

'What about you being happy?'

Francesca leaned back on her chair, she squeezed the back of her neck and sighed. 'That's a whole other story!'

It was twenty past four in the afternoon when Francesca checked the time on her watch. She'd expected Jasmine, for their session, at quarter past but she hadn't showed yet. She got up and walked into reception. Julie wasn't there, so she checked the waiting room, but it was empty. As she turned to walk back she heard the toilet system flush. Julie walked out of the rest room and was surprised to see Francesca out of her office.

'Is Jasmine not here yet?'

'No, not as far as I know. Is she not in the waiting room?' Julie asked.

'No I've checked. She hasn't phoned?'

'No. Do you want me to try her number or phone her mother?'

Francesca looked down at her watch again and wondered if she was over-worrying.

'She's only ten minutes late. I'll give it another five. It's probably nothing.' She strolled back into office and shut the door.

She got her mobile out and flicked through her contacts, to fill time. When she reached Shay's name, she paused over her number, but her phone rang before she could press the call button.

'Hello?' The voice on the other end spoke fast, but clearly. He answered all of Francesca's questions. 'What...? When...? I'll be right there...'

Francesca sped to the hospital and rushed through the entrance doors. She headed straight to the A&E department and approached the first nurse she saw walking down the corridor.

'Excuse me, nurse, a patient's just come in...Jasmine...' By the way the nurse looked at her, Francesca knew she knew who she was asking about. 'Where is she? Do you know if she's OK?'

The nurse was about to answer when a screaming howl echoed, loudly, down the corridor. Francesca's heart dropped to her stomach. The noise went straight through her. She looked in the direction of the noise and saw Debra enter the corridor from one of the end rooms. A nurse was helping to support her as she walked. Wailing, with her face red and bloated from crying, she stumbled towards Francesca.

Francesca's whole body had frozen. She couldn't move. She could tell by Debra's face, and the wailing she'd heard, that it wasn't good news.

A few metres away from Francesca, Debra stopped and bent forward. Overtaken by grief, she let out another howl. Francesca felt her eyes well up, her legs turned to jelly.

Debra seemed to gain strength from somewhere, she told the nurse that she could manage to walk by herself. She went straight up to Francesca who fumbled for words.

'Debra, I...' She could barely speak.

Debra slapped her, hard, on the cheek. Francesca felt the sting and, instinctively, lifted her hand to the pain. She could feel it burning as a tear fell down her face. Debra stared at her, with a face full of anger.

'You should have known she would do this...' Her voice wobbled with emotion. 'You're her therapist. This is your fault! I want you to know I hold you responsible, you hear me?' She walked past and away from Francesca, she left her standing there in shock.

'Are you OK?' Francesca had completely forgotten about the nurse she had approached was standing with her.

'Can I... can I see her?'

Francesca waited outside Jasmine's room while the nurse entered and checked with the doctor if she could go in. She came back out a couple of minutes later.

'Just to warn you, she's hooked up to various machines still.'

Francesca nodded in acknowledgement. The nurse opened the door and guided her into the room. As she walked in the doctor, who had helped medically treat Jasmine, gave her a look of condolence and left quietly.

All was quiet and still as Francesca, slowly, walked over to the side of the bed. Jasmine lay there, motionless, with a breathing tube taped to her mouth. All the machines around her bed were switched off, the heart monitor was just a blank screen. The nurse approached and gently unclipped the breathing tube so Francesca could see more of her face. She looked pale but peaceful. She took Jasmine's already cold hand and burst into tears.

Francesca sat with Jasmine's body until the nurse and doctor came in to move her. One of the doctors invited her into a side room whilst they prepared the body.

'I'm sorry. There was nothing we could do for her.' The doctor had lost many patients over the years but it never made it any easier when it came to know what to say.

Francesca was still in complete shock and exhausted from crying so much.

'What did she do? What did she take?'

'Not all the blood toxicology has come back yet but it looks like a concoction of tablets and insulin.'

She repeated what he'd said, just to make sure she'd heard right. 'Insulin?'

'Yes. It seems as though she injected an overdose of it. She was obviously determined for it to work...to end her life. I don't believe it to be an accident or a cry for help.' He paused and looked at Francesca. 'I understand this is a hard time for everyone involved. Do you have someone you can go to, to be with you, someone who can support you through this?'

Francesca felt numb. His words were still sinking in. 'I was her therapist. I'm not family...' She said it as if she didn't have the right to be upset or affected.

'Yes, I understand that, but still, you're clearly in shock. It's not every day one of your clients takes their own life. You still must have had a relationship with her?'

She stared at him, not knowing what to say.

CHAPTER EIGHTY THREE

Shay was alone in Yani's, closing up the restaurant. She'd lost a game of rock, paper, and scissors with Frank and had to close and lock up the restaurant by herself. She was sweeping up some broken glass from the floor, behind the bar, when she heard the door open. She thought she'd locked it so no one else could walk in. '

Sorry we're closed, we close early on a...' She turned around and looked up to see who it was, she was more than surprised to see Francesca stood there. She moved from behind the bar and walked past her to the door. She flipped the latch and locked it so no-one else could walk in off the street. She turned to look at Francesca, who looked completely drained.

'You look exhausted. Have you been working late or something?' Shay sounded flat after a long day's work herself. Francesca didn't say anything. She just stared at Shay as her body began to shake. 'Francesca?' Francesca still couldn't say anything. 'Francesca you're scaring me, what's going on?'

Silent tears fell down Francesca's face as she felt her body about to collapse with grief. Shay rushed straight over to her and, without even thinking, took her in her arms. Francesca's body stiffened from the connection, she didn't want to feel her body because she knew, then, she would have to feel the grief.

Shay, held on to her and softly whispered in her ear. 'Tell me.'

Francesca tried to swallow the lump in her throat. 'She's gone...' Her words came out cold, with no feeling.

'Who's gone?' She gazed at her and held her face between her hands. Completely dissociated, Francesca couldn't do anything but stare past her. 'Francesca, look at me...'

Francesca slowly looked into Shay's eyes, she broke down and grabbed onto her. She scrunched her t-shirt in her hands, gripping onto her as tightly as she could, and cried even harder. Francesca cried for Jasmine, for everything she'd held in, for everything she'd, hopelessly, tried to control in her life and around her. She surrendered to it all and completely let go. Exhausted, she gave the weight of her body to Shay.

'It's OK, I've got you.' Shay held on to Francesca tightly. She didn't let her go.

CHAPTER EIGHTY FOUR

FIVE HOURS EARLIER.

As Jasmine took her last breath she saw her whole life, playing before her, like a movie. It was as if someone was showing her home videos of herself as a baby, learning to crawl, walk, and then run. She saw all the birthdays she'd celebrated with her mum and Paul. She saw herself at the beach with her grandpa, both of them playing by the water and jumping over the waves.

She heard a voice whisper to her from beside her hospital bed.

'Jazzy...' She recognised her grandpa, straight away, she twisted her head in the direction of his voice, but couldn't see him anywhere.

'Jazzy...' This time the voice was louder and clearer. A light appeared next to her, brighter than anything she'd ever seen before.

'Jazzy...' Her grandpa appeared from within the light. Standing next to her bed, he put his hand out to her. Jasmine smiled at him, overjoyed to see him.

'Are you coming with me now?' His voice was kind, warm and reassuring, just like she remembered. She got out of the bed and took his hand. They walked together over to the door, her grandpa slowly opened it. The light through the door was so bright that all Jasmine could see was a colour whiter than white.

'Where are we going grandpa?'

He chuckled warmly and squeezed her hand. 'Wherever you want to go, kid!'

She grinned up at him feeling nothing but love, joy and excitement.

'The beach?' She suggested, with the biggest grin on her face.

He slowly nodded and smiled at her. 'The beach it is...'

Hand in hand they walked through the door, into the light.

CHAPTER EIGHTY FIVE

The police released Jasmine's belongings, found on her at the beach, to Debra. They then handed her an evidence envelope and asked her to read the note they had found stuffed inside a school bag, to verify that it was Jasmine's bag, her handwriting and her note.

Debra opened it. As soon as she saw the hand writing she knew straight away that it was her daughter's....

Dear family, I'm sorry it came to this, but I couldn't carry on any longer. I've grown too tired on this roller coaster that we call life. I tried, I promise you, but things just went wrong for me too many times... I guess happiness is a door not all of us can open. I couldn't open it, no matter how many times I tried.

I want everyone to know, you couldn't have stopped this, you couldn't have stopped me... I take full responsibility for my actions and I'm sorry if I have caused any of my pain to be passed on. That was never my intention.

I truly believe all of you, and the world, are better off without me. Know I'm at peace now... Grandpa will look after me.

I will see you again, one day. I love you all.

All my love, Jasmine xxx

THE END.

26461588R00287

Printed in Poland
by Amazon Fulfillment
Poland Sp. z o.o., Wrocław